DOWNFALL

TWISTED LOVE
(BOOK ONE)

DOWNFALL

TWISTED LOVE
(BOOK ONE)

ELLIE SANDERS

Would a rose by any other name smell as sweet?
—ROMEO & JULIET, WILLIAM SHAKESPEARE

TRIGGER WARNINGS

THIS BOOK IS A DARK MODERN, RETELLING OF ROMEO AND JULIET. There are a lot of triggers so please be aware of this before embarking down this road as it's labelled 'dark' for a reason.

Ideally, I'd prefer for you to dive into this book blind so as not to spoil the twists and turns but I know some people like a warning. Below are the main triggers.

For a full list please visit www.hotsteamywriter.com

Triggers include: familial abuse, emotional abuse, sexual assault, dub con, physical violence, coercion, toxic relationships, human trafficking, organ trafficking, kidnapping and torture.

There is also a lot of extremely explicit sex scenes so if this is not your thing, then this book / duet is not for you.

Reader discretion really is advised because you have been warned.

PLAYLIST

Apologize — OneRepublic
Because of You — Kelly Clarkson
Not Ready To Make — Nice The Chicks
Set Fire To The Rain — Adele
Let It Go — James Bay
Wicked Game — Grace Carter
You Found Me — The Fray
Last Request — Paolo Nutini
Can We Kiss Forever? — Kina, Adriana Proenza
Praying — Kesha
Start Again — Conrad Sewell
Easy On Me — Adele
Love Me Like You Do — Ellie Goulding
Losing You — Aquilo
Impossible — James Arthur

ROMAN

Christ she's beautiful. That's the only thought that keeps going round in my head as I've watched her.

She laughs, she smiles, she radiates the kind of warmth that hits your soul and settles in it, burning through every dark moment of your life and erasing them entirely.

Her eyes catch mine. For a second it feels like everything stops. Like the world is still spinning but the two of us are no longer moving with it.

My breath stops. My heart stops too.

Like someone's just grasped it and gripped it so tightly I can't even breathe.

She knows who I am. And she's more than aware that a Montague has no reason to be here, at her party. She tilts her head, her cheeks turning pink as if she's actually shy under all that sunshine brightness she displays and then she slips away, out the door, into the darkness.

But not before she throws me one final look. One I can read only too well.

She wants me to follow her.

I smirk, considering my options. It could well be a trap. She could be leading me out to my death right now, but damn what a way to die, if I got to touch her, if I got to kiss her just once then it feels like it would be worth it.

I glance over at Ben. He's the only one stupid enough to have come with me, gate crashing this little Capulet soirée. He's necking some blonde girl in a corner he's been flirting with for the last hour. Clearly he won't be too bothered by my absence so I do it. I walk out. I follow the little minx even though there's a good chance I won't see the sunrise if I do.

It's dark outside. My eyes take a minute to adjust but as they do I can see it's just her. No one else. No assassins waiting to slit my throat.

I lick my lips stepping closer.

She looks up meeting my gaze and suddenly it feels like the tables have flipped. Like I'm the predator and no longer the prey.

"You shouldn't be out here alone." I murmur.

She swallows, her face showing more nervousness. "I'm not alone." She says quietly. Damn she even sounds like an angel.

"No?" I make a show of looking around. "I don't see anyone else here."

She smiles, takes my hand and the shock of her flesh against mine sends something up my entire spine. She pulls me further away from the door. "That's because there isn't anyone. It's just us."

Just us. Those words do something to me. It feels like she's united us, joined us. Two mortal enemies who have no business conversing, no business breathing the same air, and yet here we are.

"This is a trap." I state.

She lets out a small chuckle. "Why would I trap you?"

I step closer, breathing her in. She's smaller than me, even in the ridiculous heels she's in. She steps back as if she suddenly realises the situation she's put herself in.

"Are you scared?" I tease. "Scared big bad Roman Montague is going to eat you?"

She gulps. Her body flattening against the wall and I wonder if all of this was false bravado, an alcohol fuelled notion on her part that's quickly gotten out of control.

I push into her, running my face across her skin and through her hair. She smells so good I groan. In my pants I can feel my dick already straining, desperate for me to be fucking her already.

"I think you want me to eat you." I murmur. "I think you want me to devour you whole."

A squeak escapes her lips that makes me wonder how experienced this girl even is because I've never seen her with anyone, never even heard her name associated with anyone.

But her hands grab at the hem of her dress and to my surprise she starts to raise it up, higher and higher, showing the top of her thighs and then her black lacy panties beneath.

"Go on then." She half whispers.

I grin. She's taunting me. But that's okay. I'm more than game. I grab her, spinning her around. If anyone were to come out right now I don't want them to see her. She's mine, all mine, as is this moment. I'll be damned if I share it with anyone. And I'll be damned if anyone sees who we are and takes it from us.

She gasps as I push her face first into the wall. Taking charge, yanking her dress higher till it's right up over her hips.

She's wearing a thong. Her perfect peachy round little ass is there just waiting to be touched. I run my hand over it and she freezes. Her whole body freezes.

"Do you want to stop?" I ask.

She shakes her head. "No." It comes out more like a gasp.

I let out a low breath, that's both the answer I wanted and not at all. I wanted her to end this. To tell me this was a joke that got out of hand because now that I have her, now that she's more real than ever, I don't want to let her go. Not ever.

She pushes back into me just a little. Just enough to show she's into this. "Touch me. Do your worst."

I grin. My worst? That's how she wants to play this? Fine, I'm all game for that.

3

I tilt my head, snaking my hand around and into her underwear, cupping her. She's wet. Soaked. The little Capulet Princess is dripping just for me.

As my fingers start to explore, she whimpers enough that she feels more like my prey than ever. And Christ do I want to devour her. I want to devour every inch of her. But not just once. Not just this time in a dark alley. I want to possess her in a way I've never needed to possess a woman before.

"I'm going to ruin you." I mutter. I don't think she hears. I don't really care if she does. I will ruin her, I will ruin her for everyone else but me. She's going to be mine now, forever. In this moment I know it, I feel it.

Rose Capulet will be bound to me.

Our souls will be damned together.

She starts writhing, her body riding my fingers as I start to thrust more. It feels like she wants this as much as me.

She lets out a moan and I snarl back. We feel like two lost people, two lost souls who've finally found our reason for existence.

I yank her head around enough to make eye contact and she half glares at me.

I don't say it out loud but I think it.

And deep down I know it's true; she's mine now.

And I'm never letting her go.

Six Years Later

THE BAR IS FULL. MORE FULL THAN I WOULD LIKE. NOT THAT IT matters.

But still.

I glance around from what would normally be a piss poor seating choice almost entirely obscured in the corner, except tonight I don't want to be seen. I don't want to be observed. I take another sip of my scotch, looking nonchalant, though I'm anything but. The pistol is tucked against my side. Concealed. With the silencer already in place.

I haven't been in this city, in my home, in over six years. Six god damn years. It doesn't feel like anything has changed, even the faces look the same. Perhaps no one noticed my absence. Perhaps no one cared.

I feel a flash of fury at that. That I was forced into exile, forced to hide, and to all these people it meant nothing. My sacrifice was nothing.

My hand tightens around the glass and I force myself to be calm. I am back. I have returned and this entire city shall feel the consequences.

And then I see her. Even from this distance, with her back to me, I still recognise her. Though her perfume may have changed I know the scent of her soul. The colours of her heart. Two men are escorting her but I pay them no heed.

She walks up, takes a seat, and orders a drink. Vodka tonic. Just like she used to drink.

At least somethings don't change.

Only the things that matter.

My anger grows then, as I take in her clothes. Scarlet silk of a designer dress that clings to her curves that seem to have only gotten better as she's aged. I guess the colour couldn't be more perfect. She is in many ways *the* scarlet woman. The betrayer. Her dark hair flows in loosely styled curls reminding me of all the times she used to play with it while we'd talk, while we'd whisper our desires, as if any of it was real to her.

But especially I take in the diamond glinting on *that* finger. She moved on. She forgot me. She married someone else.

Despite everything we'd promised. Everything we'd agreed. In the end it all meant nothing. I meant nothing.

She sips her drink, her rouge lipstick leaving a smear on the glass, reminding me of so many times she would have done the same on my lips. Suddenly I can taste it, I can taste her. She glances around. Perhaps she senses that someone is watching her.

In truth half the bar is. She's Rose Capulet for Christ sake. Her family are as powerful as mine.

Her eyes cast over the corner where I'm sat, concealed, but she doesn't see me and if anything that tells me what I need to know. That I am nothing. That she truly has forgotten me.

It should strengthen my resolve. It should make this task easier. Afterall I came here tonight for one reason and one reason alone. To make my mark. To let this city know that I am back and that this time they will pay for their insults.

Starting with her. With Rose. My first love. In truth, the only woman I have ever loved, have ever cared for, my own sister excluded. If I had anything left that resembled a heart then I would feel something akin to grief in this moment but I have nothing now. Nothing but darkness.

She turns, her legs tucked to the side on the stool like she's some graceful beauty and not some heartless creature of deception.

My hand pauses. I'm not one for changing plans. But now that I'm here, now that I've seen her it's harder than I imagined. I thought this would be easy. I thought this would feel good. To take my vengeance. She belonged to me after all, all I'm doing is claiming that, fulfilling the promise she made all those years ago, when she said she would die for me. Though I can see now how hollow those words were, I was going to make them real. To claim her life. To take it. To watch her last deceitful breaths pass over those perfect pouty lips.

But I *can't* do it. The realisation hits me from nowhere.

I can't kill her.

But she doesn't deserve to live either.

And then he walks in.

No, saunters in.

He doesn't look around. He knows where she is. His men have been stood close enough as if they're her bodyguards but I wonder with the way she seems to flit if they might be more than that.

Perhaps he senses her duplicity too. Perhaps he's learnt to keep a tight leash on her. Can't blame him for that.

He puts his hand on her back, where the dress exposes her skin and she doesn't react. Doesn't recoil from his touch. My jealousy spikes because she should fucking recoil. She should hate it.

His mouth lowers and he murmurs something in her ear. She sighs, nodding her head, her eyes fixed in front. She puts the glass down, gets to her feet, and he leads her out, her heels clacking with every manicured step she takes.

She doesn't look then.

She just walks.

Hand in hand with Paris Blumenfeld. The man she married instead of me.

ROMAN

"Well?" Ben says as soon as I walk into the house. It's dark. I was meant to be back hours ago but it felt too soon to return to the house. And I wanted some thinking time. Some processing time.

It wasn't meant to feel like this. It was meant to be easy. It was meant to feel good. To take my vengeance. To show the world what it meant to cross me and yet for the first time in my life my finger faltered. I failed to pull the trigger.

I look at Ben. For the entirety of my exile he has remained by my side. Helping me. In truth being more of a servant at times than a friend. His face bares the scar of when he took a knife for me. When Capulet sent an assassin, not long after I'd left, to ensure his enemy's only son was gone for good. Except it didn't end that way. Ben took the knife. Lost his eye for me. And the assassin spent the next two weeks enduring every minute of my furious violence until I sent him back, neatly packed up in a box for Ignatio to keep.

I shake my head just a little in answer to his unspoken question. But he must know already. If she were dead the news would already been screaming it. Social media would too. Rose Capulet executed in a bar. The entire city's elite would be dumbstruck.

And yet it didn't happen. I didn't do it.

He gets up, walks over to the drinks cabinet and pours out two drinks, passing one to me and I down it.

"I did warn you." He says. And I know he's right. I hate that he's right. That that beautiful, conniving temptress has beaten me once again. Beaten me without even knowing it.

My glass shatters in my hand as I clench my fist. How can such a woman possess such power over me? Me?

"What are you going to do?" Ben asks.

"I'm going to destroy her. I'm going to destroy her entire family. Bring them down to their knees." I snarl.

I'm going to make her pay. I'm going to show her exactly what I've become in the last six years. What she made me. She won't even recognise the man when I stand before her, not that she knew me then, not that she clearly cared. I must have been a joke to her, an amusement to fill her tedious days when she wasn't shopping, when she wasn't living the high life.

I stalk over to get another drink. I'm not usually a big drinker but today I want the alcohol to numb the bitter disappointment of my own actions. I want the taste of scotch to override the taste of her that even now, so many years later, I still yearn for.

I sink into the chair, my mind already planning it now. Each minute step I'm going to take. Each piece of the board I'm going to manipulate until eventually there is only us. Me and her. I can't wait to see it. The look on her face when she realises she's been outmanoeuvred. When she realises who it was lurking in the shadows, haunting her steps, taking each and every life she holds dear and extinguishing them the way she extinguished our love.

"The funeral is tomorrow." Ben says glancing at the fresh glass in my hand.

"Sofia will be there." I state. It will show my hand if I'm there, at the Cathedral, for everyone to see, mourning the death of Horace Montague, showing everyone my face. No, my sister will have to deal with that alone.

"Yes I will." She says tersely walking in, her eyes already judging us, taking in the smashed glass.

"Sofia." Ben says. For years he's held a soft spot for her. I wonder for a moment if she's noticed. Right now she seems too furious to take note of anything.

"Ben can accompany you." I state.

"No." She says. "His presence may give you away."

I snort. I doubt anyone watching will realise who he is but perhaps she is right. I don't want to show my hand until I'm ready. Until all the trap has been laid and is ready to spring shut.

"So who will you go with?" Ben asks, leaning against the arm of the couch, his eyes running over her in what could be mistaken for a brotherly gesture.

"No one." She says folding her arms. "I'm fully capable of going by myself. I don't need anybody holding my hand thank you very much."

"There will be a lot of eyes on you." Ben warns. "You'll need to be careful."

"Like I haven't had that for the last six years." She snaps and it's hard not to feel a pang of anger at that. She's my sister. I should have been here, I should have been able to protect her, to keep her safe and yet instead of that I was forced to run like a coward and hide.

She glances at me and her expression softens just a tad. "Roman." She says.

I meet her gaze.

"…I'm sorry you can't be there."

I shrug it off taking another sip. Letting the whiskey soothe a pain that I can't quite fathom considering the circumstances.

"He's your father too." She states.

Yeah he was. And yet he was stupid enough to be outmanoeuvred. To allow the Capulets to gain the upper hand. To accept that the entire city danced to their whims, while the Montague empire crumbled around our feet.

"I'll speak with Darius." She says quietly. "Perhaps now he will grant you a reprieve. You are our father's heir as much as me.

I snarl at that. "I don't need a reprieve." I snap. "I don't need empty words from a man balls deep with our enemy. I need retribution and by god will I have it."

"Roman…" She says walking over to me, crouching down. "You cannot always be carrying this anger."

"Wouldn't you?"

She gives me a bitter, pained smile. "You have spent too long focused on your revenge but what will you do once you have it? What then? When every Capulet is dead, when Darius himself admits he was wrong, what will your life be then?"

"What does it matter?"

"It matters Roman." She says getting back up. "It matters."

I shake my head, tossing the remainder of the drink down my throat. "Be careful tomorrow Sofia. They may see it as an opportunity to cut us down. To strike when they think we are weak."

She nods but she looks doubtful. "There will be too many witnesses. The whole thing is being livestreamed." She states, as though it were a carnival procession and not the marking of a dead man.

I watch her go. Ben watches her too and as his eyes flit to mine I wonder why he still has never made a move. Perhaps he fears my reaction. Perhaps he thinks he's not good enough for her. Would I sleep better knowing he was in her bed, protecting her? Perhaps.

"If you want I will be there. In the crowd." He says.

"You're too noticeable." I say glancing at the scar the slices down the left side of his face.

"Then how do you plan to do any of this?" He asks. "Nobody knows we are here but I doubt that will remain a secret for all that long."

I smile. "You forget old friend, I'm used to operating from the shadows. I've spent the last six years in the dark."

He narrows his eyes, choosing in that moment not to argue further but a part of him is right; I won't be able to stay concealed forever. Besides that's not my plan. What revelry is there in revenge if the person you're taking it from doesn't realise who exactly wields the blade? The city will know I am here. But they will learn it on my terms. It's just a case of timing.

ROSE

"**M**ontague." *The name slips from my lips as I writhe against his body. It shouldn't be that name. Everything in my blood screams against it and yet still this man sets me on fire. From the moment our eyes met across that expanse, I knew.*

He growls in response. His body pushing me harder into the wall. His hand pushing further inside me.

I moan, my legs shaking, threatening to give way but he doesn't stop. And I don't want him too. Despite my protestations to the contrary. Despite the insults I hurled.

"You're enjoying this aren't you?" He says. "Little Rose Capulet, being ravaged by her enemy at her own birthday party."

"Fuck you." I snarl but it sounds pitiful. I sound pitiful.

"Ssssh." He says his face right up against my ear. "It's okay to like what you like." His fingers thrust mercilessly but I'm not complaining. My body is loving it. I am loving it.

"I don't like you." I say through gritted teeth.

He chuckles. "Then why are we here? Why did you pull up your dress for me huh?"

I groan. I want to blame the alcohol but I haven't had any, at least not enough to get me drunk. I want to blame him too. To say this is all Roman, that he's forcing himself on me but that's not true either.

I did want this. I wanted him.

I wanted to make a point. I wanted to prove that I have some autonomy over my own body, over my own choices

I can feel his dick poking into me through his jeans and for a fleeting moment I wonder why he hasn't made me touch him, but then I'm relieved he hasn't, if he does he'll realise how inexperienced I am and he might just give this all up, move onto a girl that knows how to actually pleasure him.

I shudder again. His other hand moves to cup my breast. I arch my back further into him and he slides his hand under my bra and pinches my nipple hard.

My breath catches and I bite my lip to not give myself away.

"Don't hide those moans." He says. "You got yourself into this, might as well enjoy the ride."

I nod. He's right. In so many ways.

My body leaks more arousal, I can feel it dripping down my thighs. He's doing it on purpose, teasing me but not letting me come and I feel so close to tears, to utter desperation.

"Please…" I gasp.

"Please what?"

"I want to…" I trail off. Too embarrassed to say the words. Too embarrassed to admit what I want.

"You want to come is that it?" He murmurs.

I nod, my head sliding against his, feeling the stubble of his cheek.

"Beg me Rose. Beg for Roman Montague to make you come."

He's taunting me. I hate him for it but a part of me loves it. I shake my head. Refusing to say it. Refusing to play his little game.

He curls his fingers, teasing me more, and my legs shake violently. "You wanted this Rose. Don't you dare pretend otherwise. You like my hands on you. You like the feel of my fingers in that pretty cunt of yours."

I groan. Giving in. Not good enough at this game to play it with any skill. "Please Roman."

"Please what?"

"Please make me come." I gasp the words, my face flushing so red I'm pleased the darkness hides it.

He growls, pulling me tighter and his fingers find my clit. I let out a moan so loud I swear anyone nearby can hear.

"You're going to come Rose. You're going to come but when you do remember who's fingers got you there. Remember who got you off."

I lean back into him, surrendering in every way I can. I start to shriek, my body jerking, my eyes rolling back and he has to jam his hand on my mouth to silence me. But his other hand continues to pleasure me, making my body soar, making me see stars.

When I slump against him he stops and for a moment we both stay where we are, concealed in this alleyway, in silence.

He puts my underwear back in place, pulls my dress back down but his body is still up against mine, still keeping me where I am, pressed between him and the brick wall.

"Roman." I whisper his name. It's the first time I've said it in a way that isn't lust filled or scathing.

I can hear his breathing. I can feel his body heat. He didn't get off and I wonder for a moment what he got out of this. Will he use this against me? Will this one potentially stupid moment of rebellion haunt me now?

"Rose." He murmurs. He pulls my hair to the side, exposing my neck. I don't look back at him. I just stay still, facing the wall, waiting for whatever comes next as reality starts to sink in. "You're trouble do you know that?"

I bite my lip, bite back the grin. No one has ever called me trouble. I'm the complete opposite. I'm the obedient one, while my cousins Tyrone and Tybalt are the real troublemakers.

Except I just let my enemy finger fuck me in an alleyway after sneaking out of my own party.

"I didn't mean…" I begin but it feels weird trying to justify it.

His lips brush against my neck. "Definitely trouble." He says.

"Then what are you Roman?"

He tilts his head. "Maybe I'm the one who's going to tame you."

I scoff. "No you aren't."

He chuckles before lowering his mouth to my neck and sucking hard. I jerk but I can't shove him off. "I've marked you now. You're mine." He teases.

I turn my head glaring at him as I palm the spot. He's given me a hiccy. A god damn hiccy. How the hell am I going to hide that from my mother's piercing eyes?

"If anyone sees…" I begin.

"Tell them it was me." He says proudly.

"Like hell." I snap going to push past. He grabs me pulling me back.

"You're just going to pretend this didn't happen is that it?" He says.

I pause staring up at him. I didn't think about the consequences when I got him to follow me. I figured he'd see this as a onetime thing. I hoped it was. That all the need inside me would be sated afterwards.

"You don't want to?" I murmur, ignoring the voice in my own head that is practically screaming for more.

His face reacts, his eyes drop, betraying him as he stares at my body. "No."

"Oh." I gasp. God why isn't there some sort of rule book for this? I don't know how to act. I don't know what to say.

"You do?" He half snarls.

I shake my head blushing. "I…"

"You had fun. I had fun. Why should we stop?" He says.

"Because we're enemies."

He rolls his eyes. "No. Our parents are. You're not my enemy Rose."

"I doubt your dad would agree with that."

"Fuck what they think."

"Roman…"

He kisses me and the shock of it makes me freeze. I've never been kissed. I've never kissed anyone. His mouth crashes into mine. His tongue invades mine and I'm so clumsy as I try to kiss him back. I can taste the whiskey on his tongue. I bet he can taste the cheap ass punch I was drinking too.

"You're trouble Rose." He says. "But you're my trouble now."

I smile. A shy, unsure smile that he kisses from my lips until all that concern, all that trepidation melts away back into lust once more.

VERONA BAY. CHRIST WHAT A PLACE.

Full of vacuous men and empty headed women, myself included in that of course. Because that's what I am. What the world sees me as. The glittery diamond covered pinnacle of all their aspirations.

Everyone smiles at me. Simpers. Every man runs his eyes over me in a way that makes my skin crawl.

I guess I should be grateful it's so apparent. That no one thinks to put up any pretence. It makes it easier at least. Though it certainly doesn't make it more palatable.

I stayed inside, cooped up almost, for most of the day. It felt appropriate. It felt respectful. Paris of course went to the funeral. His family being who they are, it was expected of him but we could hardly make any justifications as to why a Capulet would be there, at a Montague event.

The TV has aired every minute of it. With the horse drawn carriage carrying Horace's silk lined coffin through the cobbled streets, and either side lined with ogling swathes of faces, not there to mourn. There to enjoy it. It's a spectacle after all.

Darius walked behind the coffin. Horace's daughter, Sofia, beside him. She was bold enough to match her black dress with a pair of Louboutin's that she strutted in as if she were marching into battle. I half admire her for it. The brashness. The gall. I don't think I'd have it in me to look half as fierce as she did in that moment.

The Montague Heiress.

The words hit me for a moment and that old pain stirs in my gut. I gulp, pushing against my belly, suppressing it, suppressing it all. Six years have passed. Six years and yet every time I think I'm over it another thing happens that proves quite the opposite is the case.

Already the rumours are running about him. If he'll return. If he'll be allowed back. I don't think on it. I *can't* think on it. If I even let my head go near that notion I know I'll be lost. I know all the darkness that I fight so hard to control will seep back through my veins and I won't be me anymore.

I'll be that broken thing again. The creature he made of me.

The one he discarded.

The one he left behind like trash.

I cross through the house. Though technically we own it together it's far more Paris's home than mine. A great homage to modernity. All glass and steel and cold like the man's soul. That is if he has one.

When I married him I'll admit that I wanted to love him. I'd wanted it to work out. I wanted so badly to replace what was taken but within weeks I realised Paris wasn't capable of such affection because he was too deeply in love with himself. I was a show bride. A perfect trophy on his arm. And for a while we lived a double life, pretending for the cameras, for both our families. And then I think he grew bored of the pretence, at least in private anyway.

And I grew good at hiding the bruises.

My family turn a blind eye to what we really are. He is more a son to them than I am a daughter. He holds more worth, at least to the Capulet men because Darius is his uncle and the Governor of this state. And that power dynamic alone is worth more than one daughter's happiness.

As I grab my gym bag I hear the skittle of claws across the polished porcelain and the ugly-cute face of my dog comes hurtling around the corner.

"Bella." Mae, one of the maids calls, rushing after her and then she stops a look of relief when she sees it's me and not my husband. "I'm sorry. I was watching her but she got out…"

"It's okay Mae." I say scooping her up into my arms. She's a shit-zuh pug cross with a snorty little nose and big bug eyes. She resembles more of an ewok than a dog. I rescued her from a pound where she'd been overlooked by everyone because she's allergic to absolutely everything and clearly people wanted a less costly pet.

Most of the women around me have dogs. Designer dogs that fit in their handbags and need to be groomed daily. But, while Bella would certainly fit in my Louis Vuitton, she'd probably bite me if I tried to put her in it and I wouldn't blame her either.

Besides, she gives me a great excuse to be out of the house at any given moment. To be in the park too. Because no one bats an eye at a person walking their dog. But a woman, sat alone, for hours on end? That would certainly garner unwanted attention.

I pass her back to the maid. Though my husband doesn't know it most of her duties now revolve around my dog, ensuring she is never left alone because she has separation anxiety and sadly being who I am means I have to be seen out at every big event, I have to be photographed, and having her with me is not always an option.

"I'll be back later." I say.

I need to be out of the house. I need to be doing something because this place is giving me cabin fever again.

I HIT THE GYM HARD. FOCUSING ALL THE TENSION THAT SEEMS TO have wound itself tight inside me and, as my feet pound onto the treadmill, I visualise it ebbing away. Only it doesn't. No matter how many miles I run, no matter how many weights I lift, even when my legs protest too much, nothing eases what seems to growing inside me.

The gym is attached to the clubhouse. Anyone who is anyone has membership here though it's more common to see them in the spa than it is seeing them sweat it out like I do on an almost daily basis. I'm not even a health freak. I just come here because there's little else in my life to do. I'm not allowed to work, And I can hardly sit around eating cake all day because Paris would very quickly take advantage of that. He can't have a fat wife. Image is everything to him.

After we married he put me on a diet. Though he'd never understood the reasons behind my weight gain he was quick to ensure my body was honed into something of goddess proportions. He even makes me stand on the scales for him. Bi-weekly. If he could, he'd control all my eating too, but luckily even he understands how the gossip rags would view that if it got out.

And it would.

Somehow they seem more than adept at delving out the grimiest parts of our lives, though mercifully none of them have yet to realise my darkest secrets. The one that keeps me up at night. The one that forces me out. The one that even now simmers inside, never quite releasing its grip enough to let me get free.

Two hours later and I'm done with my workout. The gym was quieter than usual. I guess most people didn't want to be seen here, today of all days. Most of them were probably at the funeral. At the wake. Eating the fine spread the Montague's put on and offering their sympathies like they give a shit.

I grab a shower, rinsing off the sweat that pools across my skin and then carefully I replace my makeup. I'm more an advocate of the French way of beauty, with less is more, but thanks to Paris's hands I often have to wear heavier foundation. It's safer to opt for more coverage, even when I don't need it, than raise suspicions.

When I've finished drying my hair I grab my bag and wonder if I have time for a 'walk' before dinner. Will she be there? I think the days she is are worse than when she's absent because seeing her, knowing I can't talk to her, interact with her in any way is like a dagger that delves deeper and deeper into my heart.

Someone barges into me as I open the door and I step back.

"Sorry." I say and then my eyes widen as I realise who it is.

Sofia.

Her eyebrows raise and then quickly the mask comes down. "It's my fault." She says. "I was distracted."

"You have good reason to be." I reply.

She frowns for a second and then steps aside. We've barely spoken. Barely ever exchanged more than a word here and there. We both know who the other is though I wonder how much she knows about me. About my past. About her brother too.

As she walks past I weigh up the consequences of what I'm about to do and for once throw caution to the wind.

"I'm sorry for your loss." I say.

She stops. Turns. Meets my gaze. Clearly she's trying to figure out if I'm being genuine or just trying to twist the blade like any other Capulet would.

"Thank you." She says after a moment.

"He was a good father." I say.

She tilts her head. "Was he?" She replies. "With whom are you comparing him to?"

"With my own." I say.

She frowns more and the air around us thickens to the point you could actually put your hand out and grasp it.

I shouldn't have said anything. I shouldn't have opened my big mouth. It would have been so easy to just walk by and not even acknowledge her but I guess some part of me wanted to show compassion, wanted to show that we're not all heartless.

And now we're stood awkwardly just staring at each other.

A Capulet and a Montague. Mortal enemies or as good as.

Two women walk into the changing rooms chatting merrily and as they spot us they fall silent. God I can just see it now, the gossip columns full of chatter about this moment.

I turn on my heel walking away before I can say anything else. Before I can do anymore damage.

ROSE

There's not really time to get to the park but I don't care. I need to clear my head. To refocus. To remind myself of exactly where I am and how I ended up here. How my actions have consequences.

Bella is sniffing around at my feet. I know Mae took her out earlier and it's not like such a small dog needs more than one walk but still. She's my cover.

I'm sat on the usual bench. There's a play area a few metres away but I'm mostly obscured by a giant oak. I can hear them, the last of the children still allowed out.

I shut my eyes, taking in the sounds, breathing the noise in like it's something physical I can cherish.

As a car pulls up the other side of the rail I already know who it is.

"Rose."

I sigh putting my game-face back on. Playing the perfect Capulet princess I'm meant to be.

Tyrone, my cousin, is stood lounging against the side of the Bentley. He eyeballs Bella like she's got fleas.

"The family are waiting." He says.

Of course they are. And we both know better than that.

I scoop Bella into my arms and get into the car. Tyrone slides in beside me and for the entire ride we don't say a word. Not one single syllable.

I stare out, watching the city whizz by. Seeing all the glitz and gold of every shop window. Seeing all the ostentatious need of every single person to project their wealth, their social status, as if that alone makes them a worthy human being.

The Bentley pulls up to the main gates. Even at this hour enough people stop to look and a few snap a picture. After all who can resist such a close call with one of us?

The gates open as if they're gliding over ice and not gravel and then we continue on. Up the long drive, to where the grand Capulet house is.

A man opens the door for me and I step out with Bella still firm in my arms.

"Rose." I hear the tone of my mother's indignation and it's hard not to roll my eyes.

"She was walking the dog." Tyrone states as if he'd found me on the moon.

My mother raises an eyebrow before clicking her fingers. A maid appears right behind her. "See to the dog." She says and the maid steps towards me.

I could fight. I could argue but there would be little point. I sigh, passing Bella over as she kicks out in protest.

"Please give her some cold rice and scrambled eggs." I say and the girl nods.

Tyrone scoffs and I do my best to ignore it as I walk in. My mother as always is dressed to the nines. Her lithe, model like frame covered in a slinky evening dress and a muslin scarf is thrown over her shoulder despite the heat still in the air.

She casts a disappointed look at my less than impressive jeans and shirt. Still, it's silk so it's not like I'm slumming it that much. But by Capulet standards I'm pretty much deadbeat aesthetic right now.

The hall echoes with our footsteps. Tyrone and I walk behind my mother and as we approach the drawing room I already know everyone else is waiting.

The doors open for us and a dozen sets of eyes fix on me in particular.

"You're late." My father says.

"I got distracted." I murmur moving quickly now to take my seat. For all my want to be assertive, I don't have the guts to fight the man. I never have.

He grunts, taking in my clothes, taking in my trainers in particular. I doubt he's ever seen me so underdressed.

He looks around and waves his hand for everyone to continue as if we're not all hanging off his every word.

He speaks quietly to Tyrone, sat beside him and we all start to eat.

No one speaks to me, not that I'm complaining; if I can get through the next few hours being ignored like this I'll be more than happy.

Our family have these 'little' dinners every few weeks. For the most part I'm just here to tick a box. I've done my duty in their eyes. I married a Blumenfeld. I guess I should be grateful that being Paris's wife protects me from the more clandestine aspects of being in this family, but in reality, I pay in others ways.

"With the funeral over, Darius will be more amenable to our wants." My father says. "He's pandered to the Montagues but we need to ensure our proposals go through." He glances at Carter, his right hand man, who nods.

Of course this would be his focus.

"The Montagues are weak. Sofia is barely more than a child. No doubt they'll try to get her married off." My mother states from the other end of the table.

"With Paris spoken for there aren't any others in Darius's immediate circle to worry about." My father replies.

"What about Otto Blumenfeld?" Carter asks and a few people pause.

"Otto is in his forties." My mother says dismissively.

"Like that would put her off. Enough women marry for power and status, you think this bitch is any different?" Carter states and enough of the men grunt in agreement.

My stomach turns at that, at the misogyny around the room as every man nods in agreement. By their estimation that's exactly what I did too. Sold myself for my family's need for power. Only they were all more than happy with the terms back then.

"Rose." My father says and all heads turn to me. "I want you to speak to Darius, ensure that Otto is not an option."

I grit my teeth. He thinks I can simply swan in and have such a conversation with him?

"I'll do what I can." I say.

His eyebrows raise at that. "What you can?" He snaps. "You will do more than that."

I nod quickly. It was a stupid response. But it's not like this isn't going to come back and bite me in the arse. If Sofia does set her sights on Otto then I doubt there's much I can do to influence anything.

He keeps his gaze on me for an uncomfortable amount of time and then he looks back across the table, thankfully returning to his usual game pretending I don't exist now that I've been given my task.

28

When the meal ends I make sure that I'm not darting for the door, though I want to so badly. I stand making polite conversation before slipping away and going to get Bella.

They've stuck her in a storage room, like she's something to be packed away. I shake my head in annoyance and scoop her up and she snuggles into me clearly relieved to be out of the dark.

"Rose."

I turn looking at my mother who's even now giving me a look half of sympathy, half disapproval.

"What is it?" I ask.

"I wanted to see how you were, to check on you, what with everything going on."

I wince. Of course she would want to have *this* conversation. Only the skeletons in my closet are buried so deep I doubt she'd be able to locate them.

"I'm fine." I say.

"I'm here if you need me. If you want to talk."

"I know." I say giving her best, reassuring smile. For all her faults, my mother at least has my back.

"Then let's catch up properly. Go out for tea. Just you and me. Some mother daughter bonding."

I nod. "That sounds good."

"Next Friday." She says. "I'll book it. We can go shopping after, maybe buy a few things to cheer you up."

I shake my head slightly. It's not her fault, but that's her go to response. When in doubt douse me with material things, as if all the world's hurts can be fixed with a credit card.

"That sounds great." I murmur as Bella begins to fidget.

"Just leave the dog at home." She says patting me on the shoulder.

ROSE

I'm awake with the sun. Though the room is dark from the blackout curtains I can still sense that it's morning.

Paris is asleep beside me. He came back in the early hours, mercifully far too drunk to give a shit about my existence which is how I like him best.

I blink, staring at the ceiling, my mind already spinning with the haunting images of another night dreaming of a life so far from my own. But the pain is still there. Lingering. The agonising hunger is still there too.

A tear streaks down my cheek before I can stop it and I'm quick to move, quick to wipe it away. Just like always I refuse to cry. I refuse to let it out, afraid that if I do I'll never come back.

I'm thirsty, parched, but I don't want to move, I don't want to wake Paris. He's at his best when he's asleep. So instead I lay there, immobile, barely daring to breath for what feels like hours while he quietly snores beside me.

In the end it's my full bladder that forces me up. I creep from the bed, tiptoeing to the bathroom and stuff enough paper down the pan to silence the sound of my pee. I don't flush. I just put the lid down, wash my hands quietly, and then tiptoe back.

As I slip into the bed he groans in annoyance and I realise the game is up.

"If you're going to move around so much you might as well make yourself useful and get me some water." He grumbles.

If I refuse I'll only piss him off more so I get up, walk as quietly as I can and come back with a glass for him. He half snatches it, gulping down the contents then puts it empty on the side.

I look at him and he's glaring at me.

"I'll let you sleep." I murmur.

"No." He replies holding the sheets. "Lie down."

I don't show my reaction but I feel it, the way my stomach twists, though I get in all the same. His arms wrap around me and I can smell the alcohol still on his breath as he presses his face against my neck.

"I heard a rumour." He mutters.

"What rumour?" I ask.

"That you were facing off with Sofia Montague yesterday at the clubhouse."

I shake my head. "It wasn't like that. I was just offering my condolences."

He lets out a sound of disbelief. "Don't lie to me Rose."

"I'm not."

"You need to back off. Whatever crap your family is up to, it needs to stop."

"I'm not up to anything."

He pulls me back. Hard. I'm now lying facing him as he stares down at me. "You Capulets are always up to something."

"I'm not."

He narrows his eyes. "You better not be. There's shit going down. I don't need you muddying the water."

"What shit?" I ask.

He rolls his eyes. "Like I'd tell you that, you'll go running to daddy dearest the first opportunity you get."

"I wouldn't. You can trust me." I half whisper it though I'm not sure why. I know Paris doesn't trust me and I sure as hell don't trust him. Not for a second. We're two vipers sleeping in the same bed waiting for the other to strike.

His lips curl with amusement as though I've said a joke. "You're only good for one thing Rose and sometimes I wonder if you're even worth that."

I look away but don't reply. He's said worse in the past. Much worse. I've learnt not to retaliate because doing so only ends in one thing. Pain. My pain.

"There's a lot going on above your head." He mumbles.

"I don't want to know." I reply. It's true, I don't. I'm sick of it. All the fighting. All the power games. It's exhausting. And more often than not it feels like it's us women who bear the brunt of it.

"We have to keep the Montagues sweet." He says.

"Why?" I ask, curious despite myself. The Montagues have been losing power for years. Why now do they suddenly matter?

He smirks. "Like I said, it's all above your head. Just for once do as I ask and don't cause trouble."

"I don't cause trouble." I snap as *that* word sets me on edge. I'm the most amenable out of all of us. I've been brought up to be just that and let's face it, my family know exactly what weapons to wield anytime I get any desire to be otherwise.

His fingers graze my cheek. He's always softer in the mornings but that doesn't mean I welcome it any more.

"My head hurts." He mutters.

"Perhaps you shouldn't have drunk so much." I reply.

He tilts his head. "How about you put that mouth to better use?"

I wince shaking my head. "How about I get you some paracetamol instead?"

He laughs, grabbing my hair manhandling me enough to show his intent. "Paracetamol isn't the kind of relief I'm looking for." He states giving me one final push which is enough to jolt my neck and make me yelp.

His cock is hard, just as I knew it would be. I end up face to face with it beneath the stuffiness of the duvet. Paris rolls flat on his back, one hand twisting in my hair and I can practically feel the expectation coming off of him.

I bite my tongue, weighing my options. I'm not in the mood. Truth be told I'm never in the mood when it comes to sex. At least not sex with another person because I can get myself off alright when it's just me but with Paris there's nothing. Not even when I close my eyes and desperately pretend I'm with someone else, desperately pretend it's *his* hands on me, I can feel the difference.

In my very soul I know the difference.

But if I don't do this there will be consequences. Maybe not right now. Maybe Paris right now is too hungover but as soon as his headache dulls and his anger grows then I'll pay. And it'll be much worse than simply having his cock in my mouth.

He clears his throat, clearly getting annoyed with the inaction on my part.

I shake my head, resigning myself to once again playing the whore and, after wetting my lips, I suck him in.

He groans. His body stretches. He's not unattractive. In fact, he's anything but. Paris Blumenfeld is undeniably beautiful. Every muscle honed by hours of dedication. His sun kissed skin is soft, unblemished, because he's never had a hard day's work in his life. It's just a shame that under it all the man is a monster.

And worse than that, he's my husband.

He starts jerking his hips, his cock hitting the back of my throat. As always he likes me to initiate and then he takes over, chasing his own pleasure while hate fucking me in the process. On some level I don't mind because this way I don't have to over-pretend. I just have to go through the motions, keeping him happy as he groans and all the while fighting the bitter resentment that festers at the notion that this is my life, my reality, what my parents wanted when they forced me into this.

Everyone else has gotten what they wanted. Everyone else has ticked their boxes, achieved their goals, and I, as always, am merely an object to be used.

When he finally comes I swallow it quickly, wanting the taste to be gone. I wipe my mouth, clamber out of the bed and he doesn't stop me. In the bathroom I'm quick to rinse with mouthwash, to rinse away the taste of him.

And when I walk back in he's lying there with his arms behind his head, eyes closed, and a satisfied grin on his face. I don't comment. I don't say anything. I just walk past into the dressing room. He's gotten what he wanted now so I can go back to being invisible again.

Paris stays in bed, nursing his hangover. I don't complain. It's the best outcome considering.

I ensure the maids know to pamper him just like he expects, and then I escape, seeking sanctuary at the clubhouse and hoping that a few hours of a punishing workout might give me some sort of reprieve from the dark oppression of my headspace.

Only it doesn't. It's like my head is stuck in some death spin. The same images keep flashing in my mind. The same trauma repeating over and over. I hunch up over the treadmill, sweat pouring from my skin. I could spend an eternity here, working each muscle group, and more often than not this is what occupies my time.

My body isn't exhausted. It's my mind that's broken.

My mind that's so far down into a blackhole of despair that I don't think anything will ever bring me back out.

But it's no less than what I deserve.

I gulp as those words echo in my head because deep down I know that's true too. I deserve this. I deserve every moment of pain, of torment. My life is what it is because of my actions. My stupidity. I fell for the oldest trick in the book. I allowed some infantile need to be actually loved, a desperate want to be seen, to overrule every ounce of common sense.

I deserve this life. I deserve every horrific moment.

I spend another hour beating the hell out of my body, willing my mind to just shut up. And then I grab a shower. Freezing cold. It's meant to be good for your hair, smooths the follicles or some such thing, but that's not why I do it.

If you stand under the water long enough your whole body goes numb. Even your head. And sometimes, if you're really lucky, your thoughts just stop.

For a second.

For a brief moment in time.

Everything turns to silence. Everything becomes silent.

Only it always comes crashing back after.

When I'm dressed and back to the perfect socialite, I sit for a while and drink coffee with the other ladies ignoring the loneliness that wants to set into my bones. I don't have any friends. No one close. No one I would trust. But everyone here would gladly give up their seat for me. I make polite talk, add a comment here and there, just like always I act exactly the way I'm expected and no one realises the sunshine princess of Verona is dead on the inside and has been for a very long time.

I say goodbye, exchange hugs and kisses as if we're all bosom buddies and again, I feel a streak of loneliness. What I wouldn't give to have just one friend. Just one person I could truly talk to.

I let out a low sigh as I walk to my car because that will never happen. Not in this life. Not for me.

The valet was more than happy to call my driver and have it brought round but right now I want some fresh air.

Only when I get there there's clearly an issue. My driver looks up at me from where he's squatted with a face of horror.

"Ms. Capulet..." He begins, getting to his feet, wringing his hands like he's guilty of something.

"What's wrong?" I ask.

He winces. "I took a break. It was only for a moment. I didn't mean..."

I give him a reassuring smile. One that I hope conveys that I'm not like my husband and no matter what is going on, I'm not going to react the way Paris would with anger and violence.

"The car..." He begins and then steps aside so that I can see.

The tyres are slashed. Every single one. I blink in shock as I walk around. And then I see the words scratched into the paintwork above the trunk.

Big angry slashes. Big angry letters that seem to shine more in the daylight as I stare at them.

'Whore'

I gulp. My hands wrapping around my body more in reflex at the fact that this *is* an attack. Maybe not on my body but on me.

"Do you know who did this?" I ask.

The driver shakes his head and the man from the Club finally speaks.

"We're pulling CCTV but there's an issue with the feed." He says.

"What issue?" I ask.

He winces too. "The film is corrupted."

I shake my head. Corrupted. So this was planned. Whoever did this knew exactly when my driver had left the vehicle unattended and was also more than capable of ensuring they'd not get caught.

A shiver runs through me and I glance around, scanning every bush, every corner, every possible hiding place that the vandal could be. No way would they leave after doing this. They'd want to see the damage, to see my reaction.

Is it him?

The thought hits me out of the blue. It can't be. He isn't allowed back. He was exiled. And yet, it feels like him. It's certainly his style.

"I'll call the house. Get another car sent." The driver says.

"Don't bother." I reply. If he's here, and he'd be damn stupid to be, but if he is, then I'm more than ready to give him a piece of my mind. It's been six years coming. Six torturous years because of him.

"Ms. Capulet?" The driver says confused. Clearly he's wondering how the hell I'm going to get home.

"I'll walk. It's a nice day."

"It's two miles." The driver replies and I smile.

"See to the car." I murmur before hiking my bag onto my shoulder and turning away.

The gravel crunches under my shoes, the air is already warm enough to tell me I'm going to regret this but I'm too stubborn, too belligerent to simply turn around and go back.

Besides if they send another car it will be one of Paris's and I know in my gut he'll twist this so that it's my fault. By taking one of his cars, I'll only be adding fuel to the fire. And in my gut, I'm hoping that somehow I can pass this off as an accident, that I might even be able to pretend the car broke down and that's why it's gone to be repaired.

Only my head tells me that's preposterous. That he'll know. He'll find out. And when he does he'll be even more furious about the fact he's been misled.

Well, I guess I can't blame him for that.

A car drives past. Two faces turning to look at me before the fade off in a blur of heat and dust.

I wince. Yeah he's going to know. The whole damn bay is going to hear how Rose Capulet was seen walking for miles like a tramp.

My heels pinch into my skin. I'm lucky I'm so used to wearing them that I know I can walk two miles without the height of them being an issue.

Another car drives past.

Then another.

I keep my face neutral, calm, as if this is perfectly normal. As if this is a regular thing I do.

I could turn back. I could.

But I don't.

To do it now would be so much worse.

I could call a taxi too. But then I'd be stood at the side of the road and no doubt there'd be comments about that. I can just imagine my father's face if he heard. The word 'whore' echoes in my head and it's enough to make me pick up my pace. Make me stomp a little faster, ignoring the sweat that's now beading across my brow, ignoring the ache of my muscles that I'd already destroyed in the gym.

"Do you need a lift?"

I blink turning, unaware that a car had even slowed.

She gives me what should be a reassuring smile. Only it's Sofia Montague. Nothing she does should be reassuring.

I glance around, my mind wondering for a second if this is a trap, a concoction between her and her brother to lure me out and then murder me. But they'd never have guessed I would have been here, on this road, they'd never have guessed I would have walked.

Except the old me would have. The young me. The naïve me.

My gut twists as I realise it. I was reckless. Stupid. Just like before.

"I'm fine." I say trying to mentally calm my nerves that seem to be spiking more and more.

She frowns glancing at the Christian Dior heels that are definitely not meant for anything other than a light walk between boutiques.

"It's not a big deal." She says.

I let out a laugh. It sounds bitter. Bitter and twisted, just like the rest of me.

"Rose..." She begins but I shake my head.

"I'm not getting in a car with you Sofia." I murmur.

"You'd rather walk?"

"I like walking."

She glances at my feet again and smirks. "Sure. Whatever. I was just trying to be nice."

I shake my head again. "I don't need you to be nice. I don't need anything from you."

She lets out a huff like she expected a different outcome from this. "Fine. Walk if you want but there's no need to be so rude."

She drives off before I can reply, leaving me in the dusty wake of her tyres.

I grit my teeth trying to ignore the guilt. Trying to ignore all the twisting words in my head. Maybe she was just being nice, maybe she was just offering a lift.

And yet I still can't believe it. I still won't believe it.

She's a Montague. But more than that she's *his* sister.

ROMAN

She's nervous. I shouldn't find it amusing but I do. We're in a nondescript car park tucked away where the cameras and prying eyes can't find us. If I'm honest I'm half astounded that she showed up.

That she didn't just block my number.

I open the door and she gets in, biting her lip, looking around before she meets my gaze. She looks more innocent tonight. I tilt my head appraising her, seeing her cheeks steadily flush pink as I take my time.

"What?" She half whispers.

I shrug. "You look better like this."

"Like what?"

"Not all dressed up."

She raises her eyebrows before looking down at her outfit. She's in a pair of daisy dukes and a tank top that scoops low enough to give a taste of her perky breasts. She's done her makeup but it's less heavy and her hair is up in a ponytail that I'm dying to yank on.

"You look better too." She replies.

"*How so?*" *I'm wearing jeans and a t-shirt. Not all that different from the outfit I was in when I'd pinned her against the wall barely a week ago. She grins.* "*In daylight.*"

Yeah that grin does something, sends the blood rushing to my cock. My eyes flit to her perfect plump lips and I'm dying more than ever to grab her face and shove it right where it belongs.

"*Are you going to ruin me again?*" *She asks.*

"*I had something else in mind.*"

"*What?*" *She says, the nervousness now apparent in her voice.*

I give her a smirk, put the car in drive and pull off. I want to keep her on edge. Maybe I'm being an ass but I'm enjoying this. And I'm enjoying the fact that she's just going with this, that she's not challenging me, not questioning me.

I'm her enemy and yet here she is, willing sat beside with no idea where we're headed or what my intentions are. I could be taking her out of the city, I could be planning anything, and yet she's sitting as calmly as if this is all perfectly normal.

I put my hand on her thigh. It's possessive but that's the point. She tenses a little looking at me while I keep my face on the road. Her skin is so smooth, so ridiculous soft, I can't help running my thumb over it.

"*You shaved for me?*" *I tease.*

"*Not for you actually. I always shave. Body hair is unattractive.*"

I let out a chuckle. "*Is that why your pussy is bare?*"

She gasps. A tiny shocked noise that makes me want to force a louder one from her.

"*I'm not complaining.*" *I say.* "*I'm sure all the guys you've been with appreciate it.*"

She clears her throat, folding her arms. "*I haven't actually.*"

"*Haven't what?*"

"*Been with other guys.*"

"*Excuse me?*" *We're at a set of traffic lights. They're red, thank god, so I take the opportunity to look at her. She's flushed. Embarrassed. Like she's ashamed of the fact she hasn't been sleeping around.*

"I've not been with other guys." She repeats, her eyes focused on the dashboard, her words all but confirming what I suspected.

"You mean you're a virgin." I state.

She gulps. *"Yes, sort of."*

"What do you mean sort of?"

"I mean I haven't been with anyone period." She huffs, her eyes blazing now as she half glares at me.

I stare back, meeting that glare head on, fully prepared to burn in the heat of it if it meant I'd get a chance to touch her again.

A car horn beeps loudly and we both jump. The lights are green. Fuck knows how long we've been sat staring at each other but I break our gaze as we drive off.

A silence sets in. No doubt awkward for her but for me it's anything but. I chew my lip for a second, thinking about how to proceed. I could easily change the conversation, ask about her day, ask her anything because let's face it neither of us knows the other that well, if at all, and quite frankly I don't give a shit for that kind of talk.

"So I'm the only one who's fingers have been inside you?" I say.

"Beyond my own." She sounds almost sulky.

I let out a laugh. *"How often do you touch yourself Rose? Huh?"*

She glares again but I can see from the way she's squeezing her thighs that she's getting turned on. If she dropped her gaze she'd see my reaction too, the way my pants are so fucking tight around my cock.

"I don't think that's any of your business." She states.

"No?" I tease. *"You ever touched yourself while thinking of me?"*

She gasps, turning to stare out the window and I wonder if she's planning on jumping out at the next junction. I guess I can't blame her. I'm being a prick I know, but I'm enjoying it, enjoying her reaction, enjoying getting under the little pampered princess's skin.

"How come you've never been with anyone else?" I ask.

She shrugs. *"It's not from lack of trying. My parents pretty much control my life. They watch me like a hawk."*

"Where do they think you are right now?" I ask. No doubt she's told some lie to explain her absence.

"In bed with a headache."

"And if they check?"

"They won't look too close" She shrugs. "They'll see the outline of a sleeping person under the duvet and be satisfied. I'll sneak back in later and they'll be none the wiser."

I laugh. She's confident of herself. She's probably pulled that stunt before.

"You're a little liar aren't you Rose?"

"When I have to." She says jutting her chin in defiance.

"Will you lie to me?" I ask.

She tilts her head, that hardness softening. "No, as long as you don't lie to me."

I take her hand squeezing it. It's odd that despite how little we know each other already I feel something for this girl. "I won't lie." I say wanting her to hear it, to hear what I'm feeling. "I'll be honest with you. Always."

She smiles like I've just promised her the world. And then her hands start undoing the buttons on her tight little shorts.

"What are you doing?" I ask.

She takes my hand, pushing it down into the hot wet fabric beneath. "I thought we agreed to be honest with one another?"

"How is this honest?" I ask as she manoeuvres my fingers right to where she wants them.

"I want you to touch me and I know you want to as well." She says as she starts to rock her hips just a little.

"Fuck." I growl, looking around, trying to figure out how the hell to get off this damn road. I cut the lane, earning a sharp toot from the person I almost crash into and then I pull off, onto a side road, pulling up as soon as I can.

She glances around, noticing how deserted this road is and then pulls her shorts down entirely leaving her in just her tiny thong.

"You're fast becoming a slut for me." I taunt.

"Like you don't want this." She says spreading her legs.

I grin, grabbing her hand and shoving it down my own pants, ensuring she gets a good hold of me. Her eyes widen as she feels my cock and how hard I am. "Don't worry Rose." I murmur as I tighten my grip around hers. "I'll show you what to do. Teach you everything you need to know."

She nods. Her eyes already dilating, her body already leaking out. "What are you waiting for Roman? Ruin me."

I grin, leaning in to capture her lips as my hands work away to bring us both to orgasm.

For someone as high-profile as Paris Blumenfeld is, you'd think he'd take security more seriously. It was practically child's play to hack into their cameras and put them on a loop. And the watchmen? They make as much noise as a rampaging elephant, enough to cover the sounds of my own feet as I make my way across the gravel and to my new hiding place.

I stare into the house. The amount of glass this place has makes it easy to see into almost every room. Though I'll deny it, my eyes are already searching for her and when I finally find those tortuous curves I'm surprised to see her curled up, with a book, and a dog no less.

The Rose I knew didn't read. She didn't have the patience for it. She never stayed still long enough. Nor was she a dog person or an any type of animal person. Not that she was cruel or anything, but again, it wasn't an interest.

I tilt my head watching her turn the page, absentmindedly scratching the belly of the little dog as it rolls on its back clearly loving the attention. Did he buy her that pet? Was that some anniversary gift *he* got her? My anger flares at the thought. At the perfect world of domesticity she seems to have built for herself.

I look around the house, taking in the stark minimalism. There's nothing but a few paintings on the walls. All pretentious art that they've no doubt chosen to reflect their highly cultured image.

Only there's also nothing that feels like her. Nothing that reflects the woman I used to know.

But then again I didn't really know her, did I? The woman I loved never existed. She was a mirage. A creature made entirely from fantasy while the real Rose no doubt laughed at how easily I was fooled.

I wonder if her entire family were in on it. If that was just another of their games. But surely if it was she'd have never let it get that far, never have actually slept with me? I shake my head. Something makes me doubt it, even now, even after all this evidence showing me what she is, I can't bring myself to admit that *those* moments were a farce.

I can still see her when I close my eyes.

I see her.

And me.

I see us both, wrapped up in the other.

I see the way her body embraced mine. The way the two of us knew what to do, how to touch, how to pleasure though we were both running off pure instinct. I can see the way her mouth opened, the way her body arched and her muscles contracted.

I can hear her too.

The way she moaned. The way she whimpered as I wound her body tighter and tighter until that inevitable release came. Until she came. Until she fell apart under my touch. Only my touch.

She was mine. In those moments she truly was mine.

The darkness twists in me, the hate, the anger, all of it churning and it takes all my strength not to storm into that house right now and show her what she did, how big a monster she made of me.

If she'd only come with me, if she'd only left, we could be happy now. We could be normal.

I smirk as I think that because I'm a fool. She was never going to leave. This life, this glided, gold plated life is what she really craved. Under all the pretence, all the words to the contrary, it was this she chose. This she fought for.

Not me. Not us.

She became a Blumenfeld. She became this creature more plastic fantastic than human.

Right on cue he walks in. I see the door shut. I see the way he tosses his jacket to the waiting maid, stalking through the house like a king and I guess in a way he is. This is his domain. His castle.

Rose looks up as he saunters in. He says something and she responds by putting her book down and getting up.

And together they walk upstairs.

Him behind her. Him overshadowing every step she takes.

I don't want to look.

I don't want to see her kissing him. Wrapping her body around his. Enjoying his touch when it should be me she desires. Me that she wants.

I should probably leave now. I want to.

But something makes me watch.

It's like a car crash unfolding. I know it's only going to hurt me. I know it's only going to cut me but I have to see, I have to witness this. To prove to myself that she is exactly what I fear. To take a stake and drive it right into the heart of my floundering hope, that still, despite everything remains.

Of course they've fucked. They've been married long enough, I don't doubt Paris has fucked her more times this year than I ever did the entirety of our time together and yet as I watch it feels so much worse than I could have imagined.

He's kissing her. She's kissing him back.

There's not the passion, not the fire that we had, but she's still responding. She still clearly wants this.

His mouth moves across her skin, removing each layer of fabric with his hands and revealing more and more of her flesh. I'm too far away to make out the finer details but my mind is more than capable of filling in the blanks and, as I watch, the current Rose turns back to the twenty year old I loved. It's her body I'm imagining as Paris goes down on her. As his hands spread her thighs. As his mouth begins to devour that part of her that once only I knew intimately.

She rolls her head, I can't tell if she's liking it or faking it but as the minutes pass she clearly grows more frustrated. She pulls him up. His mouth is back on hers. I can imagine how he tastes now, the saltiness of her seasoning his tongue.

And then I watch as he fucks her. As he thrusts over and over and she arches her back, clearly seeking more. Clearly wanting more. His hands grab at her waist. I don't doubt if I was there, in the room with them he'd be grunting away like a pig. Would she be moaning? Would she be crying out in pleasure? Something about her expression makes me think not.

And when he comes there's one obvious thing of note. That she hasn't. He lays across her, swamping her body beneath his and she stays perfectly still, half crushed by him. Her head is turned, it's almost as if she's in a daze but it's not from afterglow. I smirk more in that knowledge because that never happened when she was with me. It wasn't even a conscious thing. I just knew how to take care of her and I made sure her needs were met. All of them. Every single one. Without even having to try either.

How satisfying it is to know that Paris is either too selfish or incapable of doing the same.

When I was with her she was always satisfied. She always came. Multiple times at that. But right now her husband can't even give her one orgasm. Not even one.

It's that notion that makes my walk back to my house all the better. That keeps the smile on my face long after they've no doubt fallen asleep.

And when Ben asks what's got me in such a good mood I just shake my head. It's my secret right now. I want to savour it a bit longer.

ROSE

Paris half digs his fingers into my waist but the smile remains on my lips nonetheless. I know he's angry. I don't know what about exactly but already I know how this evening is going to end.

We're at one of the Governor's events. Technically it's a political rally but we all know it's a done deal. Darius is as good as re-elected before the ballot paper has even been finalised and printed. He holds too much sway for there to be any other outcome.

My black dress clings to me and mercifully the way it covers hides the remnants from my husband's last outburst while still looking revealing enough to be glamourous. And with my hair styled and huge diamonds dangling from my ears, I fit the part.

Darius is barely metres from us. When Paris disappears off to the bar it's Darius who notices I'm alone and he takes the moment to talk to me. We've had an easy enough relationship considering him being the Governor and me being my father's daughter has often meant we've been on opposing sides.

The Capulets are often making demands he cannot meet but as Horace Montague aged, even I can see my family's alliance with the Blumenfeld's is tightening. The only question is whether Darius is aware of it and whether it is something he will continue to encourage because, if he decides we are a threat, I don't doubt his response will be as swift as it is deadly.

"Beautiful as always Rose." He says passing me a glass of champagne and I give him a smile. He's a shrewd man. Deadly when crossed but not cruel for cruelty's sake from what I've seen.

"Thank you." I reply.

"Where is that husband of yours, to have abandoned you so?"

I glance around making a show of looking for Paris when in truth I'm pleased he's gone. Perhaps he'll sate his anger on someone else though I don't have high hopes of it.

"Stick with me then. I will keep you safe." He teases taking my hand and tucking it into the crook of his arm. I laugh while around us camera's flash. No doubt wanting to get a pretty memento to upload to social media and for the press to print later.

From the sides I can feel my family watching. I don't look. I don't want to see the ambition reflected in their stares. This will make my father happy. To have his daughter on the arm of the Governor, for the entirety of Verona Bay to see a Capulet photographed with him.

Yes, this will make him very happy indeed.

I think of asking Darius about Otto. Of bringing it up. But in truth it feels to risky in such a situation. What would I say if he took offence? For all the Capulet blood that runs in my veins I don't have the sophistication that the rest of my family do. Afterall I wasn't brought up to be that person. My only value was in the marriage market, not in the powerplay of politics.

"You know, if you weren't half my age, and if you weren't married to my nephew, I'd have snapped you up myself." He states.

I roll my eyes with amusement. "Is that so?"

He grins more. He's not *exactly* being a lech. It's just how he is. A ladies man through and through. He gets the occasional complaint every now and then about sexual impropriety, about inappropriate comments but nothing that ever sticks. The man is like Teflon. And especially so since his wife died. Apparently a long sustained illness has bought him a lifetime worth of sympathy and justifications.

"Governor."

Darius turns to see one of his men stood awkwardly.

"What is it?" Darius asks.

The man glances at me then murmurs something into his ear. Darius shakes his head. "I'm not dealing with that now." He says. "Go make yourself busy."

The man sighs and walks away.

"Everything okay?" I ask.

Darius smiles. "Nothing to worry your pretty head." He says raising his glass to chink against mine. "But let me ask you Rose, you and Paris have been together, four years…"

"Five." I say. Five long years.

"Why have you never had children?"

I gulp. The words seem to send a shiver through me. Children? In what world would I want to bring children into the wreck that is my marriage? I open my mouth to reply, to say something, anything but then Paris is back.

"What are you talking about?" He asks. His eyes fixing more on me than Darius as if he sees some sort of conspiracy, as if I'm so conniving I might be able to turn his own uncle against him.

"Children." Darius says smiling.

"Excuse me?" Paris says.

"You two have been married long enough. Is there some medical reason why you haven't had babies?"

I drop my eyes. I don't want to look at either of them. Paris slides his hand back around my waist and it's all I can to just stand there and not recoil from his skin against mine.

"No reason." He says smoothly.

"Then get to it. I want to have nieces and nephews enough to fill these halls. And with a wife as beautiful as Rose is, every single one will be a heartbreaker."

Paris smiles more. "Is that a direct order from the Governor himself?"

Darius laughs.

"Do you need an order to fuck your wife Paris?" Calvin says walking up to the three of us.

I try not to flinch as I look at him. Though Darius is Governor, we all know Calvin is just as powerful. That he has his nasty little fingers so firmly in every aspect of Verona life that he might as well have a crown on his god damn head.

I hate him. I can't even pinpoint why but I do. Something about him puts the fear of god into me. He scans his eyes over me in such a predatory way that I want to sprint from this room and never look back only Paris's hands are gripping me so tightly I couldn't escape if I wanted to.

Paris makes some comment that I don't hear. Calvin replies slapping him on the back and the three of them laugh while I'm stood trying not to look outraged. Somehow I don't think it's the drink talking right now and even if it was, it still wouldn't make any of this acceptable.

Paris leads me away and because everyone here can clearly see us, he makes a good show of giving me attention, playing the doting husband. And I make just a good show of being the perfect wife.

More cameras flash. I'd put money on our image being front page.

And when the evening is finally over we get into our chauffeured car, still smiling, and disappear into the night.

ROMAN

I've taken to stalking her. First it was just one night. One logical reason too. I needed to scope out the place. I needed to see it for myself. If I'm going to bring them down then it makes sense.

It's logical.

But then I came back again, watching the next night too. Seeing their interactions, seeing the way they lived, the way they fit together.

And tonight I took it one step further. I followed them to this event the Governor was hosting. I watched as she walked with her husband's arm lovingly around her, watched as she laughed with Darius and Calvin too.

She's done well. I'll give her that. The traitorous bitch. She's done very well in fact. No doubt her father is proud of his achievements. His little whore of a daughter has ensured the Capulets will always stay in the Governor's good books and for a moment, as I watch the three of them, Darius, Rose and Paris, I wonder if she's fucking him too. If she's fucking the Governor.

I wouldn't put it past her. I wouldn't put anything past her at this point.

They wander off. The happily married couple. His arm still around her waist and if anything that grates me more, the way he holds her, the way he seems to possess every bit of air she exists in.

She was mine. She should have been mine. And yet here she is, with her husband, happy, content, blissfully unaware that any other man exists except for him.

They get into the car, chauffeur driven of course, and then they disappear off back to their soulless home.

I shouldn't follow. I know I shouldn't.

And yet I do.

By the time I've hacked into their security system and concealed myself in my usual safe space they're inside. Rose has kicked off her heels and Paris looks like he's pleading for something.

I frown watching them. His face is contorted and I realise he's not pleading at all. Is that rage? Are they fighting? Is that what this is? A lovers tiff? The perfect couple aren't so perfect after all. Perhaps I'm the sick one here to get a perverse sense of pleasure from that thought.

That her perfect little world isn't so fucking perfect.

She turns. Putting what looks like a glass of water down and his hands grab her. I snarl despite myself. He's pulling her to him and it's more than apparent what he wants, what's about to happen. *Again.* I clench my fists.

Only she pushes back, right at the moment when I go to leave and that makes me pause.

I see her hands push against his chest. His face contorts more, his hands grab at the black slip of her dress and she pushes harder.

Apparently all is not as perfect in paradise as they like to present. I smirk despite myself. She made her bed, I shouldn't feel sorry for her. She chose this life. I offered her an escape. I offered her a chance to be with me and she turned her back. No doubt she decided that power was worth more to her than anything I could offer.

She's a Capulet after all. I shouldn't have been surprised. I should have seen it coming.

She chose him.

I let out a low breath. Something in my stomach twists as I watch the scene play out and I fight the urge to make myself known but what would be the point? He's her husband. She married him.

And then I see his fist. It happens almost in slow motion, the way his hand curls, the way he delivers the perfect side swipe and his knuckles collide with her cheek.

She jolts. For a moment it's like she doesn't register it.

But then he hits again. He *fucking* hits her again.

She falls this time, as though the force of the blow has knocked the life out of her. I can see her legs moving so I know she's not unconscious but he doesn't seem in the least bit concerned. Instead he's pulling her round, yanking her hair with one hand and her dress off with the other.

My heart thumps in my chest as it dawns on me what this is. I take a step forward, out from obscurity, only that immediately alerts one of the guards to my presence. A flash light spins round to where I am. Illuminating me.

And before I know it I'm racing from the scene. Forcing myself to move. I can't do anything anyway. I can't stop it. If I do, everything I've worked for will be ruined.

I have to leave. I have no choice.

ROMAN

I get back to my house. Sneak in through the old servants entrance but Ben already knows where I've been. I wasn't stupid enough to hide that from him, though he took his time to tell me how reckless it was to be anywhere near her.

I guess he's right.

Because this changes everything.

I kick off my muddy trainers, pull off the hooded jacket that helped hide my face and ditch it. My t-shirt sticks to the sweat along my back. I need a shower.

But more than that I need a drink.

I storm up into the drawing room. In years past my father would be in here, with his cronies. They'd be planning. They'd be conspiring. It feels like all the whispers still hang in the air and god only knows what these four walls have been privy to.

I pour a drink. Down it. Then pour another.

He hit her.

The words keep reverberating in my head. Sure I wanted her dead. Sure I even had the bullet in the chamber with my finger poised on the trigger, but somehow this feels different. I had reasons. Good reasons. She betrayed me after all. And there's a fine line between taking out an adversary and doing what Paris is right now.

I growl as I realise it. What is almost certainly happening back at that house.

As much of a monster as I am I would never have inflicted that on her. I shut my eyes. Perhaps a part of me should feel joy, she made her bed didn't she? She married him. Why should I care what their relationship is? What should I care if he hurts her? If he beats her? If he rapes her even?

But I do care. I do *fucking* care.

"What happened?" Ben says leaning against the door. He's always been so good at reading me.

I shake my head. Can I tell him? What would he say? No doubt he'd call me a fool for going back there again.

"I went back to the house." I say. I don't need to state whose. He already knows.

"And?" He says.

"Paris hit her." I state.

Ben narrows his eyes. "So what?"

I shake my head and down the second drink. "He hit her."

"She married…."

"I watched him Ben." I half yell. "I watched him hit her, and then rip her dress off and…" My words die as I see Sofia stood just behind him and the expression on her face says it all.

"It's not the first time." She says.

"What are you talking about?" I snap.

"Paris hits her regularly enough."

"How do you know that?" Ben asks.

She shrugs. "We go to the same country club. She's not as good at hiding the bruises as she thinks. Besides it's hard to hide all of them when you're getting changed."

"You've seen each other changing?" Ben says.

She rolls her eyes in response. "Of course that's what you would take from that." She mutters before looking back at me. "Roman, what are you thinking?"

I shake my head, walking over to the couch and sink down into it. I don't know what I'm thinking but right now it feels like everything I'd planned is off kilter.

"So he hits her?" Ben says. "What's the big deal?"

"It is a big deal." I mutter. If I've overlooked this, what else have I not seen? What else have I missed?

"She still married him. She still chose to stay." Ben states. I know he's right. Nothing that I witnessed tonight changes that. She *did* choose to stay. She *did* choose to walk away from everything we could have been.

So why does this feel so significant?

"Roman." Sofia says. She's sitting beside me now, though when she moved I couldn't tell you. "Are you sure she's who you think she is?"

"Yes." I spit the word. Maybe their marriage isn't what it appears but somethings haven't changed. She still walked away. She still chose him.

"Why don't you talk to her? Ask her why she did it. See what she says."

"That's not a good idea." Ben says quickly. "No one knows he's here. He can't exactly walk up to her in the street can he?"

"He's been going to her house enough times…" Sofia mutters.

"It's not just her house is it? Paris is there." Ben states.

I snarl at his name. That fucking prick.

I'm going to kill him. In this moment, that's what I decide. That will be my next move. I'm going to fucking kill him for what

63

he's done, whether she agreed or not, he married her, he took her from me and more than that, he's hurt her.

I'm going to make that bastard pay.

And then I'll deal with Rose. But more than that I'll see how she truly feels for him, when he's dead at her feet, will she cry over his coffin? Will she mourn him? Whatever she does will dictate how I treat her, whether I show her kindness, mercy even, or the rage that's been festering these last six years.

10

ROSE

"*Someone was outside.*" The security guard states.

I barely look up. It's three in the morning. My head is killing me from more than just the alcohol and the icepack against my face is making my fingers throb with the cold.

Paris is pacing back and forth. What most people would consider his killer looks contorted into something akin to concern.

He looks at me and I can feel the heat of his glare, like it's my fault, like I did this.

"What did they see? How long were they there?" He starts shouting out questions but the security man doesn't seem to have any reply. "What about the CCTV?"

"There's nothing there. We didn't pick anything up on any cameras."

I grit my teeth. Another no show on the CCTV? That can't be a coincidence can it? I don't voice it. I don't say anything.

Paris snarls tossing a glass ornament.

The security man glances at me but I avoid his gaze. I know they know what Paris is like, who he really is but none of us say the words. None of us speak it out loud.

"I want more cameras. I want more men patrolling too. No one gets inside this compound without us knowing." Paris growls. The man nods.

"You're dismissed." Paris waves his hand barely looking at him as he says it.

The security man spins on his heels and leaves the room as quickly as he can without making it obvious he wants to run, clearly relieved that he's not getting a beating too.

I let out a low sigh. The signs were there that this night was going to be a bad one but even I hadn't guessed it would be this long. I need another drink but that would only make things worse.

"If they saw…" Paris snaps.

I let out a hollow laugh. "What?" I snap.

He narrows his eyes, his body moving quickly to dwarf mine. "This was your fault."

"And how do you figure that out?" I retort. Christ my face is throbbing. It doesn't feel like the ice has done anything to help it. How hard did he hit me this time?

"If you hadn't picked a fight. If you'd acted the way a wife should."

"You mean just give you what you want?" I sneer.

His hands find my hair, yanking my neck back at an angle that forces me to look at him. Even now he's itching to lash out again isn't he?

"You're my wife. My property. I can do what I like with you."

"Then why are you so concerned about what someone might have seen?"

He snarls, his fingers twisting and I feel more of my hair break. At this rate I may well have to tie it up until it recovers.

"Why are you always so difficult?" He snaps. "I've given you everything. I've given your family everything too. You Capulets wouldn't have half the power you have right now if it wasn't for me. If it wasn't for my name attached to yours. You live a life of luxury because of me and yet you won't even show any gratitude? FOR ANY OF IT." His spit hits my face as he yells, his fingers clawing at my head.

He wants gratitude? He wants me to be thankful? I scrunch my fist up and slam it into his side. Yeah I'm not opposed to getting my hands dirty either. Though he's the one that always turns to violence, I'm not going to just take it. No, more often than not I've started fighting back, showing him I'm not going to be his eternal punchbag.

I'm not proud that I resort to his level but to some degree I can rationalise it. Besides it makes the bruises more palatable. The pain too. It makes it easier to look myself in the mirror and know I didn't just cry and beg him to stop, I gave as good as I got.

"Is that the best you've got?" He mocks, grabbing my hand in his and crushing my knuckles to the point I think they might break but he's careful not to cross that line. Never to do any more than nasty bruises. Because broken bones require more explanation. Broken bones are harder to deny. Harder to cover.

"Let me go Paris." I reply trying to jerk out of his grip.

"You're my wife."

"Then treat me like that."

He smiles. That awful crooked smile he gets before he does something unforgiveable. "Is that what you want Rose?" His hands grab me tighter and my stomach lurches. He's going to do *it* again. A repeat of earlier, not that that was the first time, but usually he slinks off after, half ashamed at himself as well as me once the moment is passed.

"You heard Darius. He wants nieces and nephews." He says into my ear as his hands begin to claw away at my flesh, ripping open the robe I wrapped around myself like some sort of shield.

"And I said no." I cry back.

He laughs. "You don't get to say no Rose. I'm in charge here. Not you. And you'll take everything I give you, because under that polished exterior you're just like the rest of your family, a bunch of grubby whores willing to do anything for a bit more power."

ROSE

I t's been a long week. I've spent most of it hiding while no doubt the world assumes I'm getting over Darius's political rally.

But in truth I'm getting over the events *after* it.

It's not the first time Paris has pulled that move. Usually I just give in where sex is concerned. It's easier that way and it often saves me a few bruises too. But after the comments Darius made, something made me want to take a stand, to assert myself, to prove that I'm more than what they all see me as.

I don't want children. Not with Paris. Not in this relationship.

Only he clearly doesn't give a shit and he'll make sure he ticks that box as quickly as he can. Afterall, for all Paris's connections, for all his money, we both know his real power comes from Darius. He needs to keep him sweet. He needs to keep in favour.

And apparently my uterus is how he does that.

But what Paris doesn't know is that I have an IUD fitted. I bribed a doctor to do it and I paid a princely sum to make sure it's not in my medical records because I don't trust any of my family, or Paris himself to not get hold of them should the occasion call for it.

So he can fuck me as many times as he wants. He won't achieve his goal. I won't get pregnant.

I let out a small sigh of relief as I tell myself that. That it won't happen. That I won't be forced to bring some poor innocent child into this horror show of a union.

That history won't repeat itself.

~~But today I don't have an excuse for hiding; I've got ten with my mother. Joy of joys.~~

The Bentley pulls up outside. I take a glance at myself in the mirror and check my makeup is still covering. I look immaculate. Presentable. The very image of perfection this city expects of me.

The whole drive I stare out the window wondering what my life would be if I wasn't a Capulet. If my family's expectations didn't overrule every aspect of my life. Would I be happy? Would I be content? I don't harbour any illusions that my life would be easier.

I know I'm privileged, incredibly so.

I've never had to worry about paying bills, never even looked at the price tag on anything I get. Nor do I pay attention when the assistant rings up the bill. I just hand over my card. The numbers don't matter.

I've never woken up hungry, wondering where my next meal will come from.

In truth, I've lived a life of luxury in so many ways, so perhaps I'm being ungrateful to want happiness too, perhaps I'm asking too much, being too greedy.

But then I'm a Capulet. That's what we are by nature. Greedy.

I get out of the car and the wind makes my hair whip across my face forcing me to tuck it behind my ears. I've styled it today in big waves to cover the damage of Paris's destruction. I would have tied

70

it up but I need the volume to stop the light from hitting my face at the wrong angle and showing the final vestiges of swollen flesh.

We're meeting in the Bay District. The most expensive part. Every bar, every restaurant has a waiting list months in advance but we're Capulets. Waiting lists are for the masses not for the likes of us.

The doormen greet me with polite hellos and I smile back with my heels clacking against the polished surface.

I'm wearing a navy jumpsuit with a subtle Hermes belt. It's understated. The kind of outfit I feel most comfortable in.

The Plaza is a homage to old time Hollywood glamour and all that entails with art nouveau panels and great palms that could almost lull you into believing you'd actually travelled back in time.

As expected my mother has her favourite table, right in the middle, where she sits like a queen. She's wearing classic Chanel with a string of pearls too.

"Rose." She says smiling before hugging me and kissing either side of my cheeks.

I don't know if she notices as I wince just a little. If she does she does mention it. Most of the bruising is gone. It's more just colouring now that I need to hide but my makeup is doing a stellar job of that.

"Mother." I say taking a seat opposite.

A waiter appears almost immediately and we order some drinks.

She fixes her eyes on me then takes my hand. Her nails are blood red, perfectly manicured, her skin looks ageless.

"He's done it again hasn't he." She says quietly.

I frown. Perhaps she has been paying more attention than I gave her credit for.

"What was his reason this time?" She asks.

I shrug. "There's always something." I murmur. It doesn't really matter anyway. My marriage isn't about me. It's about Paris. About what he brings to our family.

She squeezes my hand sympathetically. "But you're handling it well. Not making a scene. Just keeping your chin up."

I don't reply. It's pointless to say anything anyway.

"Does Darius know?" She asks.

I shake my head. No he doesn't. Not that I think he'd do all that much if he did. Paris is his favourite nephew. He's like a son to him.

"It is what it is." I say because I don't want her sympathy. After all I married him didn't I? Not that I had that much choice but still, I made this bed, now I have to lie in it.

The waiter comes back with our drinks. A cappuccino for her. A flat white for me.

I take a sip grateful for the caffeine as well as the warmth of it.

"What of Otto, have you spoken to Darius about him?"

"No." I say. "And I don't know how. Father seems to be labouring under the illusion that I have a better relationship with Darius than I do."

"You seemed pretty close this week." She states.

I let out a small laugh. "Appearances are deceptive you know that."

"Is that why Paris did that?" She asks.

I sigh. "He gets jealous." I mutter. Besides that's only half the story, the more palatable side though not by much.

"We can't afford for Sofia Montague to marry Otto."

"I know." I say. "But I don't think she's going to."

My mother pulls a face. "She's a Montague. That makes her a conniving bitch by nature. We can't assume anything."

I nod but I'm so over this argument. I've never even seen Sofia near Otto. In fact I've never seen her interested in any man for that matter. Besides she has independence, and most of the Montague fortune, why would she throw that away for a man twice her age who would clearly control every aspect of her life?

"Now that Horace is gone we have a unique opportunity to take them down."

I take another sip. That's all my family thinks about. This bitter old rivalry. It's all consuming. I don't even know what we'd do if we did truly defeat them because it feels like our whole existence is tied up with theirs, our whole purpose certainly is.

Horace was one of the lucky few; he'd died peacefully enough in his bed. Unlike most of his kin. Unlike most of ours.

For the briefest moment I think of my cousin. Of Tyrone's older brother, Tybalt. The man Roman killed. The man whose death forced him into exile.

For a moment my heart stops. As *his* name reverberates, as his face cuts to my very soul.

"Rose?" My mother says and I realise I've clenched my eyes shut. Clenched my jaw shut too. I can't think of him. I won't think of him.

That old pain. The bitter, gut wrenching grief twists inside and it takes all my strength to beat it back down.

"It's okay." I say smiling. Replacing my pain with the same false cheery mask I wear. Rose Capulet, the sunshine princess of Verona Bay. That's what they actually call me. I deserve an award for my acting performance because I truly doubt anyone, even my mother, sees the real me.

"I meant what I said. I'm here for you. Here if you want to talk."

"I don't." I say. I can't talk about it. I'm done talking about it. That part of my life is over. Gone for good. All my hopes, all my dreams, all of my stupid naive beliefs were shattered the day that man walked away, the day he showed me what he really was and exactly what I'd meant to him.

Nothing.

That's what.

And talking about it, going through it again won't make it better. It won't solve anything. All it will do is hurt me more.

And I'm done hurting. I'm done with all of it. I want to be free, I want to live the life I have, no matter how limited it is, no matter how constrained, because I don't believe I will be saddled to Paris forever.

Somehow I know our marriage won't last.

Either he'll grow bored of me and grant me a divorce or he'll do something reckless, something no one can ignore. And when that happens I'll be free. I'll be free of all of them. Of my father as well as my husband. And it's that thought that sustains me, that thought that keeps me going when I wash my blood off my skin, when I press an ice pack to a new bruise, when I clear up the mess of some object he's smashed to pieces in his rage.

No Paris will not be the end of me. One way or another I will get my emancipation from him.

"Let's do dinner then."

I blink confused. "We're out now…" I say.

She laughs. "Not just us. I mean your father and I and you and Paris. Let's spend a little time together. It'll be good for you. Good for the pair of you. Maybe remind you both of why your marriage is a good thing."

"Is it?" I scoff.

"Of course it is." She says. "You make a good couple. You just need to get past this blip."

I nod. There's not much to say. It's not a blip but I don't have the energy to argue about it and as much as I know my mother cares, she won't see it any other way no matter how much I protest.

"Dinner sounds good." I say smiling while internally I couldn't think of anything worse.

ROMAN

A week has passed. A week that I've sat here, in the dark obscurity of the great Montague house. Planning. Conspiring.

Every time the door goes Ben and I freeze. We're lurking on the top floor, in what was once servants quarters. It's despicable that a Montague should be existing like this. It's a mockery of our name, our legacy.

But it's not just the Capulets who created this situation. My father did too because he was too weak in the end, too lost after my exile to do anything constructive. He just shut down, rolled over like a dog, and let them fuck everything.

And then there was Darius. The great Governor.

Of course he had a hand in this. Though he played impartiality to the public, the fact is, he was the one pushing his nephew's marriage as much as Ignatio Capulet was because apparently he saw some alliance, some gain to be had by allying himself with them.

A part of me wonders if on reflection Rose is just cannon fodder. A pretty jewel that got caught up in the greater ambitions of the treacherous men surrounding her. But she didn't exactly fight it. She didn't do anything. She willingly walked down that aisle and said 'I do'.

When I left I gave her the means to follow. I made sure of it. I stood waiting for her for weeks and when the realisation hit me, when it sunk in that she wasn't coming, all my love, all my desire turned into a bitter twisted thing. My soul turned to darkness. My ~~heart did too.~~

~~No, she may be cannon fodder, she may be in over her head,~~ but that doesn't mean she's not complicit. That doesn't make her an innocent.

"Look at this." Ben says quietly. Downstairs are more 'well-wishers'. People intent on shoving their noses into our business, pretending they cared about my father now that he's dead and my poor sister is stuck, having to endure it like a saint.

I glance over at the paperwork.

"What is it?" I ask.

"Deeds."

"What?" I frown.

"Deeds. That name, I've been seeing it over and over." Ben states.

"So what?"

"So…" He says sliding over the extensive plan we made of Darius's extended family. He's got so many it's hard to keep track, though most of them don't bear the great Blumenfeld name, which if anything makes it more confusing. "Christos Argent died when he was six so how is he buying prime real estate in Verona Bay twenty years later?"

I frown following the line back to Darius through an illegitimate daughter no one seems to aware of. "It's interesting but I don't see how it helps."

"These deeds aren't for housing. They're for commercial buildings. All the businesses are still operating as if nothing's happened."

"And?"

"What if Darius is doing more than just playing the Governor? What if he's secretly buying up half of Verona, controlling all the major players and ensuring he has their loyalty?"

Would he do that? I wouldn't put it past him but what would be his end game? Why would he bother? He's Governor already. He holds enough property in his own name, he has enough wealth. Why would he need to take such action?

"Okay. Let's look into it." I mutter. I doubt this will be the smoking gun we're looking for but knowledge is power isn't it? Maybe there's something in there we can use.

The door creaks open and we both look up.

"Thank fuck he's gone." Sofia says.

"Who was it?" Ben asks.

"Otto fucking Blumenfeld."

"What?" I narrow my eyes. A Blumenfeld has had the audacity to come here? To our house?

"Don't know why you look so offended." Sofia says. "I was the one who's had to endure the last hour of him holding my hand and making not so subtle hints about how he could take care of me, help me handle my grief."

Ben reacts to that, his face turns deadly and just for a moment I wonder if he might do it, might finally admit to all of us how he actually feels about my sister. Only he doesn't. Coward that he is he just gets up and walks to the window, staring down, no doubt watching Otto's fucking car travelling down the drive far below.

I stare at his back and wonder how he manages to do it, to contain such emotion. But then I am too aren't I? Because even now, I still feel it. I still feel that deep longing for the deceitful creature that is Rose Capulet. *Fuck I'm a fool.*

"He wants to help you grieve?" I say.

"No. He wants to marry me." Sofia replies. "He wants the Montague fortune."

"That is not happening." Ben growls and I finally feel a bit of respect for him in how he's handling this situation. About fucking time.

"I agree." Sofia says. "I'm not stupid enough to marry anyone and, even if I were, it certainly wouldn't be a Blumenfeld."

"This is Darius's doing." I state. "I'm certain he was part of the reason he tied his nephew with the Capulets. If he can do the same to you then his family is linked to the only two houses that rival his own."

"Well I'm not interested. That is unless you think it's good idea." Sofia says.

"What?" My jaw drops. Why would she think that?

"Come on." She says fixing me with a look. "I know what you're both doing. I'm all for taking back what those bastards stole."

"No." I say. "I wouldn't ask that. Not of you."

She nods looking relieved. "Good."

"But it could help…" I say out loud thinking suddenly. Sofia is no fool. She's also not the kind of person content to sit on the side-lines. While I want to protect her I'm also not going to insult her by wrapping her up in cotton wool like she's a delicate flower. She's a Montague after all and we Montagues fight with our fists.

"What are you saying?" Ben snarls.

"Hear me out." I say holding my hands up. "Otto wants to marry her. He's made that clear enough. What if Sofia played the game? Didn't commit, just didn't outwardly refuse. If she can get into Darius's house, if she can get us some information, something of use."

"Absolutely not." Ben snaps.

"I'll do it." Sofia says smiling. "I want to bring those bastards down as much as you do."

"You're sure?" I check. I won't ask her to do anything she's not a hundred per cent comfortable with.

"Positive. I'll do whatever it takes." She says.

"No you fucking won't." Ben hisses half storming across the room to where she is.

She narrows her eyes. He's a good foot taller than her but she's not backing down. "Who the fuck do you think you are to be telling me what I can and cannot do? Huh?"

I bite my tongue. This battle isn't mine to fight but I understand the stakes well enough.

"I won't let you take such a risk." He says.

"Oh but you can? Roman can? What, you'd rather I stayed here, played the little innocent heiress, too fragile to do anything? Too scared to make any moves in case I break a nail? Fuck off."

She's grown I realise. My sister really has grown. She's not just a woman, she's a force to be reckoned with. She's every bit as fierce as me. How my father didn't see it I don't know.

"Sofia this isn't a joke." Ben snaps. "This isn't some soap drama. This is real life. You could get hurt. Or worse."

"Like I don't know that. I saw what they did to Mason. I saw what my brother had to do to save you from Tybalt. Do you really think I'm that naïve? I know what the risks are. I've spent the last six years watching it all play out."

"Sofia." I murmur.

"No. You've made your point. Now it's time I made mine." She states. "Father left us weak. I know he was broken, I know your exile all but destroyed him, but we have to fight back or the Capulets will kill us all and what's more I want revenge. I deserve it as much as you both."

I nod. It's not me she needs to convince. In truth she doesn't need to convince Ben either because he doesn't get to say yes or no.

The three of us are equals. Though he doesn't bear the Montague name he's as much one as me and Sofia are. If she wants to do this then it's her call and hers alone.

"Sofia..." Ben begins and I wonder if he might just do it, might finally have the balls. But then I see that same old resigned look. Christ the man is an idiot but a part of me is grateful. If he admits what he wants, if she feels the same then this throws the whole 'Otto plan' out the window and as selfish as I am, I need this. *We* need this.

"It's decided." She says. "I'll play his paramour and I'll get something on the Capulets we can actually use. I'll get something on Darius too. Bring the whole lot of them down."

ROSE

I've stayed out as much as I can. Hiding from Paris though in truth I wonder if he's also hiding from me. Perhaps his last act of barbarism was too far, even for him.

Whatever the reason, I'm enjoying the silence, I'm enjoying the peace.

My mother is making a big point of a family dinner though. Just the four of us. And as the hours approach my stomach is knotting more and more.

I'm out with Bella. She's been my sanctuary these last few days and this park has been both my heaven and hell. Everything I ever wanted and everything I can never have.

The children are playing. The park is packed today because the sun is out. I can hear their laughter, can hear their joy. When I think back to my own childhood I wonder if I was a happy child. It feels so long ago. The few memories I have are all peppered with death. Our family fighting theirs. Every meal, every holiday focused around how to defeat them in some way, how to win some petty battle more constructed in our own heads.

An ice cream van is doing a roaring trade and I can't help but watch as a little girl with dark brown pigtails jumps with excitement while queuing for one. She's wearing a little pink gingham dress. As her face turns to look around Bella pulls on her lead and I drop my gaze, half annoyed but half so god damn relieved. I scoop the dog up into my arms and she snuggles in alleviating that awful hollowness for the briefest of seconds.

When I dare to look back up the girl is gone. Vanished. Part of me wonders if she was really there at all and it wasn't just that my mind is playing tricks. Taunting me. Torturing me.

I grab my bag and reposition Bella to hold her more securely. If I'm going to play pretend at happy families tonight I need some alone time. I need to purge these feelings. This resentment too. I need to ensure my mask is so firmly in place it cannot slide.

And to do that I have to be away from here, away from all of this. From the haunting memories, from the haunting hope that somehow, despite everything, still pervades into my every excruciating moment of consciousness.

By the time six o clock comes I've mastered myself. I'm the perfect wife stood beside my husband.

He's wearing a tailored dinner suit that clings to his impeccably honed body. His blonde hair is coiffed in a side parting. His face clean shaven. Everything about him screams control. But when I look at him that's not what I see. I see chaos. I see danger. I see a man so used to getting what he wants that he will break the world to ensure it stays that way.

He meets my eyes. He looks almost bored.

A part of me wonders why he agreed to this evening. He didn't have to. God knows he holds enough power to tell my father where to stick it and yet he said yes before the words were even properly out of my mouth.

He takes my hand raising it to his lips and kisses it as if he were a perfect gentleman and not an animal.

"I assume we are over our storming." He murmurs.

I nod. He can think whatever he wants if it keeps things calm between us. I'm not so petty as to need to win every argument and with Paris it's safer if I don't.

His lips curl. "In that case I have something for you."

My eyes flicker to where his other hand moves to the jacket pocket. I see the glint between his fingers as he pulls them back out.

"Turn around."

As he wraps the heavy chain around my neck, I shut my eyes. It's classic Paris. This is his form of apology. Bribe me with jewels. Cover me with diamonds. Afterall, I'm a woman, I'm easy to buy in his eyes, easy to placate.

"What do you think?" His words are loaded. He doesn't care if I like it or not. It's not about my opinion on this new necklace. This is an ascent. An acquiesce to his wants. My surrender to him as the victor.

My fingers brush over the cold stone. It's a huge diamond. The necklace is double chained. With one wrapping around my neck like a choker and the second holding the massive pear cut stone that nestles just at the top of my cleavage. This would have cost a lot. More than most people's entire salary for a year.

Perhaps it's a sign of how far Paris thinks he's gone, how big a line he thinks he's crossed that he feels the need to buy my forgiveness with such a costly jewel.

"It's beautiful." I reply. It's garish too. Far to brash an item for me to choose myself but it matches most of my collection, most of the rings and jewels Paris has bought over the years.

The car pulls up and mercifully stops any further discussion. He takes my hand more firmly and I scoop the bottom of my evening dress with the other.

We look a perfect united front. We look a perfect couple. And as the car pulls away that's exactly how I intend to play tonight.

I'll be the perfect wife. The perfect daughter.

Once again folding myself away for the wants of every other person around me.

WE'RE IN THE SAME ROOM MY FAMILY MET IN LAST TIME. IT'S A ridiculously ornate space that resembles more of a great hall than a place to dine. Around us are the portraits of Capulets going back centuries right to the very founding of this city. It's a stark reminder to anyone that comes to this house of who we are, what our history is.

I wonder what Paris thinks when he sees this. His family date back just as far though his have always held the bigger swathes of authority. Somehow we've always been the supporting act. The Montagues too. For all our jiving for power, neither of us have ever achieved what the Blumenfeld's have.

That's exactly why my father wanted our marriage. Unite the Capulets with the Blumenfelds and suddenly we're on a par with them. We outrank the Montagues. For all intents and purpose we beat them.

"Will you be going away for the summer?" My mother asks.

Normally it's a given. Verona is too hot, too stifling to stay. Anyone that can afford to escapes for July and August and returns with the autumn. But this is an election year.

Paris tilts his head. "Probably not." He says. "I will need to be here, to support my uncle." His eyes turn to me and my mother asks the question before he can say anything further.

"But does Rose need to stay?"

I wince. Perhaps she's trying to buy me some respite. Give me a little breathing space. It would be exactly her kind of thing. Absence makes the heart grow fonder after all, doesn't it? Give us a little time apart and no doubt when we see each other next we'll fall madly back in love and everything will be fixed. I can practically see the plan forming in her head.

Paris tenses, just a little, just enough. "Not necessarily." He replies. "But she will."

I bite my tongue, swallowing the relief that was almost there, that was almost granted. He's making me stay. He's keeping me here, beside him, like a god damn slave.

"She is your wife. It would be expected that she stays with you." My father says pointedly, throwing my mother a look that clearly says 'shut the fuck up'.

My mother smiles, simpering. "Of course." She sips her wine and I take a gulp of mine hoping it might soothe the sting but it barely touches it.

"We've been married five years." Paris states and both my parents watch his face eagerly for any hint of what his next words might be. "Long enough for us to realise what we want."

My mother bites her lip. My father's face is hard. Does he think Paris might be saying he wants a divorce? Is that what he's thinking right now?

Paris looks across at me. Thank god the table is so big that he can't touch me in this moment but somehow I know what the next words will be. What awful thing he's about to declare.

"…We've decided to start a family of our own."

My mother gasps with visible joy. My father thaws instantly.

The necklace that Paris gave me feels suddenly like a noose around my neck. The diamond is suddenly a millstone dragging me down and I'm drowning.

Right here.

In front of them all.

Only they can't see that. My face betrays nothing. My lips are curled in the tiniest of smiles as if I'm bashful, shy even.

"Oh Paris." My mother exclaims clapping her hands. "Rose." She leans over the chair and hugs me.

I can't speak or this mask will break.

"We're not pregnant yet." Paris says. His eyes twinkling in triumph. "But very soon I'm sure we will be parents and you will have grandchildren."

"Blumenfelds." My mother says. "Our grandchildren will be Blumenfelds."

"Yes." Paris says smiling like that's the only thing he's ever wanted too.

I take another sip of my wine, only it turns into a gulp. And I'm telling myself over and over that this won't happen. That I won't let it. That for once in my life I'm not going to be railroaded into something I don't want.

"A toast." My father says raising his glass. "To Paris and Rose. My daughter and son-in-law and our future grandchildren."

"Paris and Rose." My mother echoes.

"And our children." Paris says his eyes fixed on me.

I raise my glass. Still I have nothing. No words. Just an awful, bitter pain that writhes worse than ever.

And I toast as if I'm happy about this.

Only deep down that's not what I'm thinking. Deep down I'm imagining him dead. My husband. I'm imagining that's what we're all cheering for, that's what we're all joyful about.

Paris dead and me finally free of this entire charade.

ROMAN

Yeah I did it. I took the opportunity to sneak inside. No one was around, at least none of the staff were anywhere to be seen.

And I watched the pair of them disappear into the waiting car, all dressed up and no doubt off to play the perfect couple at some event or other.

The house feels even more soulless than it did from the outside. Everything is pristine. White. Colourless. There are no personal effects, no photos, nothing out of place that suggests an actual couple lives here. It's all so stilted. As if they expect paparazzi to be peering over the hedges at any moment.

I pause looking about, savouring the moment of being here, in her space. My fingers skim across the surfaces feeling the cool quartz worktops, feeling the smooth metal sideboard and the soft sensual leather of the couch.

Sitting down into it I imagine how she would react if she knew I was here. She'd be shocked. Angry too. Part of me wants to wait it out, to sit here patiently until they return, to see the look on their faces, to hear her pitiful excuses first hand.

For a moment I think about doing it again. About ending her. I pull the gun from the folds of my jacket, running my hand over the cold smooth steel. It would feel good. Hell, it would feel more than good to sit here, to have the pair of them on their knees begging for forgiveness, begging for their lives. I smirk, my hand fingering the trigger as I imagine Paris's face contorted with fear as he begs me. And Rose, my dear darling Rose, pleading, as the ~~tears streaming down her cheeks~~

~~Yeah that would feel good.~~

Except I know I wouldn't be able to pull the trigger. Not on her. And Paris is going to get a far more useful ending than this. Useful to me that is. He'll die the way I've planned out as a demonstration not only of my power but that I know everything and that fighting me is futile.

I get up, climb the stairs. It's hard to imagine how anyone could live in such a sterile environment let alone the vivacious woman I fell in love with.

Except that's not her.

I have to remind myself over and over that that woman does not exist. That she never existed. The Rose I knew was a mirage, no more real than a character from a book. She played a part. She played a damn good part but that is all.

I wander through the rooms, this place has too many to count. Pointless rooms. Rooms they've clearly never used for anything.

As I come to their bedroom I pause. The bed is huge but like everything else it looks too perfect. The sheets looked freshly ironed, the pillows impossibly plump.

This is where she sleeps. Where she wakes beside him. Where they fuck.

That thought makes me mad. Unreasonably so. After everything I know of their relationship, at least on some level it's not all consensual but she still married him and she still chooses to be here.

I let out a snarl. A stupid noise that could give me away and proves I'm not altogether in control of myself. I pause, listening but there's no movement. Nothing. No one in the house has heard me.

The closet is filled with their clothes. Trappings of a gilded life organised onto hangers. His and hers.

I ignore his. I don't give a fuck about his suits, his shirts, any of it. But my hands flicker across hers. I feel the softness of her dresses, the richness of the fabrics.

I open a cupboard and my eyes widen just a little as I see the dirty clothes in the laundry box.

I shouldn't do it. I know I shouldn't but my hand reaches in, I grab at the maroon lace without considering the consequences, pulling it free. It's a thong. It's her thong. Worn. Dirty. I raise it to my face and like a man possessed I sniff groaning, taking in the deep scent of a creature who even now is like a drug to me.

I can taste her in this moment.

I can see her too.

As she was so many years ago, laid out, spread wide and eager for me to devour her.

I wonder what exactly she did while wearing this underwear, if Paris fucked her before she put them on, if she'd gotten aroused while wearing them and if some small residue of her still remains permeated into the stitching.

My cock hardens in my pants at the thought. At the memory of her smell, at the taste of her on my tongue. I reach down grabbing hold of myself, needing to get some release. My hand moves on instinct. I'm jacking off, grunting, burying my face into the thong surrounded by her clothes, her belongings, her damn intoxicating smell. Before I can even think, before I can register it's happening I'm coming, spunking all over a midnight blue dress. I can see the streams of it as it drips down. I could wipe it off. I could make an attempt at cleaning it up but I don't.

I want her to find it.

I want her to see what she's done.

The mess she's made.

Hell, Paris can take the blame for all I care.

I pocket the thong. I don't really care if I should or not. I don't really care if it's noticed by her. I want this keepsake, this tiny memento if you will. And god knows I'll be using it again, probably the minute I get back home.

I'm halfway back down the hall when I hear a key in the lock and I realise they're back. Sooner than expected. I've practically been caught red-handed. I move quickly, ducking back out of sight.

Voices echo through the house and it's clear they're getting nearer. I curse my stupidity for lurking so long but there's nothing to do now but hide.

I tuck myself back into the closet, concealing myself entirely by Rose's belongings.

Rose walks in first, but Paris is quick on her heels.

"Why won't you just take the damn test?" He hisses.

"Because there's no point. I'm not pregnant." She replies.

From where I am I can just make out their faces. He looks furious. She looks almost exhausted.

I guess I shouldn't be surprised they're working on starting a family. They've been together five years but the thought of her carrying his brats, of growing fat with his child, it makes me furious, so much so I'm not sure how I'm able to remain hiding.

"How would you know if you don't take the test?" He snaps.

She shakes her head, folding her arms. "I'm not pregnant. I'd know if I was."

He scoffs for a moment. "Like hell. When was the last time you even had a period huh?"

Her eyes widen like he's discovered some sort of secret and he latches onto it.

"What? Are you barren, is that it? Are you so dried up inside you can't even have children?"

"No." She says but I can hear the pain of something in her voice. God does she want that? Is that why she sounds distressed? Because she wants to have his child but is as yet unable to.

He laughs. A nasty bitter laugh and grabs her arm making her wince. "Then let's go make that baby."

"No." She says yanking back. "I don't want a child, not with you."

He laughs again. "I don't give a fuck Rose. We're doing this one way or another."

She opens her mouth to retort but clearly thinks better of it and then she just seems to give in, her body slumps, and she lets him lead her out the room like she's too tired to even fight.

I want to step out, to reveal myself but what would be the point? Paris would go running his mouth and Rose? Fuck knows what Rose would do.

So I stay where I am, thinking it over. Paris wants children, wants a family so much so he's going to force Rose into it. I don't feel bad for her, I don't feel sorry. The woman made her decision, she decided long ago what life she wanted. This is all of her own making and she deserves everything she gets.

But as the grunts from the other room begin to grow I feel the fury growing inside me. That he's in her right now. That he's fucking her barely metres from where I am and that she's willingly letting him, that she's not even trying to stop it.

I clench my fists, willing myself to calm, willing my mind to focus on all the ways I could kill him. All the ways I can ensure that Paris Fucking Blumenfeld is no more.

ROSE

I'm at the Governor's house. It's another meet and greet only mercifully Paris isn't here. Darius sent him away on some errand that was apparently so important he had to go straight away.

Not that I'm complaining.

Around me is most of Paris's immediate family. All Blumenfelds. Plus a few other faces. Big names. Big movers in this city. Though notably I'm the only Capulet not that I mind. It's rare that my father doesn't attend these things, and I wonder briefly what's kept him away but I don't dwell on it.

His absence makes tonight bearable.

Both their absences do.

I'm wearing a wraparound dress. It's not what I'd planned but the dress I had intended was damaged. Soiled. If I didn't know better I'd think Paris had spunked over it but I know better than that. Especially now. He's so determined to get me pregnant that he wouldn't have wasted any of it my clothes when he could shove it up me whenever he likes.

And he is. At every awful opportunity despite the fact that, as the weeks have gone by, he's becoming more and more convinced that I really am infertile. Still, I'd rather he think that, rather he see it as some physical defect on my part than realise what it really is.

I hide the scowl at that thought, at the notion that he might just discover my real secret.

When my eyes fall on her, on *his* ex, I realise exactly how inheriting this place is. Lynne married a real estate magnate, a distant cousin of Roman's, though he doesn't bear the Montague name, he has similar enough features that every time I see him, my heart stops just a tiny bit before I recover, before I remind myself that it's not Roman. That it's someone else entirely.

She walks up to me, greets me warmly then disappears off to speak to someone. She's a social butterfly. Better than me truth be told. Besides she has no reason to be off with me, she doesn't know my history. Nobody here does.

Darius's house is in the old colonial style with a great wooden surround and polished floors. The doors have been thrown open and the bay air is refreshing against the heat that's been steadily building.

Soon most of these people will leave, will pack up their lives and disappear off. Most will vacate to the Hamptons, or some other millionaires playground. Normally I would go too. Paris and I have a beach house, a great monstrosity of a thing, completely to his tastes but at least when we're there we are free of each other. He spends his days playing golf, drinking, sailing, whirling away the hours, while I spend as much time as I can anywhere else but where he is. It's an unspoken agreement. One we danced around at the beginning but one that's pretty much set in stone now.

Out of Verona we don't keep the pretence. He is free and I am free. And for two blissful months of the year I can actually breathe.

Only this year it's not happening. This year, I'm stuck in Verona, stuck because of his family. Because of the Blumenfelds.

I shake my head, forcing myself back to the present. Back to the room.

I'm caught in a conversation with Paula Lewinksy. She's new money and obviously so. From the way she smiles at me she's desperate for me to give her my approval. If I were more of a bitch then I could easily make her life hell but I'm not that person. Instead I force myself to engage, to be polite, to act like I care what the cost of her latest shopping trip was and that yes, the dresses she bought are beautiful as she flashes them to me on her brand new jewel encrusted phone.

Around me a few people stir. It's enough to draw my attention away and for a moment I think I'm hallucinating.

Because in the doorway is Otto Blumenfeld, beaming like a god damn Cheshire cat, and on his arm, looking so serenely beautiful, is Sofia Montague.

I blink expecting the mirage to crack. Expecting the woman to morph into someone else. Only she doesn't. It's her. It's actually fucking her.

Sofia Montague.

She's wearing a pale satin slip of a dress that makes her skin look like she's actually glowing. I don't think I've ever seen her look so put together. Not that she's a state normally but still, the Sofia I know leans towards dark hues, clothes that while stylish, cover.

But that dress is anything but.

Her eyes skim over the crowd now half gawping but she seems barely bothered. Otto murmurs something in her ear and she blushes before nodding. And then his arm is sliding around her waist, clearly keeping her beside him and he leads her over right to where I am by the drinks.

He picks up a champagne flute and hands it to her.

She thanks him so quietly, as if she's afraid of her own voice, as if she's had a whole personality switch, as if Otto Blumenfeld overwhelms her to the point of timidity.

"Rose." Otto says smirking just a little. "I trust you know my date." He emphasises the word enough for everyone to hear, like we can't see it.

"I do." I smile to hide my shock. "Sofia." I tilt my glass, hopefully showing no enmity. I have nothing against her personally. Though she might be a Montague, though she might be sibling to the man who tore out my heart and stamped all over it, Sofia has never done anything to harm me.

And besides I'm still embarrassed about the whole lift incident.

"Rose." She replies before sipping her drink.

God, what the gossip columns will say about this. A Montague and a Capulet sharing a drink. Worse still, a Montague on the arm of a Blumenfeld. My father is going to shit kittens when he hears.

And then I realise he's going to take all that rage out on me because I was meant to stop this wasn't I? Christ I'm screwed.

"Rose." Darius says quietly as he slides beside me. His eyes flit between Otto and Sofia for a moment and then they reach my face. "Let me show you this new painting I've acquired. It's exquisite and exactly to your tastes."

I smile letting him lead me away, no, relieved that he is. I need a moment to think. To process.

We walk into an empty side room. The breeze is cooling but it does nothing to ease the rising fear in me.

The painting is anything but exquisite. It's mundane. Pompous even. There's no risk to it, no expression at all. It's as if someone's taken a masterpiece and tried to replicate it with a canvas that's all 'painting by numbers'. But I don't mind. I like that I'm away from that situation, that the pressure cooker has been turned down a tiny bit.

And then I realise Darius is staring at me in a way that makes me more than a little uncomfortable.

"Where is Paris?" I ask.

His lips curl for a moment. "He's running an errand for me."

I nod like that's an answer.

"Are you missing your husband Rose?" He teases stepping that little bit closer.

I shrug playing the game. Of course I'm not. I'm enjoying the few moments of freedom I have right now, no matter how fleeting they are.

He frowns just a little as I look away.

"Do not worry about Sofia." He says quietly.

"In what way?" I ask.

"Being with Otto."

"Is she?"

He smiles, leading me further from view as if he doesn't want us to be even seen in this moment. "You're no fool Rose. Under that pretty polished exterior you're just as smart, just as sharp as the rest of us."

"I don't know what you mean." I reply.

"No?" He says. "Then what would your father say when he hears of them, of Otto and Sofia?"

I shake my head. This is dangerous ground. I've never outwardly spoken of our rift, never once dared discuss the feud with Darius, even when my father has all but ordered me to in the past. It feels too blatant. It feels far too risky to speak of such things.

Besides it's easier to play the pawn and not the conspirator.

As I step away he catches me. His hand wrapping around me and I flinch out of instinct.

"Rose?"

I look up meeting his gaze as his eyes drop to take me in.

"Let me go." I whisper.

"I would never hurt you." He says.

I shut my eyes stepping further away and his body crowds me once more. His hand scoops under my jaw, forcing my head up, all but forcing me to look at him as I try to get away and as I glare at him he sees it. I know he does. For the first time he's seeing what I've hidden these five years.

"How long?" He asks.

I don't reply.

"How long Rose?" His voice is harsher, harsh enough to make me gulp but bite my tongue. He shakes his head, his eyes flashing with something akin to the same fury that resides in his nephew and my heart hammers in response. "If I'd known…"

"What?" I whisper.

"I wouldn't have let him treat you like that." He states. "You deserve better. Far better."

I snort. It doesn't matter what I deserve, Paris is what I got. And I have to live with that fact.

"Would you leave him?" He asks.

My eyes dart about us to make sure we're not witnessed but no one is here. It's just me and him. Me and Darius. Alone. "How can I?" I reply.

"Your father would never permit it." He says.

"No."

"If I saw to it, if I told him I knew…"

"It would make no difference." I retort. Though in truth I think it would. It would make things worse. Much worse. Paris would see it as me running to Darius for help, me snitching on him, and by god would he make me pay for that.

"Rose…"

"Please just leave it."

"I can't."

"Yes you can." I snap pulling free. "You have to."

I walk away before he can say more. No matter what he says now, Paris is his nephew, his family, and we all know family comes first.

I go to the bathroom, certain he won't follow me in here and for a few moments I hide while I regain my composure. While I regain my perfect sunshine mask.

When I step back out into the corridor I see Sofia. Only she's not with Otto. She's alone, and she's sneaking out of Darius's office, fiddling with her bag like she's trying to shut it.

When she sees me she freezes. A micro-expression of fear crosses her face but before I can say anything Otto appears.

"There you are." He says and then he looks at me. "Were you two having some girl talk?" He's so much older than her that even the way he speaks makes it odd.

She shoots me a look. One that's pleading. One that feels like she's begging me to go along with this.

I smile nodding back at Otto. "Yes." I have no reason to lie. No reason to cover for her and yet in this moment I do.

"Well I'm going to steal her away now." He says sliding his arm back around her the same way Paris does with me. Perhaps it's a Blumenfeld thing but I hate it all the same.

"By all means. It was nice to see you Sofia." I reply before watching as they disappear back into the main crowd and as I do I catch Calvin's eye. He's smirking. Smiling. Like he couldn't be happier at today's turn of events.

I swallow the bile, turn away, and put on the same perfect mask I always have in public.

ROMAN

We're sat up. Waiting. It's past eight and she was due back hours ago. I guess I shouldn't be surprised that she's late, it's one of Darius's parties after all. We all know his reputation just like we know her date's.

Otto is a philanderer. A player. His first wife left him when he got the nanny pregnant and then the nanny left him after he'd married her and pulled pretty much the same stunt again.

After that it seems like he gave up on marriage, preferring to keep things simple and to no doubt save his bank account from any more alimony payments.

"She's back." Ben says as the car lights flash across the drive. He looks half relieved half furious and I know some of it is aimed at me. That I allowed this. That I permitted this.

Five minutes later Sofia is walking into the room, barefoot, though still wearing the dress she left in. Ben runs his eyes over her and I see it, more anger, more resentment.

"Well?" I ask before it turns into a blazing row.

"You could say I was successful." She says.

"What did you get?" I reply.

She smirks opening her bag, pulling out a napkin and lays it in front of me. "I couldn't take the original because that would have been noticeable but I snuck away from Otto and in Darius' office is a shit load of paperwork with this address on it."

Ben pulls up his phone, immediately looking it up and we all stare at the screen as we see google maps images of what looks like a load of industrial units in the middle of nowhere.

"What do you think it is?" Sofia asks.

"We should scope it out." I reply.

Ben nods but his focus seems less on the new information and more on the woman and what she had to do to get it.

She glances at him and rolls her eyes. "You can stop that."

"Stop what?" He snaps.

"Looking at me like a hurt puppy." She states.

Ben snarls, opening his mouth to retort.

"I'm not yours to protect." She says clenching her fists. "And even if I was I have as much right to be here, to be taking risks as you do."

"I never said…"

"No but your face does. You're acting like I'm whoring myself out."

"Aren't you?" He snaps.

"No." She cries getting up and padding over to where the drinks are. She doesn't even bother to pour one out, just takes a swig straight from the bottle, wiping her mouth after.

"Tell us about Otto then." I say. I probably have no right to ask, in fact I know I don't but perhaps if we lance this wound Ben will get over his issue or better still, he'll grow some balls and admit to what he feels.

"He's exactly what we think he is." She says smirking.

"How is that a good thing?" Ben retorts.

"Because he's easy to play. So easy." Sofia half laughs in a way that shocks me. "Oh shut up Roman." She says waving her hand when she sees my reaction. "It's not like that. I've kept myself to myself so long I can be whoever I want to be, create a completely new persona, and what better one to be than the innocent virginal heiress?"

"Excuse me?" Ben snarls.

Sofia takes the moment to swig another mouthful. It's dramatic and I wonder if she's doing it to taunt Ben more. To make some sort of point.

"Think about it." She says. "He's fucked half the city. If I'm dating him then he's going to expect me to put out right? Well, if I play the whole 'virgin trope' not only do I side step that entire sickfest but I make myself more desirable to him. Men like him love that shit. They get off on it."

"Fucking hell Sofia." I mutter.

"What?" She laughs at her own ingenuity. "He wants my money right? And I want information. But I sure as hell will not be whoring any part of me except my time in exchange for it."

If she wasn't my sister she'd scare the shit out of me. She grins like she can tell what I'm thinking.

"I'm going to shower. He had his hands on me all night and I stink." She says.

"If he…" Ben begins.

"Relax Benvolio." She says making a huge play of his full name. "I can take care of myself." And then she waltzes out of the room while he stares after her and I can't help but laugh.

ROSE

The window slides open and I hear the soft thump as his feet hit the carpet. I bite my lip, staying perfectly still. It's late but I know somewhere in the house my father is still up, no doubt plotting away.

As I feel the covers shift I let out a whimper full of need.

He chuckles in response. "How long have you been lying there waiting for me Trouble?" He whispers.

"Too long." I pout.

"Hmmm?" His hands trace up my lower legs, claiming each new inch of my flesh as he does. "I suppose you want me to make it up to you?"

"I expect you to." I gasp. Heat is already bursting from my core. I'm struggling not to just reach down and claim him.

Another chuckle reverberates through his chest. "So demanding." He replies.

"It's what I deserve." I state.

I can practically feel the smirk on his lips. He pulls the covers off and I stare down at where his head is now angled perfectly between my thighs. "I'll *show you what you deserve Trouble." He says hooking his thumbs under the elastic band of my thong, sliding it down painstakingly slowly.*

"Sit on your hands." He orders and I do it, folding them under me as if I'm bound.

"We have to be quiet." I say. "Father is still up."

He quirks and eyebrow. "Is that so?" He says curling up the thong and before I can register it he shoves it into my mouth. I can taste it, my arousal. I want to protest, to yank it out but I'm too into this to do it. So I lay there, like a slut, with the taste of myself on my tongue, and I spread my thighs wider, ~~impprovingly~~

~~He grins again, clearly enjoying the improved view. "I'm going to make~~ *you come Rose." He says as his tongue traces up my centre.*

I whimper, arching my back, immediately seeking more. Always seeking more.

"Christ you're wet." He says. "Dripping in fact. Is the thought of me ruining you that arousing?"

I moan in response. Yes. Yes it fucking is.

He licks again. Taking his time, tasting me slowly as if this is about his need and not mine. I whimper, I shimmy more desperate for him to pick up speed. "How much do you want me right now?" He says. "My little Capulet slut huh?"

I should feel embarrassment at his taunts. I should feel something at the fact that he's degrading me but what I feel is the complete opposite. I like it. I like the way he taunts as he teases. Giving with one hand and taking so deliciously with the other.

He slides a finger inside. It's slow. Deliberate. My body moulds around it. Welcoming it. I let out another moan and he rewards me with another finger.

I throw my head back, spreading my legs now as wide as they go. I need him to pick up pace. I need him to finish this. But I can't exactly say that with my undies in my mouth so I give him every visual signal I can.

And Roman as always reads me like a book.

He starts thrusting, picking up speed, curling so devastatingly inside me that my moans are getting louder despite myself.

"Sshhh." He says. "We wouldn't want daddy Capulet to hear you would we?"

I shake my head but in this moment I'm so lust filled I don't think I'd give that much of a damn. Let them find me, let them see exactly what Roman Montague is doing to their precious daughter, and hopefully they'll be so shocked they'll throw me out, disown me.

I'll no longer be a Capulet. But I'll be Roman's still.

He kisses my thigh, his eyes holding my gaze as if he can hear my thoughts, as if he's telling me that yes, he'd keep me forever. That we'll be together no matter what.

My body coils, my legs jerk. I'm so close now it hurts. My body is covered in sweat. I scream, muffled under the lace. Roman fixes me with a look and I do it again, half in pleasure and half just to push him. I like pushing him. I like seeing his response.

He grabs a pillow stuffing it onto my face.

And then he gets back to it. Only now it's like he's punishing me, he thrusts harder, my body hurtling towards release. His mouth devours my skin, nips at my thigh, sucks at my clit over and over.

I lose myself, I kick out one final time and then I fall utterly under the whim of this man. Letting my body do what it wants as my eyes roll back. The pillow muffles my screams but not enough. My hands grasp at the sheets and then at Roman's hair. I don't care if I hurt him in this moment, I'm too lost to think of it.

"That's it." He groans, licking at me as I come. Lapping up every last bit as if I were a feast. "There's my good girl."

I lay panting with the pillow still over my face. Roman crawls up the bed pulling it off, taking my thong out, and kissing me. "You were not quiet."

"I tried." I say back.

He gives me a look that says it all.

"It's your fault." I tease.

"How?"

"If you weren't so good at that."

"Good at what?" He says acting like he doesn't know.

"At that."

He smirks. I'm still shy about it. About sex. Roman is my first. For everything. Though I know he slept with his girlfriend before me he doesn't make me feel inadequate because I don't have a clue how to touch him, how to pleasure him.

"Say it Rose. Say what I did." He replies.

I go bright red. Redder than I already am from climaxing. "You licked my pussy." I say squirming.

He chuckles wrapping his arms around me. "I didn't just lick you did I?" He says.

I shake my head. "I enjoyed it."

"I know you did." He says. "That's why I did it."

I open my mouth to reply to tell him that I want to taste him now but we both hear it and freeze. Footsteps. Someone is out on the landing. I shoot him a look and he's gone, disappearing into the closest like a ghost.

I grab the covers pulling them over me and shut my eyes. Playing at sleep. My door creaks open and light from the hall cascades in. I don't react. I keep my face perfectly neutral, turned away as if I'm so deep in sleep nothing would wake me.

"I thought I heard something..." My mother's voice whispers.

My father sighs. "You're imagining things." He says irritated before half slamming door, clearly not caring if he wakes me.

I sit up, listening to their footsteps retreat and when the silence returns I know Roman is creeping back out and across the room.

"That was close." I whisper.

He shakes his head. "They won't catch me."

"They'll kill you if they do. You know that right?" I say. I mean metaphorically though in reality I wouldn't put it past my father. If he had walked in and found Roman between my legs he wouldn't have just thrown us out. Deep down I don't know exactly what my father is capable of but I wouldn't put murder past him.

Roman brushes my hair back, tucks it behind my ear reassuringly. "Nothing's going to happen. I won't let it."

"You're so confident of yourself aren't you?"

He grins. "Yeah I am."

I roll my eyes and mutter about privileged white men under my breath.

"I'm a Montague, Rose. I always win."

"And I'm a Capulet." I state. "I don't back down."

He kisses me, his lips crashing into mine so hungrily it steals my breath.

"Good." He murmurs and I can hear it, the finality of his tone. He's leaving.

"Stay." I whisper.

He shakes his head. "Better not."

"Please?" I know it's pointless. Reckless too. He won't stay. There's far too much risk.

"I'll see you in a couple of days."

"So long?" I whine.

He smirks getting up from the bed. "Absence makes the heart grow fonder."

"Fuck off." I half laugh as he creeps over the window sill and climbs back through. He pulls something out and despite the lack of light I know exactly what it is. He taps it in my direction then lays it out on the sill.

One Juliet rose. Just for me.

And then he's disappearing into the night as if that's where he belongs.

IT'S A DREAM. I KNOW IT IS AND YET I CAN STILL *FEEL* IT. HIM. Holding me. Touching me.

I can practically smell him in this moment. Not his aftershave, not his shampoo, but him, his sweat, his real aroma. In my head he's here, beside me, stroking my hair off from my face, telling me that it's going to be okay, that together we can figure this all out. That together we can survive.

Only that's not what happened is it?

My heart twists with something unfathomable.

My hands drop to hold my stomach, to clutch it, remembering how it felt, allowing myself to remember for the first time in so long.

She was taken from me.

Stolen.

As the duvet clings to my sweat covered frame that's all I can think about. Not him. But her. What she would have looked like in that moment. What she would have felt like to have held, just once.

A whimper escapes me but there's no one here. As I force myself awake, as I force those memories back down, the room is dark but mercifully it's empty because Paris is still away. Though he's coming back today.

I get up, walk to the bathroom and splash cold water on my face.

I can't go back there. I can't relive those memories because it will only end one way. I have to be stronger. I have to be better than that. This is my life. This, right here.

But as I stare at my reflection I can see the cracks. The lies settling in. My resolve crumbles and my tears stream down my cheeks and for once I don't try to stop them.

I give in. Sobbing out my pain.

My anger.

My grief.

All of it, while clinging desperately to the sink as if my legs aren't strong enough to hold my weight.

I SPEND THE MORNING IN THE GYM BURNING OUT MY FRUSTRATION. Burning out my anger too. Returning myself to the hollow, empty person I have to be to simply get through each moment of the day.

I don't want to feel any of this when I see him. I want to be back to the emotionless person I was. The person I'd formed in my head when we first married. I want to be able to zone out again. To pretend that this was my choice.

But the cracks feel like they're growing not settling. It feels like my very foundations are crumbling and I don't know how I can fix this. How I can continue on. Something is going to break.

Something inside me is going to snap and when it does, I'm afraid of what I will do.

And more than that, what the consequences will be.

When I return home he's already there. I can sense his presence. It's like a foul odour that lingers in the air, poisoning it, poisoning me too.

It's been three days. Three days of his absence and complete radio silence. But now it feels like we need to clear the air at least on some level.

I kick off my shoes, walk through the house to where his office is located. I don't think he actually does any work there. I think it's another powerplay. Another part of the image he's constructed for how he wants the world to view him. The great Paris Blumenfeld.

But a noise makes me pause.

It's a woman's voice. Only she's not speaking. She's moaning.

I narrow my eyes listening and then I hear him grunting.

No. Surely not?

I push the door open and they're there, her sprawled naked over his desk on her stomach and his body over hers.

I don't know who she is but she shrieks in shock when she sees me and Paris just smirks.

She tries to move. Tries to hide herself. Only his body is holding her in place. I see his hand wrap around her throat. She jerks more but his grip is too tight. And I know that grip. I know it only too well.

"Hello wife." He says.

The woman mutters something incomprehensible.

I don't know what to say. I just stand there, watching my husband fuck another woman because he hasn't stopped. He's still thrusting away, not giving a shit that I can see everything.

"You really are something." I mutter.

He laughs. Pulling her up more at an angle so I can see all of her as well. She's beautiful. Perfect skin, perfect curves. I can see why he wanted her.

"What's the matter Rose? You always complain when it's me fucking you? Thought you'd be happy if I found someone else to warm our bed." He taunts.

"If that's what you want fine." I say stepping back.

"Fine?" He snarls. "Fine? Perhaps I should get her pregnant." He says. "Fill this bitch up."

I roll my eyes, I still don't know why I'm here, why I haven't just walked away.

"It would be a fine lesson to you and your family. That this common slut can bear my children but you, my poor excuse for a wife is apparently barren."

"Fuck you." I snap going to leave.

He laughs slamming his body into her harder. I can't even tell if she's enjoying it or hating it from the shrieks she's making.

"That's it." He shouts loud enough for me to hear. "Come for me. Show my wife how she's meant to behave."

I rush down the stairs, I can't be in this house, I can't be anywhere near him. I'm not even mad about him cheating. He's done it before. Countless times. It's just the reality of this situation. The fact that *this* is my life.

I grab the lead, scoop Bella up and we're out with a slam of the door. I'll find a café to hide in. Somewhere with a garden.

I can't go to the park because that would tip the scales so far I don't think I'd ever come back from it.

ROMAN

Calvin Milkos always thought he was a big shot.

And I guess in a way he is up until today. He owns this city, only the minions far beneath him are blissfully unaware. He drives around in his chauffeured cars, in his million dollar suits, and he ensures Darius and every other official, every cop, every judge does exactly what he wants.

He's a leech. One that's been draining this city for decades. Between him and Darius they've turned this place into a mob town.

I stand to the side, dressed as a server, watching as he devours his dinner. He doesn't look at us. He doesn't give a shit about anyone but his meal right now.

He's a fat, greedy bastard in every aspect of his life.

He clicks his fingers for wine. The girl beside my steps forward and fills his glass with a scarlet liquid so reminiscent of blood it wouldn't surprise me if it was.

He takes a long slurp then puts the glass down before picking up his cutlery once more and barking out for salt.

I step forward, pick up the shaker, and sprinkle a little on his food. He barks for more so that's what I give him. Enough to kill a pig.

He gobbles his food down. Mouthful after mouthful as I watch.

And just as he clears the plate I step forward once more. He looks at me, his eyes flashing in fury because I haven't been called. I'm acting out by all accounts.

"I hope your dinner was satisfactory," I murmur. "Because it's the last meal you'll ever have."

He frowns before his eyes register who I am. He grabs the knife, lunges at me and I laugh, easily disabling him before pushing him back into his chair.

In one quick movement I drive the blade that I've claimed into his hand, securing it to the table. He screams out trying to fight, but his movements are languid. Slow. The poison is starting to work.

All the other waiters are gone. The door slams shut as they flee though I'm not worried that any of them will say anything. Besides it doesn't matter if they do. I'll be long gone by the time anyone arrives, I've already seen to it by having Ben creating a nice little distraction the other side of the city.

I lean in, my mouth up against his ear as he continues to fight. "The poison works fast doesn't it?" I taunt.

He groans. His legs kick out, slamming into the bottom of the table and as I watch he gasps for every last breath of air taking more delight than I believed possible.

When he slumps forward his face lands into the very dish that poisoned him.

I grab his head by his hair, yanking it back before I begin to hack it off, ignoring the spray of blood as I get to work.

ROMAN

I *stand in the shadows. Hide in them. Just like always.*

And just like always he has no idea I'm here.

He sighs sinking into the oversized leather office chair and rubs his eyes like he's had a hard day. I smirk at that because it's about to get a whole lot worse.

I take a step.

Then another.

Despite the expensive boots I have on I'm as silent as a ghost and I know he doesn't hear a thing, doesn't even realise until the muzzle of my gun presses into his neck.

He freezes. A murmur of shock passes his lips.

"Don't move." I say.

"What do you want?" The standard stupid response.

I lay out the photos. One after another. There are only three but they're the three worst. The three most incriminating of my collection.

He gulps and I physically hear his saliva slipping down his throat.

"That's not what you think it is…"

I laugh a mocking laugh. "Oh I think it is Darius." I murmur.

"Look we can sort this out. Put the gun away, let's discuss this like gentlemen."

He's trembling so much he's making my gun shake as it lies against him.

"Put your hands on the table. Keep them out front." I order.

He does it quickly. "Please." He says

"Is that what they said too?" I ask as I walk around the desk. "Did they beg you to stop?"

"I, it wasn't like that." He splutters.

"No?" I murmur picking up the middle picture and waving it in front of him. "Was she asking for it? Is that it?"

"I…" He shakes his head, blinks then forces himself to look at me.

Only he can't see my face. At least not yet. I've got a mask on to conceal it because I want to bide my time, wait to the exact moment in the conversation when he realises how fucked he is and then I'll reveal it, reveal that he's made a deal with the devil.

"This is how it's going to go down." I say laying out my terms. Instructing him that from now on all his so-called 'business' with Ignatio is over. That all dirty deals he has, all the backhands, all of it comes to me.

"There's a new power in town Darius." I say.

He lets out a low breath. "Calvin won't have that."

"Ah yes." I say grinning. The real man who's been pulling the strings, manipulating both the Montagues and the Capulets for generations. I lift the sack up emptying it onto his immaculate leather desk and he shrieks with horror as the head somersaults across it to him and his eyes connect with the dead man.

"Calvin won't be an issue." I state.

He stares, wide eyed at the head. "Who the fuck are you?" As I yank the mask off it's hard not to grin. "Surely you haven't forgotten me Darius?"

His jaw drops. He stutters words that make no sense and I let out a laugh.

"I'm in charge now. You do as I say or the entirety of Verona will realise exactly where you've been sticking your dick."

He nods so quickly. I know he's acting on instinct now, agreeing because at this moment he can't think of another option, but as I slip out of the room I also know he'll test me.

Darius isn't the kind of man to simply roll over and play ball.

No, he'll try to out manoeuvre me and somehow I know exactly who he'll chose to do his bidding. Yeah, this couldn't work out any better because Darius will all but force my hand, and in doing so I'll not only send a message to Ignatio Capulet too but I'll finally get a taste of what real revenge feels like.

ROSE

I'm nervy. On edge. My head's looking from one corner to the next waiting for him to show and when he does I feel relief and trepidation all in one.

My parents think I'm at a sleepover. I don't know where Roman's dad think he is but somehow we've managed to orchestrate a whole night to ourselves. Just us.

And I know what I want to happen. What we've both been heading towards.

We're going to actually fuck for the first time.

My heart jumps as I get in the car and look at him. He's smiling. No signs of nerves. No signs that this isn't like every other time we've managed to sneak away and have a few stolen moments.

But tonight won't be stolen moments. It'll be hours. And though I want it, I want it more than anything it feels like taking this step might be a mistake, that allowing ourselves to cross this final line might just truly damn us.

I bite my lip, willing the butterflies in my stomach to stop churning, willing the incessant thoughts in my head to just shut up.

"You okay?" Roman asks. We haven't left. We're just sat here.

I nod. "Fine."

"Rose?"

"I'm fine." My voice cracks betraying me.

His hand moves to rest on my thigh. "Why are you so nervous?"

I shut my eyes, the heat flushing to my face. I wish I wasn't always the insecure one. I wish I wasn't always the inexperienced one. It's okay for Roman, he's done this before, but for me, everything has been the first time, the first kiss, the first touch, the first blowjob, all of it.

"Nothing's going to happen unless you want it to. You're in charge." He says quietly.

I give him a smile. He's always said that, always made that clear, even the first time he touched me, when I was recklessly making moves on a man I knew I shouldn't be anywhere near. He was always clear, that at any point I could walk away. That I could stop it.

"I know." I say. "I want…" I bite my lip. "Can we go before someone sees us?"

He huffs glancing around. It's an excuse and he knows it. No one else is here. That's why we choose this spot to always meet. No one will see Rose Capulet getting into Roman Montague's car time after time.

He puts the car into drive and I jolt back in the seat as we speed off.

We don't say another word. Not one. The radio is the only sound between us and when we pull up to the motel, an hour out of the main city, we both sit there staring for a moment.

Roman gets out first, and ever the gentleman he walks around and opens my door. I hop out giving him my best, sunshine smile.

He pulls me back, pulls me into his arms and kisses me lightly. "I'll never do anything you don't want, you know that right?"

I nod. I want this. I know I do. I'm just nervous.

I fidget beside him as he collects the keys and we walk into a nondescript room. It's not bad. It's not dingy. It's just impersonal. Standard white sheets, a generic picture screwed to the wall and a bland chair in the corner.

Roman glances at me before putting the bags on the side. He pulls out a bottle and I let a nervous giggle escape me.

"Champagne?" I tease.

He grins. "I want to do this right." He says.

"And champagne makes it right does it?"

He shrugs. "I'd have laid rose petals but…"

"I prefer them on the stem." I reply and he grins.

He pops the cork, pouring the drink out and I sip nervously, letting the bubbles fizz in my mouth. I feel like a child despite the fact that I'm twenty years of age. Roman puts his glass down by the bed and lays out on it.

I watch him for a moment then take the hint and lie down.

He doesn't touch me. Doesn't make a move to.

So it's me who leans over, me who kisses him. His hands wrap around my hair and he pulls me tighter into him.

"Rose." He murmurs.

I open my eyes staring into his. I can feel him beneath me. He's hard. I've nothing to compare him to but Roman feels big, he looks big. I gulp as I realise that soon he's going to be pushing that into me.

His hands start to undo his clothes. He unzips his hoody. Then his jeans.

I fumble with my top, unable to get it off despite choosing one that should be easy to remove and in the end he helps, easing it off my head. His eyes fall to my breasts. I bought a new lingerie set especially. I wanted to show him how ready I was.

"You're so beautiful Rose." He says cupping my cheek and kissing me.

I kiss him back. Hard. He pulls me on top of him and without realising it I'm grinding against him. He's groaning, undoing my jeans and sliding them down before I register it.

His fingers skim over my back and then down under my thong and round to where I'm already drenched but, as he starts to touch me, I freeze.

He notices immediately. "What's wrong?" He asks. He's stopped touching me. Stopped grinding too.

I shake my head burying it in his chest.

"Rose talk to me."

"I can't." I whisper.

"Rose?"

"I…"

"We don't have to do this. We don't have to do anything. We can just lie here, just watch movies all night and talk if you want."

I steal a glance at him. *"I want to do it."*

"But?"

I chew my lip for a moment. *"If we cross this line…"*

"It's no different to what we've already done." He says gently.

"Have you," I snap.

He tilts his head but he doesn't reply.

"It's alright for you. You're a man. And you've had sex before." I state going on the attack because that feels like the appropriate response in my head right now.

"If you don't want to…" He says for the hundredth time.

"I do. I just." I sit up, pushing my hair back off my face, crossing my arms over my breasts to try to shield myself. *"You're a Montague. I'm a Capulet. If we cross this line there's no going back."*

"I don't want to go back."

"What if something happens?"

"Like what?" He asks.

"Like you change your mind." I half whisper it.

"Change my mind about what?"

"Us."

He blinks, sighing, then pulls me down. *"Rose, that's not going to happen. I won't change my mind."*

"What if something happens, between our families?" We've been warring worse than ever. Even the Governor has had to step in a few times and force us both into a ceasefire.

"It doesn't matter what happens. It doesn't matter what either of our families do. I'm not going anywhere Rose. I love you."

My eyes widen and I gasp. Relief, surprise, joy, so many emotions flush through me just by hearing that one word. *"Love?"*

"Yes Rose." He half growls. "I love you. I love you and I'm not leaving you. Not ever."

I nod, my eyes welling up. "I love you too." I say. "I know I shouldn't. I know we're meant to hate each other but I don't."

He cups my face kissing me. "Trust me Rose. I won't hurt you. I won't ever leave you."

I nod. I do trust him. I trust him with my life.

I curl back into him, and we lay there in complete silence for a while. It's clear tonight isn't the night. I've ruined it, ruined the moment. But it needed to be said, needed to be spoken.

And in a way I'm relieved I've done it, that we finally said what we're feeling instead of letting the lust do all the talking.

Do you ever wake up and feel restless? Feel the burning need to do something, anything? That's how I feel most days and today is no exception.

Except I'm Rose Capulet. I can't do *anything*. My role is to be a wife. To smile. To simper. To maintain my perfect photoshoot ready image at all times. To spend my hours shopping, or eating with friends, and by my husband's side each evening.

Only I don't have any friends. Not really. Most of the women I hang around with are there for what they can get, what my family name can give them, and people like that can't be trusted.

Sure I make polite conversation. Sure we sit around drinking coffee, discussing inane things with no consequence, but I know little of them and they know little of me. I don't know what their wants are, what they dreamt of being growing up. I don't know what they fear. I don't know anything beyond the plastic exterior that they keep for appearances. That we all keep for appearances.

I sip my coffee as one of these women talks about the below par flowers at her cousin's wedding. The other three women at the table pull the appropriate faces. We're at the country club. I got in a good workout before day dreaming in the sauna and after replacing all my makeup and doing my hair, I'm now here, acting like a lady who lunches, and I guess that's exactly what I am.

We look around at the sound of a commotion. This place is where people come to show off. To look their best. No one raises their voices. No one dares shatter that perfect illusion.

But as everyone in the bar falls silent he walks in, full of rage, his body practically shaking with it and his eyes set on me.

Paris.

I frown. He's never not been composed enough to let such outburst show beyond our four walls. He's not stupid. Even in Verona Bay and with who his family is, he'd be hard pushed to justify his brutality if it got out. Sometimes I wonder if I should just leak it. Get a maid to 'sneak' a photo to the press, but I'm not naïve enough to think there wouldn't be consequences for me too.

"What the fuck is this?" He snarls loud enough for everyone to hear while he waves some paper in his hand like a flag.

I gulp as my stomach twists. As my fear lurches.

"Excuse me." I murmur to the women sat with me, grabbing my bag, and cross the entire length with every pair of eyes tracing my every god damn step.

Paris snarls more as I look up at him. His hand snatches around my arm so tight I yelp and then he's dragging me, actually dragging me, through the building and down the steps to his car.

He pushes me in, slams the door and gets round the other side. I think everyone's faces are pressed against the window. I know they're itching to know what the 'perfect couple's' fight is about.

As soon as his door shuts he's there, back in my face.

"What the fuck is this?" He waves that paper again like I'm some sort of psychic, like I'd be able to tell what it contains. "You have an IUD."

I freeze. My body locks up. How the fuck did he find that out? How the hell did that happen? I paid so much money. I used a fake name. Hell, I even left this city to make sure it couldn't be tracked back but if he's discovered that, what else does he know?

"It's true isn't it?" He snaps. "You've been playing me. You're not infertile at all."

I shake my head slightly. Not because I'm admitting it but because I already know how this will end. With his fists to start and then soon, really soon, he's going to have it taken out and get me pregnant.

My stomach twists. That old, gut wrenching wound rips through me and I have to clench my stomach to try to halt it from spreading. From consuming me entirely.

"You stupid fucking bitch." He snarls screwing the paper up and shoving it into my face. "Do you have any idea what you're doing?"

There's no partition between us and the driver. He's just sat there, head forward, not reacting as this whole fight plays out.

"I don't want your child." I shout back. My anger suddenly roaring. I'm not just some vessel for him. I'm not just some slave to his wants.

"You think this is about you? You think any of this is about you?" He snaps. "Like I wanted to marry you? Like I even wanted to be with you?"

That stops me. I know he pretty much hates me now but six years ago it was different. He was the one pursuing me. He was the one practically begging my father for my hand. Waiting, even as I hid away.

Waiting a whole year till I was worn down enough by everything that had happened to consent to it.

"You dumb bitch." He says. "I had to marry you. Calvin made that abundantly clear."

"What the fuck are you talking about?" I ask.

He laughs. He laughs so loud it sends a shiver through me. "Oh you're going to find out." He clicks his fingers for the driver to move. The engine roars to life and I fall against the backseat as the car jerks away.

For a few minutes I don't talk. I don't even breathe. I just sit there, frozen. Paralysed. But then something makes me look out the window.

"Where are we going?" I ask. I wouldn't say I know most of Verona Bay but I know our usual areas and where we're headed right now is somewhere entirely new.

He throws me a look, full of hate, full of loathing. "You Capulets, you think all your money puts you on an equal footing to us but it doesn't. It doesn't even come close."

"I don't think that." I reply. "I'm not like them. Not like the rest of my family only you've never paid enough attention to recognise that."

He scoffs. "If you're so different why is it you've stayed huh? You could have walked away years ago. Could have disappeared into the night and no one would have found you. Only you couldn't. You'd be a nobody. You'd be poor too. You thrive off this life Rose. You thrive off me."

"I hate you."

He laughs. "But you're happy enough to spread your legs when I want it."

"No I'm not."

"No? What about all the jewels? Happy to exchange your body for them too."

I pull a face and look away. He's twisting it. Acting like I've intentionally whored myself out for him and it's not him forcing me to do things I don't want, then forcing me to take his apology gifts like blood money after.

"If you didn't want to marry me then why bother to pretend after?" I ask. "Once the ring was on why not simply put a show on in public and leave me alone in private?"

He leans in. I can smell his aftershave, that thick musky scent that I once used to actually quite like. "I had to get something out of this arrangement didn't I? Might as well make it worth my while."

I scowl. "You fucking prick." My hand lashes out slapping him hard across the face and his eyes widen for a second.

"You will never do that again. Never raise your hand against me." He states. "From now on, you're going to take everything I give you, and I mean everything, without complaint. In fact, you're going to thank me for it. Thank me for every scrap I throw your way."

"Like hell I will." I spit.

His hand grabs my throat. I can feel his fingers digging into my muscles and I gasp, half clawing at him but as he leans his weight further in something screeches.

The car jerks.

Paris falls on top of me, his entire body engulfing mine and his weight pushes me out of the seat and into the footwell as the car tips onto its side, skidding across the tarmac.

ROMAN

The truck rams into the car with such accuracy even I'm impressed. The air is punctuated with the sound of crunching metal and screeching tyres, and then there's nothing.

Just silence.

It feels almost poetic. It feels like I've just witness an opera performed solely for me.

The man in the truck gets out quickly. Disposing of any last bits of evidence and saunters over to where the second car is. He gives me a quick nod, job done, and gets in. He'll no doubt have a few bruises but we've paid him more than enough in danger money to cover it.

I get out of my car, gun in hand, and twist the silencer into place. I don't need it but it's the middle of the day and though this area is secluded enough I don't want the sound of gunshots to bring any unwanted attention.

Besides we've made enough noise as it is. No need for anymore.

I cross the road. There's a good chance the bastard is already dead but I want to make sure. I have to make sure. I need to see his body.

The car lies on its side. The entire length concaved from the impact and there's a steady pool of something leaking out from the engine. I can smell that sharp acrid stench of burning. I don't think the car is on fire though, I'm pretty certain it's just the airbags and residuals from the crash.

The door is hard to open. It takes all my strength to wrench it free.

And then I see him. His back is to me. He's lying on his front, his arms sprawled about his head as if the impact threw him out of his seat. As I pause I see him move. The bastard is still alive.

He lets out a groan. His fingertips flicker and his head turns. His eyes make contact with mine and for the briefest of seconds we stare at one another. Me and him. Me and Paris.

I don't know if he knows who I am. He frowns and then his eyes widen. His pupils dilate.

"Montague…" The word is a mockery on his tongue. A curse too.

I smirk, raising the gun.

He shakes his head. Thankfully he's not stupid enough to beg. Not that it would help. He was dead the moment I watched him hit her.

Dead the moment I watched him rip her dress off.

Dead.

He just didn't know it yet.

I pull the trigger. No hesitation this time. No feelings of guilt. No remorse.

It hits square between his eyebrows. A perfect round wound and he slumps back.

Perhaps I should have stretched this out. Hurt him more. He didn't deserve a quick death. He didn't deserve such an easy escape. As I lower my gun and click on the safety I hear a noise. It's quiet.

I glance at the driver. He's got a nasty gash on his head but I can see his chest rising and falling. If the medics get to him quick enough he'll make it but I don't have any real remorse. He knew what Paris was like. He not only turned a blind eye, he helped him when the moment called for it.

But as I turn my eyes register something else. Dark hair. Long dark hair.

No.

No fucking way.

I grab Paris's great lump of a body and yank it out the way and she's there, beneath him. He's been crushing her this whole time.

Her eyes are shut. Her face bruised. She looks almost peaceful except for the livid marks around her throat that I'm certain haven't come from this crash.

"Rose." I whisper her name but she doesn't react.

My fingers find her neck, I search frantically across her soft skin and thank god there's a pulse. She's alive.

I pull her up out of the hollow of the car. It's hard with Paris blocking the way but she's so limp her body bends to fit the space.

"Roman." Ben says behind me.

I don't look back. Not in this moment. My focus is her. What the hell was she doing here? Why was she here? Did she know about the Barn? Was she more involved than I realised?

"Roman we have to leave." Ben says.

We can hear sirens now. They're far off. A good few minutes away. We're not so far from view that someone couldn't have witnessed this. Couldn't have seen the crash.

"Roman. For Christ sake listen to me." Ben snaps, grabbing my arm and yanking so hard I almost drop her.

I snarl back, holding her tighter to me. She feels so light. She feels so broken in my arms. I can smell her hair as the wind flickers it across my face. I can smell her perfume too. It's light, floral. So many memories come flooding back, so many moments of us, entangled, entwined. I let out a groan before I can stop myself. But the smell of burning from the car is getting worse. I'm not so sure it's just the airbags now.

I carry Rose out the way. Carry her to a safe distance and lay her down in the dirt. She must have hit her head though there's no open wounds. I stare at her face. I want her to wake. I want her to open her eyes and see me.

"Roman we have to go "

I nod. I know. The sirens are getting louder and louder. We can't stay.

For a fleeting moment I think of taking her with me. Of carrying her to my car and stealing her away. But I can't. Not like this. Despite what I feel, despite what we had, there are too many questions still lingering. Too many unanswered wounds.

I have to leave her here. I have to leave her again.

Ben grabs my arm and I let him pull me to the car.

He yells at the driver and I stare out, watching, as her form gets smaller and smaller before it disappears entirely as we make a turn.

ROMAN

"I t's done. As far as anyone knows it was simply an accident."

Darius's voice is quiet. Muted.

There's none of the overconfidence he has in public. It feels good to hear it. It feels really good.

I nod. Darius is my pet now or as good as. Today has all but ensured it.

"Paris is dead."

I don't react. It's not like I don't know it. I put the bullet in his brain myself.

"My nephew is dead." Darius says louder.

I turn at that. "What did you expect?" I reply. The arrogant prick thought he could rock the boat? He sends his nephew off to play silly buggers, what did he think was going to happen? That I'd let them get away with it, that I'd let them undermine me?

"You really think you can just sweep in here and takeover?" He asks. I can hear the contempt in his voice but he's the one jumping when I say, so really all the shame is on him.

"Yes." I reply simply. That's exactly what I've done. I'm taking everything now. "You will call the Capulets to a meeting. Sofia and I will be there. You will tell them that after my father's death and the death of Paris there will be unity. Healing. You will tell them I have been granted a pardon."

He glares at me, his fists clenching but there's fuck all he can do right now,

"My nephew is dead." He states, like he cared for the man, like Paris was anything but a convenient pawn for Darius when he needed him. "I want a funeral first. I want an appropriate time for mourning."

"Fine." I say. No need to be hasty. I've waited long enough. I can wait a little longer. And besides I want Rose there. I want her to hear the words. I don't know how injured she is, Sofia is trying to find out, but I know she's still in the hospital. "You have two weeks."

"Two weeks?" He splutters.

"Two weeks." I repeat. "So you'd better make it count."

He half stalks away muttering under his breath and as he reaches for the door I call after him with a little reminder.

"Don't do anything stupid Darius."

He meets my gaze. His eyes flash but he's smart enough to keep his mouth shut.

"We wouldn't want your secrets to get out now would we?" I add.

His shoulders slump and he wrenches the door open letting it slam behind him. The last vestiges of his pride no doubt shattering with the sound.

ROSE

It's a party. Not mine. Not anyone I know really. But I'm here, lurking on the peripheries.

I know Roman is here too. I didn't think about the consequences of us being seen together I just had to see him.

When I spot him my heart leaps and then it's like I'm thrown in the ocean with my ankles tied around an anchor and it's pulling me down, deeper and deeper.

He's talking to a girl. Not just any girl but Lynne. His ex.

I gulp. It shouldn't matter, not after what he said, not after our promises but right now I'm so on edge that it feels like it does.

He looks up as if he can feel the heat of my gaze and as our eyes connect something flickers on his face. He mutters something. Lynne raises her hand, strokes his face and he jerks pushing her off, pushing quickly through the crowd to get to me.

Only I don't stay.

I'm gone. I've spun on my heels, half storming into the night and he has to run to catch me.

"Rose."

"Let me go." *I hiss.*

He grabs my arm and I yank myself free but not before stumbling and this time he grabs me to stop me from landing face first on the pavement.

"Let me go." *I grit it out.*

"Why are you here?" *He asks.*

"That's what you want to say?" *I reply.* "That's it?"

He frowns. "Are you jealous?" *He seems confused, like I didn't just see another woman touching him.*

"She was all over you." *I hiss.*

He shakes his head, his eyes flashing and he pulls me before I do anything into an alleyway. "I'm not interested in her, Rose. You know that."

I huff, crossing my arms, projecting all my anger, all my fear onto him in this moment because it feels like everything is spiralling so fast out of my control and I have no way of stopping it. Of stopping any of it.

"What's wrong?" *He asks.*

"You mean apart from you and Lynne?"

He shakes his head. "That's not the issue."

"No but I suppose it doesn't matter." *I state.* "She's a better girlfriend for you anyway. At least you can take her out in public."

"For fucksake." *Roman snaps, pushing me back against the wall, his hands over my head all but holding me in place.* "What is going on?"

"Paris." *I whisper his name. It feels as disgusting on my tongue as it does in my head.*

His face changes. The anger goes, replaced with confusion. "What?"

I feel my eyes welling up and I don't want to cry. Not now. I really don't want to but they're spilling over as I say the words. "My parents want me to marry him."

"What?" *He growls making the tears spill more.*

"Apparently it's been in the works for months. It's all but a done deal." *I whisper before burying my face in his chest and he wraps an arm around me.*

"That's not going to happen." He growls.

"I can't stop them. I can't…" I trail off as my tears get almost uncontrollable.

"Look at me Rose." He says but I don't.

He shakes his head, pulling my chin up and forcing me to look at him.

"You're not marrying Paris fucking Blumenfeld." He snarls.

I don't know what makes me do it but I grab him, kissing him hard, feeling my lips bruise as they crash with his but I don't care. I need him. I want him.

He groans, his tongue wrapping with mine, while his hands pull me in tighter.

I grab at his jeans, unbuttoning them and wrenching them open before feeling how god damn hard he already is.

"Fuck." He groans.

"Fuck me."

"What?"

"Fuck me." I say again.

He shakes his head. "Not like this."

"Please Roman. Please. You said I'm yours. You said we'd be together so do it, prove it."

He lets out a low breath. I can see he wants to. I can see he wants it as much as me and I run my hand over him, pumping his dick and feeling his precome as it seeps through. I'm spurring him on, doing everything I can in this moment to get what I want.

He pulls out his wallet. I gulp as I see he's already got a condom there. He rips it open, pulling his boxers down and slides it on.

I bite my lip, leaning back into the wall. An alleyway is hardly the dream location for your first time but beggars can't be choosers and that's what I've done, I've begged him for this, I'm not going to back out now because the scenery isn't to my liking.

"Are you sure?" He says and I nod not trusting myself to speak.

He pulls my skirt up, not roughly, but not gently either. I pull my underwear aside and I see another micro-expression across his face so I grab him, pulling him to me, urging him on. I don't want him to reject me. I don't want him to change his mind. This could be our last chance. This could be the only time we ever cross this line.

But more than that I want my first time to be with him. I want to give my virginity to him. Not the man six years older than me. Not the man my parents are even now plotting to marry me to. Not to Paris Blumenfeld.

"Roman." I whisper.

He grabs my thighs, raising me up, angling himself. "I'll be as gentle as I can." He says.

"I can handle it."

He shakes his head, his mouth meeting mine, and as he starts to kiss me I can feel him pressing against my core, pushing further and further into me.

I shut my eyes, trying not to tense up but it hurts. There's no denying it. A whimper escapes me before I can swallow it and Roman stops.

"Don't." I say.

"Give your body a moment to adjust." He murmurs.

I shake my head. I don't want to. It feels like we don't have time. I need him to be fucking me. I need him to be giving me this. "Please Roman. Please don't stop."

I gasp as his thumb touches my clit. He kisses me again. And then he starts to circle before pushing into me further. It burns, every inch he takes from me it burns. I try to focus on the feel of what he's doing, how his thumb is teasing me, but it doesn't override the pain.

When he bottoms out he waits for a moment and then slides back out.

I look up at him and as he watches for my reaction he starts to slowly push back in. I grit my teeth, forcing myself not to show how uncomfortable this is and perhaps he falls for it because he starts to pick up pace. Before I realise it's happening that pain, that burning is gone, and all I can feel, all I can focus on is him. Roman. His dick sliding in and out of me.

I let out a moan that echoes around us.

"Is that okay?" Roman asks.

I nod. "It's good. Really good."

"Yeah?"

138

I bite my lip, pulling him in, digging my nails into his flesh. "Fuck me Roman. Fuck me like you've wanted to."

He grips me harder, pushing me into the wall as he adjusts and as the brick scrapes against my back he starts properly thrusting. And god does it feel good. So good. Too good. I don't want him to stop. I don't want him to ever stop. I moan louder. I rock my hips, fucking him as much as he's fucking me.

His mouth finds mine and it's like we're possessed, like we're both high on whatever this is. He grabs at my dress and I hear the strap rip but I don't care, if he rips it to shreds right now I just don't care. His mouth finds my breast, his tongue swirls over my nipple.

And all the while he's sending shockwaves through me.

I shut my eyes, I bury my face into his skin, smelling him, letting him overwhelm me.

His thumb has my clit throbbing so badly. His dick has my body feeling a pleasure I couldn't imagine possible. I gasp as I feel myself getting closer and closer to the edge.

"Roman."

He smirks. "Come for me. Come around my dick."

I nod like I have any choice in the matter because my body is already so happy to oblige him.

I can feel my muscles tightening, I can feel myself coiling tighter and tighter and in an instant my climax takes over, and I'm screaming, writhing, not giving a fuck that we're in an alley, not giving a fuck who can see.

Roman growls, pushing into me, ensuring my pleasure lasts as he chases his own and as he tenses I know he's coming too.

I fall against him, gasping, as if he's sucked all the life out of me when in truth, he's done the complete opposite. He sets me down. I can feel the bruising already around my thighs from where his hands dug in and despite the pleasure at the end, I feel sore. Really sore.

I look down at Roman's dick. The condom is not only full but it's obviously tinged with blood. Roman traces it with his fingertips before pulling it off and discarding it into the pile of trash a few metres away.

"That's not how our first time was meant to be." He says with something almost like regret.

I bite my lip but I smile anyway because right now I don't care. I wanted him, I wanted Roman, and I knew he wanted me too. Who cares where we did it, all that matters is that we did.

"Should we have got champagne first?" I tease.

He rolls his eyes. "You are trouble." He says as puts my underwear back in place because somehow despite the very public setting I seem too much in a daze to make myself decent now the deed is done.

"But I'm your trouble remember." I say.

He nods. "My trouble. And don't you forget it."

"I won't." I reply tucking myself into him. "I won't have to."

But the feeling is still there, under the euphoria, under the afterglow, the feeling that all of this, us, it's slipping away.

And there's nothing I can do to stop it.

MY HEAD HURTS.

That's the first thought I have. I'm aware of the sounds around me. The beeping of a machine. The strangeness of the room I'm in. For a moment I'm thrown back to before. When I was here last time. When they had no choice but to bring me to the hospital.

My stomach knots.

I can feel it. I can feel every agonising moment as if it's happening right now. The life I wanted being torn away again.

My tears are streaming. I don't know whether it's now or just in my memory but it feels real. My heart is pumping so violently in my chest. If I could move, I'd be lashing out, screaming, fighting, just like I did before, but I'm not stupid enough to think the outcome would be any different.

That I wouldn't still be here.

Alone.

I let out a whimper. It feels like my heart breaks with the noise of it. The sound of how truly broken I am. How little I've recovered from that day. How little I've moved on.

"Rose."

The voice makes me freeze. He's here with me? He has the audacity to sit here, to be here?

God, it really is a repeat.

I open my eyes, only one of them remains shut, too swollen to respond. I push my body up but one of my arms doesn't respond either and I realise it's in a sling, wrapped against my chest. Everything aches. Everything hurts. I feel like I've fallen off a mountain. I feel like I've been in the worst fight of my life.

It takes me a few seconds to get the courage to raise my head and then I look up into his face. Ignatio Capulet. My father. The man who's meant to protect me but more often than not he's the cause of my pain, the reason I'm in danger in the first place.

"What happened?" I ask. It's a rouse but I can't think of anything else to say. I know exactly what happened. I remember the crash. I remember the awful sound of it. The high pitched screech of the tyres. The metal crunching around us. And then Paris's body collided with mine and everything went blank.

"You were in an accident." He says. "Paris is dead."

I don't react to that. I just sit there staring at him like the words aren't real. Like it's some sick joke.

Only my father doesn't joke. I doubt he even knows how to.

I swallow. My throat hurts. It feels like all my muscles are bruised as they constrict to allow the movement.

Paris had his hands around me.

He was throttling me.

That's the last memory I have of him. The last memory of us. I guess it's fitting isn't it? I guess it pays homage to the type of marriage I had, the whole damned relationship between us.

"What do you remember?" He asks. Even in this moment he doesn't sound concerned for me. This isn't about me. This is about the family, the Capulets. About ensuring that this works out in our favour. It's damage control.

I shrug then wince as my shoulder protests angrily about the movement.

"You were seen leaving the clubhouse. Apparently you were arguing?" He snaps.

I nod. "Yes."

"About what?"

I look away. Like hell I'm going to tell him those details. He doesn't have the right to know any of it. "Paris is dead." I reply. The words barely sink in even as I speak them. "What difference does it make?"

"Oh it makes a difference Rose." He spits. I can hear his anger. I can feel it, as if such a thing were possible. He gets up off the chair that he's been sat this entire time and stalks towards me. "People are going to talk. There's going to be an inquiry."

I shut my eyes. A wave of exhaustion hits me. Am I going to be blamed for this? How in anyway was this my fault?

I can feel his weight as he leans over me onto the bed, bracketing me with his frame. "Think very carefully about the next words out of your mouth..." He says.

I frown meeting his gaze head on. Whatever this is, I'm not going to be bullied, at least that's what I tell myself, because all my past behaviour suggest otherwise. Besides, he holds all the cards. He always has.

"Why were you on that road? Why was he taking you to..."

The door opens and his words stop. Immediately. He turns and his whole body language does a complete one eighty.

"Darius." He says. His voice suddenly silky smooth as he steps away from me.

"Ignatio." Darius replies before his eyes find me. "Rose." He says stepping further into the room. My mother is in his shadow, glancing between us all. No doubt trying to read the room and figure out how to play this best to our advantage.

"Rose." Darius says again walking up the other side of the bed and taking the hand that's not strung up. I don't exactly flinch at the contact but if anyone was paying attention they'd see my face react. Hear my breath halt for a second.

"Rose I'm so sorry." Darius says. "I know how much you cared for my nephew. I know how much you cared for each other."

I look away, drop my gaze. Surely he doesn't believe that? Paris said he was pretty much forced into this and who else would have been behind that than Darius himself? Besides, he knew what Paris had done. He knew he was assaulting me.

"Let me arrange the funeral. Let me take care of this and you can just focus on healing, on grieving too."

I nod. Like I give a damn what send-off Paris has anyway. The fucker can be tossed off a cliff for all I care.

His thumb traces over the back of my hand. It feels odd. It feels intimate. I pull my hand away and my mother mutters my name like I'm a child misbehaving.

"I'm tired." I whisper, just wanting everyone to leave now.

"Of course." Darius says gently. "Get some rest. If you need anything Rose let me know. You're like a daughter to me. You always have been. Nothing changes that."

I look up at him with my one good eye, being as amenable as I can because I need to keep him on my side. I need Darius to be my ally now more than ever.

"Thank you." I reply.

He leans over and kisses the top of my head. I feel my parents react. Both of them in different ways. My mother is surprised. My father seems to swell with pride as if I've achieved something.

Darius leaves the room but not before telling my parents to keep him updated and to let him know the minute I'm discharged. The minute I'm home.

As soon as the door shuts my father's face turns from one of concern to glee. His eyes snap back to me with something akin to pride.

"That was very well played." He says.

I shake my head. "I didn't do anything."

"Oh shush." He waves his hand. "Keep playing this card. Keep acting like a bird with a broken wing. We need to keep Darius close more than ever."

My stomach twists. That's all he thinks about? Even now? Paris is dead for fucksake. My husband is dead. Not that I'm heartbroken, but still, are we just going to act like it didn't happen? Act like he never existed?

"Why don't you leave us to it?" My mother says. "Rose needs to rest and you have things to do."

My father looks between us and smiles. "Fine."

I want to ask my mother to leave too. I want to just be alone, in my own space, to just process all of this. Only she settles herself down, makes it abundantly clear that she's not going anywhere. So I lay down, huddle under the sheets, and pretend to sleep while my head tries to make sense of everything that's happened in the last few hours.

Paris is dead.

Paris is fucking dead.

I never have to smile and pretend. Never have to act like he's my loving husband, like I'm his loving wife. I never have to endure his beatings. I never have to endure *him* again. Is it wrong to be happy about that? Maybe it is. Maybe I am a horrible person. Maybe I truly am. But a smile creeps across my face anyway and it's hard not to let out a sound of glee.

But I have to play the grieving widow.

144

The thought hits me and I let out a sigh. Even now, even in my newfound freedom, I still have to play this game, still have to keep up the charade.

Paris is dead and yet still, in so many ways, I am still not free of him.

ROSE

My mother rides with me in the car. My face is still swollen. My arm was dislocated in the crash but beyond that and a few nasty bruises I got away pretty much unscathed. No one comments on the obvious marks around my neck. It's as if they don't exist.

As we pull up outside so many people are there. So many cameras snapping away. I hide my face behind my hair but I still see it; the rows and rows of flowers laid out by the gates.

People mourning the loss of a man barely worth the oxygen he breathed.

The gravel crunches under the tyres and as we come to a stop I let out an exhale.

"I can come in if you want." She begins and I shake my head.

"No." I murmur. She's not left my side in two days. It's suffocating. Claustrophobic. I know she's only doing it out of concern but I need space. I need to be alone.

I give her my best reassuring smile and then get out.

Inside the house feels empty. Like it's already the monument to an old life. I walk from room to room as if seeing them in afresh. This was my home. Mine and Paris's and yet it never felt like that. Even from day one, it felt his space, his haven, and just a place I existed.

I wasn't allowed to change anything, wasn't allowed to redecorate, or hang anything up on the walls. All of this minimalist interior was of his design. The only thing that was mine were the clothes hanging in my closet and the toothbrush by the sink.

I shake my head. I guess all that changes now. I can literally do what I want. Hell, I can sell this house, sell it all and no one can stop me.

I let out a laugh and it echoes of the stark walls.

I knew I'd outlive our marriage. I just didn't expect Paris not to.

DAYS PASS. I DON'T LEAVE THE HOUSE. I DON'T EXACTLY HIDE HERE but I'm so exhausted and for once it's nice to stay in bed without fear of the consequences.

My mind keeps going back, not to him, not to my husband, but before that; to that horrific year before. For the first time I'm able to think about it, to allow myself to. To acknowledge everything I endured, acknowledge everything I suffered.

In truth, to actually grieve.

I feel drained in a way I've never felt, like opening this door has finally let the floodgates out to all the emotions I've buried, all the trauma I suppressed.

I lay in the darkness, barely eating or drinking each day beyond the forced mouthfuls the maids make me take in.

But each night I binge. Each night my hunger takes over and I lurk in the kitchen, eating everything Paris would never let me eat before slinking back into the darkness of my bedroom once more.

Only today I have a meeting with our lawyers. Paris's technically.

I've got myself showered, dressed, put makeup on and for all intents and purpose I look presentable, polished. I look how the world expects me to look.

I walk into his reception and a few people glance wide eyed at me. We've been front page news since the accident. There's been so much speculation. So much gossip. Darius pulled strings to speed up the inquest but it's not for another week.

My face is still livid with bruising but I can at least open my eye properly. I've ditched the sling too but my arm feels funny, like my body is disjointed, like it's not quite sure if it's mending itself or not.

"Mrs Blumenfeld."

I look up. "It's Capulet." I say quietly. I never changed my name. My father wouldn't allow it. He wanted everyone to remember who I was, that it was a Capulet married to Paris, a Capulet in his bed.

"I apologise Ms Capulet."

I give a small smile. It shouldn't make any difference but in this moment it does. I don't want to be associated to Paris any more than I already am. I gave that man five years of my life. Five torturous, horrific years. He doesn't deserve anything more.

I follow him through and as he shuts the door I can practically see everyone in the foyer craning their necks to get a good look at me.

"Would you like a drink?" He asks.

"No, thank you." I reply.

He gestures to the leather chair across from his desk and then sits behind it, pulling what is undoubtedly 'our' paperwork. He must be in his fifties. He's portly, with grey whispery hair and an expensive suit but he gives the air of someone you can trust, I guess he has to in his profession.

"If you're happy then, we can get straight to it."

I nod. That works for me.

"Unfortunately your husband didn't have any will in place..."
He begins, flicking through the papers.

That makes sense, Paris was the kind of man who thought
he'd live forever. He wouldn't have done anything as mundane as
sort out a will, wouldn't have done anything that attested to his
mortality.

"...But as his spouse, under normal circumstances that means
his entire estate goes to you."

"What do you mean by 'normal circumstances'?" I ask.

"At present we don't have an official cause of death."

"But it was an accident..."

"Yes." He cuts across me gently enough. "We need the inquest
to rule it as such for legal purposes. Once we have that then I can
fill in the necessary bits from my side."

"And then?"

"Then it's just a case of sorting probate. Paris had some minor
debts that will need to be cleared but his assets far outweigh all
of it."

I nod. It shouldn't be about the money. Not really. The man is
dead and that's enough for me. But the fact that I get that too? I'll
admit that amuses me. That in the end, I profit personally from
this union.

Not my father.

Not my family.

But me.

It seems right. It seems fitting. After all the violence I endured,
all the disgusting moments I suffered at his hands, it's only fair that
I walk away with something in return. I few million isn't a bad
price to set, is it?

The lawyer flicks through the papers. "In total, after taxes and debts are deducted you're looking at an estate worth two hundred million."

My eyes widen. I balk at his words. "What?" Even my voice stammers.

"That's only the liquid assets. We have the two houses to account for, so in total it's closer to two hundred and fifty."

"Jesus." I mutter. That's a hell of a lot more money than I thought he had. I mean we Capulets are rich but this is something else entirely.

"Assuming the inquest rules as we expect we should be able to release the funds in the next six months."

I nod. It's not like I'm in desperate need for money right now. I have cash in my accounts and no real expenditure beyond frivolities, which, with Paris now gone, I have little need for. I won't be going to anymore parties as arm candy. I won't be his trophy wife anymore.

A wave of relief hits me at that thought. No more pretence. No more false smiles while his hands dig into my flesh.

"Is there anything else you need from me?" I ask.

"No. Not until the inquest."

I give a tight smile shaking his hand. "One thing actually, if I wanted to sell the house..."

"Which one?"

I tilt my head. "Both?"

"You'd need to wait, at least until probate is granted."

"Fine." I say. It's not like that's all that urgent either. I've put up with the place for years. I can wait a little longer before I'm able to ditch it and find somewhere more me. Somewhere without such memories attached.

Or perhaps I could leave entirely? Leave Verona. The idea strikes me. To walk away. To finally disappear. But to do that I'd truly have to admit defeat. To admit that they all won. To surrender everything.

And I don't think I'm ready for that. Not yet.

I've still got a lot of fight left in me. I'm going to claim back everything they stole. And I've got six months to figure it all out because when that money comes in, I want to be ready.

And I will be.

I'm going to win this round. I *am* going to win.

And in the meantime I just need to bide my time and play pretend.

ROMAN

I stare at the skyscrapers. They're distant. Taunting. This is the closest I'm allowed, the closest I dare to come.

Verona glints like the entire damn city is in the midst of some sort of party, like everyone is celebrating something

I let out a snarl. How can it feel like this? How can it be like this? I've left, gone, and yet the place looks unchanged as if none of it even happened.

I glance at my phone. I've been here hours. The same as yesterday and no doubt the same as tomorrow. I'll wait here for as long as it takes. Waiting for her. Just like always.

The dirt track is bare. Though I can tell myself that a car is coming, though I can will myself to pretend, I know it's not the case. It's just me here. Alone. With nothing but the relentless heat of the summer sun beating down onto me.

Why hasn't she come? Where the fuck is she?

My instructions were clear in the message. I got the read receipt so I know she's seen it. She hasn't even replied though. She hasn't even responded. It's as if she's a ghost. As if this is all a game to her.

My phone buzzes and I jump, but it's not her. It's not Rose.

I read the message quickly. My father made sure we had medical assistance as soon as we were beyond the city limits. He made sure we had allies out here too because let's face it, an exiled Montague is still a Montague, and what's more there's a price on my head. I doubt Ignatio Capulet is willing to just wash his hands of me now. No, he'll be planning, just like always. That old bastard always has something up his sleeve. No doubt he'll send an assassin, a shadow to gut me in the night but unfortunately for him, I'm more than ready for it. Hell, I'm ready to face even him if that's who shows up.

But Rose, where the fuck is Rose?

My phone buzzes again. Another message. Ben's eye can't be saved. The medics have done their best but there's nothing else to do. I should go back, I should be with him, and yet I can't. I can't leave. I refuse to go because any minute she's going to appear. I know it. I know she will. This is what we agreed. This is the plan we came to. She's going to come. She's going to show and we'll be together, in exile, but we'll build a life for ourselves. We'll actually be able to live.

"Come on Rose." I mutter, willing her to hear it, willing my voice to carry the hundreds of miles that separate us.

I need her to be here. I need her to come.

And yet still there's nothing but the dirt in front of me.

IT'S HARD TO STAY HIDING. ESPECIALLY NOW. ESPECIALLY WHEN everything is so close.

Sofia is still playing her part. Playing the virginal girl Otto seems to lust over. Ben seems to grow more bitter as each day passes but he doesn't say anything. He just sits, brooding, while I seem to haunt Rose's every step though she seems to be blissfully unaware.

She's holed up most days in that monstrosity of a house. It feels like she seems to retreat, as if she's afraid the walls themselves might collapse in on her.

For a while I watch, wondering if she's actually mourning him but how could she be? How could she be mourning the man after the way he treated her? Perhaps it's just the shock. Perhaps it's just the realisation that all her plans have unravelled, but I'll admit I expected to see her happier.

I expected her to be more pleased.

I didn't just kill Paris for me. I killed him for her too. For the Rose I thought I knew. The Rose I thought I loved.

The last homage to a woman who never existed.

But today she can no longer hide. Today she has to face the world, face everyone, tell them what she remembers of the crash.

And I'll admit I'm nervous. Curious too. Does she remember me? Does she know I was there? Will she spill the beans on what they were doing on *that* road?

I'm stood in the crowd. I queued all morning like most of the people around me, the general population, vying for a piece of the action, vying to witness a chapter in Verona's great history books.

Rose walks in chaperoned by Darius no less which both surprises me and makes me pause.

I expected it to be her parents, for the Capulets to be all bonding together, making a big show of support.

Though Ignatio and Carla are here, they stay back. Flitting in the shadows as if they're pulling the strings but anxious not to be noticed. Ignatio hasn't taken his eyes off his daughter, not for a second. And if you look closely enough you'll see the concern on his face though I doubt it has anything to do with his daughter's welfare and more to do with what secrets she might unwittingly divulge, what ugly truths she might spill from those pretty lips.

The crowd falls silent when they see her. The bruising around her neck has faded but it's still visible. And there's still the remainders of a shinier under her left eye but despite this, despite the marks that blemish her skin, she's breath-taking.

All her apparent fragility seems to have transformed her into something even more beautiful.

My stomach knots. I have to grit my teeth to control the reaction of my body. Even from across the room I swear I can smell her. The floral, innocent scent of my Rose.

But she's not mine. *Fuck,* I have to clench my fists and dig my nails into my palms as I remind myself that she never was. It was a lie. She is a lie.

She takes a seat. Up front. As though she were on trial and I guess in a way she is. This is a public inquest after all. If she says the wrong thing, if she admits to anything then all my planning, all my forcing of Darius's hand will be for nothing.

Everything rests on the words coming from her mouth and it feels like every person in this room knows it too.

The coroner walks in. Nobody stands but Rose clearly makes a move to and Darius gently puts his hand to stop her, whispering into her ear no doubt reassuring words of comfort.

My jealousy spikes. He's guiding her. She's clearly far more dependent on him than I realised. I narrow my eyes watching her body language, watching his as he leans towards her. Is there something there or am I imagining this?

The coroner starts speaking and, though I want to focus on that thought, I need to pay attention.

It starts off as expected with the police report. The fact that the truck was abandoned and the driver had fled the scene. Witnesses, my planted witnesses attested to this, and that the driver has as yet not been identified. All particulars I've ensured are the case.

Then comes the medical report detailing Paris's injuries. Nasty injuries. Catastrophic injuries consistent with a car crash and not a single bullet to the brain. I keep my eyes focused on the pathologist as he goes into immense detail about the damage that would have contributed to Paris's death. Clearly Darius chose wisely when he picked this guy because he's not deviated once, not given even a hint that every word out of his mouth is a lie.

Darius doesn't react. His face is calm. Neutral. And curiously so is Rose's. She stares at the wooden table in front of her as if she's zoning out, as if she doesn't want to hear any of it.

When the pathologist is done he gets down and we all take a short recess. Around me everyone is whispering because we all know what's coming next. Witnesses. And that means Rose will have to take the stand. It feels like the entire building is alive with the prospect. I wouldn't be surprised if someone started handing out popcorn.

We come back in and Rose takes her place, where she sat before, but you can see she's nervous now. The first witness is called. A woman, who talks fast. Her eyes flit from the coroner to the crowd every few moments and it looks as though she wants to grin, as though all this attention makes her so uncomfortable she doesn't know how to behave.

She talks of being in the clubhouse, of being sat with Rose and how Paris apparently stormed in. How he grabbed her. How they were clearly having some sort of public argument before they drove off.

A second witness repeats a near identical story.

And a third.

To be honest I'm bored now. I don't care for bystanders. I don't care for the people who think they're a part of this.

My attention is on her. On the treacherous woman sat across from me, though as usual she doesn't even realise I'm here.

Only the coroner calls it a day. The whole room seems to groan in disappointment as if they've just been promised a treat and had it snatched away at the very last minute.

Darius stands, taking Rose's arm and leads her quietly out of a side door before the cameras and the crowds can get at her.

It's infuriating. It's more than that.

I sit in my chair long after the people around me disperse.

Tomorrow she will be back. Tomorrow she won't be able to escape this.

And something tells me it won't just be me kept awake with the promise of what that pretty mouth might divulge.

ROSE

The entire room feels on tenterhooks.

Even the coroner looks like he can't wait for the action to start.

As I get to my feet in what is technically day two of this damned inquest I hear an audible exhale. This is the show they've all come for. This is a performance for them. Some form of entertainment to brighten the dull plastic mundanity of their lives.

And yet this *is* my life. All the sordid little details that witnesses revealed yesterday. All the parts they picked over like candy. I can see in their faces that they're hoping I'll give them more.

I'm shaking. It's ridiculous but I am. I shouldn't have anything to fear after wall, I didn't cause this, I didn't make the damn truck crash into us. I wasn't even willingly in that car.

But still it feels like everyone is watching me, judging me, not that that's unusual considering who I am but today it feels worse. Today it feels so much worse, so much more pervasive.

The coroner starts off gently. I keep my eyes on him, ignoring the crowd as best I can, answering each question simply. Confirming my name. Confirming that yes I was in the car with Paris and yes we had left the clubhouse together.

"Would you mind explaining the nature in which you left the clubhouse?"

I wince. I knew this was where today would go. I knew today secrets would come out. My secrets. But I have a plan. Even now, even when I'm exposed and it feels like this entire god damn city is ready to pick over the sordid aspects of my private life, I know how I'm going to cover myself.

"We were arguing." I say. I can hardly deny that when half the damn clubhouse has sat where I have, eager to be a part of this, eager to state everything that they saw.

"What about?" The coroner asks. Like he has a right to know. Like any of these people do.

"I don't remember." I reply.

His eyebrows raise. "You remember arguing but not what it was about?"

I let out a low breath. I'm lying. Perjuring myself technically but these are my secrets. My life. This city has taken so much from me, how dare they think they have a right to strip me bare for their entertainment.

"We argued a lot." I state and that sets a murmur through the crowd. That the perfect fucking couple wasn't so god damn perfect after all.

The coroner pauses, as if he's assessing me and I take the moment to sip some water. My throat is dry. It still feels tight from where Paris's hands were around me as if he's a ghost haunting me now, continuing the abuse long after he's dead. Without thinking my hand moves to my neck, feeling where the bruising is as if I need to confirm that I can breathe, that Paris *is* dead and can no longer do that to me anymore.

He picks up some papers, flicking through till he finds the one he wants. "According to the medical report you sustained a dislocated shoulder, a concussion, as well as bruising in the crash." He says clearly changing tactic.

"Yes."

"...but the bruising around your neck is not consistent with a car accident."

I blink. I bite my tongue, sinking my two front teeth into the tip of it and it's my father who decides to take over.

"Is this relevant?" He asks standing up, as if he were my lawyer and I was on trial, though I suppose in a way I am.

"Mr Capulet." The coroner says fixing his gaze on him. "This is my inquiry, I decide what is and is not relevant."

"How is my daughter's injuries relevant to what killed her husband?"

"I would have thought that was obvious." The coroner says. Clearly he's not swayed by who my father is and as my eyes flit to Darius's I can see exactly why that is. He doesn't look concerned. If anything he looks like he's orchestrated all of this as though this is his court and we are all merely players.

He gives me a reassuring smile but it doesn't reassure me. Not in this moment.

The coroner turns back to me, ignoring my father completely and I'll admit I want to see the look on his face though I don't take the opportunity to look. I keep my focus on the man in the wig. The man who right now has power over me.

"I'll ask you in a different way Ms Capulet, the bruising on your neck was not caused by the crash was it?"

I meet his gaze. He doesn't seem a hard man, a malicious man. I don't think he's getting anything from this beyond it being necessary to his job and yet I still resent it, I still resent having to sit here and admit to it, to admit to what I am, to become a victim in all their eyes.

The room seems to brace itself, it feels like everyone is leaning forward, half drooling. I can see the journalists, pens poised, ready to scratch down whatever words leave my mouth.

"No." I say quietly. Not that it makes any difference because they all hear.

"Your husband did that?"

I nod dropping my gaze. I'm not ashamed. I have no reason to be but right now I need to be damn careful. I'm treading a very fine line between what I will admit and what I refuse to.

"Why?"

The question I knew was coming. The million dollar question that everyone in this room didn't know they wanted the answer to but now it's like their lives depend on it.

"I don't remember."

He narrows his eyes. If he weren't so professional I think he would scoff. "You don't remember?" He repeats.

"No."

"You remember arguing, you remember your husband strangling you but you don't remember any actual details?"

I can hear it, the tone of disbelief. I have to be convincing now, I have to win him and everyone over with this answer or I'm fucked. I lick my lips, feeling the cracked skin. I need a lip balm. I need to take better care of myself.

"Like I said, Paris and I argue a lot." I reply, keeping my voice steady. "He has a temper. Had a temper." I correct myself. "I don't remember what that argument was about because it could have been anything, any little thing set him off. But I remember his hands around my throat. I remember him choking me, and the screech of tyres and then I remember nothing."

He sits back in his chair. "Would it be fair to say this isn't the first time your husband injured you physically?"

I drop my gaze, frowning before I quickly recover myself. I won't admit to that. Not because I'm protecting him, not because

I'm protecting Paris, but because I won't be seen as some battered wife. That I've stood by, that I've allowed this. That I'm the weak pathetic person I really am. My pride won't have it.

And I can feel from the way my mother and father seem to bristle at that question that they don't want me to admit it either. These are our family secrets. They're not for all Verona to know.

"Ms. Capulet?"

I let out a low sigh but still he gets nothing.

"Ms. Capulet was your husband often physically violent with you?"

"Again, how is this relevant?" My father asks standing up. I look across at him meeting his gaze and it's the same hard look of a man more concerned with what the world perceives him to be instead of what his actions actually make him.

"Mr. Capulet, you have spoken out of turn a number of times today. Consider this your last warning. This is not showtime TV. This is not a soap opera and you are not a lawyer. If you speak again I will have you removed."

My father turns bright purple. He clenches his fists and it's clear he wants to reply but he doesn't dare. This is probably the first time in his entire life that he's been put in his place. If it wasn't so serious I think I might laugh.

The coroner turns back to me. "I appreciate this is not an easy question. I appreciate that you and your husband were married for a number of years and that his death must be affecting you but I need you to answer the question."

"Why?" I half whisper it. I don't want anyone else to hear though I'm certain they do.

He gives me a look that could almost be mistaken for one of compassion. "This is about the nature of his death. I need to ascertain whether his actions in anyway prior to the accident precipitated it."

"They didn't. We were fighting but that didn't cause the truck to hit us. They were two separate events."

He runs his eyes over my face, then stares for a moment at the bruising at the cause of all of this. "Would you say your husband was a kind man?" He asks quietly, as if it's just us having a quiet conversation, as if we are two friends, divulging secrets.

"He was sometimes."

"In what ways?"

I shrug. How was Paris kind? Maybe in the beginning when he was trying to seduce me but that side of him has long since vanished. "He used to surprise me with things, inconsequential things." I state, bringing up old memories. I'm not exactly lying, just embellishing the truth, using artistic license and all that.

"Like what?"

"Like my favourite cake." I don't add that he'd then used it against me after I ate it, calling me a fat whore and all but forcing me to throw it up on command. "He bought me flowers too."

"And jewellery?" He asks. It's well known that Paris bought me jewellery. A lot of it. Everyone saw it as a demonstration of a loving husband when it was far from the case.

"Yes, he bought me a lot of jewellery." I murmur.

"So he was generous?"

"Sometimes."

"Would he buy you jewellery after one of your fights? Was that his way of apologising?" He asks.

I gulp. That's close to the line. Too close. "Sometimes." My voice sounds unsure, nervy.

"So he'd hurt you physically then buy your silence with jewels?" He says simply, no accusation, no judgement, as if it's a stated fact already.

My eyes widen. I stupidly look over at Darius who is leant forward, with a face that says everything. He set this up. He did this. For some reason he's decided to expose Paris in death as the monster he was but why? What does he get out of this? What possible reason would he want to blemish the Blumenfeld name for me?

"I..." I stammer then fall silent. There's a power play here beyond my understanding but I need to figure it out and fast.

"He bought you a twenty carat diamond necklace days after you were seen with bruising on your cheekbone. That wasn't a coincidence was it?"

I shut my eyes, my stomach twisting as this whole situation gets more out of control. I tried really hard to hide that injury. I stayed inside for almost an entire week while the swelling went down.

"Why did you not leave him? You have means, clearly you have a supportive family." The coroner says looking over at my father who's shooting daggers back.

"I couldn't leave." I whisper.

"Why not?" He asks gently, reasonably, as if the act were a simple thing.

"I just couldn't." My voice breaks. It takes everything in me not to cry then but I won't. I won't let these vultures see me like that. I won't let the papers print an image of my tear stained face for everyone to leer at.

"Was that what your argument was about that day? Did you want to leave and he wouldn't let you?"

I shake my head. Would it be easier if that was the truth? Maybe in some ways.

"Did you ever ask him for a divorce Ms. Capulet?"

"No."

The room reacts to that. To the fact that I never made such a demand. And then my pride gets the better of me, that old Capulet streak because I'll be damned if they all think I was content to take his punches. "He wouldn't have agreed. If I'd asked it would only have made everything worse." I say.

"So you did want to leave him?" The coroner replies.

I shrug. "He was my husband. I married him. For better or for worse right?" I know it makes no sense. I know I should just admit it but I can't. I'm not going to show them what I really am, that I've been essentially as good as a prisoner for the last five years. My pride won't let me. I refuse to be looked at with sympathy. I refuse to be thought of in that way.

There's a moment of silence as if he's processing what I'm saying.

"Did he ever thr,airen to kill you? Did he ever threaten to harm you if you left?"

I don't reply to that. No, he never said those words but that's because we both knew I wasn't going anywhere. That in the end he could hurt me as much as he wanted but I couldn't leave, my family would never have let me.

"Did you ever fight back?" He asks.

"Whenever I did he would just hit me harder." The words slip out before I can stop them.

The room gasps and I do too. My admittance hangs about me and I stare wildly across at Darius but he doesn't look angry. If anything he seems pleased. What game is he playing? Why is he so intent on letting everyone know what was really going on in my marriage?

The coroner asks a few more questions. About the truck. About the events after but when it's clear I don't remember anything he lets me get down.

I walk back to my seat, my legs shaking and my eyes focused on the floor. But I can hear the murmurs and I can feel it too, the looks of sympathy. I sink back into my seat and Darius takes my hand squeezing it gently.

"You did good." He says quietly.

"Did I?" I whisper back. I know my family certainly won't agree with that. My father is going to be furious.

He pulls me in, wrapping his arms around me. "I'll protect you Rose. From all of them." He says and those words are enough to break me. To crack the façade entirely and despite myself, despite my determination not to, the tears fall, silently streaking down my face and I feel the camera's instantly snapping away, taking every advantage of my moment of weakness.

ROMAN

I don't know what I expected but it wasn't that. I held my breath as she spoke of the crash but unsurprisingly she didn't remember a thing, at least nothing about me because we all knew she was holding back, lying about some of it. Whatever they were arguing about she does remember - she just doesn't want to admit it.

But the revelations she did make, that he was abusive, that he hit her, and that he plied her with jewellery to keep her sweet, I'm both pleased and incensed. Sure the city now knows what he is, that the great Paris Blumenfeld was a wife beater, but it wasn't my intention for that to get out.

And I'd watched as Darius led her away when it was finally all over, I watched as her tear stained face passed me by and still she didn't see me. Didn't sense me.

He's presenting her as a martyr.

He's presenting her as a victim in all of this and I want to know why.

When his car pulls up, the dust kicks up about the track. We didn't have to meet in person but sometimes it's better to read a man this way, to see all of his body language. Besides I've got back up. I'm not stupid enough to meet with Darius in any capacity that would result in me being the underdog.

He gets out, his face hard and yet resigned and he walks slowly towards me, his shiny oxfords gaining more dirt with every step. When he stops we assess each other. He's half an inch taller than me but, where his hard body has started to go soft with age, mine is muscle. And a lot of it. I spent years in the gym, years in the ring too, fighting, brawling, turning myself from the skinny runt I was into something of worth. Someone that others would only have to look at and know not to cross.

"Roman." He says quietly.

"Darius." I reply.

"I did what you asked."

"You did." I confirm. He got the pathologist to lie about Paris's actual cause of death. He also ensured that no one focused on where the car was actually going to. Why they were on that road. But there's a big question around what else he did.

He lets out a huff as if this is an inconvenience to him.

"I'm curious as to your motives." I say

"What motives?"

"Divulging all those details about Paris. About his marriage." I don't say her name. I don't want anything to betray me.

"I thought you would have appreciated that." He says stiffly. "You clearly never liked the man."

"No, I didn't."

"So what's the issue? Now everyone knows what a shit he was. That he used to beat his wife."

"That sounds like bullshit. You had no need to sully your family's name with such salacious details…"

"Maybe Rose deserved it." He cuts across me.

"Deserved what?" I snap. My anger spiking at the way he says her name. The way he thinks he has a right to.

"Justice. He put her through enough. She deserved for the world to see what was really going on."

I tilt my head. Is that it? Is it really just a case of him wanting to make amends? It doesn't feel like that and especially not from the way he was acting towards her. Besides Darius isn't one to care for justice, for morals, for righting all the worlds wrongs.

"Why do you care? What is she to you?" I ask.

He narrows his eyes. "I helped orchestrate their marriage. It's only right I do something to fix it."

I grunt. It feels like bullshit. It certainly sounds like it. Darius clearly has a soft spot for her. I guess I can't blame him for that, Rose Capulet has a way of burrowing into people's psyche, of turning them into her pets.

I'll need to watch Darius, I'll need to ensure he doesn't cross any lines.

Because Rose is mine.

She always has been.

Whatever I ultimately decide to do in terms of delivering her particular slice of justice I won't have anyone getting in the way.

"I have an errand for you." I state.

He bristles. "The funeral is in two days."

"I don't care." I want him to focus on the bigger picture, the fact that I have the power here, that I say jump and he does it without hesitation, without any freewill to do otherwise. "If you're a good boy you'll get it done in plenty of time." I say handing him the envelope.

He snatches it, opens it and shakes his head. "I can't miss the funeral…"

"Then get it done." I say dismissively.

His eyes flash. He clearly wants to retort and a part of me wants him to. I want to smack him down, to prove that I'm not empty words, that behind them I'm more than willing to get my hands dirty. I'm more than willing to have every street in Verona pouring forth with blood if that's what it takes.

He storms away as I watch.

Once the car door is slammed his driver nods his head, just a little, his eyes on me. Yeah I bought him too. I own every man in Darius's immediate circle though the stupid fucker doesn't have a clue. Not that I'd care if he did. I have eyes on him at all times, and if he so much as thinks of crossing the line I'll cut him down like the dog he is and it feels like he's finally realising it.

ROMAN

She's slunk back into the shadows. The papers have run article after article about her because apparently this entire city is more in love with her than ever.

More flowers adorn the pavement. So much so they've had to close the street. She doesn't come out. She hides inside and only her mother seems to visit. Her father is apparently too angry to show his face.

Today is the funeral. Another funeral. If this place didn't glitter with so much gold I'd say it was cursed.

She's up early. No doubt practising her grieving widow look.

I stay as long as I can, watching from my vantage point as she moves more like a ghost than a person through the emptiness of the space around her.

I know I should stay home. I even lied to Ben that I would. Lied to my sister too.

But I can't. I have to see this. To witness this.

Afterall, I was the one to create this moment, I deserve to revel in it, to feel every second of it as it unravels.

I hide amongst the crowd, wearing a disguise of sorts, though in truth I doubt the average person would recognise me. They seem to have forgotten I exist so why would my face help remind them?

I watch as the procession goes by. It's funny that I shied away from my own father's and yet here I am watching as Paris Blumenfeld's coffin rolls past like he's some fallen knight. Like he's some great fucking saint being laid to rest.

Everyone knows his secret. Everyone knows what he is and yet still they fawn over him, still they pretend.

Behind his coffin is Darius. Just as expected. But Rose isn't there. She's not walking. She's not stood in the place where a grieving wife should be.

I guess that should tell me something. Only it doesn't. Rose is nothing if not an expert in societal behaviour. I doubt she's ever publicly taken a misstep in her life so where the fuck is she?

I look around. I'm right outside the Cathedral having waited here in this crowd for hours expecting to see her lithe form walking, just as my sister did barely a month ago.

Only the bitch isn't here.

Around me is murmuring. Speculation. It's clearly been noted that the grieving widow is distinctly absent from her duties.

And then the cars start to arrive. One after another. Dozens of them. Filled with Capulets and Blumenfelds. Amongst them is my sister. Though she's playing a part, Montagues had to be here too, this is the Governor's nephew after all, despite his connection to our enemy.

All the big names gather outside. Waiting. Talking. While the coffin is still there, on the carriage, half forgotten.

And then a final car arrives. I hold my breath without meaning to because I know it's her. She's got her hair pulled back, a black veil obscures her face but Christ is she still breathtakingly stunning even in this moment.

My heart thumps in my chest. The entire crowd falls silent as Darius steps up to the car, opens the door, and offers his hand.

She pauses, no doubt collecting herself, and lets him lead her in.

The crowd seems to love it. To love her. Women are weeping, everyone is talking about their great love story as if they had one. As if this were some Greek tragedy playing out before our eyes.

It's hard not to react to it. Hard not start shouting out the truth.

But that's not why I came. I came to see her. To figure out if she really is grieving or if even this is a charade.

Only I can't tell.

As I stand watching the woman I once loved walking inside and then, as I wait patiently for her to leave, I realise she's an enigma. A puzzle that perhaps I'll never solve.

Who the fuck is the real Rose Capulet? Because she wasn't the girl I knew and she sure as hell isn't the innocent looking woman I see before me now.

ROMAN

More days pass. More days spent with Sofia playing her game, carefully mind, while I become a full on stalker.

I've replaced all her security. She doesn't know it. Paris's men were shit at their jobs anyway but now they're mine. Every single one answers to me. So in a way I'm already controlling her. She's cornered like a wild animal in a trap blissfully unaware that it's just about to go off.

I don't need to hide. I could stand here, seen by all of them but I remain in my old spot. Concealed. I don't know what she would do if she saw me, how she'd react, but I'm not ready yet.

I have a plan. A carefully crafted one.

And, despite my heart seemingly wanting to overthrow it for the sake of a pretty face and the wish to regain something long gone, my head wins out.

She's my prey right now. And I'll admit I'm enjoying the chase.

She mooches about. Reads more than I think is normal. She also seems intent on eating the entire contents of her fridge as if her newfound freedom extends that far. As if until now, even her culinary options were constricted.

She orders takeaway. Night after night. The leftovers litter the kitchen each morning and it's the maids cleaning up after her though clearly they don't complain. It is their job after all.

And then one day she stands, staring out through the expanse of glass.

As if she knows I'm here.

As if she can sense me.

I have the biggest urge to step forward. To reveal myself.

But just at the last minute she's the one who turns away. Suddenly she's racing through the house like a person possessed. She's in the bedroom. *Their* bedroom.

She disappears into the closet and for minutes I'm just stood waiting.

Then she comes back out, her arms full of what looks like clothes. She carries them down, dumps them all outside. Then disappears again repeating the action. When she's done with the clothes she adds more items, a few paintings, a few books. All things I'd put good money on belonging to Paris.

It looks like she's purging the house.

She lights a match, and I step forward then, but I realise she's deposited it all into a firepit that's submerged right in the middle of her patio.

As the whole thing goes up in flames it illuminates her face, twisting it into ghastly contortions that make her look in this moment like some sort of apparition. But as the fire starts to clear she looks at peace. She looks like something inside has been purged. That she's cleansed her soul almost.

She sinks down sitting crossed legged on the slabs, drinking red wine from the bottle. One after another. As the night goes on she must be getting drunker and drunker but she makes no attempts to move. She just keeps drinking. And then she suddenly keels over. Like it hits her all at once and her body can no longer handle it.

I move then, out from the shadows, out from my hiding space. I don't hide my steps. I don't try to quieten them. I take each one deliberately with the intention of her hearing because she's too drunk now to remember anything.

When I reach her she's sprawled out. What looks like days old makeup smudged across her cheeks. I scoop her up, once more carrying her, but this time it feels less necessary and more of a mistake.

One of the guards appears. He pauses, weighing up his options but he knows who his boss is, who his real boss is, and he quietly nods his head and slinkers off.

I carry her through the house. The tiny dog runs to us but it does little more than sniff at my feet and it's hard to not step on it.

I lay her down on her bed, pull the covers over and then stand there. Watching. Waiting. Because I want her to wake up. I want her to see. To know it was me. To realise I was here. In her home.

Only she doesn't. She just rolls over, muttering something. It's not my name. It's not me she's calling for. My anger flares again because I want it to be, in this moment I want her to be crying her eyes out, crying for me, regretting every decision she made that separated us.

But that's not what this is. Not what she's doing. She's mourning him. Not me. Mourning their life. Not ours.

I snarl walking away before I do something I'll regret.

And as I reach the door, the little dog jumps onto her bed cuddling into her and in my fury I curse it too. I curse the pair of them.

ROSE

This can't be happening. That's the thought that keeps repeating over and over in my head.

There's no way.

We took precautions.

We weren't stupid.

But three pregnancy tests can't be wrong

I feel sick. Numb too.

What the hell are we going to do now? I'm shaking, sat on the edge of my bathtub trying not to puke. Again.

How the hell am I pregnant? I get up and start pacing. I can't just sit here. I can't just sit still.

I need to see him.

I grab my phone, calling him but he doesn't pick up and although that's not unusual in itself it sets me on edge. I know he was out with Benvolio, they'd gone hunting, but he was meant to be back hours ago.

I call him again. I keep calling him but there's nothing. No reply. Just silence.

I stare around at my bathroom. It's late afternoon. There's a fancy dinner planned this evening so I need a damn good excuse to be out but I'll figure that later.

I send him a message telling him to meet me and that it's urgent and then I grab my bag and, quietly as I can, I sneak out my window, down onto the flat roof of the veranda below and in one quick motion I jump, landing silently on the soft grass. Technically no one will stop me if they see me, after all I have every right to walk in my own back garden but I don't want to risk it. I don't want to be seen.

By the time I get to our meeting spot the air is cooling and the oppressive heat is finally letting up a bit. I stare at my phone. He hasn't replied, he hasn't even responded. It's like I don't exist. Like none of this is real.

I start shaking my head. Maybe it's the hormones already whirling inside me but it feels like everything is collapsing. It feels like suddenly the ground beneath my feet is crumbling away so fast and I'm rapidly descending into a situation I'll never be able to climb out of.

So I do it. I send the message I've been putting off. My hands shake as I type the words. My throat constricts and I don't need to touch my face to know my cheeks are wet with tears. What the hell are we going to do?

It doesn't take long for his reply. I feel relief when I see the small bubbles indicating that he's writing. Relief and anger because who the fuck types back to that? Why is he not calling me? I'm his girlfriend for fucksake. I'm pregnant with his child.

Then the words flash and everything really does fall apart. He asks why I'm even telling him, he calls me a whore. He says that I'm probably fucking half the city so it could be anyone's.

I whimper shaking my head. Roman would never say that. Roman would never behave like that. Not to me.

I dial his number but he sends it immediately to voicemail. And then more words come. More vitriol. He tells me not to contact him again. That I was nothing but a joke. A bet to him and his friends.

But I know that's not true. Not after what he said. Not after the way we were.

I call again only this time he's blocked me. Cut me out entirely.

I sink down onto the low brick wall that I've sat so many time before. Around me is so much broken glass and soggy cigarette ends. All signs that I'm in the shittiest part of town. It feels like a reflection of my life, like some sort of metaphor for how low I've sunk. How fucked I truly am.

My tears start falling harder than ever. It wasn't a joke. I know it wasn't. He told me he loved me. He didn't have to say that. Hell, he didn't have to do half the things he did but his behaviour right now says a very different story.

Christ was I that stupid? That blinded? That starved for attention that I fell for it? Did I miss all the warning signs, too high from the fun of rebelling to see it? To deeply in love with Roman to notice that to him this was all a joke?

I'm pregnant.

There's no going back from that.

No matter what games Roman was playing, no matter how twisted it all was, he can walk away but I can't, can I?

I clench my fists, trying to process it.

My father is going to kill me. My mother too. This will ruin all their plans. There'll be no Paris Blumenfeld. No fancy marriage and alliance. I'll be an outcast. Christ, I really am ruined. Roman made so many jokes about it, so much teasing, but in the end he was right; he has ruined me.

I stare across at the bay. A ferry is coming in. It's loaded with tourists eager to see the glitz and glamour of Verona as if it's not truly rotten right to the core.

I have two choices. Go home, admit to everything and face the consequences or I could leave. I have a little money. Not enough to set me up or anything but it would get me away from Verona. I could disappear, run away, start a new life and have this child. My hands wrap around my belly. It's not the life I planned but then I was never going to get that was I? Being a Capulet meant my life would always be controlled by my parents. But this way, this way I might be able to carve out a new destiny and more than that, I'll ensure my child isn't a part of their schemes.

I get up, wiping the tears. I won't cry now. No matter what Roman was to me, is to me, I won't think on it. I'm going to bury those thoughts, bury it all. I'll live my life the way I want and ensure my child does too.

That's my only option.

Fight now, fight for my child and bury every last heart-breaking memory of the man I loved until I'm far enough away to safely fall apart.

I walk over to the cash point. It's covered in graffiti, another sign that I'm in a shitty part of town. I withdraw as much as it allows. Only five hundred bucks but as I walk back I stop off at another one and another one. Slowly I drain my account and by the time I'm done I have close to five thousand dollars ~~*to play with. Like I said, it's not enough to set me up. It's pocket change really*~~ *and it irks that my entire trust fund is there, with millions in, except I can't touch it without my father's sign off.*

But I'll use this cash, I'll get a bus out of town, I'll cross the country, get as far from Verona as I can and then I'll find some quiet town, somewhere that feels safe, and I'll get a job, I'll actually work for a living, and slowly I'll build a new life.

A life on my terms.

That idea makes me smile. I'll do this for my child.

And I'll never see Roman Montague, or have to hear his name again.

I just need to get home and pack a few things. Not much, just enough clothes and essentials to save wasting my resources.

And tomorrow I'll leave.

Vanish.

Rose Capulet will be no more.

She'll cease to exist.

I'll become someone new, I'll become a real person and not the fake sunshine princess my family has moulded me into.

But as I turn the corner footsteps behind me make me freeze. As does the voice calling out.

"And where have you been?"

I gulp looking up, meeting the cold, mean eyes of Carter and, as gravel crunches behind me, I know Sampson is there at my back.

"*Just for a walk.*" *I reply trying to look as innocent as possible. I hate these two. Out of all of father's men these two men are the meanest, nastiest pieces of shit. They make my skin crawl.*

"*Is that so?*" *Sampson says grabbing my bag and I yelp trying to pull it back.*

"*Get off.*" *I snap.* "*You have no right…*"

Carter grins yanking me back and the bag falls free. Sampson's digging his hand in rummaging through like he knows exactly what he's looking for and as he does my stomach sinks further and further. He pulls my purse out and we all see the notes sticking out. It's bloody loaded.

"*What's this princess?*" *He taunts.*

"*It's my money I can do what I want with it.*" *I state.*

Carter yanks my face up so I'm forced to stare at him. "*And what would you need all this cash for?*"

"*I'm going on a shopping trip.*" *I say.*

He laughs. Sampson laughs too. And then Sampson puts his fingers to his right ear and mutters. "*We have her. Send the car.*"

"*What's going on?*" *I ask jerking to get free but already I know it's useless.*

"*You tell me princess.*" *Carter says.* "*You're the one who's been fraternising with the enemy.*"

"*What?*" *I half whisper before my brain engages enough to tell me to shut up.*

They don't reply, they just stand there, holding me like I'm some sort of escapee until the car pulls up and then I'm bundled inside.

And the whole time I'm trying to figure out what they know, what my parents know, and how the hell I'm going to get away now.

I WAKE IN MY BED WITH NO RECOLLECTION OF HOW I GOT HERE. Bella is curled up into me and I guess it's a measure of how much she's changed now that Paris is gone because he refused to allow her upstairs and certainly would never have permitted her on, let alone in, our bed.

185

My head is pounding. I know I drank too much but at the time I didn't care. Something in me snapped. I had to get rid of his stuff. I had to try to expel some of the memories and some of the guilt too.

Because I do feel guilty.

He's my husband. *Was* my husband. I should be mourning him. Grieving him but all I feel is a strange mix of relief and stagnation. If I had my way I'd be out of this house. I'd be selling it already. Selling every single item too because all of it reminds me of him.

But damn did it feel good to burn his stuff. It felt like a final 'fuck you'. Paris always took such pride in his appearance. He spent more money on clothes than I did.

And now all of them are little more than ash.

I smirk and my head responds by punishing me further.

Thankfully there's nowhere to be so I spend the day in bed, with Bella, coming up with a new plan. Deciding that even if I can't sell this place, I don't have to live here do I?

And once I come to that conclusion I start looking up houses, places to rent that are far more me.

DAYS LATER I PACK SOME THINGS AND MOVE OUT. I TELL THE MAIDS to stay all except Mae. I keep the security there as well to ensure the place is safe and I go. If I were prudent I'd take more of them with me but I'm sick of being followed. I'm sick of being watched.

So yeah, perhaps it is reckless but I trust the handful of guards that I do take to keep me safe.

My new house is tiny in comparison. With wooden shutters on the front that give it a cottage type feel. It's in the Old Town. Not far from City Hall and if I was admitting it, more on the Montague side of town. Not that that is intentional. And not that any of us adhere to the old boundaries.

Besides that wasn't what attracted me to this place. It's the little details. The fact that it's got a great view of the marina. The fact that there's a big comfy corner couch that you can feel yourself sinking into just by looking at it.

But mainly it's the fact that I have no past here. No ugly interactions with Paris in any of the rooms.

This place feels like a sanctuary.

And from the moment I step inside it feels like home. My home.

Bella runs around snorting as she explores the place. I had to pay a lot more to allow her to stay but that was never not an option. I'm sure if I want I could just buy this place when my money comes through.

I order groceries. No more chefs, no more takeaways either. I'm done rebelling and I'm done being pampered too. I'm an okay cook. Not fantastic. But I guess now is the time to learn. Besides it's just me so there's no need to do anything flamboyant.

The first night I have grilled cheese sandwiches for dinner and they taste all the better for it being me who made them.

And when I curl up in a new bed , I sleep better than I have in a long time.

ROSE

*D*arius has summoned us to his office. *Not just me. Not just my parents but the entire Capulet family.*

My stomach is in knots because I can't figure out what this is. As the car drives through the streets I try to calm myself. He's been acting more and more protective around me and I don't want to think about what that means, what his intentions are.

When I get out in front of City Hall I know half my family are there, inside already. Tyrone is lounging against a stone balustrade, cigarette in hand, scowling at no one in particular.

As I make my way up he hollers at me. "Rose."

I let out a low breath walking over. Ty has never had my back. Not once. I doubt recent events have changed that.

"Do you know what this is about?" He asks.

"Not a clue." I reply.

"You mean your dear in-laws haven't been kind enough to give you a hint?" He says.

"No."

He snorts. "Perhaps you're out of favour."

"Perhaps." I mutter. God I hope so. If the Blumenfelds decide to shun me I can only see that as a good thing for me. I can disappear into anonymity waiting till my money comes through and I can escape.

"Perhaps they're suspicious."

"Of what?" I ask.

"You're seen publicly arguing with your husband and then suddenly he's dead and you've inherited the lot."

I screw my face up. "If you're suggesting…"

"I'm suggesting nothing Rose. It's just what everyone's saying behind your back."

"Like hell they are." I reply.

"Why not ask? Oh right, because you've been hiding away, in your house, with all those newly inherited millions."

"Fuck you." I snap.

"Rose." My mother says behind me.

I turn meeting her exasperated look head on. She gives me a once over like she's inspecting my outfit choice then glances at Tyrone.

"Are you going to put that out?" She asks gesturing to the cigarette.

"When I'm done." He replies.

She rolls her eyes, knowing better than to make further comment. "Let's go." She tucks her arm into mine and walks me into the building like I was about to duck and run.

"What is this about?" I ask once we're inside. It's so much cooler inside. Like this whole building was designed to be a refuge from the sun that seems to beat down onto everything.

"I was going to ask you if you had any ideas." She says.

"I don't."

"What if this is about Otto?" She says quietly.

I pause. "What?"

"He's been seeing that Montague girl." She states, like the entire city doesn't know it. It's in all the gossip rags. It's all over social media too.

"I highly doubt we've all been called her because of who Sofia Montague is dating." I reply.

"Unless they're getting married."

"Mother really, I don't see…" My words die as I see my father half glaring at us.

"You took your time." He says to me.

"I'm not late." I reply. Darius set the meeting for two pm. We've still got fifteen minutes to go.

He snarls bearing down on me. "I told you this was going to happen. I warned you…" He focuses all his anger on me and I realise he must be thinking the same as my mother. That this is about Sofia. But I just don't see it. I don't see why she'd be so stupid. Why she'd throw everything she has away? And more than that, why would Darius summon all of us here to pass on this news? It doesn't make sense.

So I don't reply. I just fold my arms and stand in silence, surrounded by my family, until we're called into his office.

Except we're not the only ones here. Across from us are stood the entire Montague hoard. Sofia is amongst them. In this moment she looks like a queen and I'll admit I envy her. The way her family seem to protect her in a manner mine do not do with me.

Darius sits behind his desk. His eyes seem to find mine and for a moment I wonder what he thinks of us, the Capulets. Why he even bothers with my father and all his drama? Surely we're not so powerful as this? Surely we're not so necessary to his role as Governor?

"Thank you all for coming." He says quietly. He's not looking at me now. He's staring at my father. Who is obviously fighting to control himself in this moment.

"...the reason I've called you here is because I've come to a decision. It's not something I've taken lightly, but with recent events..."

A few of my family glance at me. No doubt they're thinking of Paris. Why does it feel like I'm about to get the blame for all of this? Whatever this is.

"...I think it's time this city focused on healing. Focused on repairing old wounds. Ancient wounds."

I frown. What wounds? Paris didn't hurt anyone except me. Only thanks to Darius now the entire damn city knows it too.

"The Montagues and the Capulets have been at each other's throats forever. It's time it stopped. Time this fighting between you all came to an end."

My father growls. The only show of dissent he's able to muster.

"With the passing of Horace, I have decided it is time Roman Montague was granted a pardon. That he is allowed to return home."

As he says *those* words the door to the side opens. My eyes follow the movement and he's there.

Roman is there.

Barely metres from me.

I stare at him. He looks so different and yet exactly the same. His eyes skim over us. The twenty something members of my family who are already reacting like they've just been attacked. He doesn't even look at me. It's like I don't exist but I guess to him I never did. I was something to use and discard when he was done.

I wonder if he even remembers me at all.

Around me my family are shouting, hurling insults, completely lost to any sense of decorum but I can't make out a sound. I can't hear anything beyond the scream that seems to ring out in my own head.

"Enough." Darius says raising his voice and holding his hands for silence. "I don't want to hear any arguments. It is done. There has been enough bloodshed. Enough lives lost on both sides. You will all abide by the laws of this city." He looks from Roman to my father.

"You expect them to do that?" My father snarls.

"I expect peace." Darius says more forcefully.

I can't stand here. I can't process this. And yet I'm trapped. Surrounded. I can't escape because my family as always are blocking my way.

Darius dismisses us all but he calls me back so I'm forced to stand as everyone filters past. I don't look. I shut my eyes, barely keeping my composure until the room falls to silence and I know we're alone.

"Rose." He says softly. I jump at the proximity of his voice. At how close he is to me. He's right in front of me, practically nose to nose with me.

I look up at him and he's frowning with concern.

"I wanted to see you." He says. "I wanted to check on you."

"I'm fine." I murmur.

"No you're not." He says. "I can see you're anything but."

"Why did you do It?" I ask, my voice more angry than I meant.

"You mean Roman?"

"No." I snap. "The inquest. I know that was you. I know you got the coroner to ask all those things about Paris. About us."

He sighs, his thumb brushes against my cheek, and I jerk like I've been shocked. He keeps doing that I realise, he keeps touching me in ways that could easily be mistaken for loving gestures.

Except I don't find it loving, I don't want it to be.

"I did it for you Rose." He states. "I wanted people to realise what you've gone through. I didn't want you to pretend any longer, to be burdened by it."

I shake my head as my anger unfurls more. "It wasn't your secret to spill."

"Perhaps not." He replies. "But it was necessary nonetheless."

I shut my eyes. How dare he make that call? How dare he think he can tell the world my private life without even consulting me?

"If you let me I would take care of you." He murmurs.

"I don't need that." I reply. I'm done being everyone else's plaything. Done being viewed as simply a puppet to manipulate and control.

He sighs. "Fine."

I step away to the refuge of the door but at the last minute I turn back. "Do you know what you're doing?" I ask him.

"With Roman?" He says.

I nod.

"I do." He smiles with no doubt what he thinks is meant to be reassurance.

I shake my head. There's no reply to that. None whatsoever.

ROMAN

I couldn't look at her. Not then. Not in front of all of them.

So I let my eyes skim over her existence like she meant nothing when all I wanted to do was pull her in, check her for hurts, and never let her go.

Except that's my heart talking not my head.

I can't do that. Even if we were alone, even if it were just us in that room, I couldn't touch her. I couldn't do anything until she fixed the chasm between us. This chasm she created.

So instead of following the rest of my family back after the announcement I sneak off. I know enough about her routine to predict what she'll do. What she seems to always do in moments of stress when she thinks she needs to ground herself.

I wait patiently, concealed in the trees. It feels like I'm always concealed where Rose is concerned. First when we were young, and now, while we're circling each other, trying to find our footing.

Only she doesn't know she's doing it yet. She's still so oblivious to what's been going on but I'm about to open her eyes.

I see the dog before I see her. It's running ahead, sniffing at the ground, clearly enjoying the coolness beneath the lime trees. She follows close behind. The lead dangling from around her neck. Her hair loose and floating in the wind. She looks distracted. She looks like she's somewhere else entirely and for that I can't blame her.

If she'd shown up in Atlanta would I have felt the same? Would I have, in the space to prepare? I shake my head because the two are not comparable. She didn't leave. She didn't try to find me. She stayed and lived her life here like I didn't exist. Like what we had was nothing.

"Rose." I murmur her name. I've said it so many times. In joy. In despair. In hate too.

She doesn't hear me. She's too focused on her damn dog.

I've waited so long for this moment. This particular piece of justice. To hear her excuses. To witness her, on her knees begging for forgiveness. She thought she could just continue on, she thought she could marry someone else, that she could forget me? Today she's going to learn otherwise. Today she's going to truly understand what her actions have caused. What six years of pain and suffering, six years of exile can do to a man.

I step out, a twig snaps underfoot and she turns her eyes widening in horror and she gulps.

"No." She whispers.

"Hello Trouble." The old adage slips out before I realise I've said it.

"No." She says again louder. "You don't get to call me that. You don't get to even speak to me."

I laugh. I can't help it. She looks frightened. She looks like she might just bolt. Her body is trembling. She's shaking. Retribution is a bitch isn't it love?

She glances around but there's no one else here. It's just us. After all these weeks of watching, it's finally just us.

"You haven't changed a bit." I murmur. I don't mean to. I'm just stunned by her, by her presence, by her beauty. How she can even look me in the face right now.

She narrows her eyes. "Neither have you apparently."

"What does that mean?" I ask.

"Like you don't know." She says before glancing around, checking where her dog is, though it's right there, by her feet.

"I never stopped thinking about you." I state. "Even after everything you did."

"Really?" She replies. Her eyes flashing from fear to anger.

"I…"

"No." She says cutting across my words. "You made it abundantly clear six years ago."

"What are you talking about?" I snap.

"You." She says. Her voice ragged now. Her finger shaking as she points it right at me. "You made it clear what this was. What I was to you. You walked away. You *betrayed* me. Don't act like that never happened."

I frown taking a step nearer and she reacts like a wild beast that's been suddenly cornered. She lashes out, her hands pushing against my chest so violently I stumble for a nanosecond.

"Say something." She screams. Suddenly she's feral. All that pent up energy inside her seems to go off like an explosion and it hits me full force. "Go on. Try and justify it."

But I can't. All my anger, all those bitter twisted words I'd saved for this moment are lost. I expected pathetic pleas. I expected her to try to beg her way out of this. To justify her actions with pitiful excuses and lies.

But there's none on that.

Just raw, seething anger matching the same in my own soul. It's like I'm the one in the wrong. Like I'm the one who hurt her.

"Rose…" I murmur but she's shaking now her rage has turned to something deadly.

"You left. You left me. You don't get to waltz back in and expect me to forgive you. To just expect everything to be as it was. Not after what you did. Not after what you said. You destroyed my life. You destroyed everything."

She scoops her dog up into her arms. I take a step towards her and her nostrils flare.

"Fuck you Roman Montague." She spits before turning on her heel. "Fuck you."

ROMAN

I *stare after her, watching as she storms away. What the fuck was that? She thinks I betrayed her? How could I possible have?*

But that anger was real. That belief was real too.

I think back to that day. Six years ago. The day I killed Tybalt.

Ben and I had simply been in the wrong place at the wrong time. An error that escalated, that compounded itself, barraging through every aspect of my life.

Tybalt, aggressive arsehole that he was, saw his moment. Him and his mates.

We'd broken down coming back from a days' hunting. Ben had been into classic cars, still is to some extent, so there we were sat beside his Series Land Rover, the engine steaming because it'd overheated.

Two sitting ducks.

And then Tybalt was there. Pulling over. In his ridiculously modified truck.

Ben had thought he was a Good Samaritan, that is until he saw exactly who it was.

Tybalt sauntered over, his mates already laughing behind him like jackals.

But Ben was too far ahead of me. He'd already half run up to greet them before he'd realised what this was.

Tybalt landed the first punch, knocking him off his feet and Ben slammed back head first into tarmac. I shouted out. Yelled. But I knew they weren't going to stop. These were the Capulet boys. The entire flicking gang.

When they started beating on him I saw red. I wasn't just going to stand there and watch. I wasn't going to let Ben get killed. But I also knew I was outmatched five to one.

I didn't think. In that moment I just didn't think. I jumped into the car, grabbing the rifle. I could have let off a warning shot, I could have aimed for a less serious limb, but I didn't.

I did it on purpose.

I took aim and pulled the trigger.

Firing right into his god damn skull.

Tybalt fell back. His mouth ajar. Blood already pouring from the wound. His mates froze, looking round and as they spotted me I let off another shot. It narrowly missed the one on the right and they scarpered. The four of them running back to the truck and away.

The moments after are hazy. I dragged Ben back to the Series. I hailed down a car, got him to our house and as the medics worked away to fix him, my father began working to try and undo the shit storm I'd created.

Only it was too late.

Far too fucking late.

Tybalt was dead.

And Ignatio Capulet was already at City Hall screaming for my head.

My father pulled every favour he had. Every last one. He got my sentence commuted. Life in exile instead of lethal injection. It was a fair trade considering. I was given twelve hours to be gone. Twelve hours to pack my life up and leave forever.

I called Rose. I called her over and over but she never picked up. I left messages. I told her exactly how she could get to me. Where to be.

And then Ben and I left. Him bandaged up and still half concussed. Me with every penny my father could get at such short notice.

I waited for her. I waited over and over. Returning day after day. Expecting to see her. Only she never showed.

But someone else did.

I know Ignatio was behind it. The first assassination attempt. But Rose set it up. It was her words telling me to be there. Telling me that she was coming. That she was leaving Verona. Christ, how my heart had leap when I'd finally gotten that message. I'd called her. She didn't pick up but she replied, telling me she was being watched, that her family were suspicious and she was running away to be with me.

Except it wasn't true was it? She was playing me, having one more laugh at my expense. How I'd not ended up gutted I don't know. I guess it was instinct. I was fighting for my life, and the knifeman, though strong, wasn't able to overpower me.

And as he lay bleeding out from the knife buried in his jugular I sat beside him, watching the blood streaming into the gutter, realising how truly stupid I'd been.

She wasn't coming.

She was never coming.

She was staying in Verona Bay.

And everything we had been was a lie.

I run my hand over my face bringing my head back to now. I don't allow myself to think on it. I haven't for a long time. On those last days of the old me. The stupid me. The gullible me. Rose had fooled me. Played me. And then abandoned me, right when I'd needed her the most.

And yet she'd screamed at me just now, acting like I was the one who'd duped her.

Have I got this wrong? Is it possible that all of this is the complete opposite to what I thought it was? I can't deny that I still want her. Even now, even after everything, I know if she'd confessed to it, if she'd begged for mercy, begged me to take her back I would have.

She still holds that power over me. She still holds that power over my heart.

I snarl hating that she does. I want to hate it. I want to hate her. But I can't.

I blink staring about me. I need to figure this out. I need to know once and for all if she's the conniving bitch I've convinced myself she is or whether she's as much a victim as I am.

But the only way to know that is to spend time with her and if I do that, if I allow myself to get too close, I'll burn entirely just from the exposure.

'You left me. You destroyed my life.'

Her words echo in my head and I can hear it. Her pain. Her anger. If there's even a small chance I'm wrong, even the slightest chance that the Rose I knew was real then I have to take it, and if it turns out she's playing me again, if it turns out this woman is exactly what I fear then I will kill her.

I won't hesitate this time.

I will carve out her god damn heart.

ROSE

"*You haven't changed a bit.*"

Why is it those are the words that stick?

And more to the point, how dare he? How dare he just show up and say that? Like he knows me, like he even understands what the hell I've lived through.

I have changed. I've changed entirely. I'm not that doe-eyed, innocent idiot who fell for his charms. I'm not that naïve twenty something who believes that love conquers all.

Because it doesn't.

All that love does is leave you broken and ruined.

And that's how he left me; Roman fucking Montague. Only now he gets to play the prodigal son, gets to return to a hero's welcome.

I snarl, lashing out and send everything on the side scattering to the floor.

I lean down picking up the bigger pieces of glass and yelp as it slices through my fingers. I watch as the blood swells along the tip and trickles down. I want the pain. I want the hurt. I need to remind myself of what it feels like. What being around Roman feels like.

There's a knock at my door.

I get back up, making sure Bella isn't going to hurt herself and walk over to open it.

The other side is my mother. She's eyeing the space with a mixture of dislike and suspicion.

"You're hard to track down." She says.

I grunt turning around and leave her to show herself in. She watches me as I clear the last of the mess and finally bandage my finger.

"Aren't you going to offer me a drink?" She asks.

"Do you want one?" I reply.

"Yes. Tea please." She sounds so chirpy it makes me want to scowl more.

I grab the kettle sticking it on, and search the cupboards for the mugs. I've not yet remembered where everything is but it's starting to sink in.

"Why are you here?" She asks.

"Why do you think?" I reply.

She glances around. "This is hardly the sort of place a Capulet should reside in."

"No? You prefer Paris's house do you?" I say narrowing my eyes.

"Is that why you left? Because it was his space?"

"What do you think?" I retort.

"Oh honey." She walks around and wraps me in a big hug that is both comforting and trapping. "It's going to take time. I know how much you cared for him but you will get through this."

"I didn't." I snap.

"Didn't what?"

"Care for him."

"Rose…" She pulls away to look at me.

"No, I'm done pretending." I state pushing myself free. "I'm done keeping up the charade. The man was a brute. I endured five years of horror at his hands and yet everyone's acting like he was the love of my life."

She pauses, letting out a low breath as she assesses me. "Is that what this is about?" She says quietly. "Because Roman Montague has returned?"

I wince. I don't mean to. I certainly don't want to. I hate that she knows my secrets, the parts of me I hide even from myself most days.

"Honey, he's not the love of your life either." She says so gently.

"I know that." I reply. That man is nothing to me. Should be nothing to me. After what he did, after the way he treated me, I'm not capable of forgiving and forgetting. I'm not capable of anything but a deep festering hatred.

She moves around grabs the kettle and to my surprise she finishes making the teas, putting one in front of me and awkwardly settles onto a bar stool.

"So you moved here for some space?" She says.

"Yes."

"I see." She says. "Well it's definitely quaint."

That makes me laugh. 'Quaint' is my mother's way of saying unfashionable. "I like it." I state hearing the defiance in my voice as it rings out.

"It is very you." She says.

I raise an eyebrow. "In what way?"

"Oh come on, all that minimalism was stifling. Your house should be a reflection of you. And you Rose are not cold glass and polished surfaces. You're vibrant. You're electric. You walk into a room and it comes alive."

205

I snort. "I am not those things."

"Maybe not now. Maybe not with everything that is happening but that's who you are Rose. You're a Capulet after all."

I give a half smile and take a sip. Maybe one day I'll be that again. Maybe one day I'll remember what it's like to be excited, to be happy, but right now everything just feels so flat, so grey, so utterly pointless.

She stays with me, chatting in the way we used to for a few hours. It feels comforting. It feels good. She even seems to take more of a liking to Bella though I wouldn't go so far as to say she's become a dog person but still, this moment feels cathartic, it feels like what I needed.

When she leaves I curl myself up on the couch, put a movie on and find myself balling my eyes out, crying for the person I was six years ago, crying for the person I've become too.

The twisted, bitter, angry shell of a human being that exists more than lives in the body that is Rose Capulet.

ROMAN

She's moved out. She's gone.

I don't think she knew I was here, that I was watching, but when I returned this evening everything was dark. I thought at first it was her response. To hide. To shut herself away. She's been pretty much living as a hermit this last week; I thought this was just an extension of that.

But as the sunlight started to streak across the glass I realised the house is not the same. Things are missing; the most notable being her.

She's packed up.

She's gone.

It takes me a day to locate her, to find her in the Old Town area of all places. In a place that feels far more hipster than the great house she shared with Paris.

Paris. He may be dead but that man still has a lot to answer for. His whole family do.

I slip past the men at the front entrance, creep up the drive, and when I'm there stood outside her door I pull the rose from its casing.

Silently I lay it on the ground.

She might remember it. She might not. Either way this all part of the game. Our new game. One of hunter and prey, cat and mouse.

And then I hide. Lurking in the bushes and I'll stay as long as it takes till she appears. I want to see her face, to see her confusion when she finds it.

It's like she's upped the stakes but I'm all for it.

And when she finally does appear the look of abject horror makes it so worth the wait.

When I get back to our house it's a fine thing to walk through my own front door. To not have to sneak in. Cameras are there, flashing. I'm front page news and though a part of me likes it, likes that this city has finally remembered me, it's more than a little wearisome.

Because I'm not some returning hero. I'm not some god damn lost son.

They kicked me out. They exiled me.

And now they want to welcome me back with open arms? Well, I guess they don't know who they're welcoming anymore but that's okay, I'm all for showing them. Piece by piece.

I already all but own the Governor. I just need to take a few more people off the board. Cut a few out as well. Starting with the Capulet's source of power.

Ben is already pulling out the plans, going through the blueprints. Ignatio was good at hiding his more objectionable activities but unluckily for him I had an insider, a disgruntled ex-employee if you will, who was more than willing to spill the beans given the right incentive. I guess that's the problem when you get too high up the food chain, you forget the people under you who are holding you up. It's what my father did too. How he ended up destroying half of our empire. He got too big for his boots, thought he was above everyone and ultimately, that was what helped sign his death warrant.

And now it's what will be the undoing of Ignatio.

"You ready?" Turner says.

I don't have to look at him to know he is. As are the rest of the men. We've got a small jolly planned for tonight. More of a jab than anything but I want Ignatio to feel the sting all the same.

He's got an import coming in. A nice little package that will keep the deadbeats of this city hooked for a little while.

We climb into the van, all of us are armed to the teeth, and we sit in silence for the entire thirty minute journey. All we can hear are the sounds of the tyres churning over the road and the muffled sound of the radio through the bulkhead.

It's when the vehicle stops that we all come alive.

The side door slides open. One by one, silently we get out and then we're sprinting for the cover of the building, using its walls to hide ourselves.

I'll admit my adrenaline is up and I'm itching to get started.

When the boat appears, I don't wait for the call, like a man possessed I run ahead, shooting, taking over every one of those fuckers.

Bullets ricochet off the walls. Turner and the others follow behind but their bloods up too. Gone is the restraint, gone is tactical strategy. Right now we're men on a mission.

Every fucker that comes at me gets a bullet in the head.

And when it all falls silent we just stand there looking at all the destruction we've caused.

I order them off, all my men, tell them to get back to the safety of the dock. Once it's just me, I make my final offering to the gods of war. I pour enough gasoline for this ship to light up the entirety of Verona and then I spring from the side, toss a match, and watch with glee as the thing ignites.

He's going to be livid. He's going to be furious.

Every crackhead in the city is going to clawing at him for their fix and for once he has nothing. I've pulled out the rug from under him. Given him a little hint of what's to come.

Take that Ignatio Fucking Capulet. Take that to hell.

ROSE

His hand comes out of nowhere sending me flying. I feel the pain before I realise I'm on the floor. Sprawled out.

"You stupid fucking slut." My father spits, towering over me and for a moment I think he's going to kick me too.

I shake, trying to fight back the tears that are threatening to spill. He grabs my hair yanking my head up, forcing me to look at him.

"You're a whore. A dirty, filthy little whore."

I don't reply. I don't have anything to say back because that's exactly what I am. What I let myself become.

What Roman made of me.

My mother flits back and forth. Pacing. I don't even know how they know. They couldn't have found the test. I hid it too well. So how the hell did they find out?

"What are we going to do?" She mutters over and over.

My father snarls. "There's only one thing we can do..." He says and for a second my hope flares that maybe, just maybe this might be my escape, that somehow, despite my ruin, it might just save me after all. "...Terminate it."

"No." I gasp.

"Ignatio." My mother says shocked.

"What?" My father snarls with his beady eyes still pinned on me. "You think you can keep it? Keep his bastard child? Not a fucking chance." He grabs me yanking me up from the floor. "We'll get it aborted and then we'll never speak of this again."

"No." I say louder but he doesn't pay any attention.

He turns to my mother. "Get it sorted. Get a clinic out of the city. The pair of you will go away and when you return we'll announce the engagement."

He's still pushing that? He thinks I'll just murder my child one minute and then marry Paris Blumenfeld the next?

"I won't do it." I snap forcing myself to move, forcing myself to fight.

His face contorts. "Is that so? You think you have a say?" His hand swings again and this time the blow is so much harder knocking me to the floor with such an impact I see stars. It's as if he's hoping I'll miscarry right here, in his office.

My mother steps in shaking her head. "Ignatio." She says quietly.

"What?"

"Let me handle this."

He tilts his head. I've never seen him raise his hand to her but in this moment I wonder if he might. If he's lost so much control he might just hurt her too. "I want it done."

"It will be." She reassures, putting her hands on his forearms to reassure him. "Trust me. I will sort it."

He nods throwing me a look before storming out the door and as soon as he's gone the tears start. I'm sobbing hysterically.

"Rose." My mother says. She doesn't sound comforting in this moment. She sounds just as cold as he did.

"I can't do it. I won't do it." I state.

"You will." She says walking towards me. "You don't have any choice."

"Please." I beg and she shakes her head, tucking my hair behind my ear.

"What life do you think you would have huh? If you kept this child? Paris won't marry you. Your father would disown you, I'd have to disown you too. You'd be an outcast. A nobody."

"I don't care." I reply wrapping my hands around myself. I've never even thought about kids, about being a parent but now that I'm here I can't just walk away and pretend it didn't happen.

"Rose, be reasonable."

"I love him." I say.

"But he doesn't love you does he? He left. Without even saying goodbye."

More tears spill. More of my heart breaks at how she's stating the facts I know to be true.

"...he used you Rose. He used you and now he's left. Don't let him ruin the rest of your life."

I shake my head. I want to argue, to protest, but she's right even as my heart tells me otherwise, she's right. Roman Montague used me and then ditched me like I was nothing.

She pulls me in, hugs me as I sob more. "I'll sort it Rose. I'll sort everything." She says as if it's merely a new dress I need.

I t's a rose.

My hair stands on the back of my neck as I stare down at it. The cluster of apricot petals alone mark it for what it is and even from this distance I can smell it's light, summery aroma.

It's not just any rose. It's a Juliet rose.

I grit my teeth, already knowing where this came from.

Six years ago the mere sight of one would have made my heart leap. Six years ago he would bring one with him every time we met, like a calling card.

But what it means now is that he was here. Right outside my door. Did he follow me? Has he been watching me this entire time?

How the hell did I not notice? Was I so stuck in my own head I was oblivious to everything around me?

I let out a bitter laugh. It's so very me isn't it? I do what I think is necessary to protect myself and yet all the while, all I'm really doing is causing more harm.

Bella whines at my heels, I'd promised her a walk and she clearly is feeling short changed as we stand on the threshold not going anywhere.

"Come on." I mutter stepping over the offending article and leading her out, figuring I'll deal with it later. Once I can figure out what moves to make.

I BURN THE ROSE. IT FEELS SATISFYING. CATHARTIC ALMOST. AS IF I'M burning the very soul of that man himself.

But as I watch it turn to ash it does nothing to alleviate the feeling that he's here. That he's been here. And that at any moment he could return.

I glance around, seeing nothing but the fading light between the trees. Beyond it I know my security are stationed around the perimeter.

And yet…

I feel restless.

On edge.

I eat another homemade dinner. I cuddle Bella and try to watch TV but nothing is distracting me. As the memories whirl in my head I think I snap, forcing myself up, forcing myself to get out, to escape these four walls and pretend that I'm not a total headcase.

I put on a nice dress, I slap some concealer under my eyes to hide the dark bags I have, and I make sure Bella is watched. That Mae is with her so she doesn't get lonely.

And then I slip out into the dark across to the Bay.

The bar is rammed. The music is blaring. Bodies are heaving on the dance floor and you can practically smell the pheromones in the air.

I make my way to get a drink ignoring the people who double take at me.

"Here she is, the Merry Widow herself." Tyrone says as I spot him.

"I'm hardly a Merry Widow." I reply.

"No? Paris's millions not enough for you?" He says.

I roll my eyes clicking my fingers for the barman's attention and order a vodka tonic.

"So why have you chosen to grace us all with your presence?" Tyrone asks.

"I'm allowed out." I state. "What's your excuse?"

He smirks glancing around. "Scooping out the competition."

I frown. "What competition?"

He jerks his head to the corner that's packed with Montagues. Like they've all come back out of the woodwork.

Roman is there, as is his sister and his old friend Benvolio. There's a crowd of groupies around them like they're some sort of fan club.

"Jesus." I mutter before glancing back at Ty. "You know you'd be stupid to do anything."

He grins. "Maybe right now, but you know what they say, keep your enemies close."

I shake my head taking a long sip of my drink because god knows I need it now. "How long have they been here?"

"Few hours."

"And you?" I ask.

He grins more. "Longer."

He's never been all that articulate. In fact we've never had that great a relationship. Him and Tybalt used to bully me mercilessly when we were growing up so I tend to avoid him as much as possible but tonight perhaps I'm feeling masochistic.

"Shots?" I say.

He tilts his head. "The great Rose Capulet wants to drink with me?"

"It's just drinks. Don't let it go to your head."

He snorts. "What's the matter, none of your other friends wanna come out and play?"

"Who says I have other friends?" I ask before ordering a load of tequilas - minus the lemon and salt naturally.

He doesn't reply except to start drinking and I have to race to catch up with him.

"So tell me what's got our perfect princess all riled up?" He asks.

"What do you think?" I reply, my eyes betraying me by flickering to the corner where Team Montague is louder than ever.

He raises an eyebrow. "So that shit does affect you? You always seemed so above it."

"Seriously?" I reply. "My entire life has been hijacked because of this rivalry or do you think I'm too empty headed to notice?"

"Nah, you're not empty headed. Just stuck up."

My jaw drops. I'm not stuck up. Sure I have walls. Sure I project a certain image but that's to cover myself, to keep me safe from every arsehole that seems to reside in this city.

"And it's not like you haven't benefitted." He continues. "Dear Uncle Ignatio ensured you married a Blumenfeld after all."

"Aww what's the matter Ty, you fancied Paris yourself is that it?" I tease.

"Fuck off." He laughs.

"Would it ease the pain if I split all those millions with you?"

"Like you would."

"Yeah I wouldn't." I say holding another shot up and he clinks his glass before we down them.

"Fucking bitch." He mutters laughing.

"Arsehole." I reply with a smirk.

He looks around again. "So what are we going to do about them?"

I don't look this time. I keep my eyes on Ty because I don't want to see him. "There's nothing we can do."

"Rubbish." He states before opening his jacket just a tiny bit. "Not all of us are so defeatist."

My eyes widen as I see the glint of the blade tucked neatly into his side. "Ty you can't."

"Why not? He killed Tybalt. Six years is hardly punishment enough for that."

"You heard what Darius said."

He narrows his eyes. "We're Capulets. You think we listen to him?"

"He's the Governor." I hiss as loudly as I dare. I don't want to be overheard. I don't want to think about what the consequences of that would be.

"What's the matter Rose, you too concerned with sucking Darius's cock to care about our family now?"

"I've never…" I snarl.

"Yeah but you wouldn't turn it down would you? And dear old Uncle Ignatio would be more than happy to turn a blind eye to it if it got us what we wanted. Only it hasn't." He shoots me a look like I'm trash. "Maybe you're not as good as you thought. Maybe you need to up your cock sucking skills."

"Fuck you." I retort but he just shakes his head and walks away so I'm stood, like a loser with no mates, trying not to look over at the man who despite everything, all my senses are honed on.

A man starts chatting me up. I smile politely, all non-committal and I guess he grows bored or sees better prospects elsewhere. Besides, what did he think? My husband just died. My cheating, abusive, piece of shit of a husband, but still.

I order another vodka tonic, drinking it so quickly I'm practically downing it. I could leave, I know that. I could go find another place to drink, it's not like this is the only bar in Verona, but this was my bar. My place. I liked it here, at least I used to.

I glance back to that corner and my eyes instantly find him. He's talking to a woman with all his attention focused on her. Their conversation looks intense, like it's more than just flirting and he's smiling enough to set me teeth on edge. I shouldn't be jealous. I have no reason to be. The man is nothing to me. *Should* be nothing to me. And besides, if he's with another woman then that means he's got no interest in me, and that's a good thing, right? I don't want him to want me. After everything he's done, everything he put me through, I'd rather he acted like I didn't exist. Like he doesn't even know me.

At least, that's what I'm telling myself as the green eyed monster writhes and stretches inside me.

Only it's not just jealousy I'm feeling. It's anger. White hot fury that he can stand here, that he can act like this, like none of it happened, like he didn't betray me in the worst way possible. Half of me wants to grab Ty's knife and ram it into his deceitful heart.

I wince, fighting down the twisting grief with another mouthful of vodka.

"She's his lawyer."

My head turns. I stare at Sofia for a second before I speak. "What?"

"The woman Roman is talking to." Sofia says. "She's his lawyer. Our lawyer technically. She's helping sort out our father's estate."

I blink, trying to keep my face neutral. "Why are you telling me that?"

Her lips curl just a little and she shrugs. "Just in case you were wondering. He's not interested in her."

I draw myself up as I'm a statue made of stone. "I don't care who he is and isn't interested in."

"No?" She says quietly. "Pretty certain you used to care."

My stomach drops. So she does know then. I throw her a look, downing the last of my drink and stalk off to the bathroom, if only to clear my head.

A woman passes me on the way out as I go in but apart from that it's mercifully empty. I don't even need to pee. I just need a moment of peace. A moment to gather my thoughts.

My reflection stares back tauntingly from the mirror. In what world did I even think coming out tonight was a good idea? I let out a laugh at my own stupidity. God you'd think after so many years I'd be better at not making mistakes.

The door opens and I vaguely register the shape of a man walking in. I don't need to look to see who it is. His smirk gives him away. As does his aftershave.

"This is the women's lavatory." I state before washing my hands. I don't really need to but it gives me something to do. Something to focus on.

He laughs but makes no attempt to leave.

I glance around but there's no one else here. No other cubicles being used. It's just us.

"No one can see us." Roman says.

"There's nothing to see." I reply moving past him and heading to the door but he grabs my arm pulling me back against the counter which I hit with a thud.

"Let me go." I say.

"And turn down this opportunity." His fingers brush my face and I jerk my head away.

"Don't you dare touch me."

"That's not what you used to say Rose." He murmurs. "You used to beg me to touch you. Beg and plead. And you'd be screaming my name when I did."

I push him back but his body is too big to make any real effect and his mouth is on mine, crashing into mine and for the briefest of seconds I give in, allowing his tongue to delve deeper, moaning as he wraps it around mine in a way that makes my body feel alive for the first time in forever.

But then my mind comes back, reality hits me and I break it off, pushing him harder. My hand slaps hard right across his face and he blinks staring at me.

"Don't you fucking dare." I snarl.

"You've got feisty." He says grinning and rubbing his hand along his reddened jaw. "Oh Rose, we're going to have so much fun." He says.

I don't reply, I just storm out of there before anything further happens or worse anyone sees us.

Ty is back by my seat looking more than a little bored.

"I'm going." I say.

He tilts his head assessing my face and as his eyes flicker behind me they turn deadly. "What did he do?" He says.

I glance back. Stupidly I glance back. And Roman meets my gaze with a look that sets my skin on fire. Tyrone knows nothing of our past, nothing about what we were. My parents kept it to themselves. Kept my dirty little secret just that. Something shameful, something to be used against me at every opportunity and all the while ensuring it doesn't sully the family's great reputation.

"Nothing. I've just had enough for one night." I reply.

"If he…"

"Leave it Ty, for fucksake, just leave it." I snap. If he gets it into his head this will escalate. He's been itching for a fight anyway and I won't be the cause of it.

"Fine I'll walk you out." He states.

"That's not necessary."

"It is when Montagues are around, they'll likely gut you as soon as you're out the door."

I don't reply, I just let him lead me away, wondering whether that might just be the mercy I need. A quick death. A nice ending to all of this.

ROSE

I'm sat in the park trying to ignore my blazing hangover. Reminding myself of all the reasons why I shouldn't be feeling what I am. Shouldn't be replaying that moment, that kiss.

I hate him. I hate him with every fibre of my being.

Bella pulls on the lead and I lean down absentmindedly stroking her as she sniffs.

He left another rose. A fresh one.

I threw yesterday's away but this morning it'd been replaced. Today's is bigger, like it's some sort of statement. He's taunting me. This is a game to him, I realise, a joke.

Perhaps he doesn't remember, perhaps it was so inconsequential he forgot, but as I watch the children playing on the climbing frame ahead of me that thought makes me more angry. It meant that little to him. My feelings, my emotions. Even now the fact that he thinks he can simply swanny back in and pick up where he left off shows exactly the kind of man he is.

I let out a low huff. I have to be better than this. I have to be more in control. It's not just my life at stake, and right now everything feels so precarious, like I'm balancing on a knife edge and any minute I'm going to slip.

I've got six months, six months before I get Paris's money. And once that happens everything changes. I won't have to do what my family says anymore. I won't have to jump through their hoops. I won't even have to see them if I don't want to.

My eyes flicker to the playground once more. Six months – in six months I can make my move, I just have to hold out till then.

Someone sits down on the bench beside me. I barely glance over before doing a double take.

"Why are you here?" My mother asks quietly.

"I'm just walking the dog." I murmur.

Her eyebrows raise. "Here?"

"This is a park isn't it." I state.

She looks pointedly at the children's area before looking back at me. "I don't think this is helping you."

"What would you know about it?" I snap.

She shakes her head, putting her hand on mine. "Rose, you come here almost every day."

I pull my eyes away from the distance to look at her. "And?"

"Maybe you need to move on. Stop living in the past."

"How can I?" I snarl. "You think it's that easy?"

"I didn't say that."

"Then what…"

"It's like you're torturing yourself. Punishing yourself for what happened."

I narrow my eyes hoping she hears the venom in my next words. "I'm not the one doing the punishing."

Her hand squeezes mine more firmly. "We have your best interests at heart."

"Is that so?" I mutter. My mother might but my father certainly doesn't. I know what he sees me as. And I think he gets some sort of pleasure out of this situation, he's certainly keen to use it to his advantage at every opportunity that comes knocking.

"Your father wants a word."

"What?"

She jerks her head to where I can see the car waiting.

"He's here?" My stomach twists with alarm. That he's this close. That he might see everything I have planned out.

"He's at the house." She says.

Of course he wouldn't come here. He expects me to go to him. That's the nature of our relationship, me constantly breaking while he refuses to bend even a little bit.

"I have Bella." I state.

"The maids can watch her."

I want to refuse. I want to tell her that I'll go in my own time but with where we are it feels too dangerous. I can't afford to be petty, after all, they hold all the cards and it's never been more evident than in this moment.

The journey takes less time than I would like. I wanted to gather my thoughts. To lock them away but I'm still half spiralling as we pull up to the Capulet house. It's so long since I ever considered this place a home but the more I come here like this, the more it feels like a prison.

A man opens the door and my mother is there, walking around quickly as if she needs to control my behaviour. She takes Bella before I can object and passes her over to a maid who stands awkwardly like she's never seen a dog before or knows what to do.

"Take her around the grounds." I say. "But keep her out of the sun or she'll over heat."

The maid nods and my mother keeps her face blank before gesturing for me to go in.

I steel myself for whatever this is because clearly we're about to have a 'conversation'. Carer and Sampson are stood in the corridor outside. Just like usual. They both eye me with suspicion and I do my best to bite down the retort I'd dearly love to hurl at them.

My father is in his study stood by the window, staring out. He doesn't even turn as we walk in. Doesn't even acknowledge we exist.

So we sit, waiting, like obedient pets for him to grace us with his attention. I don't know how my mother does it, how she puts up with him but she never seems to mind. In fact, it feels like she soothes his rougher edges. It's an odd, almost symbiotic relationship that they have but I don't know what I'd do if my mother wasn't here; if she left I'd be thrown to the wolves.

"Rose." My father says eventually.

"Father." I reply hoping I sound more congenial than I feel.

"It's time we had a proper conversation."

"About what?"

"Paris."

"What?" I frown. That's the last thing I expected him to say.

He turns, his eyes boring into me. "The day he died you were arguing. I want to know what it was about."

I look from him to my mother. They brought me all the way here just to ask that?

"Why was he taking you to the Barn?" He continues.

"The what?" I repeat.

He leans over the desk, his hands planting onto the antique leather cover. "Don't play games. I am not in the mood."

"I don't know what you're talking about." I state. "I didn't even know where we were headed."

He glances back at my mother and I swear I see something exchanged in that look. "What were you arguing about?"

"What does it matter to you?"

226

He tilts his head before slamming his hand down. "Do you forget yourself? Do you forget who you are? You're my daughter Rose Capulet."

I push back from my chair, clenching my fists. "It would be nice if you remembered that." I retort. "If you remembered I'm actually your flesh and blood and not just a thing to be used."

"We don't think like that." My mother says quickly grabbing my hand but I jerk away out of her hold.

"You might not." I mutter before fixing my gaze on him again. "But he's certainly not above using people is he?"

"Rose." She says.

"Rose." My father growls. "You are a Capulet and you will behave as one."

"Or you'll what? Punish me further?" The words are out of my mouth before I can stop them.

He narrows his eyes but I see that glint in them. "Is that what you want Rose? You want to test me?" He says quietly. "Because I know exactly how to respond to that…"

"No." I say shaking my head. Cursing my own stupidity. I don't care what it takes, what I have to do, I won't let him do that, to resort to that. I have six months. I just have to bide my time. Play it safe. And then I'll finally get away.

"Then tell me." He growls slamming his hand once more and this time I flinch at the noise.

"Paris wants to start a family." I say. "Wanted to." I correct myself. God, when will I get used to the fact he's dead? No present tense anymore. He's the past. My past.

"So?" He replies.

"So I didn't want that. That's what we were arguing about."

My mother lets out an exhale that sounds almost like something of relief. "Rose." She says taking my hand.

"Don't." I reply pulling away further.

"That's it?" My father asks like he's not quite convinced, as though there's some bigger secret I'm hiding.

"That's it." I state.

"Fine." My father says dismissively. "But it still doesn't explain why you were on *that* road."

"I can't answer that. Paris must have told the driver where to go before I even got in."

He huffs.

"Is that it? Can I go now?" I ask.

"No." He says waving his hand. "Sit down."

I shake my head but I can't refuse so I'm forced to sink into the chair, hearing the leather squeak in protest.

"We need to discuss what we're going to do now Paris is gone." He says.

"What do you mean?" I ask.

He throws me a look like I'm an idiot. "You're back on the market technically. We need to make sure your next match is as advantageous as your last was."

"What?" I grip the arms of the chair, digging my nails into them till it hurts.

"We'll give it six months, that should be enough time to be prevent any idle gossip."

I shake my head. "No." I say but he doesn't hear. He's too busy planning this out.

"You'll need to behave of course. Need to keep up appearances." He fixes me with a look. "I know you were out drinking so that will have to stop."

"Excuse me?"

"You need to act chaste. Everyone knows you're not a virgin, what with your first marriage but still, you need to present yourself as the ideal wife nevertheless."

"I'm not doing that." I state. "I won't do that."

"Rose." My mother says gently.

"No." I snap. "You already sold me once. I did what you wanted. I'm not sacrificing myself again."

"No?" My father grins. "Not even for…"

"Ignatio." My mother says cutting across him. "She just needs a little time. Her husband has just died. You can hardly expect her to be entertaining such an idea so soon."

"We don't have time." My father growls. "The Montagues are gaining ground. We no longer have a link to the Blumenfelds while their whore of a daughter is all but engaged to Otto and now that Roman has returned our very existence is threatened."

"So that's what this is about." I say. "The old rivalry. Us vs. them."

He glares at me. "That's what all this is about Rose and you of all people should remember it better than most."

"What does that mean?" I retort, my anger blinding my now to any sense of reason.

He smirks, his eyes dropping to take me in like I'm a piece of meat he's appraising at the butchers. "I think you know well enough, you were happy enough to spread your legs for him last time. It'd be prudent of me to ensure the past doesn't repeat itself."

I spring up from the chair so quickly I'm surprised it doesn't flip backwards. My mother is quick to step in, to play the part of go-between.

But I'm gone. Storming out the door. With his insult still burning my cheeks.

ROMAN

Though I'm calm on the outside my adrenaline is pumping furiously through my veins.

I'm stood beside Ben. Both of us in balaclavas though in truth I'd be more than happy with them seeing my face.

Around us my men are getting in position. Creeping silently towards the massive building they call 'the barn' though in truth it's more of a warehouse.

My hand twitches. I'm itching to just burst in and start shooting but I know that's just the old Roman, the impulsive Roman coming to the surface.

"Ready?" Ben murmurs and I nod. I can hear from the tone he is too. We've been planning this for weeks, ever since we found out about this place. Ever since we located it.

This is where the Capulet's source of power comes from. From places like this. While Ignatio walks around like he shits gold, in this dark crevice his people are trafficking women, children, you name it. Not just for sex mind. Although I'm sure he makes a tidy sum from the flesh trade but he's savvier than that. He's diversified his portfolio better. No, many of them end up being cut up, butchered, their organs sold for insurmountable sums to extend the lives of people who deem themselves more important, more worthy than the victims they steal from.

I snarl at the thought. I wonder if Rose knows of this place, if she knows what her father really is. Paris certainly did because that's where they were headed the day I eliminated him. The day I took him off the board. And I know Darius does as well; I have photographic evidence of him being here, of him enjoying some of the 'stock' before it's sold on. Just a few leaks would be enough to ruin Darius's entire political career, ruin his life too but I'm not stupid enough to do that. No, I'm not after normal justice. I'm not after seeing him locked away in a federal prison. I have my own means of making him pay.

And he will.

But on my terms.

I'm going to bleed the man dry, make him jump through every fucking hoop I choose and when I'm done then I will make him pay for all the women he's hurt, all the children he's helped sell too.

"Ready when you are."

It comes over the earpiece and I grin. It's showtime.

I give the signal and moments later a blast echoes as the strategically placed bomb takes out the reinforced doors. They thought locks could keep me out but they're about to learn how wrong they were.

My men rush in. Guns raised. Charging through the building and securing everyone in place.

Ben and I walk in quietly after them. It's not that I'm afraid of the fighting, it's more a case of being smart. My men are ex-military. Trained assassins. And while I'm damn good I'm not ashamed to admit that they're better.

Besides, the intel we have suggests there are victims in here. I won't risk their lives simply to nurse my own ego.

Inside it stinks. I wrinkle my nose as the acrid smell of urine hits me. I can hear murmuring, whimpers. It's hot. Stiflingly so. As my eyes adjust my eyes widen at what looks like a god damn cattle market. Around the perimeter are countless chairs, no doubt where the low life scum sit watching the merchandise as they're brought out.

In the centre stand a dozen men held at gunpoint. I take them in. Seeing their sullen faces. They don't even look ashamed.

"Where are they?" I ask.

"Out the back. They have them in cages." Turner says jerking his head.

I grunt following him past to where he indicated and my stomach churns at the sight. They really are in cages. Like god damn animals.

My eyes fix on the one nearest. Two eyes stare back filled with terror. The girl can't be more than twelve. She's wearing a ragged, dirty dress that's two sizes too big and she's pushed her body as far back into the darkness as if she could fade into it. Beside her is a bucket and from the stench we all know exactly what it's for.

"How many?" I ask.

"Twenty six." Turner replies.

Twenty six. Twenty six women and children. All kidnapped. All specifically targeted because they are low risk, have no immediate friends or family that would notice them gone. Ignatio is no fool. If the city realised that dozens of people are going missing each week there'd be uproar but as it is no one looks for these people. They're the dredges in their eyes. Easily expendable.

"Get them out. Get them to the trucks." I state.

Turner gives the signal and slowly they start breaking apart the cages. We have a facility all ready and waiting to receive them with doctors and therapists because god knows these people are going to need it.

"Fucking hell." Ben says as he walks up beside me.

I meet his gaze. I knew this would be bad. We both did. I guess we just couldn't imagine exactly what hell looked like until we saw it for real.

The girl I first saw starts struggling, fighting tooth and nail to stay in her cage as if it's a sanctuary but Turner extracts her, taking the hits as if he himself deserves them and calmly he walks past with her over his shoulder.

"Let's start the clean-up." I say.

Back in the main section the men have been made to kneel. I walk up to them, wanting to see the shame in their eyes but it's not there. I guess Ignatio knew exactly who to pick when he chose these men.

I take off my balaclava letting them see my face. None of them react. Not that I expected them too.

"Do you know who I am?" I ask

One of them spits in response. It lands narrowly missing the tip of my boot.

"I'm your worst nightmare." I say pulling out my gun. It's smaller than the assault rifles my men are carrying but that's okay, my dick is more than big enough for me not to feel the need to compensate for it.

One of them snorts like it's some sort of joke. I take aim, pulling the trigger and blast a hole through his knee cap. He cries out like a baby and it's hard not to smirk.

"This isn't a fucking joke." I state. "I'm not here to play games. I know everything that's gone on here so we can make this easy or hard. I want to know where the records are kept."

"What records?" The man nearest me asks.

I tilt my head. We all know there are records. Ignatio is nothing if not meticulous. He wouldn't have bought or sold a damn thing without a carefully maintained trail because in the end he would be protecting himself with it.

I pull the trigger, shooting through the man's leg. He snarls, grabbing at the wound as his blood starts to pour out.

"Like I said I can make this easy or hard." I state.

"Like fuck we'll tell you." Another shouts.

I roll my eyes before blasting his fucking head off. They need to know I'm serious and they need to know now. This place fucking stinks and while the victims are all being carted off I'm itching to get the fuck out of here.

"Alright. Alright." One of the others says holding his hands up. "They're at the docks."

"What?" I reply.

"At the docks. There's a container there. It's all kept there."

I smile. Ignatio owns half the docks, it'd be a smart place to hide them. It'd be a logical place too.

I look around at my men. Nodding once they all take aim and pull the trigger. Within seconds every last one is neutralised. I don't feel guilty. I don't feel anything. These men deserved death for what they did. But I'll save the real torture for the highers up.

And for Ignatio himself.

Once the last of the women are out we pour petrol all over the floor. All over their bodies too. I don't care if they burn or not. I just want to make sure they get the message and more than that I want to ensure that this place can never be used again.

I stand staring as the flames lick the skies. The air is thick with smoke but it helps cover the rancid smell of human piss and shit that still lingers.

And when I'm certain the barn is destroyed beyond repair I get in the truck driving away, smiling at the thought of what Ignatio will do when he finds out because boy is he going to be pissed.

ROSE

*I*t feels like the city has finally moved on from gossiping about me.

I guess I should be grateful. Not every front page is dedicated to the revelations I made. Not every headline is screaming out in scandal about my marriage and what was really going on behind closed doors.

No, now the focus is on Roman. On his great return.

My stomach turns and I scowl at the thought. At the way he's being treated like a god damn hero. Already women at the clubhouse are talking about how they want to date him, or get their daughter's to date him. Apparently the fact he's a murderer doesn't make him any less appealing when the Montague fortune could be up for grabs.

I stay inside. Hiding mostly from the sympathetic looks I'm still getting but in reality I need to plan, I need to strategize. If I'm really going to make a break for it, I need to be prepared. I need to have everything ready so the minute the money hits my account I can cut and run.

I won't be outsmarted this time.

I refuse to let my father win. To let any of them win.

The only issue I have is that I have no one to help me. I don't trust anyone. Not even Mae, despite the care she takes of Bella. Any one of the people around me could be on my father's payroll and they probably are in some capacity or another.

So I spend my time researching, scheming. I have the route planned out, memorised. I have the tickets bought and stashed away where I know no one will find them. I rent a container. Cash only of course. It's on the outskirts of town. The complete opposite side from where my father's empire is by the docks and inside I begin to put everything I would need.

I buy some high cash items, diamonds, necklaces, generic things that could easily be pawned should I need it. I sell Paris's jewels too. Every single awful one. It was him trapping me in this city in the first place and now it is his death that's setting me free.

If that's not poetic justice I don't know what is.

I stash clothes. Nothing fancy. Nothing noticeable. Just normal, regular clothes, regular items for someone who wants to blend in. Who doesn't want to be noticed.

And I get a gun too, paying a small fortune for it. It's nothing fancy. A pistol barely bigger than my hand but just having it, just knowing that it's there, helps alleviate some of the tension in my head.

And every time I go to the container, I'm careful, so very careful. I check I'm not followed. I double back on myself so many times it's impossible for someone not to give themselves away. I won't make the same mistakes as last time. I won't give myself away.

I sink into my bed every night, knowing that as each one passes I get a tiny bit closer to my goal. One tiny step closer to my freedom. Except my brain seems fixated on that long after my body is ready for sleep, my mind won't switch off and I lay here, exhausted and yet wide awake.

And tonight is apparently going the same way. I'm here, with the air con humming away and my own thoughts whirling in my head.

For a second I glance around half convinced someone is here, lurking in the shadows, watching me. But I can see nothing.

I shake my head, letting the vivid hyper-exhaustion take over again. No one is here. It's just me. Me and my crazy headspace.

I sink back into the sheet. Perhaps I should leave, should make some excuse to escape to the Hamptons after all, but that thought is pointless because I'd never be able too. My father would use everything he has to keep me here, under his control, and as always I would be obedient. His perfect fucking puppet.

Besides, if I do leave then it will only make my plans to disappear even harder to enact.

I scowl shutting my eyes, willing my head to just shut the fuck up. I want to sleep. I need to sleep. And yet I know when I do, my dreams will be plagued by the same images that torment my waking hours.

A movement of light makes me jolt. My adrenaline jumps and I look around again. Am I imagining this? Is someone here or have I really lost my mind? All I can hear is my breathing, all I can feel is my heart hammering in my chest.

I put my hand out, reaching to the bedside table to grab my phone only it's not there. The side is bare. I wince through the darkness, my mind too muddled by lack of sleep to really register what's actually going on. Something wraps around my wrist. It's quick. Suddenly I'm clawing, snarling, trying to get free as I realise I'm now tied to the bedframe.

Someone *is* here.

My other hand is yanked back, more forcefully than the first. I can make out the person over me now. Their body framed by the dark but if anything they're all the more horrifying for it.

I scream hoping my security will hear. Hoping it might scare this person away but all they do is tut. As if my fear is an inconvenience to them.

When both my wrists are tied I start kicking out, using my legs as a last defence. I can feel their weight on the bed, I can feel them moving closer and closer to me. My panic is all consuming as I fight so hard to get free.

"Stop."

The words chill me. The sound of that voice. His voice.

"Roman." I gasp his name and he tilts his head as if he's amused. "Let me go."

"Where would the fun in that be?" He murmurs.

"Let me go you bastard." I scream.

He shakes his head letting out a laugh as his hands run down my sides. He loops his fingers around my thong, teasing it down, as I thrash more and more violently in my attempt to stop him.

Only it does no good. He half rips it off, curling them in his hand and leaning back over my face.

"Remember this?" He says and then rams the lace into my mouth.

I growl under the fabric but all he does is brush the hair from out my eyes as if this is some sort of seduction, some weird sex game we're playing and not a thing of force.

He takes in a deep breath, running his nose against my skin and I can feel the way his stubble pricks mine. "I missed you Rose." He says quietly. As if he has a right.

I snarl screaming out that I didn't miss him. That I hate him. That I wish he was dead. Only none of my words make any sense with this damn fabric in my mouth.

I can smell him now. That delicious, deadly scent that is like a poison to me, that beguiles me into thinking he's something of safety. Someone to want. Someone I can trust.

He yanks on the straps of my night dress and we both hear the rip as the flimsy fabric gives way. Then he slides it down off my shoulders. Slowly. His eyes fixed on my body more than my face. Perhaps he doesn't want to see the anger, perhaps he doesn't want to see the fear too. Is he trying to pretend that I want this, that I'm as up for this moment as he is?

"Let me go." I articulate each word as loudly as I can.

He looks up at me grinning. Yeah he understood well enough didn't he? The prick.

"That's not how this works." He says. "I let you go when I'm finished remember."

I shake my head. "Not anymore."

He ignores me yanking the silk so that my breasts are exposed. My nipples harden almost instantly and though I will die on the hill that it's simply exposure to the air I can't deny the flash of arousal that permeates through to my core.

Even my stupid body is betraying me now.

He lowers his mouth, peppering each one with soft kisses. I can feel his saliva wet against me. I can feel the way his lips caress me long after he removes them.

I shut my eyes, turning my head away. There's nothing I can do. I'm trapped. Caught in his game until he's done and while he no doubt is enjoying this new form of torture, I refuse to show that I am. On any level.

He runs his fingers down, removing more of the silk nightgown and revealing more and more of me as he goes. I jerk. I kick out. Landing a perfectly aimed strike to his face but still it does nothing. It's like he doesn't even feel it.

He grabs my thighs, forcing them apart as I try to lock them.

"No." I say as loud as I can. Where the fuck are my security? How have they not heard any of this? How the hell have they not intervened?

He lowers his face and I can feel it, his hot breath hitting my core. I freeze, caught between the undeniable want for him to continue and the bitter hatred festering inside me at that realisation.

He takes in a deep breath groaning. "Your pussy always smelt so good." He mutters.

I pull my hips back into the mattress, the only movement I can make now, trying to gain whatever few inches I can between him and me.

He sweeps his tongue up. One long languid lick that sends shockwaves through me and I grit my teeth so hard to force down the moan of both shock and pleasure.

He smirks as if he knows and then he turns his head biting my inner thigh as I shriek. Only he doesn't let up. He just releases his grip and takes another bite. Tearing into the soft flesh enough that I know he's made me bleed.

My tears stream then. My body shakes.

The old Roman never hurt me. Not once. Even when we did play pretend, he never crossed that line. No, the pain he gave me was so much worse. So much more devastating. I pull my leg free enough to aim another kick and he snarls narrowly avoiding it before biting me again even harder.

I thrash more, trying to throw him off and he grabs my legs, tying each one so that the last of my defence is gone.

I'm spread eagled now. Like an all you can eat buffet for him. I whimper as I realise it. Too ashamed now to do anything as he maims more of my flesh.

His fingers grab at me, spreading my labia apart and baring me wide open for him and then he pauses fixing me with a look.

"Pretend you don't want this Rose. Pretend you're not as eager for me to be in your cunt as I am."

I shake my head screaming that I don't.

He laughs, running one finger right up to my clit which throbs so hard in response. The needy traitorous bitch.

"Why are you wet then? Huh?" He mutters. "You're dripping for me."

I shake my head again. Refusing to give in. Refusing to give him any satisfaction.

"You're going to come Rose. You're going to fall apart right here for me to enjoy." And then he lowers his mouth, his tongue devouring me like a lost lover finally returning home.

I try not to react. I try so hard. I scream in my head over and over that I don't want this. That I don't want him. That he's forcing this on me. Raping me in some sense. But my body doesn't get the message. My body responds exactly as he wants and I can feel my core coiling tighter and tighter as I fight each breath, fight each gasp, fight every second of pleasure.

He slides a finger inside me, curling right where he knows he'll hit that sweet spot and I arch my back in spite of myself, my hips bucking against his mouth as the pleasure swells.

"That's better." He murmurs. "Seems like you can be a good girl after all."

I glare at him hating the mockery of his words and yet loving how good his touch is.

My pleasure feels like it's peaking too much now for me to do anything to stop it but I refuse to give in. I refuse to not fight this right to the end.

Clearly he sees my resolve and, as he curls his fingers more and more inside me, he clamps down on my thigh, biting once more into my flesh. I scream. The mixture of pleasure and pain too much to ignore. Too much to fight.

ELLIES SANDERS

It feels like something inside me breaks, like everything I stand for, everything I am collapses under the ministrations of this man's fingers alone. I let out a moan so loud I doubt my panties ever stood a chance of muffling it. He plunges another finger inside just as I fall over the edge and the ecstasy that is cataclysmic. I thrash, I scream, I forget even my own name as I come so hard for a man that I hate, I man that has all but forced himself on me right now.

But I don't care. In this moment it's like nothing exists beyond my own pleasure. Nothing exists beyond the feel of him fucking me so deliciously with his fingers. He crawls up my body, lays beside me, watching my face as if I were the one consuming him and not the other way around.

"I love the way you come." He groans. "I love the look on your face. Nothing in the world is more beautiful than your face in this moment."

I keep my eyes shut. The comedown all the more shameful for how much I truly enjoyed the ride. My body is shuddering, jerking as if every cell is shot with electricity.

Silence hangs between us.

He doesn't move. He just lays there, watching me as I pant.

And then mercifully he unties me. My hands drop the minute the rope frees them but I'm too exhausted, too ashamed, to do anything but just lie here.

He gets up, creeping back into the shadows like the demon he really is.

"Remember this Rose." He says. "Remember who owns you. Who has always owned you."

I gulp, forcing myself to sit up. To hurl back an insult. To say anything but he's already gone. Slithered back into the darkness like the arsehole that he is.

I spring out of the bed, grabbing a robe to cover myself and run through the house determined to gut him if I can. Downstairs the back door clicks shut giving me a hint of where he is. I grab a knife from the side but a weird chewing distracts me. I frown trying to place it and then suddenly I do. Bella is sat, gnawing on something. I gasp, snatching it from her. He bribed her with a treat? The bastard. I scoop her up, hugging her more for my own comfort that hers because she's already grumbling at me like I'm the arsehole in all this.

On the table I spot the only too familiar outline of another rose and I scowl, staring out, seeing his outline disappear into the treeline.

He isn't even trying to hide.

He clearly doesn't care if my security see him.

And as always he's left me behind without a moment's thought. Left me to deal with the consequences.

I HIDE INSIDE. SULKING. ASHAMED AT MYSELF FOR MOST OF THE NEXT day.

But tonight I can't hide. Tonight I have to be all of my sunshine brightness.

It's the Summer Gala. The last soiree before every fucker who can leaves the city and escapes to cooler climates.

I'm half tempted to bail. To feign a headache, or grief, or anything that will get me out of this but my father clearly guesses my plan and sends a message making it clear under no uncertain terms that he expects me to be there. No doubt he's wanting to show me off for whoever he's lined up to marry me. Like that will ever happen. Like I'll make that mistake a second time.

When the hair stylist and makeup artist arrive I'm almost relieved. They chatter brightly both to each other and to me. I'm sipping champagne as if this were a fun event but I need the alcohol. I need something to take the edge off everything.

My hair is twisted half up into a French plait with the rest hanging loose in boho style curls. It's simple but it suits my face. Besides I don't have the patience to sit for anything fancier.

My makeup is light. With the heat there's little point going for anything too heavy and risk it smearing under my eyes come nightfall. I stare at the perfectly presented image of myself. You wouldn't know I'd spent almost the entire night awake, restless, convinced that a man who'd already tied me up was going to come back and finish the job.

My pussy throbs for a second. As if I want that. As if that would be the solution to everything. Christ, she gets one good hit and she's like an addict, screaming for more.

I'm trembling. I can see it. My hands shaking just enough to give me away.

He's going to be there. That's the thought that keeps running through my head.

Roman is going to be there.

And I'm going to have to pretend that he is nothing. That last night didn't happen. That none of it happened.

My stomach turns.

It's another reminder of what he's done.

That his past trespasses still haunt my life as if he's a ghost possessing me, some sort of demon intent on dragging me the entire way down to hell.

ROMAN

The room is heaving. Around me all I can hear is the incessant noise of people talking. I let out a deep breath looking around. Surveying the place.

All of Verona's elite are here. Every person of consequence dressed up to the nines, no dolled up. Diamonds and rubies seem to cover every woman and the mixture of a dozen different perfumes makes my head hurt.

Everyone smiles at me. It's been a nonstop parade of women, of mothers, desperate to make friends, desperate for me to meet their daughters. I smile politely of course. Playing the perfect gentleman because I know I can't afford to piss people off. As much as I hold the balls of the Governor in my hands I don't want the general population to realise what I am.

A wolf.

Dressed in a fine suit, walking amongst the sheep.

My eyes meet Sofia's. She's uncomfortable but I know only I can tell it because she's the perfect actress, almost as perfect as Rose in that regard. Otto's arm is around her waist, his hand skimming lower when he thinks he can get away with it but she's quick to reposition herself, quick to ensure he gets nothing more than what she's willing to offer.

Ben isn't here. He couldn't trust himself not to react when he saw them and, though I'm less than impressed by his no show, I can't blame him. I know first-hand it's hard to stay calm when the woman you love is on the arm of another man.

Across the room Ignatio Capulet's eyes are burning into me. Beside him, his wife is doing her best to distract his attention, but he hasn't even blinked. Hasn't looked away from me once. I smirk before I can stop myself and I'll admit the urge to provoke him is growing stronger by the minute.

I cross the space, making for the prefilled champagne glasses despite the fact I'd rather have a whiskey. It's intentional. Bringing myself this close to him and he takes the bait just like I knew he would.

My fingers curl around the stem. I take a sip and the fizz bubbles across my tongue like the perfect accompaniment to the steps of the man stalking towards me.

I raise an eyebrow infinitely aware that we're being observed.

"You've got a lot of nerve." He snarls.

"Have I?" I reply. "I assumed the champagne was for everyone."

He prowls from side to side, trying to box me in, only I'm far bigger than him, far stronger than him too, so the effect is all but lost.

"Don't be smart with me boy."

I smirk more. "I'm not a boy Ignatio. You would do well to remember that."

"No, you're a murderer." He says. "And everyone in this city knows it. No matter how fine a suit you put on, underneath it, we all know you're scum."

"I guess the question is how long will it be before everyone knows what you are Ignatio? Before everyone discovers exactly how dirty your hands really are."

He narrows his eyes stepping right up into my space. His shoes practically toe to toe with mine. "I'm going to destroy you."

I let out an amused exhale.

"I'm going to bring every last one of you down." His eyes glance over at Sofia. To where she's stood with Otto. "And don't think he'll be able to save her either. I'll make sure your little whore of a sister is ruined too."

"Like I ruined your daughter?" I murmur.

His eyes flash. He opens his mouth to spit more venom only at that exact moment Rose appears.

Our heads turn in unison to take her in.

She's stood in the entrance, teetering almost, on the top of the five steps and half the room is already turning to look, to stare, to admire. The dress she's in shows her body to perfection.

My gut twists, my body physically reacts to her like this is the first time I've laid eyes on her.

I take a step towards her without thinking and Ignatio grabs my arm, creasing the fabric of my sleeve.

"Stay the fuck away from my daughter." He says.

"Or you'll what?" I reply.

His grip tightens but I pull myself free and straighten up my jacket with a smirk.

"You can't do shit Ignatio." I murmur. "And by the time I'm through you'll realise that."

I walk away, half convinced he's going to smash his glass over my head and I'll admit I'm surprised that he doesn't and also a little disappointed because I'd love to have an excuse to knock him out right now.

Rose moves further into the room. She doesn't look at me. She makes no attempt to. It's as if I don't exist and for once that notion amuses me because last night I proved to both of us exactly how much she still wants me.

She takes a glass offered by one of the waiters, thanking them, and then gulps it as if she needs to steady her nerves. Already people are flocking around her.

I watch as she makes what I assume to be polite conversation. She laughs. She smiles. She beguiles more than ever. She's the very epitome of the sunshine princess this damn bay sees her as.

And then Darius walks up to her. She stiffens a tiny bit but recovers as he replaces her finished glass with a fresh one. She blinks replying to whatever he says, and, as he leans in, murmuring something into her ear with his hand running down her arm, my jealousy boils over. My anger does too.

I cross the room walking right up to them and her eyes dart to me as she falls silent.

"Roman." Darius says it before she does.

"Darius." I reply before looking back at the beauty beside him.

Her hair is tousled in a way that makes me want to run my fingers through it. Her makeup is less heavy than usual. You can see the faint scattering of her freckles, the smoothness of her perfect skin.

He glances between us as if he's considering introduces us. As if we were strangers. As if I didn't know Rose better than anyone else in this room.

"What do you want?" She says.

"A dance." I reply.

Her eyebrows raise. She gulps, shaking her head, taking the tiniest of steps back, looking at Darius and if anything that pisses me off more. Because she's clearly wanting *him* to save her.

"I'm not sure that's appropriate…" Darius begins but I talk over him making my position clear.

"What better way to demonstrate the peace between our families?" I state.

Darius opens his mouth, his brain clearly trying to come up with something only he's too slow to do it.

"Surely as Governor you'd approve." I say and I see it then, the miniscule flinch. The way he registers the silent unspoken threat in my words.

"Of course." He says.

Rose looks between us. Her eyes widening. "No."

"Come." I murmur taking her still full glass and passing it back to Darius before intwining her arm around mine. "Don't make a scene."

She lets out a ragged exhale, her eyes darting to all the people watching. I'm playing her and she knows it. It's mean. Cruel even. But I won't deny I enjoy the moment of using her perfectly poised persona against her.

She stiffens more as I lead her towards the dancefloor. There're enough people already on it for us not to stand out and yet it feels like we're the centrepiece. The focal.

I take her hand, wrap my arm around her waist, feeling the delicious warmth of her body and she takes the moment to glare at me.

I let out a low laugh which if anything clearly infuriates her more.

"This is all some joke to you, isn't it?" She snaps.

"No." I reply as we begin to move. As the music allows me to direct her body as I wish. As I feel the way her beautiful curves seem to meld against me.

"You forced yourself on me." She says, glancing about as if she thinks everyone can hear.

"You enjoyed it Rose so don't try to deny it. Your body may have been tied down but you still rode my mouth like you wanted it."

She shudders shaking her head. "I didn't want it. I didn't want any of it."

"And yet you still screamed out in pleasure as I made you come."

She drops her gaze, her cheeks heating enough to tell me the effect my words are having on her. "Could you at least pretend to be a decent human being for once?"

"Is that what you want Rose?" I reply glancing around, making eye contact with her father of all people, who's practically purple in the face and I'll admit part of this is to make a point to him. To show him how little his words truly mean. "You want me to pretend the way you do? To put on a pretty façade and smile sweetly for the cameras like all these people wouldn't stab you in the back if it was worth their while?"

She shakes her head. "You're disgusting you know that?"

"At least I'm not living in a deluded fantasy world."

She scoffs. "I'd rather be deluded than live like you do."

"Is that so?" I murmur, pulling her body just a tiny fraction closer to mine, lifting her face so that she's forced to look at me. The dance is long gone. Both of us are stood immobile in the centre of the room too focused on each other now to care what anyone thinks. "I think you're lying Rose. I think you're telling yourself that because it's easier than facing up to what you did."

She blinks, her face visibly paling. "I've done nothing wrong."

"No?" I murmur. "So you didn't set your sights on me just because of who I was? Because your dear daddy was eager to strike another blow at the Montagues? Tell me Rose, did he order you to fuck me or was that just you using your initiative?"

She pulls away. Her perfect mask slipping entirely from her face. She looks like she might just start crying here, in front of us all.

And yeah I'll admit that has an effect on me.

Something deep in my chest reacts to that and for an instant I contemplate pulling her back, pulling her into my arms, and never letting her go.

"The Roman I knew was never this cruel." She murmurs so I only just hear the words and then she walks away, leaving me staring at her retreating body.

ROSE

"**...**" *ell me Rose, did he order you to fuck me or was that just you using your initiative?"*

The words ring in my head as I walk away. I can feel the stares. The shock of everyone around me. I know none of them heard. The music was too loud. The chatter too distorted.

No doubt it was how we were, how our bodies reacted to one another, that's what they're reacting to.

But that doesn't stop the twist of the knife inside me. Because that's what he thinks, what he believes. No wonder he acted the way he did. At least this explains it. He saw me as a whore. He believed I was one, that I was simply following orders.

And yet the reality was he was the one that turned me into one.

He was the one who ruined me, not the other way around.

It's hard not to laugh. Not to cry too. The swirling bitterness of my emotions feels like a tempest I can't get control of.

I thought he knew me. I thought he understood me. And yet those words alone show how completely and utterly I'd fooled myself.

I pick up another glass, half knocking it back, no longer caring what anyone thinks. My hands are still shaking. I can feel the bruising between my thighs throbbing from where Roman's teeth marked me. For a second I wonder if he did it on purpose, if last night he broke in simply because I'd be forced to face him tonight.

I scowl taking another gulp of champagne. The bubbles are stilted. The taste is flat. They've clearly chilled it for too long but no one else seems to notice. Either that or they're too polite to comment.

"Rose."

I let out a low breath as both my parents appear before me. I can see from my father's face exactly how furious he is with me.

"What the fuck was that?" He hisses.

"I didn't have a choice." I murmur. "Darius all but forced my hand." It's a lie. A bad one. But in this instance it spares me.

He clenches his fists and for a moment I thank god the crowds are here because they're tempering his anger.

"Come." He says taking my arm, leading me away from the drinks like he's afraid I might just guzzle them all.

"Where are we going?" I ask.

"I have someone I want you to meet."

I gulp already knowing exactly where this is headed. My mother gives me a reassuring look but there's an underlying message to it all the same. Be obedient.

I let him lead me like a prized cow to the man all but salivating just behind him.

"Henry, may I introduce my daughter Rose." My father says.

Henry smiles charmingly enough. "It's a pleasure."

I smile back as best I can. He's got ten years on me. And they've not been kind to him. He's clearly indulged in everything money can buy from the looks of his body. We make awkward small talk. It doesn't help that my father keeps interjecting, trying to keep the conversation going while I do my best not to cringe.

"I'm sorry for your loss." Henry says after the conversation becomes stilted for the sixth time.

I frown.

"Your husband." He says.

I bite my lip. Maybe I've drunk too much but for a moment I'd actually forgotten about him, I'd forgotten about Paris. I barely thought it was possible but the reflection gives me hope. Maybe one day I'll forget about all of this. All the heartbreak. All the trauma. Every last horrific moment.

"Thank you." I say as demurely as I can.

"I used to play golf with him." He says like that might endear me more to him. "He was very good. Beat me a number of times in fact."

I give another smile and take a sip of my drink. This is awful. He's like a cardboard cut-out of a man but he's clearly a big enough player in this city for my father to want to tie me to him.

"We should organise a round." My father replies.

Henry nods enthusiastically like a puppy that's being offered a nice juicy bone.

As Darius appears the conversation drops once more.

"May I steal Rose for a moment?" He says.

I frown but I don't argue as he all but wraps his arm around me and guides me away and though I'm relieved to be away from Henry, I'm not sure this is any better.

"I thought you needed rescuing." He says quietly.

I raise an eyebrow. "What made you think that?"

He smiles. "Henry Theroux's a nice bloke but he's not your type."

257

"And what's my type?" I ask feeling my heckles rise. He's so familiar with me now. It's as if we share some intangible level of intimacy, only we don't.

He runs his eyes over me and for a second I think I'm mistaken. That it must be the alcohol. Or the light. Or something.

"Not him." He says.

I look away unsure how to reply. This entire evening has been worse than I imagined. Longer too. A part of me wants to simply walk out, go home, and curl up with Bella

"I'm sorry about earlier." He says.

"About what?" I ask.

"Roman."

I look up meeting his eyes wanting to say something, only it's not exactly his fault is it? Though he didn't help, it wasn't necessarily his place to do anything anyway.

"There are things going on above your head." He says. "A situation. I'm managing it as best I can but I need you to trust me."

I frown, scanning his face. His words echo the same thing Paris said months ago. My spine reacts as if someone's just walked on my grave. What exactly is he trying to say right now?

"I said it before Rose, I will protect you but I need you to let me."

I shake my head. "I don't need you to."

"I know you think that." He persists taking the minutest of steps towards me, closing the distance between us further. "But you're wrong. Something is happening in Verona right now."

"What?"

He glances around like he doesn't trust anyone to not be eavesdropping. "I can't say. Just, let me take care of you." His hands wrap around me again. That intimacy that he's trying to build between us feels like a new cage, a bigger one. One with spikes, and locks that I'll never escape.

"No." I reply stepping back. I'm not going to do this again. I'm not going to let someone else take charge, railroad me into a situation I don't want, when I'm so close to finally escaping all of this.

"Rose please."

I shake my head enough to make a point without being obvious to everyone who's got eyes on us and then I make my exit.

This night has been long enough. I've done what my father wanted, I showed my face, I put on a good enough performance.

I'm ready to go home, to shut the door, and stop playing the part everyone expects of me.

ROMAN

I'm a fool to do it.

Reckless too.

Just like I used to be, just like I was six years ago, before I knew better.

And yet I'm here, stood outside her house, staring in, as if I'm possessed. As if something has bound my soul and tied it to hers.

No lights are on. It's completely pitch black.

And yet somehow I know she isn't asleep. That's she's just as awake in this moment as I am.

I creep quietly up to the same door I slipped through yesterday jimmying the lock until it gives way with a click. Inside it's silent and yet I can feel it, it's like everything is on tenterhooks. That the very house is waiting for something.

I take a step. Then another.

Somewhere her little dog should be sleeping. I don't want to startle it into barking and then give myself away and yet as I look around I can't see it. Yesterday it'd been waiting, as if it too knew I would come and yet tonight it's surprisingly absent.

That thought makes me pause. Just for a millisecond.

And then I feel it; the cold, unmistakeable feel of a gun pressed against the back of my neck.

"Hello Rose."

Her only reply is to ram the thing harder into my neck which if anything makes me smirk. She forces me to take a step, then another, but as I take my third, I spin, wrapping my hand around hers and forcing the muzzle under my chin.

As our eyes meet, hers widen in both surprise and fear. She tries to prize the weapon from my hand but I tighten my grip refusing to let go.

"The thing about wielding one of these is you have to be prepared to pull the trigger." I say.

She shuts her eyes. Her face contorting. "I'd happily pull it on you."

I tut, shaking my head at the blatant lie. "No Rose, you just proved that was not the case."

"So what?" She hisses. "So I'm not a murderer like you are?"

I let out a low breath, tossing the gun onto the couch and she follows it with her eyes as if she'd leap after it. Only I won't let her. She's in my grasp now, at my mercy and she isn't going anywhere.

"You really think you could kill someone?" I murmur.

She juts her chin up. Her eyes flashing with that same delectable level of fury I saw before. Christ, she's exquisite in this moment. The urge to press my lips to hers is practically overwhelming.

"Get the fuck out of my house." She snarls.

"I rather thought you were enjoying my visits."

She pushes me but I don't give her enough space for it to have any effect.

"What the fuck do you even want huh? Showing up here like you're invited. Like you're wanted."

"I'm setting new terms." I murmur.

"Excuse me?"

"I told you last night. I made it abundantly clear. You belong to me."

She pushes me again. "Fuck off."

I pull her tighter, my hands digging into the softness of her skin. "This is how it's going to work, you belong to me. Not that Henry guy, not the Governor...."

She lets out a hollow laugh. "Oh is that it? You couldn't bear to see me with someone else?" She sneers. "God you're pathetic."

I twist my hand into her hair, yanking it roughly as my jealousy spikes more in response to her behaviour. "You're with no one else Rose. Not that fucker your father is trying to marry you to now Paris is dead and certainly not fucking Darius."

"I'll be with whoever I want." She hisses. "You get no say on what I do."

The way she's responding makes me wonder if she really is sleeping with Darius. If this *was* something I missed. Well that would be easy to rectify. Easy to stop. "It's over. Whatever thing you have with Darius. It stops."

She seethes more, her body physically shaking as if she can barely contain the fury in her.

"Fine." I murmur, releasing my grip, brushing her cheek in what would normally be a loving gesture. Only this isn't about love, it's about possession. My possession of her. And she's about to realise how far it goes. How far my power stretches too. "Then I'll make a call to the Governor. I'll make it clear that you're off limits."

She scoffs. "Like he'll concern himself with your wants."

"Oh but he will Rose." I say tracing the outline of her face with my fingers, feeling how soft, how malleable she really is in this moment. "You see Darius is my pet. He does what I tell him. Exactly what I tell him."

She lets out a mocking laugh.

"How do you think I was able to return? Who do you think has been pulling all the strings? Manipulating everyone to do what I want?"

She gulps shaking her head slightly.

"I'm in charge now Rose. Not Darius. Not the Governor. Me. This entire city dances to my tune, only they're too stupid to realise it."

"It's you." She whispers. "You're what he referred to. You're the reason everything is changing."

My eyes glint as I realise she does get it. "That's right Rose." I murmur. "So you see it's pointless to fight me." I drop my eyes taking in the hint of her curves below the robe she has on. "It's all but inevitable."

I know I could hammer my point. That I could strip that fabric off her and spend the next god knows how many hours lost in the delights of her body, proving exactly how inevitable this all is.

Except I don't.

Something in me, some weaker part perhaps, allows her the space she obviously needs to come to terms with this.

I step back. Let the beauty slip through my hands once more and disappear back into the night.

She'll be mine soon enough.

Afterall, we both know this is a game we've been playing with each other. For six long, torturous, years.

The end is finally in sight.

We can both feel it and soon enough she'll be coming to me. Begging me to fuck her. Begging me to forgive her.

She just has to get over her pride and admit it to herself first.

ROSE

I'm up early. In truth I barely slept.

I hit the gym hard, burning through all the fury that's raging inside me. The only good thing is the clubhouse is all but deserted because everyone is up and leaving today. I guess I should be happy about that.

For once no one is watching me, sucking up to me, trying to get something from me.

For once I'm actually left in peace.

I keep mulling over what Roman said. What Darius said before him. And Paris before that. If it's true, if Roman really is pulling all the strings, then my situation right now is even more precarious than I thought because if he finds out what I've done, what happened *after* he left, then I know every carefully constructed plan for my future will be ruined.

He will ruin it.

And worse he will never let us leave.

I gulp at the thought. At the irony of the fact that the man I once considered to be my hero, my every dream, will now be responsible for continuing the nightmare I'm locked in.

I have to see Darius. I have to know for sure if this is some sort of bluff because only then will I know how to act.

I make my way to City Hall, trying to come up with some smart way of asking him, some clever way of getting him to confirm or deny it but in the end it seems silly. Better I come straight out and ask and at least then I can gauge his reaction.

The building is quiet. Not that I expected anything different. The polished marble extenuates every step I take and for some unknown reason, the closer I get to his office, the greater a sense of foreboding starts to build in my stomach. Like a knot, twisting and tightening, though the cause of it I can't wrap my head around.

Maybe this is a mistake.

The thought hits me just as the door opens. I haven't even knocked. I'm just stood, with my hand up, knuckles ready to strike the wood.

Darius covers his surprise quickly with a warm smile.

"Well this is a nice surprise." He murmurs.

I smile back, trying to cover my reservations, trying to act like this is perfectly normal behaviour. "I, I hope you don't mind…"

"Not at all." He says, taking my arm all but pulling me into the room before shutting the door.

I frown glancing around at the state of the place. His office looks an absolute mess. Papers are strewn everywhere as if someone has had some sort of paddy. I turn around to face him. "If you're busy I can come back another time."

"I'm not busy." He says gesturing to the couch as if he has nothing better to do than spend the next god knows how long pandering to my whims.

I clear my throat, sinking into the soft leather, and he immediately sits beside me. Not across from me. Not in the armchair. But *right* beside me.

I swallow, ignoring the uncomfortable feeling that churns in my stomach again.

"Last night you said something was going on." I begin. "You said there was something happening in Verona."

He nods, taking my hand, and in that moment I don't flinch, I don't react. I guess I'm too shocked to do anything but just let him. "There's nothing for you to worry yourself about. I'm dealing with it." He says gently.

"That's not what I meant." I reply.

He's running his thumb over the back of my hand. Slowly. I stare at the movement as it sinks in what I've been trying to ignore for the last I don't know how long. He's not just being friendly. He's not just looking out for me. Darius *is* hitting on me.

I gulp, pulling my hand away like I've been shocked.

"Rose?" He says tilting his head, studying me.

"It's Roman isn't it?" I reply.

He raises an eyebrow. "What makes you think that?" His voice sounds harsh now.

"It's obvious." I shrug. "At least to me. Suddenly he's allowed back. Suddenly everything is forgiven."

He lets out a low sigh and scoots himself just that bit nearer to me, as if he wasn't already right up in my personal space. "I'm taking care of it. Taking care of him."

"How?"

"There's nothing for you to worry about. You're not in any danger." He places his hand on my leg, on my thigh, in what could be, if I didn't overthink it, a reassuring gesture.

"That's not what concerns me."

267

He smiles, leaning closer and there's nowhere for me to go, no space I can move into. "Are you concerned for me Rose, is that it?" He says.

I shake my head quickly. "No. Not like that."

He lets out a low laugh, dropping his eyes to stare at my chest. "Don't play coy. You've been teasing me long enough."

"I haven't..." I begin but he's already pushing himself on top of me, his lips pressed against mine, his tongue shoving itself into mouth as his whole weight covers me and his hand squeezes my breast.

I cry out, pushing him back even as his hands grope me and for one moment I think he won't stop. That he's suddenly become a mad man. I slap him hard, pound my fists into his back and he stills.

"What are you doing?" I gasp in shock and outrage.

"What do you think?" He replies moving to envelope me again.

I cry pushing him off, half falling onto the rug in my attempt to escape him.

He shakes his head moving to grab me and I scramble to my feet before moving far enough away that I'm out of his reach.

"Don't be a little cock tease." He says.

"I'm not." I snap. "In what world did you think I was interested in you like that?"

He laughs getting to his feet as if this is a challenge. "You've been flirting with me for months."

"I haven't." I shake my head. I mean I haven't intentionally. I might have flirted a little, just like everyone does. It's Darius for fucksake, everyone behaves like that with him. Besides he's old enough to be my dad and more than that, I was married to his nephew.

"Drop the pretence. We both know you what you want." He states.

"Not you."

"No?" He smirks running his eyes over me. "Then why did you come here?"

"I told you." I hiss.

"Don't lie. You didn't come here to talk about Roman Montague."

"Yes I did." I reply.

He moves closer to me as I step back further towards the door.

He glances behind me and shakes his head. "That's not how this is going to play out Rose. Not this time."

"I'm not interested in you like that. I don't want anything like that."

That makes him smirk more. Like I've poured gasoline onto a fire. "It doesn't really matter what you want because the truth is you need me Rose. You need my support because without it who else is on your side?"

"What are you saying?" Even I can hear the tremor in my voice.

He eases his suit jacket off, clicks his neck like he's preparing for some sort of fight. "Do you not understand how precarious your situation is? Your father is happy to marry you to whoever will write the biggest cheque."

My stomach lurches. I know it's true but to hear someone else say it… "So what, you want me to be grateful you're on my side?"

His lip curls. "I am Rose, and I will be, but I expect recompense for it." He undoes his belt, slowly, making clear exactly what 'recompense' he's after.

"I was married to your nephew." I cry in disgust.

"You really think that would stop me from fucking you?"

My jar drops. I don't know what to say. I know I'm responsible for getting myself into this mess, that for weeks, months even I've been telling myself that this is nothing, that his advances haven't really been that, that he's just being friendly and I'm oversensitive. And yet here it is, plain as day, no longer possible to deny.

He jerks his head to the couch. "Take off that pretty dress and spread your legs like the good little slut we all know you are."

I whimper, my hand moving behind me to grab the door handle and just as he sees the movement and lunges, I manage to get out, to get into the corridor and then I'm running, sprinting down the hall and out into the blazing, blinding summer heat.

I barely get around the corner before I start puking. It's not even what he did, it's the way he did it, the expectation, the entitlement, it was as if he expected me to just be grateful, to just roll over and happily be used like that.

I retch again but nothing comes out. I didn't eat breakfast nor dinner last night, so I'm not surprised. I have nothing to puke up.

A hand rubs my back and I flinch spinning around, expecting to see Darius but it's not.

It's Sofia.

She's crouched down, on her knees, comforting me.

"You okay?" She asks quietly.

I shake my head. I'm anything but.

She glances around. We're in a side alley but not exactly hidden from view. She pulls me up and takes me to what I assume is her car. I sink into the passenger seat feeling pathetic now. After all, I endured a lot worse from Paris. In reality Darius hasn't done anything near as heinous as his nephew has, so why am I acting like this?

I wipe my face, feeling how wet my cheeks are. I didn't even realise I'd been crying.

"Why are you here?" I say. Like I'm not in her car. Like any of this normal.

"I have a meeting with Darius. He wants to discuss my engagement to Otto." She pulls a face like she's been poisoned.

"You're getting engaged?" Christ could this day get any worse?

"No I bloody well am not." She snaps. "But Darius is trying to force my hand."

"Oh." I look away. I guess he's more of a bastard than I realised. God, how was I so stupid not to see it?

"What happened? Why were you so upset?"

I grit my teeth. "Darius. He…" I whisper before biting my lip. I don't trust her. Not entirely. Besides saying it out loud, admitting that I was stupid enough to get myself into that situation. My cheeks heat with shame. I'm an idiot. A stupid, stupid idiot.

She tilts her head, giving me a look that says all I need to know. "Roman will kill him for that."

"Can't you just stop?" I hiss. "Can't all of you just stop?"

"Stop what?"

"These games. All you do is make everything worse."

"Your family started it. And Darius more than deserves what's coming to him."

I let out a shudder. "I can't do this. I can't live like this."

"Rose…"

"No." I snap forcing myself to get up, to get out of her car. "I don't want this to be my life. I don't want all this hate, and anger."

"Then help us. Help us create a new Verona. A better Verona."

"Like hell that's what you're trying to do." I snarl. "You're just as bad as my family. All you care about it the old rivalry. Bringing us down."

"That's not true." She says calmly. "Even you know that."

"Why else would you need me?" I spit. "You want me to pass on secrets is that it? You want me to give you juicy little titbits about my family so you can bring them down?"

"No." Sofia replies. "We don't want that. We don't need that."

I shake my head. "Don't lie…"

"I'm not lying Rose." She cries. "I'm trying to help you. How can you not see that?"

"Because I'm a Capulet and you're a Montague."

"But you're not just that are you?" She says quietly.

271

I frown staring at her like she's lost her mind. Of course I am. That's all anyone ever sees when they look at me. Capulet blood. The pretty Capulet princess.

"You're the woman my brother is in love with."

My heart stops at her words. My breath catches. And for a second it's like I can't process it, like this is all some sick twisted joke. My stomach twists, that old pain churning worse than ever.

"I can't do this." I whisper, forcing myself to move. I can't be here, where anyone can see us, see me.

"Rose..."

"No." I say not looking back. Not doing anything other than forcing myself to walk, to take one step after another until I'm back at my car and away.

ROMAN

"T hat better be a fucking joke." I growl.

"It's not."

I stare at my hands. At where they're clenched so tightly I think I might just crack my very bones.

"Are you not going to say anything?" Sofia asks, stepping further into the room.

Ben looks between us clearly trying to decide whether he should leave us to it. We were in the middle of planning another strike. Taking out another of their damn money-making enterprises when Sofia stormed in here.

I take a deep breath, trying to calm myself. I know she's not deliberately goading me and yet for weeks now she's the one pushing me, she's the one telling me that I should be honest with Rose, like that worked the first time. Like that didn't end up contributing to all the mess we're currently in.

"Roman…"

I snarl, picking up my glass and throw it as hard as I can against the wall. The shattering pieces help bring some level of control, as if the physical manifestation of my rage has actually unleashed the monster within myself.

"Tell me what he did." I say.

She meets my gaze and winces slightly. "I don't know for sure."

"Then how do you know he did anything?" Ben asks.

I glare back at him. Sofia is not an idiot. If she says something happened then I believe her. Besides we all know what Darius is like, we all know his true nature. But the thought of him touching Rose, of him laying his hands on her. The image of them, of how intimate they'd been last night flashes through my head. He's been treating her like she's his for so long now I doubt he ever stopped to question it.

I'm going to cut his dick off, I'm going to severe his fucking hands for laying them on her, even for just a second.

"You didn't see her." Sofia says. "You didn't see how messed up she was."

I blink, running my hands over my face. It's been a long day and this was not how I anticipated it ending.

"Did she say anything to you?" I ask.

Sofia shakes her head. "No. I tried to talk to her, to reason, I told her we could help."

"And she refused you?" I guess, though it's not like it's hard. If she'd agreed we'd all be having an entirely different conversation right now. And she'd be here, in my arms. Safe.

She nods with an apologetic look. "I tried Roman."

"I know." I reply gently. Despite her hard exterior Sofia has a heart of gold and I won't for a minute take out my bitter resentment on her.

"You should go see her." She says.

"What?" Ben cuts across.

"Go." Sofia says ignoring him entirely.

I shake my head. I don't have time for distractions.

"She needs you right now."

"No she doesn't." I state because if she did she would have sought me out. The fact I've had to hear this from Sofia proves it.

"For fucksake." Sofia snaps. "Don't you see? This is your chance, to prove to her you're not just here for revenge. To prove that you actually care about her."

"You think I don't know that?" I half shout back. "You think I don't want that? I love her for Christ sake."

"Then go see her."

"No." I reply. It's not enough. Love is not enough. In this moment I realise it. Because it's not about my feelings, not about my wants. It's about Rose. It's about her proving it to me.

And the only way she can do that is if she comes to me.

Not the other way around.

"You're being a fool." She cries. "A stubborn, stupid fool."

Perhaps she's right. Perhaps I am. But as I storm out of the room I know I'm right. I have to wait for Rose. It's the only way for us to clear the chasm between us.

Yet, in the meantime, that doesn't mean I have to stay here and do nothing. In fact I think it's about time our dear Governor learnt what happens when he touches things that aren't his.

ROMAN

I t's late but *I know the fucker is still awake. No doubt he's sat in his office plotting how to rid himself of me.*

I grin at the notion. That such a thing is possible.

I kick the door open and he jumps back looking at me in shock before he quickly recovers himself.

"Roman. Bit late for a chat isn't it?" He says as if we have the kind of relationship where we just 'chat'.

"It is but apparently this is needed." I reply.

"What is?" He asks.

"Rose Capulet."

He frowns. "What?"

"Stay the hell away from Rose."

"She's my nephew's wife." He says acting like that's all it is. Like he hasn't put his hands all over her. Like he hasn't dared to imagine what she would feel like to fuck.

"Dead nephew." I reply. "Which means she no longer has a connection to you."

"I care for Rose. I'm not simply going to…"

"You will." I say. "If I so much as hear you've looked in her direction there will be consequences. Big consequences. Ones you will not enjoy."

He frowns and then the realisation hits him.

"Oh you fool." He says quietly. "You absolute fool. You think her family would let her near you? You think her father would ever permit such a match."

"She's a grown woman. She can be with who she wants." I snap.

He laughs. He actually has the audacity to laugh. "No Roman. That's not how this works. You know that. Ignatio is head of his family. He controls Rose."

"And I control you." I smirk. "So whatever game you have going on it ends. You don't speak to her. You don't look at her. And god help me, you don't touch her."

"What's your plan here boy? You think you can just ride off into the sunset? Win the girl and get your happy ending?" He mocks.

"I'm not riding off anywhere. I own this city." I say pulling out a knife, making sure he takes note of it.

"And what does your precious Rose think of that?" Darius says back, obviously trying to buy himself some sort of reprieve. "Of you becoming everything she despises?"

He's trying to twist this only it won't work. I'm doing this for us. I've become this for us. Rose will realise that. She will understand that. We're not the naïve teenagers we were six years ago. We've both grown. We've both been forced too. Life is not all fairy tales and princes. It's not all black and white. Good and bad. To win you have to muddy the water. You have to be prepared to cross the lines or else there's no point even getting in the ring.

"You're overstepping Darius." I growl stepping closer to him.

"Is that so?" He says smirking but I can see it, the concern in his eyes anyway. "Tell me, did you love her all this time?"

I give him a look like 'what the hell do you think?'

He sighs sinking back into his chair. "If you'd come to me six years ago, if you'd asked, I would have cut you a deal."

I let out a laugh. Sure he would have. And then what? Me and Rose would have had our happy ending? Not a chance. I would have been tied to him. His pet fucking monkey.

God, he would have loved that. A Montague and a Capulet right in his pocket.

No, if I'd taken that path it wouldn't have worked out better for us. I knew not to trust anyone then and that hasn't changed.

"I'll cut you a deal. Get your sister to marry Otto and I'll take care of Ignatio, clear the path for you and Rose."

"No thanks." I don't need him to do my dirty work and I certainly won't be making any deals that involve Sofia being tied to one of them.

"Don't be a fool Roman…"

I snap then. All but jumping across the desk to pin him into his chair.

"You dare to speak to me like that." I snarl. "After what you've done."

He splutters. His eyes focused entirely on the blade millimetres from his eyes.

"You touched her didn't you?" I spit.

He shakes his head with as much movement as he dares to make right now.

"You've made a habit of that." I continue. "Of taking things, of touching things that don't belong to you…"

"I've done nothing…" He begins but the knife turns his words into a shriek.

I drag the blade down his cheek. It slices through his flesh like a hot knife through butter. He's going to need a good amount of stitching to fix that back up.

"The only reason I'm not gutting you where you sit is because you still have a use." I say. "But the minute you stop being that, the minute you outlive that, I'm going to enjoy ripping your throat out..."

He's trembling now, though I can't blame him.

"...So let this be a lesson to you Darius." I state. "Every time you look at yourself in the mirror, every time you see your reflection from now on, you'll remember this. You'll remember what happens when you take things that don't belong to you."

"She doesn't belong to you either." He says.

His blood is streaming down his cheek. I've a good mind to cut his damn tongue out for that statement but I don't. I'm saving that for another time. A future I can barely wait to come into fruition.

I step back, wipe the blade on his overpriced shirt, and grin.

"Rose Capulet is mine. She's always been mine." I say before driving the blade into the leather top of his desk.

He can keep that as a souvenir. Another gift from me.

Along with the four inch scar he'll now have on his face.

ROSE

I've stayed away from everyone. I don't know what to do. I have five months now. Five months before I can leave. Before I can finally get away from this awful place and all these awful people.

Only right now, I feel more trapped than ever.

It feels like someone is twisting the screws, that they know exactly what I have planned and are doing everything they can to trip me up.

Only I can't let them.

Not this time.

I have to get free.

I have to do it, because it's not just me who depends upon it. Not just my future that's at stake.

Before I can overthink it I'm up, packing my bags, chucking them into my car, putting Bella into the car too and then I'm speeding off.

This is reckless. Really reckless.

And yet it feels like if I don't do this, if I don't take action now it'll be too late.

So screw the deadline. Screw the millions that I'm due to inherit because it all means nothing if I'm still a prisoner. If I don't get away from this place.

I pull up to the park. Bella is curled up half asleep on a blanket. It's too hot to leave her in the car for long and I make sure to keep a window open enough to help ensure she'll be okay.

I put my hands in my pockets, feeling the heavy metal of the gun. If this is to work, I have to be quick, I have to come out of nowhere. A blitz attack. I have to strike hard and then get the hell out before anyone is able to locate me.

I cross the park quickly. I can hear the screams of children. The laughter too. It feels like everything is disjointed. Everything is off.

My heart is thumping so loudly now I can barely focus. My adrenaline is making me want to puke.

I finger the trigger. The safety is on but I'll be sure to take it off as I strike. I'm not going to give any opportunity for this to fail. If I have to shoot my way out of this when I will. I'm not going to just let them win this time.

Ahead I can see them. The three of them. The usual two guards. I take a deep breath stealing myself.

This is it.

This moment here.

If I can do this, if I can pull this off I'll be free. We'll be free.

"Rose."

I freeze, not daring to even look around.

"Rose." Ty repeats my name again.

I gulp as my heart sinks. As I contemplate the consequences of shooting him and then continuing on.

"Rose." He snarls it this time.

And with that sound I know it's gone.

My moment.

My entire plan is ruined.

"What is it?" I ask.

"You're wanted." Ty says jerking his head to the waiting car.

I don't look. I keep my eyes fixed on the three figures still so far from me. If I'd been five minutes earlier, if I'd gotten through a few more lights I would have made it.

Regret, anger, bitter, festering disappointment racks through me.

Once again I'm a failure.

"Rose."

I let out a huff.

"I said you're wanted." Ty snaps.

I turn meeting his gaze with a glare. "Fine."

His steps back towards the car and I shake my head. "I have my own."

"Leave it."

"No."

He raises an eyebrow giving me that arsehole look of his.

"Bella is in it. I'm not just leaving her." I state.

"Fine then. I'll see you at the house." He snaps.

I narrow my eyes wanting to tell him to stick it. Wanting to scream. To wail. To completely and utterly lose myself to my despair but the three figures are gone. Whether they saw me, whether they knew, I don't know but it's too late.

It's all too fucking late.

I shake my head storming back to my car. Bella is still asleep but I'm quick to get the engine running, quick to get the aircon on and to drop the temperature. It was cruel to leave her like that. Cruel and unnecessary as it turned out.

Because once again, the odds were not in my favour.

Once again I risked it all for nothing.

"WHAT TOOK YOU SO LONG?" MY MOTHER HISSES BARELY LETTING me get out of the car.

"I was busy." I say.

She huffs and then huffs more as I pick Bella up and carry her out.

She snaps her fingers for one of the maids and they half snatch her from my arms and carry her off.

"What is going on?" I ask.

She shakes her head pulling me inside. "We have a lot to discuss."

"If it's about me marrying some arsehole…" My words die as my father stands arms crossed glaring at me.

I gulp feeling like a child again.

He drops his gaze, giving me a once over like he's disgusted and then turns obviously expecting me and my mother to just follow in his wake.

When we walk into his study I'm surprised to see no one else there. Not even Ty.

"What is this?" I ask.

"There has been an incident." My father replies.

"What incident?" God I hope he doesn't mean me. I hope he doesn't realise what I was up to, what I was in the process of doing because if he does I'm screwed. He'll never let me leave this house. Never let me leave his sight until he's married me off again.

"At the docks." He says.

I frown. What does that mean?

"While you've been simpering away with our enemies they've been making moves against us."

"I wasn't simpering." I snap. "I didn't have a choice…"

He waves his hand like he doesn't give a shit what my excuses are.

"The facts remain the same." He says.

"And what are those?" I retort.

"That the Montagues have been on the attack." He says. "That since your dear loverboy returned we've lost half our revenue, half our businesses have been destroyed."

"What are you talking about?" I reply. In truth I don't know anything about our businesses beyond the fact that we make a lot of money from them. It's naïve I know but I doubt all of it is above board and it's easier to ignore it when you don't know the dirtier facts. Ignorance is bliss and all that.

"I'm saying your boyfriend has destroyed half our warehouses. Half our supply and distribution. He's set fire to the lot."

I screw my face up. "He's not my boyfriend." I snarl.

My father smirks sitting back in his chair and the leather squeaks against his frame. "No?" He murmurs. "You looked pretty cosy dancing with him the other night."

I huff rolling my eyes. Here we go again.

"…And the way he watched you. He didn't take his eyes off you for a moment."

"I don't give a shit." I snap. "I haven't done anything. I'm not…"

He smiles with that glint in his eye telling me he's about to say something I'm not going to like. About to make me do something I'm not going to like. "We can make this work to our advantage Rose." He states. "For once your little indiscretion might actually prove to be useful."

I gulp at that tone. "What are you saying?"

"I'm saying…" He leans forward over his desk, looking from me to my mother and back again. "You seduce him, get something on him, a location, something we can use so we can enact our revenge."

"What?" I gasp.

He smirks more. "Come now, I saw the way you two are. Clearly you both still want each other. We can use that Rose. For once you being a whore is useful."

I shake my head, clenching my fists. "I'm not a whore."

"No?" He says folding his arms and giving me that same look of contempt he always has. "Your past behaviour says otherwise."

I get to my feet, my body physically shaking. "I'm not a whore and I won't be treated as one." I snap before turning on my heel and storming out.

I want to find Bella. I want to get the fuck out of this house. But more than that I can feel the weight of the gun still pressing into my leg. So much of me wants to turn around and use it that it actually scares me.

My mother follows me. She's quick on my heels only I don't look back. I don't stop.

I storm through the house down to the servants quarters and to where Bella undoubtedly is and when I see her I snatch her back out of the maids hands before making for the door.

"Rose..."

"No." I snarl back. Not looking at her. Not giving my mother a chance to try to justify this.

"Just wait, listen."

"To what?" I snap. "More insults? More abuse? You're just as sick as he is if you think I'd willingly do that."

She shakes her head. "I know it sounds crazy but..."

"But what?" I repeat. "You want me to do that?"

She shrugs. "We do what is necessary. That is the Capulet way."

"No. It's not my way." I snap.

"Rose, don't you see? This is your chance."

"What?"

"After everything he's done to you." She says putting her hand on my shoulder, reassuring me almost. "After the way he betrayed you, don't you want your revenge? Not even just a little bit?"

I gulp. Yeah I do want that. I want to hurt Roman as much as he hurt me and yet I know this isn't it. This isn't the answer.

"He used you." She states. "Used you and ditched you like trash. Doesn't he deserve to know how that feels?"

She's twisting this. I know she is and yet my head is agreeing. My anger, my bitterness, all those years of festering rage are telling me that this is not a bad option. Not a bad way to take back some control. Afterall he's still playing games isn't he? He still snuck into my house, tied me up, all but forced himself on me...

But I wanted it.

I know I resisted but it wasn't exactly one sided. I still want him. I still love him. On some crazy level, for some unfathomable reason a part of my soul still yearns so desperately for him.

I brush away the tear. How can that be? After everything he did, everything he said, the way he left, the way he ruined me. How can I want him still?

"This is an opportunity Rose." She says. "A chance for you to get some retribution."

"No." I reply fixing her with a look. "If I do this then I want something else. Something far greater than mere revenge."

"And what is that?" She asks.

I let out a huff. Like it's not damned obvious. Like she doesn't know exactly what I'm asking for.

She bites her lip, frowning. "Let me speak to him. Let me see what I can do."

"No. No false hope. No bullshit." I snap. "You give me this. You agree or you get nothing."

She takes a moment then nods. "Fine. I'll sort it."

"Fine." I reply.

"But you have to make your move tomorrow."

I wrinkle my nose in disgust. She knows exactly what she's asking and yet she doesn't even seem to care that she's all but making me the whore she named me as six years ago.

"I'll do it." I mutter before turning on my heel, heading to my car, not looking back.

ROMAN

I'm sat in my study, going through all the evidence we've gathered so far. The most shocking of it being that Ignatio wasn't the one to come up with this idea. And neither was Darius.

No, worse than that, it was my own father. He was the one who started this 'human harvesting' program decades ago and then Ignatio found out and all but took over the business ensuring Calvin got a healthy slice of the pie and thereby securing his place in the shit hierarchy of this city.

The people we've rescued are being kept safe at one of my father's old offices. It's off-grid. Discreet. For all intents and purpose it's perfect. Once they're recovered we'll give them enough money and the means to get as far from Verona as they want. It's the least I can do considering we're as tied to this as the Capulets are.

Ben is off somewhere, sulking.

And Sofia, Sofia is on another high-profile, high visibility date with Otto.

I've already seen her image flash up multiple times across social media, and to be fair I can't blame her for picking somewhere as public as she has because we both know it contains him. It keeps Otto under control, and it ensures that Sofia doesn't have to give any more than she's willing.

The radio crackles. I look across at it and then back at my screen just as a voice comes through.

"We have a visitor."

I frown, pulling up the tab to see the front door but no one is there.

Would Darius be so bold as to send someone to 'fix' me? Fuck I hope so, I'm itching for an excuse to be rid of him. To just butcher him and the consequences be damned.

I scan through the other cameras and then I see it, the shadow, the figure, and, as their body comes into view on the next angle, I recognise who it is.

Well, well, it appears the mouse does sometimes come to the cat after all.

I can't help but grin, getting up, making my way silently to where the beauty is. She's walking quietly, hesitantly almost, as if she's not convinced that being here is an entirely sane move. I come up behind her, one hand wrapped around her mouth, the other around her upper body pining her back into me.

She freezes, a whimper escapes her lips, muffled against my palm, and I lean in getting a good breath of her.

"And why would a Capulet be creeping around my house?" I murmur.

She relaxes a tiny bit at my voice, at the knowledge that it's me that found her and not someone else who'd misinterpreted what this is.

Because we both know why she's come. Why she's here.

I let her go just enough that she can spin around and face me. She's wearing a silk dress, beneath I can see her nipples already poking through. Her breasts are heaving and I'm dying to just grab them, to feel them in my hands again.

"You've been creeping into my house." She says. "I thought it was about time I did the same to you."

I let out a low laugh. "I've done a lot worse than simply creep into your house Rose." I state and her cheeks seem to blush with memory.

I push her back into the wall, as my hands begin to explore her. Even the silk of her dress can't compare to the softness of her perfect skin. "I used to creep into your bed too. I used to spread those delicate little legs of yours and feast on that pretty cunt."

She shudders, her hands raise to my chest and she pushes enough to put a tiny bit of distance between us. "I came here to talk." She says.

I raise an eyebrow and make a point of staring at her body. "In that dress?"

She shakes her head, using that resolved tone she has when she's trying to be serious. "Roman…"

"Fine." I say stepping back, but I don't let her go, not really anyway, I stalk her steps, stalk the very air she breathes as I gesture to where my office is.

The door shuts loud enough to crack the pressure between us. She turns, her eyes darting around to take in the space.

"Talk Rose." I say.

"Aren't you going to offer me a drink?" She replies all haughty.

I should fuck that attitude right out of her. I should pick her up, throw her over my desk and prove to us both what she's really looking for because it's definitely not a conversation and nor is it a god damn drink.

Fuck, how does she do this? How does she seem to just take over all my sense of logic, of reason? I walk over pouring her out a glass of whiskey and she wrinkles her nose.

"You know I don't drink that stuff."

"Fine." I murmur, putting it down before stalking off to get a bottle. The little minx wants something more refined, then I'll give her refined before I show her how much of an animal she really is.

I grab a bottle of champagne, Boërl & Kroff no less, so let's see her make a fuss about this one and I pick up two glasses too.

She jumps as I walk back in, putting her bag down, leaning against the desk, watching me as if I might strike at any second, and in truth, with the way I feel, I probably will.

"Good enough?" I say holding the bottle up.

Her lips twitch. "Champagne?"

"Just like old times." I murmur.

She shakes her head just a little and murmurs. "This is nothing like old times."

"And how do you figure that?" I reply, popping the cork, noticing how she jumps again at that sound. She really is scatty, on edge, but I'll admit I like that too. She was scatty the first time we met up, the first time I touched her. It feels like we've done full circle. Returned right back to the beginning again and I'm about to claim my flower once more.

The bubbles threaten to spill over as I pour the contents out into the flutes.

"Neither of us really understood what we were getting into." She says. "Back then we were both too ignorant of all of this."

"All of what?" I ask handing her a glass.

She takes it from me but doesn't take a sip, instead she puts it down and I see it, that flicker that tells me she's hiding something from me.

I step back into her, all but pin her between my body and the antique wood.

"Why are you here Rose?" I ask.

She lets out a sigh before meeting my look head on. "Why did you come back? Why did you return?"

292

My lips curl, is she trying to find out my secrets now? I'm more than happy to spill them if that's what it takes to reassure her, to persuade her even, that she's safe in my hands. Darius's words echo in my head, about how she would despise me for what I've become. Maybe some honesty now would prove to her that I'm not her enemy. That she can actually trust me, love me the way I know she did before.

"I'm taking this city." I say. "That's why I'm back. I'm reclaiming everything Darius stole from my family, and I'm making them pay."

She doesn't look like that's the answer she wanted. If anything it seems to make her more conflicted but right now I don't care. Right now she's in my kingdom, my domain. And I'm going to show her what happens when an angel walks into the depths of hell simply to tease the devil.

I put my glass beside hers. She drops her gaze to stare at them both.

"Roman…" She half whispers.

"I always liked how you said my name." I reply, tracing my fingers up her back. The little slip of fabric she has on is backless, giving me free rein to enjoy her exposed flesh.

"I didn't come here to…"

I silence her with my mouth. Silence those protests with my tongue. I'm done talking. Done explaining myself. She doesn't resist, but of course she doesn't, because, no matter what little lies she's told herself, she came here for me, she came here for this.

My fingers loop in the string like straps of her dress, I yank them down in unison and she gasp as she's suddenly there, topless.

I stare at her breasts, at those perfect, fucking delicious breasts and I groan. If anything, she's gotten more beautiful with age and though I've already feasted on these once, they're so much better in the light.

My mouth is on her, devouring her. I suck on one nipple and then the other. She arches her back as her hands twist into my hair.

And then she whimpers. That desperate, needy little sound she used to make when she was hopelessly lost in her lust for me.

I dig my hands into those orbs, manipulating them as I swirl my tongue over those hardened little bullets. She can protest all she wants but her body is already telling me what she's really seeking. What she so desperately needs.

I push her back, ignoring the sound of both glasses as they topple over and spill their contents.

"We have to stop." She says.

But it's a lie and we both know it.

"You're mine Rose. You always have been." I reply.

She shakes her head trying to sit back up. "No I'm not."

I let out a laugh, wrapping my hand around her throat, not tight though, not in any way like the way her husband would have held her. She stares up at me, gulping, and I feel it, her trachea moving beneath my grasp. She feels so fragile, so breakable, my dick hardens to the point of pain at how much I hold her life in my hands right now.

"I'll prove it to you then. I'll spend the next god knows how long proving how much your body is mine, how much your heart is mine, how much all of you is mine. I'll make you come so many times you won't be able to deny it anymore. And as you lie there, soaked in your own pleasure, you'll know it was me, that I'm the one who did that to you."

"Roman…" She gasps but it's clear she's torn between denial and demand.

I push her back again, push her flat onto the desk, right into the spilt champagne, and then I push that sexy little dress of hers right up over her hips.

She's wearing a thong. It's pale. Barely darker than her skin tone and from what I can see she's drenched already.

I pull her legs apart. She shakes her head as I do it but she doesn't protest. She doesn't tell me to stop. She doesn't try to close them either.

"I used to own this cunt." I say. "I used to be the only man who'd savoured you. Who knew what you tasted of."

Her face reacts to that. Is it remorse? Regret? Guilt even?

I shove my face right there, not even caring that there's fabric separating me from paradise. She raises her hips, rocking against my mouth, clearly wanting me to go further.

"Did you miss me Rose?" I taunt. "Did you miss the feel of my lips on you?"

"Yes." She gasps.

Of course she fucking did. Because from all the nights I watched them, all the times I witnessed Paris and her fucking, she never once came. She never once reacted even remotely close to the way she is right now.

Her body was designed for me, designed to respond to my caresses, my teases. All this time she's been starved. Waiting. Longing. Knowing nobody would ever sate her desires the way I can.

"My little whore. That's what you are, my Capulet whore." I taunt.

She snarls at that. Her hand raises and she slaps me.

And I'll admit I think I get even harder then. This new Rose does have some spark. Some bite. I pin her arms back, holding them against her body. And then I lower my mouth to paradise once more.

"Beg for it Rose." I say. "Beg me to claim you again."

She whimpers shaking her head as her pride clearly overrides her need.

I grin, taking hold of her thong with my teeth and tease it to the side, revealing her perfect, pouty cunt. I'm salivating at just the thought of this, of being able to taste her again.

"Fuck." I groan staring at her. She's so ready for me right now. My tongue is on her, licking, swirling, reminding myself of how she feels. She writhes as I do it, her hands jerking as if she wants to get free only I won't let her. This feast is for me. This moment here has been six years in the making and I'm going to have this my way.

She starts whimpering more, moaning. Her body rising to meet every single tease of my tongue. She's chasing her climax, desperate for it. I add my fingers, circling her clit, watching her rub herself against me.

"Little Rose." I taunt. "You always did enjoy what my tongue could do."

She glares at me but she can barely hold it for more than a second before her expression turns to ecstasy. And I know by looking at her, I know from all the times before, the way her face flushes, the way she gets that tiny frown, she's about to come.

She's about to fall apart entirely.

She shakes her head, as if she's going to deny me, deny us. I lower my mouth, sucking around her clit hard. The little minx isn't going to get out of this now. She's going to come. She's going to give me everything I deserve.

She wails.

She writhes.

And then finally she's arching her back, screaming. Her hair is covering her face. She's lost incandescently in the feel of what I'm forcing her body to do. What she's been desperate for. What she's been longing for from the moment I left.

She screams so loud I swear my ears pop. Her come pours out of her, hot, sweet, fucking delicious on my tongue.

Her legs jerk, her fingers flail, she's shut her eyes so tightly and that mouth of hers, the way it opens, the way it gasps out each miniscule moment of her orgasm.

"There's my good girl." I taunt. "There's the Rose I love."

She whimpers, her body sagging but I'm not stopping here. I'm not leaving this here. I've already made her come once since I retuned and we both know she continued to pretend. I'm going to fuck all the last of her resistance out of her. I'm going to fuck her over and over until she can't even think straight. Until the only word she can utter is my name.

I pick up her up, toss her over my shoulder, not caring that she's all but naked right now and I march out of the office, down the hall and to my room.

She starts twisting, moving, trying to get free and I toss her onto the bed.

She glares at me then looks around. I can see she wants to argue. To say some shit about how we shouldn't be doing this and I smirk, undoing my shirt, undoing my belt.

"Roman…" She murmurs with that same warning tone in her voice.

But I'm on her, pushing her back, laying her out so I can sink my cock into her.

"Roman…" She says again but this time it's less of a refusal and more of a moan.

I capture her lips, grasp her face in my hands and then push my cock into her as her body welcomes me home.

We both moan in unison. Fuck she's still so tight, so damn perfect. For a minute I think I forget myself. Forget my name. Forget everything. I've found nirvana. I've found my reprieve. I've found the very meaning of life.

She wraps her legs tight around me, digs her nails into my skin.

But I can't resist the taunt. I can't resist the twist of the knife. "Tell me Rose, who do I compare to your dead husband? How do I compare to Paris?"

Her eyes widen. She grabs my throat, pulling me down so we're practically nose to nose. "You're nothing like him." She says and then she loses what tiny bit of restraint she's been holding onto.

She starts rolling her hips, fucking me like I'm her salvation. I grab her, half snarling as I fuck her just as hard in return.

We're both lost now.

Both gasping, grabbing, biting at each other.

I run my teeth along her skin. I trace those beautiful curves as my cock slides in and out. She's gripping me so tightly I wonder how long I can last. Every move of her muscles, every caress, it's all coming back, the memories, the way we were.

My heart swells in my chest, I grab her head, forcing her to look at me.

"I fucking love you." I growl, staring at her face, wanting to see her reaction. Needing to see it too.

ROSE

My eyes widen at his words. At those words.

I didn't mean to do this. To take it this far.

My plan was to sneak in, at worst have some sort of conversation. But I wasn't going to cross the line. I wasn't going to fuck him.

And yet here I am, on his bed, writhing beneath him, feeling his incredible cock hitting that spot that makes me lose myself.

I let out another moan. I don't want to reply. I don't want to admit what I feel. That I love him. That I've always loved him. That I've never stopped loving him.

And yet right now I've already betrayed him. I've stabbed him in the back.

Just as he did me.

In the few minutes it took for him to get the champagne I'd sent my father the address I'd found written on some of the papers.

I don't know if it means anything. I don't know what's there. But it's enough.

Enough to give me what I want.

And enough to ensure that Roman and I will never have a future. That we will forever be enemies from now on.

He kisses me again. I kiss him back, trying not to cry, trying to savour this moment because this will be my last, our last. Tomorrow I will leave. I will flee this city and I will never see Roman or any other Montague again

I'll be free. Finally I will be free.

And yet, even as that thought settles in my head I can't help feel the anguish that I'm leaving him. That right now he thinks I'm giving in, that I'm allowing us to be what we were.

Only he was the one who ruined us the first time. He was the one that twisted this all.

What I'm doing now is justified.

What I'm doing now is necessary.

And yet I hate myself for it. I hate that I'm tricking him. Hate that this moment, us, it's just as tainted as all the ones before.

I shut my eyes, trying to focus on the physical. On the now. On it just being me and him. On how on so many levels this feels right, it's always felt right.

I've dreamt of this, longed for this, hungered for Roman's touch for so long and now that I have it I can't truly enjoy it.

"You're so fucking beautiful." Roman murmurs.

I kiss him to shut him up. I can't hear his praise, his adorations, because it's only making this worse.

My body hurtles closer and closer to climax. Somehow Roman's always known how to make me come. It's like we're uniquely attuned to each other's needs that we know exactly how to touch, how to tease. But it's more than that too, we connect on level that's more than physical, that makes this more than just sex.

And I think that's what makes what I'm doing all the worse.

Because Roman is my soulmate. Deep down I know it. Deep down I've always known it.

And what kind of person fucks their soulmate over the way I am?

I gulp, shuddering. I'm so close now that my guilt and my ecstasy are merging into one, causing tears to stream down my face. If Roman notices I don't know but his lips are against mine again. His hands are holding me to him and I'm lost in those kisses, in that embrace.

We come as one. Him groaning into my mouth and me clinging to him desperate for this last moment, desperate for this last memory.

We slump together, a mass of sweaty limbs. Tangled. Intwined.

"Rose." Roman murmurs.

I blink looking at him, then looking away. I can't meet his eyes. I can't face him.

He lays back, sinking into the sheets.

And before he can say anything, before he can speak more about his love, I slink away, sliding my dress back into place, disappearing into the darkness.

I am a whore.

I'm exactly what my father called me six years ago. I'm exactly what he called me yesterday to my face.

I'm a whore and a coward.

And yet I did it for us. I had to do it. I had no choice. I won't let history repeat itself. I can't let it. I have to escape. I have to get us both out of this city before this rivalry once again turns the streets into a battlefield.

ROMAN

I wake and it's just me. Alone. It wasn't like I expected her to have come back. I watched her go, watched her sneak away after like we were still teenagers and yet I'd hoped I'd imagined it, that she was here, in my arms all the same.

I roll onto my back staring at the ceiling. My Rose came back just as I knew she would but in so many ways she's still not mine. Not really. We're still circling. Still trying to find our feet.

And the fact that I'm lying alone right now testifies to it more than anything else.

I run my hands over my face. She might have left hours ago and yet I can smell her as if she's still here. My phone buzzes. I glance at it but don't make any move to touch it.

Then it buzzes again.

And again.

I sigh sitting up, reaching over. *No rest for the wicked today apparently.*

But as I stare at the screen my stomach drops. What the fuck has happened? I spring from the bed just as it rings and I half fumble to swipe the damn screen.

"What the fuck is going on?" I snarl.

"I don't know." Ben says quickly. "I'm here. I'm sorting it."

"How did they find out where they were?"

"I don't know Roman." Ben snarls. "But there's something else…"

"What?"

"Sofia is missing."

"What?"

"She messaged me to say she was headed over here, I've searched everywhere. We can't find her."

My anger soars. If they've touched her, hurt her, kidnapped her even then by god will they pay for that.

"I'm on my way." I say.

"Make it quick." He replies hanging up.

MY TYRES SCREECH AS I COME TO A STOP IN FRONT OF THE COMPOUND. For a moment I just sit there staring at the destruction. The security gates have been blown up. It looks like a missile has blasted into the concrete walls. Part of the building is still alight and the acrid smoke is pouring up into the air.

I grab my gun, not that I think I'll need it, and get out. My boots crunch across the gravel and before I realise I'm sprinting, racing inside.

Around me my men are salvaging what they can. I make eye contact with Turner and he freezes, his face no doubt echoing the same emotions as mine.

"Have you found her?" I ask.

He shakes his head. "We have CCTV footage. We didn't see anyone taking her."

I grunt in reply. That means shit when we both know there are ways around it. Hell, I'm practically an expert in avoiding cameras when I need to and everything about this attack tells me it's a professional hit.

"Roman." Ben says from behind me and I turn seeing the ashen look on his face.

"We'll find her." I say.

He nods before jerking his head. "You need to see this."

Christ, what is it now? I follow him through the destruction, and as my eyes realise where we're headed I meet his gaze.

"Tell me they got out."

He winces which tells me enough.

I can smell the smoke even more now but I can smell something so much worse. The stench of flesh. Of bodies burnt beyond recognition. I stop as my eyes find them. The women and children we'd rescued. They've butchered them. Massacred them.

I start shaking. Not from fear but from cold unrelenting fury because this is my fault. My mistake. I left them here. I thought this place was safe. I left them like low hanging fruit to be picked off and killed. I let out a snarl so loud as my anger flashes through me. Capulet is going to pay for this. And I mean really fucking pay this time.

"Roman."

We both turn at the sound.

"Sofia?" I gasp her name. She's covered in blood, covered in dirt.

"What took you so long?" She mumbles before rushing to me and burying herself in my arms.

"I'm so sorry." I reply.

She starts sobbing as I brush her hair back. Christ what's she's been through? I pull her face up to examine it. "Are you hurt?" I ask.

"I'll be okay. The others are being seen too." She says with a tight smile that I don't let fool me for a second.

"What others?" Ben asks.

She looks over at him then back at me. "We heard them taking out the gates. We tried to get out the back but they'd surrounded the place. Some of us were able to hide but…" She trails off as her eyes fall on the mass of people who didn't make it.

"Let's go." I say pulling her away. She's seen enough shit already. She doesn't need to see anymore horror.

As we get out the front she takes a deep exhale of air. Ben is hovering, obviously wanting to comfort her but she's making it more than clear that she doesn't want that.

I can see the others now, the women and children that did manage to survive. Amongst them is that same small child we pulled from the cages. She looks so traumatised I wonder if even a lifetime worth of therapy will make any difference.

"Get Sofia out of here." Ben says.

"What about you?" I ask.

"I've got this." He says. "You focus on her."

I nod tightening my grip around my sister. She might not be seriously injured but what she went through is enough.

I help her into the car reaching around to pull the seatbelt over her.

"I'm getting your leather dirty." She mutters looking down at where the blood and dirt is now smeared across it.

"It doesn't matter." I say.

"You love this car." She replies.

I cup her cheek. "Cars are replaceable. You are not."

Her eyes swell at that. She starts sobbing again and I hug her once more.

But as we drive away back to our home the question keeps reverberating through my head. How the hell did they know about this place? How the hell did they find out?

ROSE

I *take a shower. Then another. I feel dirty. Used. Disgusting.*

I know why I did it. I know it made sense and yet right now those reasons aren't enough to rid myself of the guilt and disgust.

I tricked him. I betrayed him.

I'm just as bad as he is now. Just as hateful.

And there's no comfort in that.

No reprieve.

I get dressed. Slap makeup on my face. Make myself presentable to the world as if I'm still something to look up to and I drive over to my parents' house.

I can't stand the thought of being in this city any longer than I need to be.

I did this for one thing and one thing only.

It's time they pay up. By god, it is finally time.

I step into the house. It feels empty. As if every one of my father's cronies is off somewhere. I grit my teeth trying not think of the implications of that because deep down, if they hurt Roman, if they kill him, I'll never forgive myself.

As I walk down to my father's study I pause. Carter is there stood talking to Sampson. Neither of them seem to notice me.

My stomach twists with the same anger I get every time I see them because even now I still blame them. They were the ones who brought me back. They were the ones who have helped keep me trapped all these years.

Carter is laughing. Sampson says something, mumbles it and Carter laughs again.

"Yeah maybe." Carter says. "Perhaps we'll ask the boss."

Sampson smirks. "Like he'd agree to that. His precious daughter?"

"She's not precious though is she?" Carter replies. "She's a fucking slut. She always has been."

I grit my teeth. I don't care what they say, what they think. Their opinion of me means fuck all.

Sampson mutters something else and Carter shrugs with a look of contempt.

"Ignatio has to be careful though. She'll see through it eventually." Sampson states.

"No she won't. She's a dumb bitch. She'll do whatever she's told to because she has no choice."

"What did you say?" I snarl before I can stop myself.

They both look at me and neither of them seem the least bit concerned that I've overheard them.

"You heard." Carter says running his eyes over me.

I clench my fists. They're baiting me and I know it, but it doesn't matter, not anymore. After today I'll never have to see either of them again.

"Where is he?" I ask.

Carter points to the door.

I scowl at him and push past. He can think what he wants but one day I swear to god I'm going to put a bullet in his head.

I storm into the office, slamming the door shut behind me.

My father looks up and his eyes narrow as he realises it's me.

"What do you want?" He asks.

"You know exactly what I want." I reply.

He leans back in his chair like a dictator sat on a throne.

"I did what you asked." I state walking towards him. "I held up my end of the bargain. Now it's time you pay."

He smirks. "Oh Rose. Did you really think it would be that easy?"

For a second it's like the words don't register. My stomach drops. "What?"

"Did you really think I'd just hand her over? Hand over the very thing that keeps you where I want you?"

I swallow putting my hands on the desk in front of me as I get right in his face. "We had an agreement."

"Did we?" He says smirking even more. "Maybe you should have made sure of that before you fucked Roman Montague. Again."

"You promised me…"

"I promised nothing you filthy little whore. All I had to do was suggest it and you were practically salivating at the mouth. How long did it take huh? How fast did you drive to get to him, to beg for his cock?"

"Give her to me or I swear to god…" I begin.

"You'll what Rose? Huh?" He says standing up. "What will you do?"

My hand slips into my pocket, grasping the gun that I know I shouldn't have brought with me but in this moment that's all I can think of because I'd happily blast his fucking face off.

"…It's about time you realised where you stand in this family." He continues. "You are nothing but an instrument to be used and the more you fight, the more you resist, the worse it will be for you."

"Not anymore." I snarl pulling it out, cocking it, and pointing it right at his god damn face.

He laughs. He laughs right back at me. "Oh please." He says. "You're going to shoot me now is that it?"

"GIVE ME MY DAUGHTER." I scream, pulling the trigger, pointing just past his shoulder and the bullet blasts out hitting the wall.

He jumps back, no doubt shocked that I did it. That his weak, easy to manipulate daughter finally made a stand.

"I won't repeat myself again." I snap.

From behind me someone grabs me, jerking me back. The gun is wrenched from my hand but not before I manage to fire it again. I lash out screaming more. Fighting like some deranged animal.

"Stupid bitch." Carter says as he gets me in a head lock so tight I think he might just snap my head.

"Where did you get this from?" Sampson asks.

I screw my face up, fixing my gaze on my father.

"Toss her out." He spits.

"Please." I cry. "Please give her to me."

He doesn't even blink, doesn't even react, just watches as I'm dragged out and thrown onto the drive like trash.

And as I lay there, my palms cut from the stones, I realise the enormity of what I've done. What I've thrown away and for what? I thought this was my chance, my redemption, but it's not is it? He played me again. His own daughter. He was never going to let me see her. Never going to let me near her.

Everything I'm trying to save her from, I've just condemned her to instead.

My stomach twists. That awful grief rises up worse than ever.

I force myself up, force myself to move.

A voice in my head keeps telling me over and over to go to Roman. To tell him. To confess it all.

Only I can't.

I know I can't.

He must know by now what I've done. How I've tricked him. But if he realises what else I've been concealing, if he realises what's really going on, then he's going to despise me even more.

ROMAN

I'm sat at the table with my men are around me. All of us going through the evidence, trying to work out where the mole is.

Because someone talked. Someone betrayed us.

Sofia is upstairs. Asleep. Thankfully she's unharmed bar a few cuts and bruises. Ben is with her. I don't know if this drama will be the catalyst they both need to finally admit their feelings but either way I won't intrude.

And then it hits me. What's been staring me in the face. What's been so fucking obvious.

It was Rose. She did this.

That's why she came here. Not for me, not for us.

She must have gone through my desk when I was off getting champagne to impress her. She must have sent it to dear old daddy and then internally laughed her fucking head off as I'd fallen for the oldest trick in the book.

I've been a fool.

A stupid fucking fool.

She didn't come to me last night because she wanted me. No, oh no, she was playing me just like she has so many times before. The perfect Capulet princess was once more screwing me over, only I was too much of an idiot to see it.

Too desperate to get my dick wet.

I snarl, picking my phone up, sending some of my men to go get her.

I'll have her fucking dragged here if that's what it takes.

But she will come.

She will answer for what she's done.

The rest of us sit in silence. Waiting.

And when the door opens and the beauty appears I glare at her. She looks battered. She looks awful. Her face is strewn with tears. She's physically shaking.

She gulps as she looks back at me, wrapping her arms around herself. In truth I've never seen her look so vulnerable, so broken, and my heart reacts. It takes all my strength not to wrap my arms around her. Not to comfort her. Not to forgive her.

My anger flares. My fury rages. Because once again that stupid weakness inside me is letting this she-devil off Scott free.

"It was you." I snarl.

She winces. "Roman, let me explain…"

I grab her by the throat, she gasps, struggling, but it makes no difference, and I haul her across the room, throwing her onto the table. Her body slams into the wood and everyone looks between us in confusion.

"We found our mole." I state.

"Roman." She gasps trying to get up, pleading with me with those devastating eyes. They say the devil will be beautiful, but no one told me how much I would want her.

I growl back wrenching her head up by her hair. "Do you realise what you've done? Do you realise how many people are dead because of you?"

"I didn't mean…" She begins.

"Didn't mean what?" I retort. "Didn't mean to hurt anyone? What else did you expect? What else do you think your father would have done?"

"I didn't know…"

"You almost killed Sofia." I shout. "You almost killed my sister."

"I'm so sorry." She sobs.

"No." I snap back. "That's not good enough. Not this time." I pull my knife and start cutting at her clothes, wrenching them off her.

She shrieks trying to stop me but it makes no difference. "You want to act like a whore Rose. You want to behave like one then fine…"

She whimpers more as I rip the fabric from her, as I expose more of her to everyone sat around. I haven't even got a plan right now, I'm just so fucking angry and I need to make her pay.

Make myself pay too.

I need to realise that this is as much my fault as it is Rose's because I fell for her tricks. I knew what she was, what she was capable of, and yet still I willingly let her charm me, just like the first time around.

But not anymore. No, now I see her for what she is. The harlot that she is.

She starts hyperventilating. She starts heaving as if she's having a full panic attack.

A part of me wants to stop, wants to comfort her but I know that's the weak part. The stupid part. The lovesick part that allowed her to trick me in the first place. I have to bury that part.

I have to kill that part off because I realise now how much I am betraying us all by still feeling that.

"Fuck her." I say stepping back.

"What?"

I look up meeting the eyes of my men. "She behaves like a whore, then she gets treated like one." I state yanking her up, wrenching the last of her clothes from her, and they all stare at her body because how could they not? She's beautiful. Devastatingly so.

"The great Capulet whore." I spit.

She sobs harder, tries to hide herself, tries to curl herself into my body as if I might just protect her.

Only I won't this time.

Not anymore.

I shove her back onto the table. She cries out as she slams once more into the wood.

My men look at me for approval and then they're on her like rabid animals, grabbing her, wrenching her around.

She screams more. She cries out begging me to make them stop. I can see the panic in her eyes and for the first time I know it's real. She's actually afraid.

I clench my fists, forcing myself to do nothing. She deserves this. She deserves everything she gets. She got my men killed. She got hundreds of innocent people killed and for what?

The door crashes open. Sofia runs into the room before I can stop her.

"What the fuck are you all doing?" She shouts, yanking one man off and then another.

In truth they've barely gotten started. I pull my sister back and she swings a right hook hitting me in the jaw.

"She deserves this." I shout. "She's the reason you were attacked. She gave them the location."

Sofia spits something back but in my anger I don't hear the words.

She grabs Rose, tries to help her stand but she's in such a state she's hysterical now. Her chest is heaving, she's gasping for breath like she can't breathe.

"It's okay." Sofia says. "No one is going to hurt you."

"That's not the case." I spit back.

Sofia glares at me.

And then Rose speaks. Sobs. I barely hear the words but they reverberate through me anyway. It can't be true. What she just said. There's no way.

Sofia's jaw drops in horror.

We both look at each other like we don't know what to do and Rose sobs harder repeating the same thing over and over again.

"They stole our baby. They stole her."

ROMAN

The doctor sedated her. She was in such a state we had no choice. Sofia stayed with her while I've been sat like a mad man in my office.

I've pulled up every record I can find. I've checked every hospital but there's nothing. If Rose really did have a child then where the hell is the evidence of it?

Ben's sat opposite me. Watching. Like he's too dumbstruck by all of this to even speak and a part of me is wondering how I'm even functioning.

The door opens and Sofia slips inside.

"She's asleep." She says to no one in particular.

I grunt back. It's not like she's suddenly forgiven. She still fucked me over. Fucked *us* over.

"Roman." She says softly putting her hand on mine. "We need to talk about this."

"No we don't." I snap keeping my eyes fixed on the computer in front of me.

"Yes we do. If it's true then it could explain a lot."

"*If* it's true." I state. "But so far there's no evidence. Nothing to prove it. If Rose Capulet did have a baby don't you think this city would know? It's very foundations are built on gossip and scandal."

"Not just a baby." She says. "Your baby."

"You don't know that." I mutter.

"Who's else would it be?" She says yanking my arm, forcing me to tear my eyes off the screen and look at her.

"It could be anyone's." I say but I know it's not true. Something already tells me that this is it. This is the answer to everything. And yet it doesn't explain why she stayed. If she was pregnant why did she not tell me? Why did she not leave with me?

I snarl, rubbing my face with my palms.

"Where have you looked?" Sofia asks.

"What?"

"Where have you looked?" She says again.

I glance at the screen. "The hospitals. Clinics. You name it. I've hacked into them all. There's nothing."

"Well there wouldn't be if she was under a false name or if she had the child at home." Sofia says.

I raise an eyebrow. I guess that makes sense.

"Try birth certificates. And not just for Verona, try the nearby cities. If they're going to hide it they'll have registered the child somewhere else."

I smirk at her wisdom. "Since when did you become so smart?"

"Since you became an idiot." She snaps back.

I shake my head. I know she's talking about what I did, with Rose, with stripping her like that, but I won't apologise. She might have been manipulated into what she did but she still kept this secret.

She kept our child a secret.

I have to take a deep breath, to calm myself again because every time I think about it, that for six years she's been hiding this from me, it makes my blood boil.

My child is out there.

My child that I never even knew existed.

I pull up a new screen and try searching for any and all births that might just fit the parameters. There are thousands. I run a system, searching for Rose's name. Searching for my name too. I don't expect anything to come back but it does. Barely two minutes after the scan begins it pings.

I pull up the record. My heart thumping in my chest. The words as plain as day. It's logged from a city two hours away.

Lara Marie Capulet. Mother Rose Capulet. And father... I gulp seeing nothing but a dash.

I look at the date, mentally calculating it even though I know I don't need to. I know exactly what it means. That Rose was pregnant before I left. That maybe even the last few times we were together that life was growing inside her. Did she know? Was she aware?

They may not have put my name on the certificate but it makes no difference. This child is mine. I know it. I know she's my daughter as much as I know it's oxygen in my lungs.

"Where is she?" Sofia asks.

I glance at her. She's peering over my shoulder.

"Rose said they stole her." I murmur sounding more like a ghost than a human as it sinks in. Lara. My daughter's name is Lara. "I think Ignatio must be keeping her away somewhere." I add gritting my teeth.

Ignatio has my child. My daughter. I clench my fists, driving my nails into my palms. We know enough about his activities for me to be fearful of what he might do to her. But she's leverage right now. She must be.

I pick up my phone, call Turner, and start shooting off questions. We've been watching everything Ignatio has been doing. We've been tracking his money too. Linking most of it back to his illegal businesses.

But then Turner reminds me of the not too inconsiderable sum that goes to a charitable organisation each month. An organisation no one seems to have heard of. An organisation we all thought was a way he laundered his dirty money. I narrow my eyes. Is that where my daughter is?

The only details we have is a registered mailbox. There's no address beyond that. I get Turner to go there, to all but break into the damn place and find out anything he can.

He calls back nearly an hour later and this time he has an address.

"Is that where she is?" Sofia asks.

I look back from the scrawled note I've just made to her face. "Let's go find out."

She nods looking across at Ben. "Should one of us stay? In case Rose wakes?"

I'll admit right now Rose is not my concern. She's safe. She's asleep. I know exactly where she is. While out there somewhere my daughter is in danger.

Fuck, *my* daughter. I *have* a daughter.

"No." I say grabbing my gun. I don't care if I have to shoot every fucker between me and Lara, I'll do what's necessary to get my child out. To get her safe.

"I'll get Holden to guard her door." Ben says.

I pause for a second. Holden was in the room, was there when I stripped her. I don't want him or anyone else thinking that's still an option.

"No one touches her." I snarl.

Ben nods quickly.

"No one does anything to her. No one goes in her room. No one even speaks to her till I'm back. The door is locked and that's how it remains."

Ben meets my gaze and I don't wait to hear his reply. Sofia is giving me a look that tells me she thinks I've seriously fucked up. Like I don't know it. Like that's not bloody obvious.

I storm from the room, calling as many of the men as I can. If this is a fight then by god am I going to win it.

The vans pull up outside. It's late afternoon now but the heat is still stifling. I wipe my brow, give my sister one final look and then I clamber in, leaving her and everyone else to follow.

ROMAN

The building is dilapidated at best. The windows are dirty. The front door has paint chipping off it. I look around at the barbed wire fencing. It looks half derelict down this non-descript street. There's no one outside but the amount of cameras about says enough.

It is guarded. It is watched.

I pull my laptop, in less than a minute I've hacked in and put the system on a loop. Anyone looking now will see the videos from yesterday not anything live - and by the time they notice, we'll be long gone.

"Ready?" Ben says beside me.

"Never more so." I reply.

Sofia is to my right. She doesn't say anything but I can see from her face that she's just as on edge as me.

I give the order. Let my men go around the back securing the outside because I won't risk anyone escaping that way. Once the affirmative crackles through my ear piece I walk right up to the front door, as if I've been invited, and I kick it open.

Someone yells. Someone else screams. I raise my gun making instant eye contact with a middle aged woman who's skin is mottled pink like she's spent her entire life on the booze.

"Where is Lara?" I snarl.

The woman blinks confused. "Who are you?"

I tilt my head, I've not even covered my face. Not thought to. "Where is the girl?" I say.

She gulps looking between us, focusing mostly on the gun in my hand and then she's pointing to the uncarpeted, rickety staircase. As I take her in I realise this woman might be all my daughter has ever known. She might even think she's her mother. I can't just storm up there and get her like this. She'll never trust me. She might never forgive me.

"Go get her now." I state.

She nods and, as she half stumbles away, I shout after her.

"The house is surrounded so don't try anything."

Sofia, Ben, and I stand taking in the room. There aren't any toys out. There's nothing remotely child friendly either. The furniture looks old, moth infested. The wallpaper is peeling. The air is musty. This is the environment my child has been brought up in? Ignatio lives like a king and yet my child has been growing up in squalor.

I snarl as I realise that for six years she's existed like this. Lived like this.

And I've been completely unaware.

We turn at the sound of the woman returning. In her hand she's gripping the arm of a little girl, barefoot, dressed in grubby unicorn pyjamas. She's staring at us wide eyed. Petrified.

But as I look at her all I can see is Rose. Her eyes, her face. Her dark hair.

My lips curl as I holster my gun and get down on my knees before her.

My daughter. My child.

"Who are you?" My daughter half whispers.

Her eyelashes are so long. Her cheeks are scattered with freckles. She looks like an angel. I blink realising that I'm just staring at her.

"I'm your father." I say.

The woman holding her gasps, before yanking her arm in shock and my daughter yelps as she falls back roughly into her side.

"Let her go." I snarl.

"No. We have strict orders…"

"I don't give a shit what your orders are." I snap. "You will let my daughter go."

She shakes her head. "Montague scum." She spits.

I don't think, I just react. It's stupid. Reckless. Damned fucking idiotic to do it but she has my child and in that moment that's where my head is at. Protecting her. Getting her back.

I reach for my gun, pull the trigger, blast a hole right through her damned blackened heart.

Lara screams. Covering her face. Cowering.

Sofia springs up beside me and scoops her up into her arms. "It's okay. It's okay. You're safe now."

Lara is sobbing. Crying. And as I put the gun away I know it's my fault. Christ, I'm fucking this up already.

"I'm sorry." I say quickly. "But I needed to protect you."

She's got tears down her cheeks, more than anything I want to brush them away but I don't want to crowd her, to cross any further lines, than I already have.

Lara blinks at me wide eyed. "She wasn't very nice to me." She mutters.

"That lady?" I reply.

Lara looks at her, at the bloodied mess, and then back at me visibly paling. "She was mean, even when I wasn't naughty."

I let out a low breath. "No one is ever going to be mean to you again." I say.

"Are you taking me away?" She sounds so hopeful.

"Yes." I smile.

"To a castle? Like they do in fairy tales?"

I let out a laugh. Sofia laughs too.

Before I can think not to I've pulled her from my sister's arms and I'm holding her to me.

My daughter. My child.

I kiss her forehead. Breath in her scent. "Just like a fairy tale." I reply before carrying her out.

WHEN WE GET BACK TO THE HOUSE I LET SOFIA TAKE HER TO PICK out a room. We have so many here that I wanted to give her a choice. While they're gone I check on Rose. She's asleep, still heavily sedated by the looks of it, and though my heart twists at what she went through, I still feel it, my anger, my fury that she never told me.

That she concealed this from me.

If she'd come to me, if she'd admitted it when I first returned, I would have helped her. I would have done everything in my power to get our daughter back. I just don't understand why she didn't.

I guess she'll have to answer that when she wakes.

I turn shutting the door and lock it once more.

Silently I make my way through the house to look for my daughter. She's picked a turret room. One with a ridiculous four poster bed. A throw back to when this house was built hundreds of years ago.

When she sees me leant against the doorframe she grins.

I smile back glancing around. "This is a good choice." I say.

"Princesses always live in towers." Lara states.

"Well I'm not well versed on how princesses live so you might have to teach me." I reply.

She nods with a serious look on her face. "Okay. But you'll need to pay attention."

Sofia starts laughing. I laugh too. And that ice in my heart seems to melt more.

"Are you hungry?" I ask.

"Starving." Lara says and her eyes light up with expectation.

"Want to come have some food?"

"Yes please daddy." She says and my heart leaps. Daddy. She called me daddy. She's barely known me a few hours and yet already she sees me as that?

I hold out my hand and she takes it before giving me a hug around my waist. "Thank you."

"For what?"

"For rescuing me."

I hug her back, meeting Sofia's teary eyes over her head. Christ what has my child been through to be reacting like this?

"Come on." Sofia says. "Before Ben eats all the cake."

"Cake? There's cake?" Lara gasps.

"Of course there is." I say.

She gives me the biggest grin and I scoop her up. I know she's more than capable of walking. She's almost six years old but still, I want to hold her, to keep her close to me and never let her go.

As I carry her down I make a mental note of the things I need to buy. She needs clothes. Shoes. Toys too. When we've eaten I'll let her pick whatever she wants online and send one of my men to go get it.

Because from now on my daughter will want for nothing.

ROSE

The pain is unbearable. My skin is dripping with sweat. I can barely think. Can barely register what is happening but I know I'm on some sort of drugs only they're not having any effect.

I scream again. I thrash but nothing helps.

A nurse tries to soothe me. Another nurse flits about.

My mother and father stand to the side watching like they want no part of this. Like even in this moment, no, especially in this moment, I disgust them.

The machine keeps beeping through it all. That same piercing sound that seems to rip right through everything.

"Okay Rose." A man says drawing my attention away. He's knelt between where my legs are up. Where they're strapped into stirrups and my entire lower half is exposed. "I need you to start pushing."

I shake my head. I can't do it. I won't do it. Something tells me that the moment I let this child out of me, the moment it's no longer protected by my body then I'll no longer be able to protect it. That it'll be at my family's mercy. Just like I am.

"Push now."

"No." I wail, even as the contractions writhe through me. Even as instinct takes over and my body does it anyway.

"Good job. And again. Another strong push."

I shake my head. My face is streamed with tears and sweat.

I can't do this. I won't do this.

They're going to take my child.

I know it.

In my heart I know exactly what my father has planned because why else would he have changed his mind? Why else would he not have forced me into terminating it?

"Come on Rose." My mother says taking my hand, finally giving up the whole observer part she's been playing since my waters broke.

"Please…" I beg as she soothes me. As another contraction racks through me and I feel the mass of something start to push out. Start to move its way out of me.

"I can see the head." The doctor says. "You're crowning now. Keep pushing."

I wail, I weep, I sob as my body releases my poor child into the world.

A baby's scream echoes out. High pitched. My heart clenches as I hear it, as I hear my child. My poor innocent child.

"It's a girl." Someone says but I don't know who. I don't care. In that moment I'm staring at the mass of towels in the midwife's arms. At the tiny pink legs that are kicking out in protest and the very top of the head of my child that I can't even make our properly.

My child. My daughter.

They cut the cord. I try to sit up but the stirrups are still strapped around my legs holding me in place.

My mother steps up taking my baby and she frowns staring at her.

"Please." I say.

She looks at me, at my hands as I desperately reach out, as I beg her to let me see my child, to let me hold her.

And then my father steps up, out of the shadows, taking her from my mother and my daughter screams louder than ever as if she can sense the danger she's in.

"Please." I cry again. Trying to move, trying to get out of this damned bed.

He meets my gaze then looks back at my child as if she's a piece of dirt on his shoe.

"Father...."

He turns as I speak, starts walking away, and in that moment I lose it entirely.

I scream, I fight, I thrash against the damn stirrups not caring if I break my legs, not caring if I seriously injure myself.

I won't let them take her.

I'll fight to my last breath if that's what I takes.

I lash out, sending a tray of something crashing to the floor. I'm not even finished giving birth, there's still the afterbirth to go. I still need to be stitched back up and yet none of that matters. The only thing that does is the fragile life my father is stealing away from me.

One of the nurses steps up, I feel the jab of the syringe, feel the prick as she rams it into my neck and as the awful drugs slip into my system I see him walking away. I see him disappearing out of the room with my daughter.

And I know in that moment that I'll never get her back.

That she's lost to me.

Gone before I could even do anything to stop it.

THE MINUTE I WAKE I KNOW I'M NOT IN MY BED. I'M NOT IN MY home. My mind flickers back to yesterday and everything feels hazy at best. Someone sedated me, I remember that much, I guess the drugs are still in my system.

The sun is shining like it's a new day, like I slept the entire night. I feel disorientated. Unsteady.

But I know where I am, somehow instinct already tells me.

And I know he's here.

Watching me. I can feel his energy, his anger even now.

I sit up. My arms shake as I force the muscles to move. I'm wearing borrowed clothes. Sofia's by the guess of it.

He's sat in a chair, one leg thrown across the other with his ankle on his knee. Glaring.

"How did I get here?" I ask. I can see it's not from the kindness of his heart that I'm where I am, still in the Montague house.

"Sofia carried you up. You were hysterical. We had a doctor check you. You've got some nasty bruises but nothing serious."

I don't reply. I don't know how to. It feels like he's still raging about what I did. How I betrayed him. I drop my gaze with my shame hitting me at how he'd stripped me, how he'd treated me, how he'd almost let his men use me.

He leans forward in his chair, his knuckles white with the intensity of his grip. "Tell me Rose, how long were you planning on keeping Lara from me?"

"What?" I gasp as my stomach begins doing actual somersaults. I didn't tell him. I know I didn't. And yet somehow he knows.

"My daughter." He snarls. "How long were you planning on keeping her existence from me?"

I shake my head, my body trembling as he gets up, stalking towards me.

"You had no right…" He begins.

"No you don't." I cry back cutting him off. Scrambling up. Forcing myself to move. To respond. "You made it more than clear what you thought. You made it more than clear what you wanted me to do."

"What are you talking about?" He snarls.

"You." I half scream. "You didn't want to know. You made it clear you wanted me to get rid of her so you don't get to come back now and play the hero."

"Rose." He says screwing his face up. "You never even told me you were pregnant."

"Yes I did." I reply. I'm practically hysterical again now but I can't calm down. I can't. My heartrate feels erratic, I feel so close to completely and utterly losing it. "I called you. I called you over and over. You just ignored me. And then when I messaged you, you…" I shut my eyes, blinking back the tears at what he'd accused me of. What he'd insinuated. "You left. You washed your hands of me. Of us. You don't get to come back now and say otherwise."

"Rose that's not what happened. I called you. I messaged you. You didn't respond. I told you where to meet me. I fucking told you." He shouts the last bit slamming his fist into the wall.

I stare at him wildly for a minute.

He never did that. He never once said anything like that.

"You think I would have stayed?" I reply. "You think I wouldn't have followed you?"

His face tells me exactly what he believes; that I deliberately cut him off, that I was the one who chose this awful life instead of being with him.

He shakes his head, looking away for a moment. "Why wasn't she with you? Why was she locked away? Why does no one even know about her? She's your daughter for fucksake."

My arms wrap around me as if it could somehow comfort me from the rest of what I'm about to say, the truth I'm admitting to. I can't even look at him right now as the words come out.

"They took her from me as soon as she was born. I didn't even get to hold her. To see her." My tears stream down my face as I admit it, as I feel it too, all the pain, all the torture of what had happened that day.

The grief and the loss that I've never gotten over. The longing that's twisted inside me for years, festering into something bitter, something twisted.

I sink onto the end of the bed as it feels like my legs might give way.

"Who?" He asks pulling me back to face him, narrowing his eyes that are flashing bloody murder right now.

"Who do you think?" I reply. My parents of course, though I know it was my father's doing.

"And nobody knew?"

"No." I reply. "I never got much of a bump but my parents put out that I was too broken at Tybalt's death to leave the house. And as soon as she was born they did everything they could to hide the evidence and make sure my marriage to Paris went ahead."

"So Paris never knew?"

I shake my head. "No one did." I half whisper. "I kept it secret and my father kept her like a weapon to use against me. To ensure I did whatever he wanted."

His face reacts to that. Pure fury at the fact our child was held to ransom this entire time.

"How did you find out?" I ask.

"You were hysterical." He says. "You started muttering about our child. About someone stealing our child so we looked into it."

"I thought all the records were expunged."

He shakes his head. "Not all. There has to be a birth certificate doesn't there? After that it was a case of tracking where she was from your father's activities."

I look away in frustration. Why hadn't I thought of that? Could I have figured it out? Got her out that way? I know the answer already. That my father would have known, that for me, I'd only have put her in more danger.

"So what now?" I ask quietly. Fearfully too. Roman has all the cards now and once again I have nothing.

"Lara stays with me. No more hiding her in the shadows. No more pretending she doesn't exist."

"You have her?" I gasp.

He nods back with his eyes blazing. "She's safe now. She's going to be brought up as a Montague."

"No." I gasp, grasping at his shirt and he stares at me like I'm mad. "Roman please. Don't take her from me. Please, I'm begging you."

"What the fuck are you talking about?" He says confused.

"Please. I'll do anything, just don't take her away."

He shakes his head, gripping my shoulders as I cling to him. "Rose, you're her mother. Do you really think I'd be that cruel?"

I blink at him but his words don't register. He still looks so impossibly furious right now and I know what he's capable of. How ruthless he can be when he wants to.

"I'm not your father Rose. I'm not going to use your own child against you."

My tears start to stream. I'm shaking again as I desperately try to understand what the hell he's saying. He pulls me into his arms and starts soothing me as if he's not angry, as if he's not furious at me.

"That's why you did it, isn't it?" He says. "That's why you told your father where the compound was."

I nod. "I'm so sorry. I know I was betraying you but I had to. I had to try and save her. They've had her for almost six years. Six years. I couldn't see any other way."

"It's okay." He says.

"No, it's not." I sob into his chest feeling a lifetime worth of pain and grief hitting me. "It's not."

"I'd never have walked away." He murmurs. "I'd never have left you."

I don't reply. I just let him hold me and for the first time it feels like we might just understand each other. That it finally all makes sense.

He pulls away just enough to lift my chin up.

"Do you want to see her?"

My eyes widen. "She's here?"

"She's outside in the gardens. I can take you to her if you'd like?"

I nod wanting that more than anything.

ROSE

We walk down through the house. As we get to the conservatory I pause, ahead I can see her, playing with Sofia. Her hair is loose instead of the usual pigtails. Her laughter fills the air as she runs. As Sofia chases her.

I feel a flash of jealousy at that. That Sofia is with my daughter. I know it's absurd. I know it's unwarranted but I can't help it in that moment.

"You okay?" Roman asks quietly.

I gulp. I've waited so long for this. So incredibly long. I blink trying to get some sort of hold over my emotions.

"I just…" I trail off. "What does she know of me?"

He frowns. "What do you mean?"

"What did they tell her about me? About her mum?"

"You've never met her?" He replies.

"No."

He screws his face up. "What the fuck?"

"They wouldn't let me." I state. "They kept promising but never actually followed through. The most I got was seeing her in the park but I could never get close because her carers were there and the one time I tried she was rushed away before I could even get near."

"Why the hell did you put up with that?" He snarls.

"You think I had a choice? You think I didn't try? I fought as much as I could but then my father talked about sending her away and I couldn't risk it."

His face softens. He shakes his head muttering.

"What does she know? Does she know who you are?" I ask.

"Yes." He says. "She's confused. Understandably so. I didn't get why she wasn't asking for you but I guess that makes sense now."

"We have to protect her."

"That's exactly what I'm going to do." He replies. "I won't have anyone using my child, threatening her either."

"I'm sorry." I half whisper it, ashamed that I wasn't able to do anything. That ultimately I'd failed her right from the minute she was born.

"No, you don't get to apologise." He says.

I flinch because I know he's right. I should be doing more than simply apologising. I'm her mother for fucksake.

His hand cups my face, he lifts my chin to make look up at him. "You are as much a victim in this as Lara is." He says.

"You really believe that?" My hope swells. I hold my breath as he meets my eyes.

"Yes Rose. I'm just sorry that I didn't see it sooner."

I give an awkward smile but I'm not sure what to say. How to even respond to that.

"Come on. You've come this far." He says. "It's time you properly met her."

I gulp, swallowing down the lump that's building in my throat. I can do this, I tell myself but I'm afraid I'll be a blubbering mess.

Roman opens the French doors and both Sofia and Lara come to a stop. Lara smiles at Roman and then looks at me.

We've never made eye contact. Every time I've seen her in the park I've looked away, I've had too, but as I stare at her I realise she has my eyes. Roman's face shape, but my eyes.

"Lara." I whisper her name, but no noise comes out, I just silently mouth the word.

She tilts her head a little then looks back at Roman. Already I can see that she trusts him. And that feels like another stab right into my heart.

"Lara, this is your mummy." He says.

She bites her lip, frowning, and looks back at me.

"Hi Lara." I say, feeling stupid, feeling like I should have something better to say. Something more.

"They said you were away." She says. "Are you back now?"

"I am." I say. "And I'm not going anywhere again."

She steps closer, clearly she's hesitating but as Roman holds out his hand she takes it readily and he leads her closer to me.

"What happened to your face?" She asks.

I frown running my hand over my cheek, feeling the bruising, the cuts from all the fighting I've been doing. "I… it doesn't matter." I reply not sure what else to say. I can hardly tell my child what I've been through, what I've done just to get this one moment right here.

"Lara." Roman says. "From now on you're going to live here with me, like a proper family."

She frowns more, looking at me. "What about you? Do you live here too?"

"I…" I glance at Roman. This is his house. The Montague house. I don't even know if he wants me here, I can hardly say yes despite how much I don't want to leave her.

"Your mum will be here as much as she can." Roman says which seems to answer it. That he doesn't want me here, that Lara will be in his custody. That I'll be a part time mother at best.

I fight the bile that rises in me. It's still better than what I had. I have to remind myself of that. At least this way I have some sort of a relationship instead of nothing at all.

"Why can't you stay too?" She asks.

"Lara." Roman says gently in a tone that already makes him sound more like a parent than I ever have. "Your mum and I have some things to work out. But she'll be here as much as you want."

"Promise?" She asks.

He smiles holding his little finger up. "Pinky promise."

She grins wrapping her finger with his and shaking it.

"How about I sort some cake?" Sofia says.

I'd almost forgotten she was here and as I look at her she's giving me a sympathetic look that I know I don't deserve and it takes all my focus to stop the tears prickling my eyes from falling in this moment.

"Cake would be good." I reply.

"Can we have chocolate cake? That's my favourite." Lara says.

"We can have whatever cake you want Larabell." Sofia says laughing.

She's given her a nickname already?

Lara laughs as Sofia ruffles her hair. God, she fits with them. It's been barely more than a day since he found out she exists and already Lara is slotting into the Montague household and further away from me than ever.

"Why don't you go with Aunty Sofia? Help her cut the slices." Roman says and Lara nods following Sofia into the house before I can object, so I'm forced to just watch her, my daughter, disappear away from me.

"Rose." Roman says gently.

"What?" I say more aggressively than I mean to.

"I know how you're feeling…"

"You know nothing." I snap.

He sighs. "I'm not taking her from you."

"But she's staying here with you. She's already comfortable with you and Sofia's even given her a nickname…" I'm ranting I know but all my pent up emotions are coming out like a tsunami I can't contain. "I'm her mother."

"And I'm not denying that." Roman states. "If I had my way I'd move you in too. Have you both here but I know you'd refuse."

I blink, shocked at his admittance. "What?"

"I meant what I said. I'm not going to keep her from you. You're her mother. She needs to get to know you and right now this is all new territory. Her head is spinning from the last twelve hours. We have to take this slowly for her sake as well as ours."

I know he's right. She must be as messed up as me from all of this so I nod agreeing because what else can I do?

"Trust me in this Rose. I'm not going to screw you over."

I grit my teeth realising that I have to trust him. I don't have any choice because he's got all the power but right now I want to, I want to believe him so badly. I just hope I'm not making another mistake.

"Come on. Let's go join them." He murmurs.

I follow him out but as we head down the hallway I voice the words spinning in my head. "I'd say yes. If it wouldn't endanger her more, I'd say yes to staying here."

He pauses. "Why would it endanger her?"

"My father. If he knows you have her, if he knows I'm here…"

He lets out a huff. "I can manage him."

"He's dangerous." I state.

"I know." He replies. "But aren't you done having him dictate your life?"

"Yes." Of course I'm sick of it. I'm twenty six years old for fucksake. Most teenagers have more freedom than I do.

"Then stay here. We'll be careful but Lara needs you."

I want him to say he needs me. I want him to say it more than anything but he doesn't. He just opens the door to the kitchen and I see them there, laughing and scoffing cake.

I smile at the scene before me. As much as my heart feels like it's breaking, I have my daughter and that alone is enough.

It will be enough.

ROSE

We spend the day together. Me, Roman, Sofia, and Lara. The whole thing feels surreal to the extent I keep wanting to pinch myself, to make sure this isn't some dream.

Too often I seem to catch Roman's eye as Lara says something, or does something, but I'm quick to drop it. I can't look at him right now because all I feel is confusion and guilt.

He's so natural with her. So confident too. I don't know how to tally this with the man who betrayed me six years ago. The man who essentially told me to kill our child. To murder the girl who he so happily accepts now.

He said he didn't know so how does he explain those messages? Those replies? Because it wasn't like I imagined that.

After dinner Roman and I both read Lara a bedtime story. She seems to be into fairy tales and I take my time reading her a simplified version of Cinderella. When she drifts off we just sit there, staring at her, like we're both in some sort of trance.

And then Roman gets up quietly, signalling for me to follow.

I creep out behind him and he shuts the door. He has a man guarding it. We know the house is safe and yet he's not taking any chances and for that alone I'm grateful.

"We need to talk." He says once we're far enough out of earshot.

My heart sinks. I don't know why but it does. Already my head tells me that this is it, this is the moment where he lays down the law, when I can be with her, how much time he's allowing me to have.

I nod biting my tongue ready for whatever this is.

We walk into what looks like a drawing room. All around are paintings, faces of the Montague Family, all testament to their heritage, their history. It's odd to be here, to be even seeing them, considering who I am.

I sit opposite him, trying to ignore the butterflies. Trying to ignore the trepidation.

For a few moments he doesn't speak. He just seems to watch me until it becomes practically unbearable.

"Were you ever going to tell me about Lara?" He asks.

I hesitate before replying. "I, I don't know." I admit. "I was scared too. Scared of what your reaction would be."

"Because you thought I wanted her aborted?"

"Yes."

He shakes his head slightly at that.

"I'm sorry." I blurt out. "I'm sorry I betrayed you, that I gave my father that address. I just, I was trying to save her. I couldn't face the thought of her growing up in this environment. Of living the life I have. I wanted to save her. That's all I wanted."

He narrows his eyes for a second. "And now?"

"Now what?"

"Lara is safe here so what do you want now Rose?"

346

I gulp. In truth I don't know. My life is in freefall. I can hardly go back to my house, can hardly expect my father not to take some sort of action against me.

"I don't know." I admit.

He frowns like he expected something else, like he was hoping for some other answer. "Fine. You can stay here as long as you need."

"I want to help." I state.

He shakes his head. "I don't think I can trust you. Not yet."

I guess that's fair considering everything I've done.

"Focus on Lara. Focus on our daughter." He says.

"I need to go home." I reply. "If I'm staying here then I need to get my things and my dog too."

"I can send a car. They can grab anything you want."

I narrow my eyes. "You mean you won't let me leave?"

"No." He says. "That's not what I meant."

"Then why can't I go?" I half hiss.

He gets up moving to sit beside me. I shift with the memory of what Darius tried suddenly fresh on my mind.

"We don't trust each other." Roman says. "It's to be expected. But I need you to believe that I'm not trying to screw you over. You're free to leave whenever you want. I won't force you to stay. But I want you here, not just for Lara's sake but for mine too."

"What?" I half whisper as my heart seems to do some sort of flip.

He takes my hand and despite myself, my body still reacts to it, to him touching me. To his skin against mine.

"I know what Paris did. I know how he hurt you." He says gently.

I gulp, looking away.

"I know I fucked up too." He adds. "I know what I did the other day was reprehensible but I was just so angry. And that doesn't excuse it. Nothing excuses it. I just wish I'd known, I wished you'd come to me, I wished you told me about Lara."

I shut my eyes fighting the wave of emotion that's once more threatening to overwhelm me. "You told me to get an abortion. How could I now admit that I didn't, and worse, to admit that my father's been using our child as a weapon to make me do whatever he wants."

"I never said that." He growls before taking a deep breath as if he's trying to calm himself as well "I never said that Rose, I'd never have reacted like that either."

I can feel it, my tears threatening to spill over again.

"I don't know what you want me to say." I reply.

"You don't have to say anything." He states. "It's not about words, it's about us learning to trust each other again, about us rebuilding what we had but this time ensuring no one can fuck it up."

"You, you want us to be together?" I half whisper.

He gives me a half smile. "Don't you?"

Yes. In so many ways I still do. Because no matter how much we've hurt each other I still love this man more than anything else.

But he's right.

We can't just start again and expect everything to work out.

"I need time." I murmur.

He squeezes my hand. "We both do. We've both done awful things. Have hurt each other. We're not the same as we were six years ago, so much has changed but I want to make us work."

I nod, staring at where his skin is touching mine. At where our fingers are now intwined. "What about my father? What about Darius?"

He draws himself up. "I'm sorting them."

"Darius is just as bad as he is."

"I know." Roman says and his eyes flash like he knows what he's done. But I guess he must. Sofia must have told him.

"He tried to blackmail me. To force me into some sort of relationship." I mutter as my cheeks heat with shame.

"I know. Sofia said. And I made him pay for that."

My eyes widen. "How?"

He grins. "Let's just say our Governor has had a hard lesson on what it means to touch what isn't his."

I bite my lip. Whatever he did I hope it works. And I hope to god it hurt him too.

"I'm going to bring them down Rose. Bring the whole system down. Darius will no longer be Governor and your father, if he survives, he'll be locked away for a very long time."

"You mean that?" I can't keep the hope from my voice as I speak the words.

He nods. "I'll make sure of it. They won't win this time around."

I feel the tears dropping. It's silly to be crying like this but I can't stop it. They've taken so much, from me, from us, from our daughter too.

I brush them away quickly but he still sees.

He sweeps my hair back, tucks it behind my ear. "She looks so much like you." He says.

"She has your face." I reply.

"And your freckles." He grins.

I smile back as my heart seems to melt with the look on his face. The way he's talking about our daughter.

"Promise me something." He murmurs.

"What?"

"Promise me no more secrets. From now on we're completely honest with each other. We don't hide anything. We always know what the other is thinking, is feeling. We confide in each other. We trust that we have each other's back."

"Okay." I whisper.

He kisses me lightly. Before I can register it he's pulled away but the ghost of where his lips pressed against mine still linger.

"It's been a long day. We should get some sleep." He says.

I swallow, nodding. He's right. It's been emotionally exhausting.

I follow him up to where my room is, as he holds the door open I wonder for a moment if he's going to stay here but, just as I turn, he shuts the door quietly leaving me alone.

For a while I pace. Though I'm exhausted I can't seem to switch off. I wash my face, brush my hair with the one left in the bathroom and pull on what I'm assuming is one of Sofia's T-shirts to sleep in.

As I clamber into the bed I realise this is the last place I want to be so I scoop up the duvet, wrapping it around me and sneak out into the corridor. I'm on the floor below Lara's. I take each step feeling like I'm doing something naughty. Something forbidden.

When I get to her room the man guarding it just nods, like he expected me almost.

I sneak in, shutting the door behind me quickly so the light doesn't disturb her and, as I creep up to her bed and make myself comfortable on the floor, I freeze.

Roman is here, the other side, watching me.

"I couldn't sleep." I whisper feeling like I need an explanation, a reason to be here. Some sort of justification to stop him from throwing me out.

He just smiles glancing back at Lara. "Me neither."

I lean back against the wall. It's cool in here with the aircon blasting and I wrap the duvet around me. He doesn't move. He just sits there the other side for a few moments.

And then he gets up, walks around the bed and for a minute I think he will tell me to go now. To leave. Only he doesn't, he sits down beside me.

I watch him warily. I'm nervous, unsure what to say. What to do.

I can hear his breathing. It's soft. Low against the soft hum of the AC.

I look back at our daughter who's somehow still sound asleep. I guess I'm grateful that so far, despite what she's been through, she doesn't seem to be having nightmares about it.

"Where was she?" I ask quietly.

"In a house by Charters."

I nod. I guess that makes sense. It's walking distance from there to the park. If I'd been smarter perhaps I could have followed them back, seen where they were keeping her and rescued her that way. I shake my head slightly, knowing that's nonsense.

"I did something." Roman murmurs.

"What?"

"When we were getting her, I killed a woman. Shot her right in front of Lara."

My head spins. I gasp looking at him.

"I just lost my temper. She was taunting me. She was holding Lara, she wouldn't let her go." He says like he's trying to justify it. Like he needs to.

"Do you regret it?" I ask.

He shakes his head. "Only that Lara saw. That she witnessed it."

"What did she do?"

He pauses, his eyes drifting to the sleeping child before us. "She told me that the woman was horrible to her."

I let out a deep breath. "So she wasn't scared?"

"She was but Sofia was there comforting her."

"That should have been me." The words leave my mouth before I can stop them. I hear the bitterness once more and start to apologise.

"No." Roman whispers. "You're right. If I'd known what I know now we would have gone together. Have rescued her together."

I meet his gaze, fighting the tears. His hand slips into mine and he squeezes it just a little as he says. "She's safe now. Safe with both of us."

ROSE

The next day I go to my house.

Bella half throws herself at me as I open the door and I only just manage to grab her in time. Mae comes rushing behind asking me where I've been, if I'm okay. I make up some excuse, then tell her that I'm going away for a bit, that I'm taking some time out and that she's free to stay in the house while I'm gone.

She gives me a sympathetic look and mutters something about the 'grieving process' as if I'm still heartbroken over Paris.

As if I ever was.

I don't reply. It's easier to let her think that.

I rush up to my room, pull out a suitcase and pack only the things I need. I know the men Roman sent with me will be more than happy to help carry all my stuff but right now my senses are on edge, being back here, being away from Lara makes me feel nervous, vulnerable even.

I toss in the clothes, jewellery, items that in truth could be replaced if needed but I'd still be upset to lose and then I haul the bag down the stairs before Mitch, steps in and takes it off me.

"Anymore?" He asks.

"Just some things from the living room." I reply.

He nods, wheeling the case out as I turn with Bella hot on my heels.

I scoop up her bed, make sure her favourite blanket and toys are inside and dump it by the front door then make my way into the living room. There's only a few things in here that I want, a book, my jacket, nothing overly important but as I walk in I freeze.

My mother is stood, staring out through the bifolds with her back to me.

"What are you doing here?" I ask.

She turns giving me a disappointed look. "Where have you been?"

"Away." I say through gritted teeth.

She lets out a low sigh. "How is that helpful Rose? You can't just have a paddy and then pull a disappearing act."

"I didn't have a paddy."

"No?" She says looking more disappointed. "So how do you excuse pointing a gun at your own father? You put a bullet in his bookcase."

I narrow my eyes, crossing my arms. "He bloody deserved it." I snap. "He's kept Lara from me from the last six years, dangling her like a fucking carrot."

She shakes her head, stepping closer to me. "Is that how you see it Rose?"

"Isn't it?" I retort. "The only reason he didn't force me to have an abortion was because he wanted her as leverage."

"No." She replies. "You're wrong there. It was me that wanted her as leverage."

My jaw drops. What the fuck?

"Excuse me?" I manage to say. I'm shaking with anger already and it's taking all of my self-control not to completely lose it.

She steps closer, that look of sympathy on her face. "What else was there to be done? You were acting out, misbehaving. I needed to ensure you wouldn't whore yourself out further. This was the best way to protect you, to protect us, to protect our family name."

"You…" I gasp as my heart clenches. I always thought she was on my side. Not entirely. Not a hundred per cent but at least she always seemed compassionate, caring.

"You think we didn't know? You think we didn't realise you were having sex with that boy. Carter told us, he'd seen you sneaking out, saw you with him." She states. "So we slipped some sleeping pills into your food, switched your phone out while you were asleep. Made sure all the numbers were correct, and every time he messaged you on the right one, we'd ensure you got it. We knew everything that was going on, right up to when he killed Tybalt."

I gulp stepping back, putting it all together. "You sent that message. You're the reason I thought he left us."

She lets out a sigh. "Yes Rose, I had no choice, I had to protect you."

"How was that protecting me?" I snarl.

She gives me a look like I'm an idiot. "He's a Montague. And besides, we had a future planned for you. A good future. With Paris. We needed to ensure your marriage went ahead. Calvin had ordered it and we weren't going to lose any of our standing because our daughter had grown up to be a slut."

She says it so calmly, so logically it's hard to put her actual words with the tone.

"Did you even stop and consider what I wanted?" I ask. "Did you ever even ask yourself that?"

She shakes her head. "You're being ridiculous. You never had a future with that boy. You would have ruined your life and ruined

355

ours too. It was better we took charge. Better we took control seeing as you'd lost leave of your senses."

"I trusted you." I reply. "Out of everyone, I trusted you."

She steps closer and my body reacts, my adrenaline spikes, my fists clench and it's all I can do not to launch myself at her and rip out her very eyeballs over what she's done to me.

"You were a fool Rose. You always have been." She states.

"I'm your daughter." I half scream. "How could you have treated me like that?"

She pulls herself up. "Because you were meant to be a boy. A true heir not some useless girl. I saw the look on Ignatio's face, I saw how disappointed he was, and then the doctors told me that I'd never be able to have anymore, that you'd ruined my body."

"I was a child, your child."

"You were unwanted." She says emotionlessly. "The only thing we could do was ensure we made a good match, ensure that our future was secure despite your failure. I wasn't going to sit by and watch you throw that away for all of us."

"You're not even a Capulet." I spit. "You married into this…"

"Yes I did." She replies. "And I will give my last breath to ensure our future, our legacy, our family comes out on top."

"You're fucking mad." I hiss. "All of you are."

She laughs and as I watch in horror she sees what I don't. That Bella is right there, within reaching distance. She snatches her up before I can stop her. Bella yelps, kicking out but, my mother's grip is too tight for her to get free.

"Let her go." I snap.

"You want your precious dog then you come with me. Come back to the house. Face your father like an actual adult and stop rebelling."

I shake my head. "Not a fucking chance. It's over. All of it. You don't get to play these games anymore, because I'm over them, over you."

"So what," She taunts. "You think you can just slink back to Roman Montague, that he'll protect you?"

"He will." I state.

"He used you Rose. I wasn't lying about that. He used you just like everyone does. And you want to know why? Because you're not worthy of love. You don't deserve it."

Her words sting, even though I know they shouldn't, even though I tell myself they mean nothing.

I hear the footsteps of Mitch behind me, and as I glance I see both him and Turner in my peripherals. Mitch has his gun up, pointed right at my mother.

I take a step forward, crowding her almost. "Give me my dog back."

"Not a fucking chance." She hisses.

Bella yelps as she tightens her grip, and I see red then, launching myself at her, flooring her as my body collides with hers. Bella jumps out of the way, suddenly freed, and yapping manically at the pair of us. My mother grabs for her, grabs for me, and I land one punch and then another, hearing the satisfying crunch as her nose breaks.

"You're the one who doesn't deserve love." I snarl. "You and my fucked up father."

Blood is streaming from her face. She tries to fight back but I doubt she's ever gotten her hands dirty before and in this moment all she seems to do is slap.

I get to my feet, scooping Bella up. "Go back to him. Go back to my father and tell him that I know everything. That I'm no longer his puppet. That I'm no longer a Capulet." I spit.

She crawls onto her front, one eye already swelling with the bruising. "You can't survive without us Rose. You have nothing without us, no money, no home, nothing."

I let out a laugh at that. Is that really the best she can do?

"Oh but you forget mother, you forced me to marry Paris Blumenfeld. And now that he's dead I get his entire estate. I should thank you for that, after all, you made me far richer than you are but I guess I more than earned it from all the beatings I took, all the abuse I suffered at his hands."

With that, I turn around and storm out, leaving Turner and Mitch to grab the bag by the door.

If either of them decided to just finish her off I doubt right now I'd even care.

ROMAN

I know she came back hours ago. I watched from the window as Mitch helped carry her bags in, while she had that tiny dog in her arms, and then Turner told me what had happened.

Who'd been there, waiting for her.

I thought about going to see her straight away, to check she's okay, but instead I stayed where I was, waiting.

The Rose I knew is gone. She's been gone a long time. But the Rose I thought she was, the conniving, treacherous creature, she also never existed, at least, not in the way I imagined.

I realise that I don't really know who she is. Who she's become.

And more than that, I don't think I know who I am anymore.

I came here, back to Verona with the intention of destroying everything, of burning it all to the ground, but especially burning her, making her pay.

Only now I feel the exact opposite. It feels like we have a chance, a future even.

And more than that, I have a daughter - I don't want to destroy this world, I want to build a new one, a safer one for Lara.

As I stand here, in the drawing room, thinking, I know that it's possible, that I can change course, that everything we've done so far will still give us what we want, revenge yes, but if I can take down Ignatio and Darius and all of the twisted shit they have going on, then my daughter really will be free.

And so will Rose.

I hear the tap at the door, grunt in reply, and only turn at the sound of her voice.

She looks pale. Tired. And yet at the same time that fire in her eyes, that fierce determined spark that I used to lose myself in, it's there, blazing brighter than ever.

"Are you okay?" I ask.

She nods, shutting the door, walking further into the room before sinking onto the couch.

"I heard what happened." I say.

"From Turner?" Rose guesses.

"Yes."

"Did he tell you everything?"

I frown. "He only told me your mother was there."

She lets out a sigh. "She was the one who did it. She swapped my phone out and tricked me into thinking it was you replying, that you wanted me to get rid of Lara."

My eyebrows raise. I know her father is a piece of shit, but I always thought her mother was more of a pawn in all this, that she alone was looking out for Rose at least on some level.

She palms her face with her hands. "I just... my family are so toxic. I know my father was but I didn't realise my mother was exactly the same."

"I'm sorry." I murmur sitting down beside her.

She leans into me and it's hard not to let my body respond as I feel her warmth, her softness.

"They'll know now. They'll know that I'm with you. That I'm staying here."

"Don't worry about it." I reply hearing the hint of fear in her voice. "I am more than a match for them."

"Please tell me that's the truth. Please tell me that you're not just saying that."

"I'm not Rose." I growl. "I spent the last six years planning this."

She nods shutting her eyes as if she's willing herself to believe it. I want to reach out, to touch her, to hold her properly but I don't. I realise that I don't even know how to be around her, how to act.

She lets out a sigh. Blinking. Looking at me with those beautiful eyes. "How is Lara?"

"She's good." I smile.

"She's settling in okay?"

"Ben took her shopping today, she's pretty much turned her bedroom into a fairy tale castle."

She snorts but then her face turns serious. "Is it safe to let her out? I don't want them…"

I place a finger on her lips. "Ssssh. It's safe. I wouldn't do anything to risk her life."

She glances down, her eyes looking at where I'm touching her.

"I love you Rose." I say before I can stop myself. "I never stopped loving you."

She blinks. "I know." She whispers back.

I lean in, capturing her face with my hand and kiss her softly. Only she pulls away, shaking her head.

"I can't." She says. "I, just, I need time, I need to clear my head with everything that's happened."

"It's okay." I say. "Take all the time you need. I'll be here."

She nods but I can see she's still not sure. Not convinced.

I take a deep breath leaning back into the couch beside her. I can take this slow too. I can show her through my actions that

I mean it, that I really am here, and I'm waiting for her, just as I always have.

"You broke my heart." She whispers pulling me out of my own thoughts. "When you left. You broke my heart."

"I'm so sorry, if I'd known, if I'd realised, I would have done everything I could, I would have fought with everything I had to make sure you were with me, to get you out."

She shuts her eyes, palming them with her hands. "I was a ghost I wasn't even a human being after you left. I just became this shell of a person. And all the while Lara was growing inside me and I wanted to be happy, I wanted to treasure this precious life we'd created, but I knew what would happen, I knew my parents were going to steal her."

I don't think then, I just act, wrapping my arms around her, comforting her the only way I know how. "It's okay." I murmur.

"It's not." She says. "None of it is okay. She deserved better than that. She deserved to grow up knowing who her parents were, knowing that she was loved, that she was wanted."

"She knows that now." I reply. "She knows she has a family now who love her."

She shakes her head, curling further into me. "I didn't want to marry him. I hated him but after what you did…" She stumbles on her words. "What I thought you did, I didn't fight it, I'd lost Lara then anyway, so I tried to replace you."

"You don't have to justify yourself Rose. You don't have to explain yourself. You did what you needed to survive."

She meets my gaze and that fierceness is there, alongside her pain, alongside her grief. "I want him dead. I want them all dead. For what they've done, for how they've hurt us."

I can't help the way my lips curl. "If that's what you want, then I'll kill him for you."

"For you too. And Lara. For all three of us, for our family."

I smile more. Our family. God, it feels good to hear that from her lips.

I hold her, keep her body pressed to mine, and when she falls asleep I don't move, I just lay there, with her curled into me and for a moment, for the most incredible moment in time it feels like everything is well in the world. It feels like finally everything is right.

I carry her to her room. She's still clearly exhausted by everything she's gone through. I tuck her into bed and for a fleeting moment I think of joining her.

Of sleeping beside her and holding her tight to me until she wakes.

But it feels like a step too far. It feels like even that is too much right now. We have to start right at the beginning, and to do that, to make her trust me, I have to prove that I'm not like every other arsehole in her life.

I kiss her forehead, watch her for a moment more and then walk away, letting the beauty sleep and instead I turn my focus to fulfilling that promise. To continuing planning out exactly how Ignatio and Darius are going to pay.

And soon.

Because now that she's here, now that my daughter is here too, under this roof, the timeline I had planned is out the window. There's no need to be subtle. No need to drag this out. I'm going to annihilate them. I don't need to show the world who they really are, I don't need to publicly shame them. Not anymore.

I'm going to butcher them.

And I'm going to enjoy It.

ROMAN

I *place a rose outside her door.*

I know it's cheesy. I know it will probably bring back certain memories but I want to do it anyway.

And then I walk through the house, down to where I can hear the chef already in the kitchen. It's early. Most of my nightshift are switching over and I nod to a few of the guards as they take leave.

"Daddy." Lara cries running up behind me and I laugh as she wraps her arms around my legs.

"You're up early." I say.

"I always am." She replies proudly.

"Come on then. Everyone else is asleep."

"Even momma?"

My heart warms at that. I don't know why her calling Rose that affects me so much but it does.

"Yeah they're all sleepyheads." I say and she laughs loudly.

We walk into the kitchen and I pour out some coffee before telling the chef to leave us to it. I want to make Lara's breakfast myself, I want to provide for her not just with my money but with my time, with real effort.

She perches in a chair and watches me drink. "Can I try that?"

I raise an eyebrow. "You won't like it."

"Maybe I will." She says so assuredly I let out a laugh. This girl is so like me.

"Fine then, I'll make you a bet, if you don't like it then you have to give me a kiss."

"And if I like it?" She says grinning.

"Then I have to give you a kiss."

She laughs. "Fine. Deal daddy."

I hand her the mug. She sniffs it before looking at me like she's regretting her life choices.

"It's hot." I warn her.

She takes a sip, clearly trying to decide if she likes it and then she pulls a face before she can stop herself. "Yuck."

I laugh loudly and she puts the mug on the table. "How can you drink that daddy?"

"I like it." I reply. "And now it's time to pay up…" I tap my cheek.

She rolls her eyes, getting off her seat and goes on tiptoes, as I bend down, and plants a kiss on my face.

"What is this?" Rose says looking between us.

Lara's face lights up. "You're awake."

"How could I not be with all the noise you two are making." Rose says grinning.

And then Lara spots her dog. She gasps, crouching down, scooping it up.

"Her name is Bella." Rose says. "She's super friendly but you can't give her anything to eat except her special food or she'll get sick."

Lara nods but we can both see she's too transfixed by the animal to have really taken on what Rose said.

"I always wanted a pet." Lara says. "They said if I was good I could have one but I wasn't naughty and they never gave me one anyway."

Rose lets out a sigh that I can tell is to hide the rush of pain, of guilt too. "Well, now Bella is as much your dog as mine. We can take care of her together if you'd like?"

Lara grins before hugging the dog so tightly I'm afraid she might suffocate it. Rose smiles back, not looking concerned so I guess it's more durable than it looks.

"Do you want a coffee?" I ask.

"Yes please." She says sinking into the chair beside Lara. She's wrapped a silk robe around herself. Her hair is dishevelled from sleep and she doesn't have even a smear of makeup on. She looks beautiful. Radiant.

I force myself to look away, to pour her a cup, and put it in front of her. She reaches for it and our fingers brush making my skin erupt into goosebumps. God, I'm acting like a teenager, like this is some romcom romance.

"How can you drink that? It's disgusting." Lara says.

"We had a little bet." I tell Rose. "And our daughter just lost."

"I see." Rose says. "And what were the terms?"

"If she loses she has to give me a kiss."

Rose raises an eyebrow. "So your dad gets a kiss but I don't?"

Lara smiles before putting the dog down and hugging her tightly. "You don't have to make me drink coffee to give you a kiss."

Rose laughs as she hugs her back. And then I notice what she's put on the table. What's right in front of her.

I smirk looking at the flower.

"Someone left this outside my door." Rose murmurs.

"I couldn't imagine who would be that bold." I reply.

She smiles. "Want a hand with breakfast?"

"Nope, I've got this." I say.

Her eyebrows raise at that but she doesn't try to change my mind. Instead she sits beside Lara, talking to her, while I cook up some eggs and bacon and pancakes.

When I put the plates in front of them Lara doesn't wait for permission to dive in. Rose studies it, like she's comparing it some five star meal she's had.

"You can cook." She says.

"I had to learn." I reply before scooping up some eggs and putting them in my mouth.

She studies me then, like she's trying to figure something out but whatever it is, she doesn't tell me, she just frowns a tiny bit and then begins eating.

I smirk as I see her reaction. She's clearly surprised it tastes as good as it does.

And then I realise, I've never cooked for her before, never taken care of Rose like that. I can feel my body reacting to the idea, of taking care of both of them, of providing for them.

That's how I'm going to show her, that's how I'm going to win Rose over. I'll show I'm not all flashy money and big words with no substance, I'll prove I'm the complete opposite of every other man in her life.

I'll win her by my actions. I'll turn us into a real family and she'll realise she can trust me, that we can trust each other.

WE'RE OUTSIDE, JUST THE THREE OF US. ME, ROSE, AND OUR daughter.

And her dog technically, although it seems more interested in hiding in the shade, not that I can blame it.

Lara is fidgeting because she knows she's getting a surprise and like her mother she clearly has no patience whatsoever. Rose is eyeballing me, but looking away whenever I catch her gaze.

I had this planned out yesterday. Another gift. A memory too for Lara to savour.

The gates open, a Land Rover drives in pulling a big animal trailer behind it and Rose turns to look at me again.

"Daddy? What is it?" Lara says, squeezing my hand, hopping from one foot to the other.

"Patience sweetpea." I murmur. "You'll see in a minute."

She bites her lip, scrunching her nose, and I let out a laugh.

The man gets out of the car, greets us, and goes around to the trailer. He drops the ramp and disappears from view and then we all hear it, the sound of hooves.

"Roman…" Rose murmurs.

I look at her and grin.

"Daddy?" Lara says before pulling herself free and running full pelt to where the trailer is.

The man leads the tiny little black pony out and Lara actually squeals as she sees it. It's already all tacked up, ready to go.

"Roman." Rose says shaking her head slightly.

"What?" I reply.

"You got her a Shetland Pony?"

"All princesses should know how to ride." I state picking Lara up, putting her in the saddle and looping her feet into the stirrups.

She'll need jodhpurs, riding boots, and a hat too but right now she can have a ride around the garden on the lead.

Lara grins from ear to ear. "Is she really mine?"

"It's a boy." I say. "His name is Bramble."

"Bramble." She says before throwing her arms around the pony's neck.

"You know Shetlands are absolute shits right?" Rose says smirking.

Yeah I'd heard that. But it's not like Lara's going to be doing any of the maintenance. She just gets the fun of riding. The man starts leading the pony on, and Lara sits there, looking around, clearly loving every minute of this.

Rose lets out a chuckle as she watches.

"You're spoiling her." She says as I walk back to her.

"Maybe I am." I reply taking her hand. "But she deserves to be spoiled. You both do."

She bites her lip, echoing that same expression our daughter made. I wrap my arm around her waist and she tenses just a tiny bit before she relaxes into me.

"Can you ride?" She asks.

"No." I reply. "Can you?"

She shakes her head. "I had lessons when I was a kid but I don't remember any of it really."

"Sofia can ride, she can teach you both if you want?"

She pulls a face then looks over at where our daughter is perched only a few strides ahead. "I think Lara would like that. She's trusts her already."

"She trusts you too." I state. "And the more time we spend together the more of a family we'll become."

She looks at me, meeting my gaze and I see that confusion for the briefest of seconds. Yeah, she's a tough egg to crack but then she always was.

ROSE

He's trying to charm me. I know it. I can see the way he's acting, see the way he's spoiling us both.

I'll admit that I'm enjoying it. Mostly. Though every now and then I get this fear that this might all be a trick, that he might just change his mind, that he might decide that he doesn't want to share Lara after all and then I'll be thrown out, left to face my father's wrath and Darius's too.

But each time I feel that, it's like he knows, it's like he senses it and he's there proving that that's not the case, that it's just my crazy head, just my crazy insecurity.

He cooks us dinner, we all sit around this massive table together. Ben and Sofia are there. Sofia is chatting away with Lara and Ben keeps looking between me and Roman like he wants to say something.

I guess he hasn't forgiven me yet.

So I try to ignore him, to keep my focus on my child, on Roman too.

Roman keeps piling Lara's plate up, making sure she's eaten enough and Lara keeps sliding the veggies off when she thinks we don't notice.

"You have to eat them." I say to her. "They're good for you. They'll make you grow big and strong."

"I'm already strong." She replies. "Strong just like my daddy."

I let out a short just as Sofia does and we catch each other's eyes. Roman looks so proud. "That's right Sweetpea." He says.

"Sweetpea?" Sofia repeats.

"You have a pet name for my daughter, I don't see why I can't." He states.

Sofia smirks before looking across at me. "What's yours then?"

"My what?" I say.

"Your pet name for Lara?"

I frown. I haven't even thought of one. It's hard enough to say her name, to believe this is all real, that it's not about to be ripped from me, that my daughter is actually sat here in front of me.

"Sofia." Ben says gently and I look across at him then.

He looks back giving me a mix of sympathy and something else I can't read.

I let out a deep breath, realising that I'm making this awkward now. "I haven't thought of one." I say. "I'm still trying to get my head around this."

Roman reaches across, taking my hand and he squeezes it. "Take your time." He murmurs.

I feel my heart leap, I feel my grief almost ease a little at his words. I look back at Lara and she's smiling back at us. "Do you know what your father used to call me?" I say to her.

She shakes her head.

"He used to call me Trouble." I state.

She laughs. Roman laughs too.

"You were trouble." He says. "My trouble."

I shake my head. "I think we both know you were the troublemaker out of the pair of us."

He grins more. "Nah, you were the one leading me astray, from that first day I laid eyes on you, I would have given you my soul. All you had to do was ask."

I clear my throat, glancing at Ben and Sofia, as my cheeks heat. How have we gotten onto this?

Sofia is smiling, and Ben, he's looking at Sofia as he understands, as if he knows exactly what that feels like.

"We should get you to bed." I say to Lara. "Bath and bed."

"Can't I stay up?"

I shake my head. "Nope, we need to start instilling some sort of rules."

"Urgh." She groans before looking so hopefully at Roman. "Daddy? Please can I stay up?"

"No Sweetpea." Roman says. "Your mum is right."

She mutters about us being 'unfair' but she gets down, taking my hand we leave the rest of them to it.

ROMAN DOESN'T COME UP. I GUESS HE'S GIVING ME AND LARA A little alone time.

I read her a story after her bath. Try to answer the questions she still has about why we never saved her sooner. Why we left her in that house to start with. It breaks my heart to hear the pain in her voice as she speaks because she clearly has not had a happy childhood to date. She was clearly suffering.

"I love you." I say to her, pulling the sheets up, tucking her in. "Both me and your daddy love you. And we're not going anywhere now."

She smiles at me. "I know." She says. "This is our happy ending. Just like in the books."

I bite my lip. She's got such faith in me, in us. I kiss the top of her head then once she's fallen asleep I slip out of the room.

I could go back to my room now, could take some time out and part of me wants to but the other part wants to find Roman. So I head down the stairs, back into the main part of the house.

He's in his study, in that same room where I'd tricked him. I look around as that knowledge sinks in, as I feel that guilt again.

He's sat in his chair, clearly in the middle of something.

"I'm disturbing you." I say.

He smiles, shaking his head. "It's fine." He replies, getting up, stepping away from the desk.

I make a point of not looking at any of the papers, I don't want him to think I'm snooping again. I want him to trust me even if that means I'm kept in the dark about all of this from now on.

"Is she asleep?" He asks.

I nod. "Yeah, she's shattered."

"I'm not surprised." He says. "These last few days have been a lot for her."

"And me." I say.

He places his hands on my shoulders. "You okay?"

I bite my lip before I answer. "How do you do it? How are you so natural with her?"

He frowns, tilting his head to the side. "What do you mean?"

"You act like you know how to be a parent, you act like you know exactly what she needs."

"No I don't." He says. "I'm making this up just as much as you are."

"It doesn't feel like it." I state. "I feel like I'm in over my head. I feel like I've been so desperate to save her and know that I have, I don't know how to actually be a mother."

"Rose, you don't have to be anything, you *are* her mother."

I let out a sigh. There it is again, that natural wisdom. Meanwhile all I have is my own thoughts telling me I'm not good enough. That I'll never be good enough. That Lara is better off without me.

He takes my hand pulling me gently to sit on the couch. For a moment neither of us speak. We just sit there, staring in front of us, sharing this trauma as if the silence is a comfort.

"I wish I'd seen you." He says. "I'd give anything to have witnessed it."

I frown in confusion. "What?"

"You pregnant. To have seen how big you got, to have seen how beautiful you were."

I shake my head, shutting my eyes. "I didn't get big, not really. My belly didn't really swell, and I wasn't beautiful."

"No, that's not true." He says. "You were beautiful they just wanted you to think that. They wanted you to believe that. But you were beautiful. You had a new life growing inside you. You had my child growing inside you. Of course you were beautiful. How could you not have been?"

I can feel them, my tears, they're running hot down my cheeks. I know he's not meaning to make me cry and yet I can feel it, all those emotions, all the pain of those months locked away, hidden away, only seeing my parents, only hearing their hateful words day after day.

His hand cups my cheek, he brushes the tear away, and I all but nuzzle into him.

"I wish you'd been there too." I half whisper. "I wish so much that we could have done it together."

He pulls me into his arms, holds me to him.

And, before I can think of all the reasons not to, I lift my face, I brush my lips against his and I'm kissing him.

He lets me do it, lets me take charge. I pull him closer to me, and for once I don't think, I don't consider the consequences, I just know that I need Roman, I need his love, I need his touch, I need him.

I wrap my arms around his neck, deepen the kiss, as our tongues swirl. Normally he'd be dominating me by now but he's not, he's just letting me take what I need.

I'm moaning, wrapping my legs around him, moving so that my body is on top of his and I'm grinding slowly, but so necessarily against him.

"Rose…" He murmurs breaking off, looking at my face.

I stare back at him, wondering if he's going to refuse me now.

He cups my cheek, sweeps my hair back and then slowly, lovingly he kisses me again.

My hands fumble for his shirt buttons, he helps me to undo them, all the while not breaking the connection of where our lips are joined. I stare at his chest. I know we've technically had sex since he returned but this time it feels real, this time it feels like a beginning, a healing, and not an act of treason.

He's got a scar, right down one side, where it looks like someone tried to butcher him. I run my finger along it, tracing the raised outline.

"Your father." He murmurs.

I look back at him wide eyed. "When?"

"After I left. He sent assassins to kill me. He pretended it was you."

I don't know how to reply. What to say to that. They played him too then, they used the fact they had his number to try to kill him.

I lower my lips, kissing along the damaged skin. Kissing along his abs, where his muscles are still so defined. He's grown with age, bulked out, lost that lanky muscular look he had when we were younger and now, now he looks like a man capable of waging war.

When I reach his belt I don't stop. Slowly I undo the buckle, undo his trousers and he shifts enough that I can get them off him.

I pull his cock free, he's hard, just as I expected and for the first time what feels like forever I actually want to do this. I run my lips up his shaft. He lets out a groan throwing his head back.

I look up, watching his face, watching his expression as I slowly suck him in.

He stares back at me, his face morphing into one of ecstasy but I love that we're keeping eye contact. I swirl my tongue around his head, savouring the taste of a man I've loved and lost so many times now.

His hand twists into my hair. He murmurs my name as if it's a prayer.

"I love you." He says as I suck him in again, as I pick up pace.

I think it back, I show it in this one action, feeling as his body responds, as his hips start to lift, as he's thrusting into my mouth.

He hits my throat, I can feel that need to gag but I manage to override it. I drop my hands to fondle his balls, and he lets out a long throaty groan.

I can't take my eyes off his face, I can't look away as he begins to chase his climax. He starts thrusting more, thrusting harder. His breathing picks up, he's almost panting, and those abs, it's like his entire body has clenched in preparation.

He roars as he comes, burying his cock so far into my throat but I'm here for it, desperate for it. I swallow him down before he pulls me up into his arms.

And then he's sliding my dress off, peeling it off my skin. If I'd planned this better I would have put something sexier on, something more alluring, but the way he's looking at me, the way he's taking in my body makes me realise that it doesn't matter. It's not about cheap gestures, it's not about the physical, it's about us, the two of us coming together again, healing, showing how much we love one another.

I reach around, unhook my bra, and take it off. His lips curl, he reaches up, traces a pattern across my exposed breasts till he's lightly circling my nipples, making them so hard.

I lean in and kiss him and, as he kisses me back, he wraps his arm around me and pulls me so that I'm laying flat on the couch.

He runs his hands up my sides then lowers his mouth, peppering my skin with kisses. I arch my back, moaning as he makes his way so deliciously down my body.

When he reaches my stomach he pauses, planting a kiss right below my belly button.

"Next time I'll be here." He murmurs. "Next time we will do it together."

"Do what?" I ask.

He grins up at me. "Have another baby."

I meet his gaze and so many thoughts swirl in my head. He tilts his head like he can tell but before I can speak he's moving lower, pushing my thighs apart.

I let out a moan even before he touches me and when he does I think I lose myself. He doesn't play games this time, he doesn't tease, he swirls his tongue, making sure to taste me fully before he's sucking hard, feasting away.

I raise my hips, I ride his mouth as my moans get louder and louder. My entire body feels alive, my heart is racing so fast, I can't think, I can't even put a sentence together.

I start crying out, screaming about how much I love Roman, how much I need him, and all the while he's pleasuring me in a way that's so close to heaven I think I really have died. As my climax hurtles towards me, he scoops his arms under my legs, lifts my lower half and devours me.

"Fuck Roman, fuck." I grasp, grabbing his head, burying my hands in his hair as his fingers slip inside me.

"Show me how much you love me Rose." He murmurs.

"I do love you. I love you so much." I gasp.

He grins before sucking on my clit again, curling his fingers inside and I lose it, I writhe, I flail so much he has to hold me down as I come so hard I'm afraid I might actually have a heart attack.

As I slump back down Roman creeps back up my body, kissing me slowly. "I love the way you come for me." He says.

I cup his face, kissing him back, tasting myself on his tongue and I know he must be able to taste him on me.

He rolls us over, so that I'm on top and then he nudges himself so that I can feel he's hard and ready but he doesn't push into me. He waits, as if he's checking I'm happy to take this step, as if I wouldn't be.

I kiss him again, raise my body and sink down onto him.

We both groan as he buries himself inside me.

"You feel incredible." He says.

"So do you."

We lay there, not moving, just savouring the moment as he strokes my face, as he stares at me as if I'm some sort of heavenly creature.

And then as he leans into capture my lips once more he begins thrusting. Long, slow thrusts that seem to reach my very soul.

I bury my face in his neck, surround myself by the scent of him and gyrate my body in time with each and every thrust.

One of his hands cup my arse, the other holds my back.

It doesn't feel like fucking. For the first time in our lives it feels like we're not just responding to the world around us, responding to our own emotions, or our lust. It feels like love-making, true genuine love making. It feels like our souls are uniting, that right now we're healing each other, forgiving our sins, connecting on a level we've never been able to before.

I kiss him. I can't stop kissing him. I run my hands over his body, reminding myself of every muscle, every line. I've never touched someone the way I've touched Roman. Never been touched the way he touches me.

He groans as he gets nearer and nearer to his climax and I rest my head against his, staring into his eyes as we both find our release.

We lay there, curled up in each other's arms, listening to the others breathing.

And then Roman shifts, getting off me for a moment.

I frown watching him walking over to the desk, pulling out a drawer before he turns walking back to me. He's got that wry grin on his face, and his eyes, they're sparkling more than ever.

"What...?" I begin.

He slips onto the couch beside me. "I wanted to wait till the right moment." He says holding what looks like a small box up.

I frown, my head already telling me what's in it, even as I process what's happening.

He pops it open. Inside is a sapphire surrounded by diamonds. It's old, vintage. I know just by looking at it that it was his mother's. That this is a family heirloom. That this means something very special to him.

"Rose, will you marry me?"

I nod, half laughing, half crying. "Of course."

He kisses me, sliding the ring onto my finger. "I already had it resized."

I raise an eyebrow shaking my head. "You were that confident I'd say yes?"

He grins. "Why would you not?" He replies before scooping me up and he's carrying me, through the house clearly not concerned that he's naked, that I'm naked, that anyone could see us right now.

He lays me in his bed. I sink into the mattress and then curl into his body as he gets in beside me.

"I kept that ring, the whole time I was in exile I kept it with me." He says.

I gulp looking up at him. Is he saying what I think he's saying?

"I was going to ask you. I was going to propose, I knew we couldn't continue as we were and that time was running out. And then, when I was exiled, I kept looking at it, every night, thinking of you, wondering at first why you hadn't come, why you never replied."

"I'm so sorry…"

He puts a finger over my lips. "We need to make a new rule. No more apologising to one another. What is done is done."

I nod. Yeah I can agree to that.

"Why did you do it?" I say. "Why did you kill Tybalt?"

He pauses, frowning, before meeting my gaze. "What do you know about that day?" He asks.

I shrug. "Not much. I found out I was pregnant the same day. I was trying to contact you and well…" I trail off because we both know how that turned out.

He tilts his head. "Fuck." He murmurs. "I'm so sorry…"

"I thought we agreed not to apologise anymore." I say.

His lips curl. "I guess old habits die hard."

"So Tybalt?"

"We broke down. Me and Ben, on the way back from our trip. Tybalt used to have that gang he hung out with."

"I remember them." I say cutting across him. They were a nasty bunch of shits. Used to bully the hell out of me when I was too young to get away from them.

"They happened to be passing at exactly the right time. They pulled over. Started beating the shit out of Ben."

I gulp. "That's what happened to his eye." I say.

"Yes. I got my rifle, and I shot him."

"Sounds like he deserved it then." I reply.

His eyes flash, for a second I think I can see it, the murderous Roman Montague again. "He did deserve it. But Rose, I want you to understand, I knew what I was doing, I'm not making excuses, I wanted him dead."

"Tybalt was always a bully." I say cupping his face with my hand. "And if you didn't kill him he would have killed you."

He puts his hand on top of mine. "If we'd not been on that road, if we hadn't broken down, then maybe you and I..."

"Stop." I reply. "Stop the what ifs. It's too late now. We are where we are."

He grins. "And I have you back."

I grin too. "I guess you do."

"And I'm never letting you go again. Never letting anyone take you from me."

I kiss him before I reply. "They'd have to kill me to separate me from you."

"Till death us do part eh?" He murmurs.

I nod back. I might not have said the words. We might not be married but I have his ring on my finger, and I have his love. Nothing my family do, nothing they say can change that. I know Roman is mine as much as the birds fly in the air and the fish swim in the sea.

We are one and the same me and Roman. We are united now. Nothing my family can do will ever destroy what we feel for one another.

And as I look at Roman, as I meet his gaze I know he feels the same.

ROSE

I wake to his mouth on me, to his kisses on my skin. It feels like a dream. Like I've slipped into a fantasy world but as I open my eyes and see his face staring back at me I know it's real. I'm here, in the Montague House and Roman, Roman is here with me. That we're together now. United.

I want to lie here all day. I want to savour this moment and let it replace every awful one I've experienced leading up to it.

Only I can't. I have to leave. I have to go out into the Bay. My lawyers have called a meeting. I don't know exactly what they want but they say something about Paris's will, like I care right now. I don't need his money. I don't even think I want it now. It feels like blood money. An awful reminder of a life I'm still in some ways trying to escape.

Reluctantly I leave the safety of the Montague house and re-emerge into the wider world.

And that's how it feels.

Like I'm some sort of butterfly finally breaking free of the cocoon that's been locked around me for so long.

Roman was insistent that Mitch and Turner came with me, acting as bodyguards, and though my pride wanted to say no, common sense prevailed. Afterall, my parents know where I am and I wouldn't put it past them to do something to get me back.

I walk into the big glass building, noticing once more the glances, the murmurs. I've been MIA for over a week now and I know social media has been rife with speculation as to where the 'grieving widow' has been hiding and what I've been up to.

But none of them have a clue. No one does.

My relationship with Roman has somehow managed to become my best kept secret and for the moment that's how I want it, I'm so sick of this world feasting off the titbits of my life. For once I have a sliver of privacy and I want to cherish it for as long as I can.

I cross the main atrium, head over to where my lawyer's office is but as I reach it I tense up, my body recognising the sound of *his* voice before my head registers who it is the other side of the door.

I step closer, making sure I'm out of the line of sight. I can see them now, through the crack, tucked away, with their heads bowed together, looking exactly like the conspirators I know they are. Only my lawyer's sat there too.

He's with them.

My adrenaline spikes as I realise this *is* a conspiracy. A ploy to get me away from Roman and back under their control.

"…Except we have a problem with that don't we?" Darius voice carries and the words make me pause. I lean further into the door, though anxious not to give myself away.

"Roman Montague to be exact." It's my father who replies. Just the mere tone of his voice sets my nerves on edge.

"Yes Ignatio." Darius says. "But this is your fuck up. Your mistake in not eliminating him years ago. " There's a pause, like Darius is weighing something up. "It will cost you this time."

"Fine." My father replies. "Name your price."

"Rose."

"Excuse me?"

"You heard. I want your daughter. That's my price."

I hear the leather of the chair squeak and I can imagine it, my father leaning back, probably smirking as well. "That's it?"

"That's it." Darius says.

More silence. More weighted moments.

"If she's worth so much to you why let your nephew marry her? Why not ask for yourself all those years ago?"

Darius shrugs. "Calvin wanted that. Besides she was a girl then. Barely anything of note. But now your little Rose has grown on me."

"So what, you'll marry her? Marry your nephew's widow?" My father doesn't sound shocked, it just sounds more like he's confirming the plan. Shoring it up. Ensuring he understands all the parts in play.

"Bigger scandals have happened in the past. We'll play the angle of me comforting her and us falling in love. The masses will soak that shit up and with her on my arm it will help secure my re-election."

My father laughs. "I see you've thought this through then."

"Why do you think we're here?" He replies. "Rose will be my wife. And you, Ignatio, will be the Capulet who actually defeated the Montagues."

There's a pause there and I can feel it, the way my father likes that idea.

"Fine. But I want a contract written up." My father states. "I want this all in writing. All my business interests are to be protected, and whatever businesses the Montagues have, I want that too."

Darius nods his head waiving his hand. "The lawyer can do it."

"Fine." My father says. "And I won't be held responsible if Rose goes AWOL."

Darius laughs. "Don't worry about that, she'll be going nowhere after today. Nowhere but my bed that is."

"Roman won't like it." My father muses. "You'll have to deal with him quickly."

Darius waves his hand dismissively. "It's in hand, I know he's sniffing around."

"Do not underestimate him." My father says. "Because it's more than just sniffing. They had a fling, years ago and it's obvious he's still keen." My father says. As if it was just that, something inconsequential, as if the repercussions of it are not still evident, as if Lara doesn't even exist.

"Rose and Roman? A Capulet and a Montague?" Darius says half disbelieving it.

"Does it change your mind? That my daughter fucked him?"

Darius laughs. "No. Rose fucked my nephew too, and pretty soon she'll be riding my cock just as happily."

My father doesn't comment at that. I know he's not offended though. That's all I am to him. A possession to sell. A hole to fuck.

"I'll deal with Roman." Darius says. "Like I said, it's in hand, just leave him to me."

"And what of the others? What of Sofia?"

"Sofia will marry Otto. She'll be made to see that's her only option."

"So the Blumenfelds get the Montague fortune." My father says almost bitterly.

"Yes but you get a Capulet in the Governor's bed, keeping him warm at night and ensuring you have my favour."

"Not a bad trade I guess." My father states and they both laugh.

I step away, walk as quickly as I dare because I can't bear to hear any more and I don't want to get caught here. I don't want to fall into this trap they've set.

It's happening again though isn't it? It's like a literal repeat of six years ago. I'm being sold to a Blumenfeld for the supposed greater good of my family. In this moment it's so hard not to panic, not to give myself away.

Only, as I turn the corner Carter is there, stepping out of the shadows with that awful grin of his.

"And where are you going princess?" He says.

I shake my head, my fear overriding my senses, but Turner and Mitch spring into action, pulling me back. Mitch pulls a gun and Carter lets out a laugh producing his own.

I look around, at all the people that are in the vicinity of this. If this turned into a fight god knows how many people would get hurt.

"Rose comes with me." Carter says.

"Not a fucking chance." I snap back. I'm not doing it, I refuse to. Maybe I am selfish but I won't sacrifice myself again, I won't continually fall on my sword for the sake of everyone else.

Carter takes a step forward. Turner points his gun at him and then it's like it all happens at once.

Someone sees. Some random person realises that this little standoff is happening.

A scream echoes out around the atrium. I recoil further into Mitch's massive body but as I do I can see we're out numbered. I can see all the armed men rushing to us.

"No." I murmur shaking my head. It can't end like this. It just can't.

Turner snarls, pointing his gun up in the air and he lets off a round. I don't know where he hits. I only hear as he shatters the glass.

Half the room drops to the floor. The other half seem to go berserk, in full panic mode. I flinch even further into Mitch and he grabs me, throwing me over his shoulder, and the two of them make a run for it with Carter hot on our heels.

ROSE

Somehow we manage to get to the car park. Me still on Mitch's back and Turner taking strategic shots when necessary.

But they're hunting us.

Armed men are streaming out of what feels like every damned juncture.

The car is barely a hundred metres from us and yet it might as well be at the ends of the earth. Mitch and Turner are sprinting for their lives. I scrunch my face up, grit my teeth, as my body jolts with every move Mitch makes. They all but toss me inside. I don't complain, I'll take a few bruises, hell I'd take broken bones too if that's what it takes to get away from them.

Turner starts the engine, revs it, as Mitch is yelling into the radio that I know connects to Roman. The tyres screech as we're pitched back into reverse.

And then suddenly someone is shooting. I duck, burying myself in the footwell as a hail of bullets seem to hit the vehicle.

But Roman put bulletproof glass in so even as the sound is terrifying it has little effect beyond some nasty chinks.

We hurtle out into the main road. Sending a group of our attackers flying. I can hear the beeps, hear the carnage of the other road users as we speed off.

But I can hear Mitch and Turner too.

I can hear from the way their talking that their concerned.

"They're following." Mitch says.

"We've got this." Turner replies. "If we get to the Interstate we can lose them there."

I pull my phone, dialling Roman's number as quickly as I can. I know it's silly, I know right now he's doing everything he can to help but I need to hear his voice. It's like my life depends upon it in this moment.

He picks it up immediately. I can hear he's in a car, in a vehicle. He must be coming to me.

"Roman..." I gasp as my voice chokes up, as I start to really panic.

"It's okay." He says. "You're going to be fine. We're coming to you now, we're on our way."

"They're following us." I reply. "It's Darius and my father. They made a deal..."

"Rose, listen to me, they're not going to win. You're going to get away."

I gulp, feeling the tears start to stream. "I don't want to lose you." I whisper it. "I don't want to lose Lara, not now, not when everything is finally going right."

"You're not going to." He growls back. "You're not going anywhere. Just hang on Rose. Just hang on five more minutes."

I sob harder. I shouldn't have come. This was such a stupid fucking thing to have done. To have fallen into their trap.

More bullets ring out. I duck again. It feels like they don't even care if they kill me, just as long as Roman doesn't get me back.

"Rose?" Roman says.

"Yes." I whisper back.

"I love you. I love you so much. Nothing is ever going to happen to you, do you hear me?"

"I love you too." I cry. "I love you so much I can't even…"

A bang makes the whole car shake, we swerve, spinning around and I have to clutch the seat in front to stop myself from being slammed into it. We pitch forward, as if the vehicle is no longer on four wheels but somehow, miraculously we pitch back, landing with a thud. When we finally come to a stop it feels like everything is silent and yet there's a ringing in my ears so high-pitched it makes me wince.

The air is thick with smoke. I start to choke but after a moment it clears and I realise it's not actually smoke, it's just the airbags.

I hear Mitch groan. I peer up over the seat and he's there, covered in blood, with the airbag deflated and splattered too.

"Rose?"

I grab the phone, my hands are shaking so much it's hard to even hold it.

"Roman."

"What's happening?"

"I don't know. I think we crashed." I murmur.

"Don't get out of the car." He says. "Do you hear me? Don't get out of the car."

But even as the words leave him I can hear it, they're cutting the damned door off. I scream as the sparks seem to go flying, as they rip through the very metal, and then all too soon someone's hands are grabbing me, hauling me out.

I want to grab the phone. I want to tell Roman that I love him, I want to tell him to tell Lara that I love her too. That I want her to be happy, that whatever happens, whatever the consequence of this, he has to take care of her, he has to ensure she's protected now.

But as I'm dragged from the wreckage I can't even do that.

I can't even say goodbye.

I kick out, I scream harder. Someone clamps their hand around my mouth and their other arm holds me to their body. I can feel the hard material of their bulletproof vest as I'm pressed against it.

I don't know where Mitch and Turner are. I don't even know how injured they are.

As I try to look for them the man holding me tightens his grip, forcing my head to remain forward.

Carter struts towards me. That same arsehole smirk of his plastered across his face.

"That was fun." He says.

"Fuck you." I spit back, but it's only a muffled sound under the grip of the man holding me. I should have bought a gun too. I should have bought my own weapon and put a bullet in his god damn skull.

He looks across at the wreckage. "Are they alive?" He asks.

One of his men smirks, cocking his gun. "Not for much longer." He replies.

I scream, jerking, kicking out as I realise what he's saying. That he's going to kill them. He's going to murder them.

Carter grunts before holding my gaze and watching with clear enjoyment as I flinch with each awful bullet.

They're dead. Mitch and Turner. Murdered. Because of me.

And as if that's a cue the man holding me releases his grip. I jerk, half trembling as I face off against Carter. I know I've lost, I know I don't stand a chance now but I refuse to go without a fight. I refuse to be the cowardly, complicit girl I was before.

"It's over princess." Carter says stepping up to me. "Time to stop playing the rebellious teenager."

"It's not over." I reply. "It will never be over."

He lets out a laugh, yanks my head by my hair at such an angle I think he might snap my neck and then he jabs a syringe into me. "No one's going to save you now." He murmurs as that awful cold drug seeps into my veins.

I slump, despite myself, despite every screaming thought that's telling me to fight this, to keep moving, to not give in.

And as my body crumbles it's Carter who's scooping me up, carrying me to the waiting car and I know where I'm headed.

I know exactly where he's taking me.

And worst of all, I know there's no escaping this. That this time I will never get free.

ROMAN

’m yelling, shouting, screaming down the damned phone. But there's nothing I can do.

I'm too late.

Too fucking late.

I hear the taunts. Hear the gunshots too.

And I know what they mean; that Mitch and Turner are dead.

That they've killed them.

I snarl, punching the dashboard. My men are dead. And Rose, my beautiful Rose has been taken from me again, stolen right as everything was starting to work out.

"Two more minutes." Someone says.

But it makes no fucking difference if it's two or two hundred. I'm too late. Too fucking late.

"Roman…" Ben murmurs.

I glare at him. I know he's trying to help. I know this isn't his fault and yet right now I can't even think straight.

"Perhaps we should go back. Regroup. Plan a counter attack." Holden says.

"No fucking way." I growl back. I'm not giving up. I'm not turning back. They have Rose, they have her and if we have to run them off the road, storm the very building to get her back then that's what we'll do.

"Roman." Ben says grabbing my shoulder.

"I'm not leaving her." I state. "I'm not letting Darius get anywhere near her."

Someone else says something. Mutters something. But I don't hear it. I don't want to hear it.

We turn the corner, my eyes fixed on the road in front and then I see it, the wreckage. It's up on the bridge. The car's half twisted as if it almost ripped in two and it looks like they cut the entire door off.

"Fucking hell." Ben growls.

But as he does a hail of bullets come our way. My men duck down, even though we have bulletproof glass. I guess it's instinctual but right now I'm running off pure adrenaline.

I twist around looking for the source and spot the fuckers over by the trees. Grabbing an assault rifle, I drop the window just enough, and shoot a volley back.

My men in the truck come up behind us. They've got a machine gun attached to the roof. Ben had said it was unnecessary when we'd come up with the idea but it doesn't feel unnecessary now.

We watch as a stream of bullets start flying off in the direction of the woods and I'll admit when I see them start to fall, when I see them lying their dead, I do get more than a little sense of satisfaction.

But as my men are cheering all I can think about is the fact that they have Rose, that right now she must be utterly petrified and worse, she knows I've let this happen. That after everything I said, I've failed her.

We don't have time for this, with every second that we are caught here, in this fight, she is being driven further and further from my reach.

A roaring noise brings me back out of my thoughts, we all turn, staring in horror as an actual fucking tank comes at us.

"Jesus fucking Christ."

I don't know who says it. If it's me, if it's Ben, Holden, or all of us together.

We don't have time to react, time to do anything as the damned thing roars towards us and we're rammed, hard, right across the tarmac before we come to an abrupt halt.

"We can't get out. They'll shoot us if we do." Holden says but we can't stay in this damned car either.

The tank rams us again. We all grab the sides as the vehicle lurches and then we're rolling. Over and over. Down the bank and with a thump that feels like the very earth is shaking we land in the deep water below.

"Get out." Ben yells. "Get out of the car."

But the water is already filling up. We're trapped by the pressure and the doors won't open. They won't even budge.

We're sinking so quickly we can't escape it and as the murky water overcomes us a hail of bullets rings down from what feels like the very heavens itself.

ROSE

I wake with a groan. My body feels heavy, like I've been in a serious fight. As I shift I realise my legs are exposed; it feels like I'm half naked. I jerk violently, kicking out as I sit up.

"Slowly now." Darius says. "The drugs are still wearing off."

I stare over at him, blinking rapidly as my mind catches up.

The room I'm in is dark, like it's night time. I'm on a couch. Laid out on it while he's sat across watching me. I'm no longer wearing my dress. I'm in a shirt. Just a shirt and my panties.

I glare at him. He's got a gash down one side of his face, it looks fresh, painful. I hope it fucking hurts.

"Your dress was dirty so I took the liberty of putting you in something more appropriate." He states.

"This is appropriate is it?" I reply trying not to think about the fact that he's essentially stripped me all but naked while I was out.

"My shirt." He says. "My clothes."

I shake my head at what is a pathetic attempt at asserting dominance. But as I do it I realise my ring is gone. That it's no longer on my hand. He's taken it, removed it while I was unconscious and that hurts me more, because I know what that ring meant to Roman, and more than that, it's what it represents. What we'd agreed. It was a symbol of our whole future and Darius has no doubt tossed it away like it means nothing.

"Why am I here?" I look around again. I can't be sure but judging by the decor I'd put money on us being in the Governor's House.

"You've been out for a few hours so let me bring you up to speed with events." He smiles but it feels more of a smirk. "Roman is no longer with us. The Montague's have been neutralised. And you belong to me now."

I let out a half laugh moving to stand. "You really think that's the case? That I'm just going to agree to that?"

Darius walks up to me, grabbing me before my still drug-addled body can properly respond and then he's pulling me back, onto the couch, with his arms around me. I kick away but his grip holds me. He takes his phone out, holds it in front of me and presses play.

I can't help but watch it. It's Roman's Range Rover. It's driving over the bridge where we crashed and then suddenly something massive careens into it, smashing it off the side. I moan shaking my head, refusing to believe it but unable to deny it either.

"I took a leaf out of your boyfriend's book. It seemed an effective way to remove Paris so why not make the same move on Roman?"

I gulp as a wave of crippling grief hits me.

He's dead.

Gone.

Waves of emotion hit me like a tsunami.

"No." I gasp clapping my hands to my mouth. "No."

"Yes." Darius practically purrs. "Roman is dead. And you are mine now."

I shake my head, glaring at him through the tears that are already streaming uncontrollably down my face. "Just kill me. Kill me and get it over with."

He lets out a chuckle stroking my cheek with his fingertips. "Why would I do that Rose when I want you warming my bed?"

I jerk my chin back. "I don't want you. I never wanted you. Whatever you think you're achieving here…"

His hand slaps me into silence.

"You are going nowhere but my bed." He snarls. "You will smile, you will simper, you will do everything from now on solely to please me."

"I will not."

He slaps me again, the sting is harsher this time. I shudder, clutching my cheek. Paris used to hit harder than that. It's a ridiculous thing to think, to compare him, but that's the thought in my head. If he means to bully me into submission then he should know how many years of training I endured at his nephew's hands.

We stare at one another, as if we're waiting for the other to break and then he picks up a bell from the table beside him, ringing it loudly and the noise clangs in my head like an echo.

The door opens Sampson of all people walks in, with his hand gripping my daughter's shoulder so she can only move as he directs.

"No." I cry. I don't know how he has her but my heart breaks at the fact that she's here. That she's in danger because of me.

Her hair is sprawled, her face is so ashen from fear. She's trembling under his massive grip. I can see how much she is physically shaking but Sampson only seems to grip harder.

"Lara." I cry springing from the couch but my legs don't work. It's like they've not yet got the message that the sedative is gone. I half stumble and Darius grabs me from behind wrapping his arms around me and pulls me back against his body.

"Let her go." I say.

He takes in a deep inhale of my hair and murmurs 'no'.

"She's a child." I hiss.

"Yes she is." Darius replies louder. "Yours and Roman's to be exact. Both Montague and Capulet. Imagine my surprise when I found out that little titbit from your father."

"Let her go." I say gritting my teeth, unable to take my eyes from Lara's petrified face.

Darius jerks his head and Sampson steps back pulling her with him.

"No." I scream fighting harder but it does nothing but tighten Darius's grip on me.

"Momma." Lara cries as she's dragged from the room.

It's the first time she's called me that and if anything it makes my heart crush more because a parent is meant to protect their child and yet that's the one thing I've never done. I've failed her from the moment she was born.

My stomach knots worse than ever but I can't let myself fall into this, I need to be focused, I need to stay in control of myself for Lara's sake. But it's taking all I have right now not to cry, not to sob, not to crumble into the grief that is twisting worse than ever.

Roman is gone. Roman is dead.

"I'm going to offer you a deal Rose." He says brushing my hair back. "It's a good deal."

"I don't give a shit…"

"Rose." He tuts. "Listen to me. Hear me out."

I bite my tongue. Like hell I'll agree to anything. He takes my silence as acquiescence.

"You'll marry me. Be the perfect wife to me just like you were for Paris and in exchange I'm willing to let you keep your daughter with us, to let her live with us."

I shut my eyes. "No." I say.

"You don't have any other options." He replies as he gently caresses my cheek with his finger.

"Why do you even want me?" I snap.

He smirks. "Because Rose, I've watched you carefully, watched the way you tolerated my nephew, the way you smiled for the cameras. This city loves you. You're exactly what I need, you'll be the perfect Governor's wife."

"I won't marry you." I growl.

"Yes you will. You're obedient when you need to be and I'm far more congenial than my nephew was. I'll treat you right and in time you'll learn to love me." His hand moves to grab my stomach and I tense even more. "And once I put a baby in you that'll be enough."

"Enough what?"

"To give you purpose. That's why you've been so restless. I saw it when you were with Paris, you had no focus. Children are a woman's focus. Their purpose. I'll make sure you have enough of mine to be content."

"I have a child already." I snap. Lara. The child he's right now holding to ransom.

"Yes but publicly we'll have to say she's adopted. A distant relative or some shit. We can't let people know who she is."

"I won't do it." I state.

He tuts, pushing me back with his weight now holding me down. His hand moves to gather the ends of the shirt up as my entire thighs are exposed. "You will Rose." He says. "You'll grow to love me."

As his hand skims over my panties I whimper. I already know where this is headed. What he's about to do.

Roman is gone. Roman is dead.

There's nothing to stop him now. Nothing to stop any of this.

His face presses into my neck and I try to fight him but his one hand grips me too tightly to do anything. I can't even kick my legs out.

"Such a beautiful body." He murmurs. "You deserved to be treated better than what Paris did. Better than Roman too. I can show you that. I can show you what it means to be with a good man."

"You're not a good man." I reply. "You're a coward. A piece of shit…" His hand grasps my mouth clamping it shut.

"Shush. You're going to learn. Day by day. I'm going to take my time and soon you'll be moaning my name as you come, enjoying everything I do, just like you did with Paris and Roman."

His hand slips my thong aside and I screw my face up as I feel his fingers begin to spread my lips apart.

I shut my eyes but I can't blank it out. Not any of it. He spits down to where his fingers are and then I feel him spreading his saliva over me, making me wet because I'm so blatantly not into this.

As he pushes two fingers into me and I jerk more.

"You're so tight Rose." He groans. "You're going to feel so good wrapped around my cock."

I shout out an insult but his hand swallows it.

He starts thrusting, trying to stimulate me but it does no good, he can hardly force my body to comply. After what feels like forever he grows frustrated. His thumb finds my clit but it makes little difference. I'm not going to come for him.

He shakes his head pulling his fingers out and holds them up like a trophy. "Resist all you want but this is your only option."

His hand comes away from my face and I half hiss at him seizing the opportunity to fight now that I have some movement.

He responds immediately grabbing me and hauling me through the room by my hair to the one beyond which, to my horror turns out to be a bedroom. His bedroom by the looks of it.

He dumps me on the bed and my head jars at the impact but he barely notices, he's too busy walking back to the door and slamming it shut.

When he turns back his face is all fury.

"Did you really think this would end any other way?" He snaps. "You really thought Roman could blackmail me forever?"

I screw my face up in confusion. "What are you talking about? What blackmail?"

He smirks. "Ah so you're innocent on that part at least. In that case let me explain. Your boyfriend has been all but holding me to ransom, forcing my hand for months now."

"About what?"

He tuts, shaking his head. "I'm not stupid enough to give you ammunition Rose."

"That's why you let him back. Let him out of exile." I say as the pieces finally slot into place.

"Very good." He replies. "He's been manipulating me. Only he was stupid enough to think I'd just lie down and take it. That I wouldn't make a few moves of my own."

"Like what?"

"Like eliminating him as a threat." He says simply. "And ensuring all the other lose ends are tied up, including marrying his slut of a sister to Otto."

"She won't do it." I snarl.

He lets out a laugh, undoing his shirt buttons and revealing a toned chest speckled with grey hair. For a man twice my age he at least is in pretty decent shape, not that that thought doesn't repulse me

"She'll do exactly as she's told." He says before moving to his trousers.

I look away, averting my eyes. He doesn't deserve such privacy but I'm not going to give any indication that I want him.

"Just like you will Rose." He adds yanking at the covers as I spring up and away backing into the wall behind me. "Get in."

"No."

"No?" He says arching an eyebrow.

"I'm not sleeping in your bed. I'm not going anywhere near you after what you just did."

He snorts. "Oh sweetheart, you're still labouring under the illusion that you have a choice so let me make this plain and clear. You don't. You are mine now. You will do exactly what I say, just as you did what Paris said before me because if you don't you can say goodbye to that precious daughter of yours forever."

"No." I cry, knowing I'm giving him the exact reaction he wants but I can't help it. Not in this moment. I think I'd agree to anything just to keep her safe, just to keep her with me.

"Get in." He says stating each word through gritted teeth.

I feel it then, the rising bile, the fury too, I'm going to fight this, I just need to figure out how. Roman is dead, I have no one coming to help, and with a sinking feeling I know I need to play along until then because Lara depends upon it and her needs far outweigh any and all of mine.

I drop my gaze, my body slumping with submission and I get into the bed ignoring the obvious smirk Darius is now giving me. He slides in beside me, his arms already wrapping around and it takes everything inside me not to push him away.

As his skin presses against mine he murmurs loud enough for me to hear. "I'll treat you right Rose. I'll take care of you and in time you'll learn to love me just as much as you did Paris and Roman."

I bite my tongue swallowing the reply that I don't want him to, that I don't need him to. And as a wave of exhaustion hits me I realise that I'm falling asleep, that the drugs are definitely still in my system and that in this moment I'm submitting more than even I intended.

Vaguely I register him kissing the side of my head. Clearly this moment is enough for him but I don't want to think about what tomorrow will bring, what more parts of me I will have to sacrifice so I let myself go, let myself sleep, hoping that at least in the morning I might have more strength to fight.

ROSE

His hands are all over me. I lie still, frozen like a god damn statue, but he doesn't stop, he doesn't relent. He takes his time, no doubt enjoying every second of this as I fight back the tears, as I fight to keep myself from lashing out at him.

He doesn't fuck me.

I guess he knows even that is a step too far at this point.

But he does enough to prove he's in control. To prove he has total power over me.

And every time I whimper, every time a sob escapes me he just soothes me, as if this is what I want, as if he is what I want.

Roman is dead. Gone.

There's nothing I can do now except focus on saving Lara. And if it means enduring this, then I'll do it. I'll do whatever I have to, to ensure my daughter survives.

Mercifully, he leaves the room long enough for me to get dressed. I didn't dare shower for fear he'd come back and find me there so his stench is still all over me. My skin feels like I'm covered in hand marks.

And now I'm just pacing, in a far too clingy dress because that's all there was to wear. He didn't even give me underwear so I'm wearing the same panties from yesterday.

The door opens and though my stomach lurches with fear, I can't think of me right now, I have to put Lara's needs first.

He walks in, runs his eyes over me in approval and I fight the almost overwhelming urge to punch him.

"I want to see Lara." I say.

He meets my gaze, clearly considering it.

"If you want me to play along then you have to acquiesce to my demands." I state.

His lips curl and he steps forward, wrapping his arm around my waist, pulling me into his frame. "If you promise to be good then you can see her."

"I will." I say quickly.

His eyes drop to my lips. "If you misbehave, if you try anything then I will not only punish you but I will punish her too."

I gulp nodding. "I won't." I half whisper.

He leans in, his lips hovering just a fraction from mine and it's clear what he wants, what he's expecting. I hate myself for it but I do it.

I kiss him.

Lightly.

As quickly as I can.

I'm doing this for Lara, I tell myself, I'm doing everything for her now. Christ, I would sell my soul to the devil himself if it meant it would protect her.

He drops his hold, grasps my forearm and leads me from the room as if he doesn't trust me to simply follow him. We walk down a set of stairs, pass two surly looking men stood guarding the door and into a room with no windows. Just a huge couch and a TV above a fireplace.

"Momma." Lara gasps running to me.

I wrench my arm free, rushing to her, and hold her so tightly as she starts to cry. She's earing the same clothes she was in yesterday. Did they force her to sleep here, on the couch? Has she even eaten?

"It's okay baby." I murmur. "It's okay. I'm here. You're safe."

She cries harder and I sink to my knees, holding her, comforting her, but all the while more than aware that Darius is still here, in the room, watching us.

"Where's daddy?" Lara asks.

"Your father is dead." Darius states.

Lara looks at me wide eyed and then sobs even more. "I want daddy. I want daddy."

Darius stalks up to us, wrenches her from me and, as I try to fight him, he delivers a perfect backhand sending me flying across the rug.

"Now you listen here brat." He says to her. "Your daddy is dead. Gone. He's not coming back. No one is coming to save you. From now on you do what I say, just as your mother does. Do you understand?"

Lara screws her face up and cries even harder. I scramble to my feet, scramble towards them and Darius sends me flying once more.

He grabs her face, forcing her to look at him. "You'd be so easy to break." He murmurs. "Your little neck would snap so easily."

"Darius please." I cry crawling back to them, to her. My head feels fuzzy, my face is throbbing but I don't care, nothing is going to stop me from protecting her.

He turns to look at me, turns Lara's head too. "Look at her. Look at your mother." He says. "You did that. You're the reason I had to hit her."

I shake my head slightly but one look from Darius makes me stop.

"Do you want to do that? Do you want to keep hurting your mummy?" He asks.

"No." Lara whimpers.

"Then be a good girl and do as you're told."

"But you didn't…." Lara begins and Darius half snarls.

"I don't want you ever to speak about your father. Do you hear me? From now on I'm your daddy. You call me by that name. Not Roman. As far as you're concerned he never even existed."

I stare at Lara seeing the confusion and fear in her face and hating that I can't do anything to stop this. "She's six Darius. She doesn't understand any of this."

"She's old enough to understand consequences." Darius snaps back.

I get to my feet, my legs are shaking, my head is throbbing, but I'm not going to back down.

"If you want me to play along then I have some stipulations too." I say.

He turns his attention on me, but he keeps his hand around her jaw, holding her in place. "And what are they?"

"You never lay a hand on my child again." I spit.

"You mean 'our child'." He says smirking.

I narrow my eyes. I don't give a shit what games he's playing, he isn't her father, he never will be.

"You never talk to her like that, you treat her with respect. I won't have her suffering because of your ego."

He pushes Lara enough that she falls back onto the couch and then he steps right up to me, towering over me. "No Rose." He says. "That's not how this works. I'm in charge, not you."

"If you want me to behave then you will." I state. "Afterall, the elections are coming up, how can you rerun for Governor with me on your arm, if my face is all black from your beatings?"

He narrows his eyes, his hand flies out and he grabs me around my throat, all but hauling me up onto tiptoes. "You'll do as you're told or they'll be consequences."

I let out a laugh. It sounds strained and it catches in my throat from where he's gripping me so tightly.

"I won't do shit." I reply. "Not when you're endangering my child."

He casts his eyes over at Lara then back at me. "Fine. The child is off limits but you Rose, I can do whatever I want to you."

If that's the deal I have to make then fine. I can handle it. I nod, ignoring the bile as it swirls in my stomach. I'd take each and every beating, endure it with a smile, if that's what it takes to protect Lara.

Roman is gone. Roman is dead.

It's just me now.

He drops his grip, lets me crumple to the floor at his feet and then turns his back on us. "You have one hour then I'm coming to get you." He says before slamming the door shut as he leaves.

I rush to Lara, hold her so tightly, as she cries and cries.

"Mummy." She sobs. "Is Daddy really dead?"

"I'm so sorry baby." I whisper.

"No." She gasps. "He can't be. He can't be."

"I'm going to get you out. Do you understand?" I say to her. "I'm going to do everything I can to ensure you're safe."

"I don't like that man."

"Me neither."

"He hurt you Mummy and then he said I did it."

"Don't listen to that shit." I reply. "He's a bad man but for the moment I need you to be careful okay?"

"Careful how?"

"Don't provoke them. Don't answer back. Be careful what you say. What you do. These men are all bad. Really bad."

"I don't like it here Mummy." She says. "I want to go home. I want to go back home and see Daddy."

She sobs harder as I hold her, as I brush her hair from her face, as I try to comfort her.

But all too soon the hour is up.

And Darius is back, taking me away, leaving her alone, scared, and absolutely distraught.

ROSE

He keeps me by his side all day. It's a powerplay. It's fucking pointless because he's just sat there, working and all I can think about is my daughter. About where she is, whether they've even given her food.

In the evening he has me dressed up all fancy in a far too revealing dress with a split up the side so high it feels like I'm at a very real risk of flashing my vagina with every step I take.

He made sure there was a makeup artist on hand, and someone to do my hair. Neither of them comment on the bruises. They act like they can't even see them.

And now I'm here, stood, with his awful arm around my waist, dressed like I'm going to the Oscars, and surrounded by his men. I grit my teeth, keeping my gaze on the view out the windows because I can feel it, the looks I'm getting. I feel like a piece of meat on display, and to everyone here, that's no doubt exactly what they think of me.

Darius is talking away to a man I know by sight but have never interacted with. I barely pay attention to what they say. It's all about his campaign. About ensuring he looks above board for the voters.

For a moment I wonder how I was ever stupid enough to think this man might be a decent human being. That all the rumours about him were just that, rumours.

I let out a low huff. Christ I really was an idiot. A stupid, naive idiot. No wonder my family were able to manipulate me so easily. I swallowed every lie, every trick, without hesitation.

"Something amiss?" Darius asks me.

I tense, looking between him and the man he's talking to. "No. Just a little hot." I give my best fake smile.

And, as Darius scans my face to try to see the lie, I register *him* from my peripheries.

My head turns, my eyes catch his, and he's got that same smug expression he had back in his study when he kicked me out.

"Why is he here?" I hear myself saying the words before I can stop them.

"Ignatio is big donor to my campaign. It would be rude not to invite him. Besides he's your father Rose, aren't you happy to see him?" Darius says as my stomach twists.

As it really registers that *that* conversation has come true.

That they won.

They beat us.

Roman is gone. Roman is dead.

As I shut my eyes, as I take a slow breath trying to keep calm, I tell myself that it's not over yet. That I can still beat them, I just don't know how.

Dinner is called. Everyone starts making their way into the formal dining room but Darius doesn't move, meaning I'm not going anywhere either. When the room empties my father steps up and smirks all the more.

"You move fast." He says.

Darius nods. "Roman is dead, so as agreed, your daughter belongs to me now."

Despite myself I jerk, trying to get out of his hold.

"You'll want to keep a tight leash on her. She's very good at sneaking around." My father replies.

Darius laughs, his fingers digging into my flesh more. "Oh don't worry about that. I'll make sure she's so busy entertaining me that she doesn't have the time to even think about escaping."

They both laugh. The bastards.

I curl my fists up. "Fuck you." I hiss.

Darius grips my face, his amusement turning instantly to anger. "Keep up those little outbursts and I will be, on that table in the next room, for every one of my men to watch."

I shut my eyes, all but giving in. I can't fight him, not now, not in this moment, and besides, I wouldn't put it past him to do what he's threatening, to strip me, to humiliate me further.

"Let's eat." My father says.

Darius grunts leading me like a dog into the room as all eyes snap to us. Darius sits at the head, I'm placed to his left and as I sink into my chair I rub my arm where he keeps holding me like I'm some sort of trophy and where a very obvious bruise is starting to show.

I don't look up, I just stare at the place setting in front of me, picking at the food when it arrives and when a toast is made I don't even reach for my glass. I just let their cheers and amusement wash over me like it means nothing.

But when the plates are cleared, when a load of fresh bottles are brought out I do look up.

And my jaw drops in horror as I see what's been right in front of me the whole time.

Sofia.

She stares back from where she's obviously being forced to sit in Otto's lap. Her dress is just as revealing as mine. No, it's worse. It's semi-see through. And we can all see she's got nothing on underneath.

Her lip is busted, her cheekbone bears the evidence of where someone has obviously hit her hard her.

But it's her eyes. She's staring at me, no doubt looking just as petrified as I feel.

A hand pulls me from my chair. I let out a yelp as Darius all but deposits me in his lap. A few of his men look on but most are too drunk right now to care.

"Did you think we'd let the little slut off?" Darius murmurs. "Did you think Sofia could simply string my cousin along like a cat?"

"I don't know what you're talking about." I say quickly.

"No?" He teases. "Little Sofia Montague dangling her virginity like a trophy. Only she wasn't a virgin was she?"

I gulp, my eyes darting to Sofia's, whose are shut now.

Otto lets out a laugh. It's cruel. And it sets the hairs on the back of my neck on end. "My little Montague whore." He mutters as his hand grabs a part of her he has no right to touch.

"She's not part of this." I say turning to face Darius.

He tuts shaking his head. "You think I'm that stupid? You think we all are? You think we didn't know she was playing a game from the start? Only you know what they say, you mess with fire you have to be prepared to be burnt."

"Sofia's learning that lesson right now." Otto growls as he raises her arm, showing where all the circular cigarette burns are. He's been fucking torturing her.

I snarl, moving to react and Darius pulls me back as his hand wraps around my throat. "We had a deal remember." He mutters.

"Let her go." I hiss.

"No. She's as big a part of this as you are."

"She has nothing to do with this."

He rolls his eyes like he's bored and then he leans around me, tapping his wine glass with a spoon, making the whole room fall silent.

"I've invited you all here this evening to make a few very special announcements." Darius says. "Firstly, it grieves me to inform you all that Roman Montague is no longer with us."

A cheer rings out. Half the room raises it's glasses and it takes all my effort not to react, not to launch myself at them and gut them as they celebrate.

"…Secondly, I'd like to inform you all of Sofia Montague's engagement to my cousin Otto. She is of course beside herself with happiness, as you all can see."

I don't look at her. Not in that moment. But I know the tears are falling down her face despite her best efforts not to cry while Otto is laughing, like the pig he is.

"And finally, we come to my own happy news."

I tense as he speaks. I know what's coming and yet my body still reacts, I still feel all the anger, and the fear, and everything in between as he says the words out loud.

"…Rose Capulet, my beautiful Rose, has agreed to become my wife."

I hang my head as the cheers ring out. They all know what this is. They must do. It's obvious isn't it, that Sofia is being forced to marry Otto just as I am being forced to be with Darius. Yet none of them seem to care. None of them clearly give a shit. They're all just as fucked up as Darius is, as my father is.

Roman is gone. Roman is dead.

My heart lurches for a moment as I realise this is the environment Lara will grow up in if I don't do something. She'll become a pawn for them, just as I am. They'll use her, sell her, inflict god knows what sort of emotional and physical abuse and

I'll be helpless to stop it, just as I was helpless to stop them doing it to me.

I glance at the knife in front of me. It's a butter knife. Blunt as hell. And in this situation it might as well be a rubber chicken for all the good it will do.

"Rose."

I hear the voice through all the commotion. Somehow I hear it I look up seeing Ty sat there, frowning. He's looking around like he doesn't understand what the fuck is going on. His eyes keep darting to Sofia, to how Otto is practically molesting her as she struggles so violently against him.

As he looks at me I wonder if the penny is dropping for him too. If he's going to take a stand, help me, help us in some way, or simply sip the fine champagne and continue the Capulet party he's enjoyed for the entirety of his adult life.

And then we both turn our heads, watching as my father slips from the room, as he makes his exit, and Darius takes that as his cue to start touching me too.

I jerk against, him, grab at his hands, despite the fact that I've all but agreed to do anything he wants if he leaves Lara alone.

He groans into my ear as he grabs me. "Keep fighting me Rose, keep fighting this, and it will only hurt you more."

"You're a bastard." I spit. "And one day I'm going to put a knife through your heart."

He lets out a laugh before planting a kiss on my cheek. "No you won't." He murmurs as if it's a sweet nothing he's saying into my ear. "Because your daughter depends upon you complying. You're going to spread your legs for me, you're going to ride my cock over and over and you'll learn to enjoy it, because that's what you do Rose, that's what you are. You're a good little whore so stop pretending otherwise and play your part."

I snarl, I kick out so hard my leg bangs into the table.

Darius lets out a chuckle before suddenly he's on his feet saying something disgusting to the men around him and then he's dragging me out.

And we both know where he's taking me. What he's going to do.

I don't look at anyone then, I shut my eyes, I shut down.

I withstood Paris for five years. I withstood every awful minute.

I can do this. I know I can.

I can withstand all of this and I will, for Lara's sake. For my daughter.

END OF BOOK ONE

Continue The Story With Book Two: *Uprising*
Out May 17Th

UPRISING

BLURB

ROMAN

Dead. That's what I am. What Verona believes.

Darius has all but erased me. He's destroyed my house, stolen my sister and forced her to marry Otto to ensure they get my millions.

And worse, far worse, he has his grubby hands on my Rose, and my daughter too.

But what he doesn't realise is he's put the nail in his own coffin. Because now I have nothing to live for. Nothing else left. I will have my vengeance this time, I will save my family, even if I have to destroy this entire city to do it.

ROSE

Dead. He's dead. Murdered.

And now I'm stuck, playing the sunshine princess once more only this time I have to endure far worse than Paris's disgusting treatment.

And I will. I will endure everything they send my way. I will do whatever it takes to protect my daughter, the last part of Roman that I have left.

But what they're starting to learn is that this princess isn't just enduring, oh no, I'm changing too. I'm twisting, evolving, becoming like the very monsters around me and very soon I will rise up and make them pay for every insult, every hurt, every bit of abuse we suffer.

SNEAK PEEK

UPRISING

ROSE

We're in his house, in his bed, curled up. I don't know what the time is. I don't care.

I only know Roman is here, that he's with me, and in this moment that's all that matters.

He leans in and kisses my lips gently, softly.

I feel the lingering imprint of that kiss so deeply in my soul as he does it.

"Rose." He murmurs.

Even the way he says my name does something to me.

I blink, feeling a wave of sorrow, a wave of guilt. My tears are falling hard down my cheeks.

He brushes each one aside with his thumb but more fall.

They keep falling. They don't stop.

"I'm letting you down." I whisper it.

"No." He says.

"I am. I'm betraying you."

He shakes his head.

"I can't do this, not without you."

"You can Rose, you're so much stronger than you realise."

I sob then. I'm not strong, I'm weak. So weak. I keep ending up in this same shitty situation and every time I'm out manoeuvred. Beaten. Pathetic.

He pulls me in, holds me to his body, and I can smell him as I bury my face into his neck.

"Forgive me." I say.

"There's nothing to forgive." He says back.

"Yes there is." I sob. "Because it should be us."

"I know."

"It should be us." I snarl. My anger surging, every pent up emotion I've been trying to numb suddenly there, boiling, erupting up inside me.

"It will be one day."

"How can it?" I gasp. He's dead. He's gone. There is no 'us' now. There is no anything and there never will be.

He tilts his head. "Maybe not in this life. Maybe we will have to wait until the next…"

I let out a whimper. I can't spend my life without him. I can barely manage one day, how can I live for years like this? For decades?

"Love like ours doesn't die Rose. Love like ours never dies."

"But you did." I say. "You died. You left me, you left me and Lara."

I know it's unfair to be angry at him, to see this as his fault but he promised, he promised he would save us and yet here we are.

But then I promised too didn't I? I promised to marry him and here I am about to marry another man instead.

My body slumps as that realisation hits me. "I let you down." I murmur. He shakes his head, cups my cheek. "You've never let me down."

I stare back at him, no longer capable of words. This man changed my life, this man is my life. My soul and his are connected, joined, one and the same.

And yet he is gone.

He is gone.

And I am here, stuck in this world, stuck in this hateful place, knowing I will never wake and see his face, that I'll never see his smile, never hear his laughter or feel his touch ever again.

"I can't do it." *I gasp.* "I can't do this. I can't live without you."

Only he doesn't reply. He just fades away, leaving me with my tears and my pain and the knowledge that when I awake the man beside me will no doubt punish me for daring to speak his name again. For daring to utter it.

I'M WOKEN BY THE ALARM. DARIUS GRUNTS, TURNING IT OFF, CLEARLY he drunk enough last night to ensure he didn't have to hear my usual cries. I guess he didn't want to sour the moment with the thought that I was still pining after another man, still wishing it was Roman beside me and not him.

He rolls over grinning at me. His pearly whites almost glowing against the morning light.

"Show time." He says.

I fucking hate him. I hate that smile, I hate the way he speaks, most of all I hate the way his smell seems to wrap around me like a vapour from the pits of hell.

He didn't let me sleep alone. He refused to honour that tradition. I guess it doesn't matter because it's not like we're honouring any of the others. There's no love. No honour. No consent. This is a forced marriage in every sense of the word.

He gets up, walks to the dressing room and comes back fully clothed, though thankfully not in his wedding suit.

"Tell me you remember." He says.

I meet his eyes, wanting to argue, wanting to show defiance.

"Rose." He half snaps. "Tell me you understand what the consequences are if you fuck this up."

I grit my teeth and nod. I'm not a fucking child. I know exactly what the consequences are. He's made that abundantly clear.

"Tell me then." He persists.

"You'll hurt Lara." I state, my voice as hollow as I feel, as powerless too.

His lips curl, he kneels onto the bed. "Not just Lara." He states. "I'll punish you both."

I let out a shudder. I don't care if he harms me, he's done it so many times now it feels like the pain doesn't even matter anymore, but I won't let him do that to Lara. I won't let her get hurt because of my actions.

He plants a kiss on my lips as if he hasn't just threatened both my life and my child's. "Hair and makeup will be here in an hour." He states like I don't know it.

And then he walks off.

And I stay here, staring out the window, staring off as the memories, as his face, as the longing, as all of it haunts me.

When I do get up, I'm barely out of the bathroom and my mother is there, all smiles, with a bottle of champagne and glasses already filled and bubbling away in her hands

"Might as well start the celebrations now." She says. She's so happy she's practically vibrating with joy right now.

I grunt in reply. I'm not celebrating. I have nothing to celebrate.

She tuts, taking my hand and all but wrapping my fingers around the stem. "Drink Rose, it will steady your nerves."

I blink back at her. Is she an actual idiot? Does she really think that I'm nervous? That I'm some sort of blushing virginal bride? It's not nerves I feel. It's uncontrollable, unimaginable fury.

I'm so close to tossing the champagne in her face, to smashing the glass into her eyeballs.

Only the knock at the door breaks off the glare I'm giving her.

The makeup artist walks in, all smiles, and with that the charade begins.

I'm perched in a chair, everyone chats away happily around me. I don't speak. I don't do anything but stare at myself in the mirror as if I still can't believe all of this is real. My mother flits back and forth, she laughs, she drinks glass after glass.

She really is having the time of her life.

My makeup is finished long before any outsiders get here. It's intentional to keep up appearances because when the cameras arrive we wouldn't want any record of the bags under my eyes, of the bruises marring my skin even if they are faded. No, I have to be flawless from the get go.

My bridesmaids arrive right on time. They smile at me, they simper appropriately but we are all aware of the part we're playing today. They're tick boxes. They get to live off this for the next few years, live off the fact that they were part of this particular piece of Verona history.

My hair is styled, in long flowing waves that pin against one side of my head so that a pearl and diamond piece of jewellery can slide in.

I slip into my dress and walk slowly back out to the ooos and ahhhs of everyone around me. My mother especially relishes this moment as she looks on at the fine creation she imagined now brought so artfully to life.

It's so tight now I feel like I can't even breathe. I take shallow breaths but it doesn't help.

I slip my shoes on, they're ridiculously high but exactly what I'd be expected to wear and then my mother pops the long cathedral veil onto my head.

"Perfect." She says.

"Am I?" I reply.

She looks at me smiling. "Today you are." She states and I can see it, that flash of something in her eyes.

I'm doing what she wants, giving her what she wants, of course I'm perfect today.

I drop my gaze, my eyes searching the room for the face I know I won't see. The person who's been banished to her room. Locked away, with only an iPad to entertain her.

Lara.

Darius has made it clear under no uncertain terms that she is not allowed out today. That she is not even to be seen. Not that I argued with him because I didn't want her to see me like this, to see me doled up, to see me marrying another man, betraying her, betraying Roman with seemingly such little resistance.

I let out a sigh, swallowing the lump in my throat.

"It's time." My mother says, handing me the bouquet, all but ramming it into my hands.

My heart sinks further as I realise she's right. I can't put this off any longer.

We walk down together with the bridesmaids chattering merrily as they walk ahead.

At the very bottom of the stairs my father is there, just like the last time I was in this situation. He runs his eyes over me before holding out his arm for me to take.

I can't do it. I can't play this part.

So I walk past him, towards the waiting car.

Only he grabs me back snarling. "You don't learn do you?" He says.

I can feel it, my body trembling, my heart fluttering more rapidly. More panicked. I hate that he's touching me right now. I hate that today is going to be everything he's dreamed of; all his ambition coming to life.

He takes me out to the car. I clamber in and once he's seated we sit in stony silence the entire way, down the streets, down past all the masses of faces that are out staring at us, waving, throwing roses.

By the time we get to the Cathedral I'm shaking so much I can't stop my hands from moving. My father stares at them then at my face with that hard look on his.

And I see it, that warning.

That message in his eyes that he will hurt me, that he will hurt Lara, if I fuck this up.

The door opens, he walks around holding his arm out as the crowd cheers so loudly. I don't hesitate then, I take his arm and we walk up the stairs that now feel like a mountainside and into the hushed silence beyond.

There must be over a thousand people in this building. Over a thousand sets of eyes that snap to me.

Someone crouches down at my feet, rearranging my dress making sure I am the picture perfect bride everyone expects and then that god awful lilt begins.

I can smell the flowers that fill the space, I can hear the sniffles of people. My footsteps seem to echo so loudly, above the music that's playing so merrily.

I look ahead and I can see him, stood at the very end. He's smiling.

Roman.

My heart lifts, for a second I want to pull myself free, to kick off my heels and run down the aisle, tossing the flowers and to throw myself into his arms.

But then I blink and it's not him.

It's not him at all.

He's dead. He's gone. I'm all alone now.

Roman's face changes, his beautiful features mar into those of Darius's. Those soft lips become chapped. That stubble becomes clean shaven, and those eyes, Roman's dark eyes turn pale watery blue.

431

I wince, my breath hitches again, thank god the veil is covering my face because I need it now, I need every little bit of help I can to get down this aisle.

My father sets a quicker pace. I know he can tell that I'm too jittery. I know he knows that I want to run, to scream, to escape so badly. But we both know too that that's not an option.

The bridesmaids walk behind me in a way that feels like they too are guards, bringing up the rear, ensuring I make progress, ensuring I cannot get away.

By the time I'm halfway up the aisle I swear the music has finished and it has to be repeated.

Why is this aisle so long? Why is this Cathedral so long?

Darius stands there, his eyes fixed on me as if he can will me to his side.

I'm afraid I'm making noise, I'm afraid that I'm whimpering like a dying animal but my father isn't showing any sign of it so I guess that too is in my head.

I stare at the tiles beneath my feet. Some of them aren't tiles at all. They look like grave markers. God, I'm walking over dead bodies to get to Darius and if that's not a marker for what this relationship is and how it started then I don't know what is.

When we finally reach the front Darius takes my arm from my father's hold.

"You're so beautiful." He murmurs.

I don't reply. My throat feels too tight, my airway feels so constricted, I don't think I can even formulate words.

The bishop stands in front of us. He clears his throat, instructs everyone else to take a seat and I so desperately want to join them.

I think my legs might collapse, I think I might just fall here, in a heap, in front of everyone and this charade, this entire thing will come out and everything I've endured to save my daughter will be for nothing.

"Dearly beloved, we are gathered here today to witness the union of this man and this woman…"

I zone out, I'm looking at Darius, seeing that smile on his lips but I can't hear the words, I can't pay attention.

I shouldn't be here.

I shouldn't be stood, at an altar with this man. Not after everything he's done to me. Not after everything he's done to my daughter.

This was meant to be Roman.

Roman and me.

We were the ones meant to be standing before an altar, declaring our love, declaring our lives for one another.

This man, holding my arm, forcing me into this, he means nothing. He is nothing.

Roman is gone. Roman is dead. I'll never see his face again.

"Does anyone know of any lawful impediment why these two cannot be wed?" The bishop asks.

I stand there wishing, hoping, screaming in my head of all the reasons why but no one speaks. No one says a thing. The only noise made is from a man coughing and he looks around embarrassed as he does so.

The bishop continues. Darius speaks his vows. He talks of love, of honour, of respect, as if he understands what any of those words truly mean. As if he has any intention of adhering to those vows.

It's so hard not to scowl then. Not to drop that perfect mask painted across my face.

I want to say it then, to shout, to scream out what this really is, that he has my daughter, that I don't want him, that none of this is what I want, but even as that idea sets in my head all I can think of is Lara.

Of what Darius will do to her if I don't obey him.

"Rose..?"

I blink. What the hell did they say?

"Do you promise to love Darius, to honour him with your body, to honour him with your words, to respect and obey him?"

I gulp. "Yes." I say somehow finding enough movement in my voice to get the word out.

"And will you forsake all others, will you commit yourself for the rest of your life solely to this union, solely to this man?"

"Yes." I agree again. Like I have any fucking choice in the matter.

A ring is all but shoved onto my finger. I don't remember putting one of Darius's but as he says the words 'man and wife' and Darius lifts my veil planting a less than chaste kiss on my lips, it's like something latches onto my heart. Like someone is squeezing it so tightly I can't breathe, I can't even pump blood around.

I let out a whimper but no one hears. No one even notices. They're too busy soaking up the dream that Darius is selling them. The romance of our love that he's created in their minds.

I try to take small breaths but even those aren't getting in.

Roman is gone. Roman is dead. I have to save Lara.

"Please sit for the sermon." The bishop says pointing across to the two chairs at the side clearly placed for us.

Darius leads me to them. I sink down feeling like my legs are collapsing. I just have to hold on, I just have to keep this up a little bit longer.

But as the bishop starts droning on, as he reads some part of the bible out, I don't think I can. My hands move, I don't mean too, I don't even register it but they're there at my throat. Clutching.

I can't breathe.

I can't fucking breathe.

My head goes dizzy. It feels like I'm actually having a heart attack and then I'm falling, off the chair, and those tiles that have laid here for hundreds of years are coming up so fast and I know when my face collides with them that it's going to hurt.

It's really going to hurt.

PREORDER TO GET YOUR COPY OF UPRISING

ALSO BY ELLIE SANDERS

BlackWater Series:
Skin in the Game
One Eye Open
Pound of Flesh

Sexy Standalones:
Good Girl
Vendetta: A Mafia Romance
At The Edge of Desire

Twisted Love Duet: A Dark Romeo & Juliet Retelling
Downfall
Uprising – Out May 17th 2023

ABOUT THE AUTHOR

ELLIE SANDERS LIVES IN RURAL HAMPSHIRE, IN THE U.K. WITH HER partner and two troublesome dogs.

She has a BA Hons degree in English and American Literature with Creative Writing and enjoys spending her time when not endlessly writing exploring the countryside around her home.

She is best known for her series of spy erotica novels, 'The BlackWater Series', as well as standalone novels including Good Girl, and Vendetta: A Mafia Romance.

For updates including new books, please follow her Instagram, TikTok, and Twitter @hotsteamywriter.

AUTHOR'S NOTE

THANK YOU SO MUCH FOR READING THIS BOOK. I HOPE YOU ENJOYED it as much as I enjoyed conjuring up all the twists – just wait for book two because there are even more shocking revelations plus some much needed revenge (no spoilers!)

I would be eternally grateful if after reading this you left a review. Reviews really are an author's lifeblood, not just because it helps beat back the crazy amount of imposter syndrome we all have but because it helps us get noticed / builds our community on places like amazon and ensures we can continue creating more stories for you to read and indulge in.